D0481864

SAVAGE GARDEN

L.A. *Times* reporter Eve Diamond has a date at the theatre with her new man, Silvio Aguilar, but when the beautiful and unstable lead actress, Catarina Velosi, fails to appear Eve learns that Catarina and Silvio share a complicated past. Her journalist's instincts lead her to approach the players in this tragedy, including Alfonso, Catarina's sometime lover and director, and his highly-strung and jealous wife Marisela Reventon. An enigmatic drama tutor, a powerful movie mogul and a lecherous political yes-man are also involved, and from stage to newsroom nothing – and no-one – can be taken at face value.

SAVAGE GARDEN

SAVAGE GARDEN

by

Denise Hamilton

Magna Large Print Books
Long Preston, North Yorkshire,
BD23 4ND, England.

British Library Cataloguing in Publication Data.

Hamilton, Denise
   Savage garden.

A catalogue record of this book is
available from the British Library

ISBN 0-7505-2644-0
ISBN 978-0-7505-2644-9

First published in Great Britain in 2006 by Orion Books
an imprint of The Orion Publishing Group

Published in Large Print 2006 by arrangement with
Orion Publishing Group

Magna Large Print is an imprint of Library Magna Books Ltd.

Printed and bound in Great Britain by
T.J. (International) Ltd., Cornwall, PL28 8RW

For Roberta, Marc, Camille, and Evan

CHAPTER 1

All day the sun had baked the concrete, sending waves of heat shimmering skyward. Now a breeze blew through the canyons of downtown and people crept from buildings and sniffed the air like desert animals at the approach of night.

Perched at the edge of a fountain outside the Dorothy Chandler Pavilion, I felt my mood lift along with the crowd's. It was opening night at the city's premier theater, and soon we'd file inside and leave the pavilion empty, save for the saxophonist nestling his instrument in its blue velvet case, the bums sifting the trash for crusts of panini, and the cashier savoring a cigarette before closing up for the night.

I sipped my Pinot Blanc and watched the café grill send up wisps of woodsy smoke. It felt delicious to be anonymous and alone, the crowd swirling around me in a way that suggested New York or Budapest or Paris. This was as good as L.A. street life got, even though it wasn't a street at all, but a concrete slab ringed by theaters and concert halls.

My city had been wrenched from the desert, willed into being by brute force and circus barkers who sold people on a mass hallucination that became a reality. And for generations, the loudest of those barkers had been my newspaper, the *Los Angeles Times*, and its onetime owners the

Chandler family. Their name graced this square, with its reflecting pools and shimmering fountains. It was sheer hubris to send water cascading skyward in the heat of an L.A. summer, but then, water had been the original currency of this land. Without it, the city would sink back to chaparral and sagging clapboard, a provincial outpost doomed to fitful dreams.

Then a man was walking toward me. He wore a guayabera, the accordion-pleated shirt of Mexico. His black wavy hair cascaded over his collar. As always when I saw him from afar, before recognition hit, a wave of impersonal pleasure passed through me at his beauty. Then the pleasure grew personal as I realized it was Silvio Aguilar, the man who occupied an increasingly large part of my heart.

We had met the previous year when I profiled the music promotion business that his family had built from a swap meet stand into a multimillion-dollar empire. The attraction had been instantaneous and mutual, but Silvio was grieving the death of his brother and I wasn't supposed to date sources so we tried to control ourselves, which only made things more explosive when we finally did get together.

I loved his complexity, his Old World chivalry, the masterful control with which he ran the family business and the utter abandon I saw in his eyes when he made love to me. Straddling the formal Mexican culture of his parents and the easygoing American ways of his home, Silvio grappled daily with the duality of his existence and wondered where he belonged. Sometimes he turned inward, retreating into pride and moody secrecy, and then I wondered how well I really knew him.

But tonight promised to be perfect. One of Silvio's childhood friends had written *Our Lady of the Barrio*, the play that would premiere in less than an hour, and we had front-row tickets. It was a triumph the entire city could celebrate, because Alfonso Reventon was a gangbanger who had been saved by the arts, a playwright whose tales of streetwise magical realism brought him growing acclaim and commissions. *Our Lady of the Barrio* was poised to be a smash hit.

As Silvio drew closer, I saw a harried look on his face. He looked at his watch, frowned, then took my hand and caressed it absently.

'Hullo, Eve.'

'Is something wrong?' I asked. My lover's mind was clearly elsewhere.

'I was just backstage, dropping off flowers for Alfonso. The stage manager says he's hysterical. It's forty-five minutes to curtain on opening night and Catarina hasn't shown up.'

'Who's Catarina?'

'Only the leading lady.' A hint of incredulity in his voice.

'She's probably running late. You know those temperamental actresses.'

I was determined not to let his words shatter my good mood, the Old World theater aura, the air like crushed velvet against my skin.

Silvio's cell phone rang and he answered sharply. 'Yeah?'

On the other end, a man's voice spoke too fast and garbled for me to make out anything. Silvio listened, then said, 'Absolutely. You can count on me.'

He hung up and scuffed his feet against the concrete, refusing to meet my eye.

'Look, uh, Alfonso says Catarina's not answering her phone. It's a fool's errand, but he's asked me to go by her house. It's only ten minutes away.'

My vision of a romantic evening, a shared drink at the fountain, holding hands in the darkened theater, vanished.

I looked at my watch: 7:20. Curtain was at 8:00. There was no way I'd be able to sit still, knowing Silvio was out there, hunting down the star.

'I'm coming,' I said.

By the time we wheeled his truck out of the underground lot, seven more minutes had elapsed.

'At this point, it would take a medevac helicopter landing on the roof to get her there on time,' I said.

Silvio grunted and kept driving. Tense and focused, he swerved in and out of traffic, his eyes on the road.

'So what's Catarina's story?'

Silvio explained that Catarina Velosi was a fiery Latina. For years she had been Alfonso's muse and his lover. But she was capricious. Unstable. The final straw came when she took off to Berlin midrun with a composer who had scored one of Alfonso's plays. An understudy took over the part and Alfonso had no choice but to get over the actress too. He married, fathered a child, and grew increasingly prominent. His gangbanger past, when it was mentioned at all, lent him a greater nobility for his having escaped it. His plays

14

received critical raves and he won a MacArthur 'genius' grant. Eventually the Mark Taper Forum commissioned a play. In Los Angeles, it was theater's holy grail, and Alfonso yearned to be its Latino Lancelot and Arthur combined.

'He wrote *Our Lady of the Barrio* for her, you know,' Silvio said. 'Every woman he creates is based on Catarina.'

'What a burden.'

Silvio shot me an insulted look. 'It's an honor,' he said. 'But the director didn't want to cast her. He had heard the diva stories. So Alfonso got on his knees and begged. Then he had to beg Catarina to audition. She thought it was beneath her.' Silvio exhaled through clenched teeth. 'Oh, he ought to kill her for this.'

The truck shot out over Glendale Boulevard and up around Echo Park Lake. Silvio turned right, making his way along a hillside street above the water.

Catarina Velosi lived in a freshly whitewashed duplex draped with bougainvillea and banana plants and set back from the street by a wooded hillside. We trudged up a short flight of stairs to the entrance. From the house next door came the loud thumping of Spanish rap, the faint smoky scent of something sweet. Pot?

Silvio knocked, then stepped back. He knocked harder, calling her name. He swore in Spanish and yelled something at the rapper's window. A young man with a shaved head and a scraggly goatee stuck his face through the yellow curtain.

'Can you turn that down for a second, I'm trying to reach the lady in there,' Silvio said.

15

The man scowled and withdrew his head. A moment later, the volume was lowered. Silvio knocked again and tapped his foot. He tried the knob. It wouldn't turn.

'Poor Alfonso,' he said. 'Every critic in town is there tonight.'

'How do you know she hasn't turned up by now?'

'He promised he'd call.' Silvio tapped the mute cell phone in his pocket.

He stood there, undecided, for a moment. Then he said, 'Do me a favor. In my glove compartment, there is a screwdriver. Could you please get it while I check the window?'

Eager to help, I walked down to the truck, somewhat encumbered by my outfit, a scoop-necked 1940s cocktail dress of raw silk that curved nicely around my hips before ending just above the knee. It was a frock made for sipping Cosmopolitans and clapping for encores, not hiking down a stone staircase. The high-heeled black leather pumps didn't help, either.

Inside the truck, the glove compartment held only papers. I looked on the floor and groped under the seats, to no avail. Then I ran up to tell Silvio the bad news. He was standing at the front door, now ajar, and shoving something into his pocket. I heard a faint jingle.

'I thought it was locked.'

'I jimmied it.'

'That's good, because I couldn't find the screwdriver.'

He gave me an odd look. 'Well, never mind.'

And with that, he stepped into the house. From

somewhere inside, we heard a low, guttural growl. Silvio stumbled backward. Something soft brushed against my bare legs. I shrieked. Craning my head, I saw a fluffed orange tail disappear into the shrubbery.

The cat's eerie *rrowwwllll* reverberated up my spine.

Silvio straightened, pulled a tissue from his pocket, and sneezed several times, his allergies distracting him momentarily from the task at hand. Then he grasped the door with renewed determination.

Inside, the windows were closed and the curtains drawn against the heat. Silvio flipped on the light. When my eyes adjusted, I saw the room was empty. An overhead fan chugged at high volume, its blades whipping the hot, tired air.

From the recesses of the house came faint music, male voices singing plaintively in Spanish, their voices twining in the style of long ago.

'Someone's home,' I said.

Silvio ignored me and moved into the living room. Mexican serapes were slung over a leather chair. There was a rattan couch upholstered with toucans and tropical flowers. A low coffee table scattered with Hollywood trade publications. I saw a purse tipped on its side, spilling out coins, a brush, a leather wallet, and a cell phone.

'Catarina?' Silvio called.

I followed him, sniffing the air. The sickly odor of gas from a tidy two-burner stove in the kitchenette mingled with the overflowing contents of an ashtray, each butt kissed by bright red lipstick. Two mugs of half-drunk tea sat on a

1950s chrome table. Above the sink, colorful Fiestaware cups marched along the windowsill. A bleeding Jesus crowned in thorns gazed out from a dispenser of Wash Your Sins Away hand soap. An avocado seed stuck with toothpicks sprouted in a cloudy glass, its vines tumbling to the floor.

'Catarina, are you here?'

The tiny house seemed to absorb and muffle his words. Silvio walked into the hallway, floorboards squeaking under his weight. The singing was louder now, voices naked and anguished. He pushed the bathroom door open and called again, but the only answer was the slow gurgle of a toilet tank. He headed for the bedroom and I followed.

The music seeped out, crooning a silvery ballad. I could make out the lyrics now and they seemed sinister, at odds with the soaring melody and sweet harmony.

'Eres una flor carnivora
En un jardin salvaje.
Bonita pero fatal
Devorando mi corazon.'

I went back over the words in English to make sure I had it right:

You are a carnivorous flower
In a savage garden.
Beautiful but deadly
As you devour my heart.

As the strings died away, I heard a scratchy

18

whir, the pop of a record ending. Then the click of a phonograph arm rising, moving then dropping, the needle nestling back into the vinyl groove in a blur of white noise. The song started up again. It was plaintive and mournful, like the cry of a heron at dusk when the river holds no more fish.

But Silvio wasn't listening. At the bedroom arch, I heard his sudden exhale.

'Maybe you should wait here.'

His voice was unsteady. He turned to block the doorway, but I was already looking beyond him.

The bed was empty, its white eyelet sheets pulled back and tousled. A torn screen balanced precariously against the pillow. The sash window above the bed, which looked out onto an alley, gaped open. I craned over Silvio's shoulder.

'Is she there? Let me see. For God's sake, I'm a reporter.'

'Catarina?' Silvio said.

You are a carnivorous flower

Silvio stepped into the room. He walked to the closet and threw it open, pushing aside clothes and meeting only empty space. With a cry of exasperation, he strode to a large hamper and lifted the lid. Nothing. His eyes roved, considering where else a woman might hide.

In a savage garden.

He brushed past me and soon I heard him outside, calling hoarsely for Catarina.

19

I walked over to examine the bedsheets. There was no blood. Maybe the screen was old and warped and had fallen in. Maybe it had been torn for years.

Beautiful but deadly

My gaze went to the window and I thought I saw a faint smear of red on the sill. I bent closer. It was rusty, already dry and slightly ridged, like a furrow in a field.

As you devour my heart.

Why was this song playing over and over? It was as though someone was trying to tell us something.

'Silvio?' I called, but he didn't answer.

I moved to Catarina's bedside table, filled with framed photos. All held the same pale-skinned woman with long black hair, an oval face, and dark eyes. She had a disquieting way of staring directly into the camera, the force of her will radiating through the photo and into the room. My eyes flittered over more frames. There she was, clad in a negligee and cradling a cocktail in her 'Thin Man' phase. Defiant with a group of zoot-suited men, her arms filled with flowers. Dressed in a T-shirt and boxers, her thin, sculpted arms flung around a boyfriend. One of the photos had fallen to the sisal carpet. It lay facedown. I squatted to pick it up, then thought better of disturbing a potential crime scene. Slowly, I stood up.

'Don't touch anything,' I called to Silvio. 'You already have to explain to the police why your prints are all over the knobs.'

I considered Catarina Velosi. A single woman who lived alone. I pictured her putting on her favorite album and twirling around the room in the arms of an imaginary lover. Sliding between those sheets for an afternoon nap before her Taper debut tonight. Then someone raising the window, left unlocked in the heat, slashing the screen and climbing in. Every woman's nightmare. Did he have a gun or a knife? Had he put it to her head? Had a struggle ensued as she tried to fight him off, a struggle in which someone's blood was spilled on the windowsill?

Or had she put on the record for a lover before they headed to bed, then left in such a hurry that she forgot to take it off? What if Catarina Velosi was striding onto the Taper boards to mass applause right now, her biggest concern a case of preshow butterflies? And Alfonso so relieved he'd forgotten to call?

I pictured us two hours from now, gathered backstage. We'd make toasts and drink champagne and Silvio and I would turn this into a funny little anecdote. Remember that night Catarina gave us such a scare ... but what if that wasn't it?

There are pivotal moments in everyone's life, when they see the future laid out clear as a seer's vision, and there's both a hallucinatory and a hyper-real quality about it. Can this really be happening? Is it what my gut tells me it is? Should I go on my instinct, even though I'll be roundly embarrassed if I'm wrong?

21

As you devour my heart, the man crooned.

Slowly, I pulled my cell phone out of my purse.

'There's something that looks like blood on the windowsill,' I yelled to Silvio. 'I'm calling 911.'

'No,' he said, his footsteps echoing back into the house. 'Wait.'

Amazingly for L.A., an operator came on immediately. I took a deep breath.

'I'd like to report a break-in,' I said. 'A woman is missing. There's a dried substance that looks like blood. Echo Park, above the lake. The address is—'

'Don't,' Silvio said. He ran up, a queer look on his face as he realized I was already talking.

'I'm waiting, miss,' the operator said.

'What's the address here?' I asked.

Silvio stared at me for a long moment.

'Eight sixty-two Lakeshore,' he finally said.

It was only after I hung up that I considered the apprehension I had seen on Silvio's face.

'Why did you tell me to wait?' I asked.

The corner of Silvio's mouth twitched.

'Because there's got to be some logical explanation,' he said. 'Catarina's pulled these stunts before. And frankly, I'm worried that bad publicity could kill Alfonso's play.'

His answer seemed anything but frank.

'What if Alfonso's not the one getting killed,' I said, leading him to the rusty red mark on the sill. 'What do you think that is, nail polish?'

He looked at it and repeated that there must be an explanation. I thought he might be trying to convince himself. But then I thought of something else. Again, I heard the jingle in his pocket.

As the sirens drew closer and the singers wound up again with their beautiful and disturbing song, I asked my lover, 'You have a key to her apartment, don't you?'

CHAPTER 2

Silvio stared off into the hills, calculating something. 'Look,' he said finally, 'I can deal with the police. But someone needs to go back to the theater and tell Alfonso.'

It was as if my words hadn't registered. I crossed my arms over my chest. 'Why don't you answer my question first.'

Silvio took my shoulders and tugged me toward him. I saw myself reflected in his measured green irises and didn't like the pleading look on my face.

'Because it would take longer than we've got,' he said softly. 'I will tell you everything, I promise. But right now, I need you to do this one thing. Trust me, *querida*.'

I stepped back. I didn't want to get lost in those eyes.

'She's probably shown up by now and everything's fine.' Silvio's voice was cajoling. 'But I promised Alfonso an answer. Leave me to deal with the police. Take my truck. Here.'

He pulled out his ring of keys, unhooked one, and handed it to me.

'How will you get back?'

'Cab.'

'Why can't you call and tell him yourself?' I said, not understanding why I had to leave.

Silvio shook his head. 'I've already tried. He's not answering his cell.'

'Maybe something's wrong with your phone. Why don't you try hers?'

I pointed to an antique rotary on the bedside table. It was painted bloodred.

'Eve, you said yourself, we don't want to disturb any prints.'

My voice rose. 'And *you* just said there's a logical explanation—'

He took my elbow and squired me away from the house, down the steps and to his truck.

'You'd better be gone before the police arrive or they'll tie us both up for hours. Call me after you find Alfonso. And be discreet. You can't imagine the politics.'

Silvio wasn't telling me the whole truth, but I was worried enough about what he might be hiding to go along. For now.

Clambering into his truck, I put it into gear and drove back downtown. Along the lake, I passed a police car barreling down Echo Park Avenue in the opposite direction, its lights flashing. Heading, no doubt, for its own rendezvous with my lover.

Despite Silvio's upbeat tone, I knew that women, even absent-minded, narcissistic ones, didn't leave the house without their purse. Especially if it was crammed with a phone and a wallet. I dreaded what lay ahead. How was I going to tell Alfonso Reventon what we'd found? This

24

was not at all how I had imagined meeting the celebrated playwright whom Silvio was so proud to call his friend.

I parked in the underground lot and trudged up the concrete stairs of the Music Center, ignoring the stares of the attendants, who hadn't expected to see a woman in a cocktail dress and four-inch pumps hop out of a primer-splattered pickup. Emerging into the cool emptiness of the square, I walked to the box office, collected my ticket for *Our Lady of the Barrio*, and handed it to the man at the door.

'I'm afraid you've missed quite a lot,' he said, tearing it.

So the play had begun. Was Catarina onstage? I looked at my watch. It was 9:15.

In the foyer, crowds of well-dressed, tanned, and perfumed people mingled, drinks in hand. Was it already intermission? Catarina's house had seemed to exist outside of time.

Then came the trilling of three musical notes. Around me, patrons hurriedly gulped the remains of their drinks, plonked down glasses, and headed back into the dark of the theater. I stepped inside.

Spotting an usher, I told him I needed to find the playwright.

'And you are...?'

'Eve Diamond, *L.A. Times*,' I said firmly, in the tone I used to get past velvet ropes, receptionists, and emergency tape.

'I'm afraid you'll have to wait until after the performance,' the usher said smoothly. He had

25

freckles, a shock of red hair, and a name tag that said *Brad*. 'Why don't you enjoy the second act and then we'll see what we can do... Front row, you really scored. Shall I escort you to your seat? Once they start we can't let anyone in until there's a break.'

The warning notes went off again and the lights dimmed.

'Why don't you get me the manager instead?'

I could feel the gears turning as he appraised me, calculating the odds of my lobbing a bomb into the crowded house or rushing the stage with a submachine gun cleverly concealed in my purse. Telling me to wait right there, Brad took my ID and scurried away.

The doors to the theater closed. I walked over and pressed my nose to the crack. The last stragglers were finding their seats. The stage lights went on. Then a young and beautiful woman in baggy pants and a wife-beater shirt sauntered onto the stage and began a monologue. A man wearing the brilliant plumage and paint of a rooster wandered after her, pecking at the ground.

Was this Catarina? She had the same dark features as the woman in the framed photos, but it was hard to tell at this distance. Why hadn't I asked the usher if she had shown up?

'...he's not a bad boyfriend, really,' the girl on-stage was saying. 'He never hits me. We got two kids now.'

The rooster raised himself up, flapped his wings, and crowed. He waddled over to a nest, and with much waggling of his feathered butt, sat down on two eggs and fluffed himself out.

'My homegirls, they say, Angelica, why you settle for a goddamn bird? With your smarts, you could have anyone, but I tell them...'

I pulled away, scanning for Brad, but saw only a bartender at the far side of the bar, polishing a glass. Someone backstage would be able to tell me where Alfonso was sitting. Trying not to attract attention, I walked through the lobby and into a corridor, turning doorknobs, but this roused another usher, who came hurrying over.

'I need to find the playwright,' I said. 'It's important.'

He shot me a look that said 'crazy.'

'I'm with the *L.A. Times* and I've got a message for him.'

The usher crossed his arms.

'His subscription lapse?'

'Big-time,' I said. 'Has Catarina Velosi shown up?'

'Who?' he said politely, clasping his hands together.

Just two hours ago, I had asked the same thing. Now, having stood in the sanctum of her bedroom and seen the blood, the tousled sheets, it seemed I had known her forever.

'The lead actress,' I said, biting back the words *you idiot.*

'It's opening night,' the usher said. 'Of course she's here.'

'Did you see her arrive?'

'Not personally.'

'Did they announce any substitutes before curtain?'

He inclined his head. 'You'll have to ask one of

27

the ushers inside.'

'Good idea.' I walked back to the lobby. He caught up to me at the theater entrance and blocked my path.

'We're under strict orders not to let anyone in once the second act starts.'

'Oh, for Christ's sake, I need to speak to Alfonso Reventon.'

I reached into my purse to show him my ID before remembering I had given it to Brad.

'You'll have to wait until the show's over,' he repeated firmly.

I groaned, and stalked back to where Brad had told me to wait. Onstage, the action was heating up. I pressed my nose against the crack.

A guy dressed like Che Guevara was explaining to a young blond woman why people of color can't be racist.

'We've been oppressed all our lives,' the proto-Che said. 'We wouldn't turn around and oppress other people of color.'

The young woman threw up her hands. 'But you just said you wouldn't want your daughter to marry a Guatemalan.'

'You're right! See how insidious it is! Your racist attitudes have even infected me.'

'Me?' the woman said. 'I can't tell the difference between a Mexican and a Guatemalan. You're all wetbacks to me.'

'That's exactly the attitude I'm talking about.' The man's voice grew heated. 'I'm working on overcoming it. But I still don't want my daughter marrying no Guatemalan.'

A Spanglish rap song started up, punctuating

his words.

'Ms. Diamond?'

Reluctantly, I wrenched myself away. Brad was back. From the stage came raised voices, a slap, then a woman screaming. A rooster's hoarse *cock-a-doodle-doo.*

'The house manager will see you now,' Brad said.

I followed him through an unmarked door, down a set of stairs, and into the bowels of the theater. In a small office with exposed piping, a plump man with a receding hairline and tortoiseshell glasses adorned with twisting gold snakes sat behind a desk. My press pass lay in front of him. He picked it up as I sat down, held it at arm's length, then flopped his meaty forearms onto the desk.

'I know all the *Times* theater critics, honey, and you ain't one of them.'

'I never said I was. I'm a news reporter, and I've got an urgent message for Alfonso Reventon. I need to find him.'

A salacious look shot from Brad to the manager. This time I thought it said 'groupie.'

The manager held out short, stubby fingers heavy with rings. 'Give it to me. I'll see that he gets it.' He winked.

I flared with rage that he might mistake me for a theater groupie, but a more evolved part of my cortex also wondered: Did playwrights have groupies?

'I'm waiting,' the manager said in a singsong voice.

Torn between my concern for the missing act-

29

ress and the desire to remain loyal to Silvio and his friend, I stood up. My back prickled with nervous heat. I was supposed to tell Alfonso, not this guy. But now the police were involved.

'It's about Catarina Velosi,' I said in desperation. 'Is she here?'

That got their attention. I took advantage of their momentary stillness to snatch back my reporter's pass.

From above, the sound of clapping began.

'She was a no-show,' the manager said in a calm, deliberate voice. 'You know something about that? 'Cause I don't care what excuse Alfonso's got this time, they're firing her diva ass.'

I hesitated. Silvio had told me to be discreet. But didn't management deserve to know?

'My message is for Mr. Reventon. And no one else.'

Still, I couldn't resist a parting shot as I walked out.

'From what I saw in her bedroom just now, your leading lady has made a dramatic exit.'

CHAPTER 3

He might have been yelling at me to stop; it was hard to hear over the clapping and whistling as I swam against the stream of early departures and into the cool dark of the theater.

The audience was on its feet. Onstage, the cast was holding hands and taking a collective bow.

As I got closer, I scanned the actors. The woman from the bedroom photos was not among them.

Now the actors flung their arms out in synchronized welcome and the playwright strode down an aisle and hopped onto the stage. Alfonso was a slight man with a hawk nose, rounded shoulders, and a goatee. He had thick black hair pulled back in a ponytail. His brown eyes, piercing behind round glasses, roved over the crowd. With his collarless black jacket and severe manner, he looked every inch the Chicano intellectual.

Placing one arm over his heart, he bowed deeply, then allowed himself a thin smile to acknowledge the full house, on its feet and clapping rhythmically. As he straightened, a pretty young woman thrust a bouquet of flowers at him. The applause grew, swelling the theater.

I spotted another usher and gave him my most professional smile. 'L.A. Times,' I said, flashing my press pass. 'How do I get backstage?'

'This way, miss,' he said, and I followed him through two unmarked doors into a room filling up with well-wishers.

Soon the actors filed in from the stage, glowing and exuberant. First came a flood of the minor characters – Che and the earnest blond woman, a ravaged older woman in jeans and a T-shirt, a priest in a Roman Catholic collar, a gaggle of haughty gangbangers and their molls, and finally Angelica the homegirl and her rooster, a tall, bronzed man smeared with feathers and paint whose fierce Yanomami getup was undermined by dimples as he smiled.

Last came Alfonso, and people's heads turned

like flowers basking in the nimbus of his celebrity sun. Such was his magnetism that it took me a moment to see the woman who hung on his arm, laughing and greeting people. By herself, she would have had her own celebrity glow. But next to Alfonso, her light seemed diminished. Could this be Catarina? As they drew closer, I knew I had never seen her before.

She was taller than Alfonso and curvy, poured into a red halter dress, with a fringed black shawl thrown over bare shoulders. She had flowing hair, strong features, and large, startled eyes. As patrons paid their respects, she embraced them loudly, but there was a nervous trill in her voice and an affected nonchalance as she surveyed the high-octane crowd.

The mayor of Los Angeles was there, Carter Langdon III, whom I knew as a millionaire philanthropist and keeper of secrets. Forming a rear guard behind him were the affluent white theatergoers who kept formal culture alive in Los Angeles. The East Side power brokers were out in force as well – U.S. Congressman Henry Duarte, who owed his seat to Latino redistricting, and a heavyset L.A. city councilman named Julio Cortez who had gone to Dartmouth and returned to govern his people at age twenty-seven. Around him clustered labor activists and community organizers.

Off to the side stood an edgy movie director from Mexico City, a popular DJ, a graffiti artist whose work commanded six figures in the best galleries, and an East L.A. rock band. I moved closer and heard them pledging money to a slight and bearded Jesuit priest who was beloved throughout the tough East Side projects – and the violence-weary city at large – for brokering a truce among Los Angeles' Latino gangs. Realizing that lack of jobs bred trouble, the Jesuit had opened a *panadería* – a Mexican bakery – and hired sworn rivals to work side by side turning out tortillas and *pan dulce.*

A little girl darted through the crowd dressed in her Sunday best, only to be swept up into the arms of a man in huaraches with hollowed cheeks, a graying ponytail, and the pious serenity of a modern-day Jesus. Next to him stood a man with jailhouse eyes who looked like he lined up every morning for his methadone cocktail. Next to them were three animated Latino yuppies in slick suits. The crowd was a mixture of low-down street and aesthete, and it struck me that here was the crossroads where Alfonso situated his plays. He was *humilde,* a humble man of the people, and that was why they had turned out in droves to honor him.

Anxious to deliver my message to Alfonso, I pushed my way through, only to see the man with jailhouse eyes cut to the front of the receiving line and grab the playwright in a headlock. A collective 'oh' issued from the crowd as people flowed backward, unsure whether to call security. The two tussled for a moment, then broke apart. Alfonso jabbed his attacker playfully in the stomach.

'I wrote that thing you said,' Alfonso told him. 'When you left the other day. I wrote it down and then the words kept coming. Like an *ángelito* perched on my shoulder whispering in my ear. It felt like I was taking dictation.'

'*Carnal!*' the man roared. He grabbed Alfonso's shoulders. 'Just tell the truth, man,' he said, pulling him closer. 'Speak for us. Be our voice. That's all we ask.'

He stared into Alfonso's eyes, seeming to want to say something more, then turned and stalked off. The West Side theater patrons stared, his queue-jumping already forgiven as they salted away this anecdote for their next dinner party. Here were Alfonso's roots laid bare, a character stepping into life from one of his plays.

Just as I reached him, Alfonso Reventon was whisked away by a well-groomed couple, immaculate in summer whites. His dark ponytail bobbed and disappeared into the crowd.

Alfonso's consort saw me staring and stretched out a long hand. 'Marisela Reventon,' she said by way of introduction. 'I'm nobody important, just the wife. But it's nice to meet you anyway.'

Taken aback, I shook her hand.

'Glad to meet you. I'm a friend of...' but before I could finish my sentence, she hitched up one foot to adjust the strap of her high-heeled sandal, balancing precariously. She tilted and I stepped forward and caught her. A lock of her hair fell against my face, and I smelled lilacs and something else – liquor – coming off her in waves.

'Ah, thank you,' she said, finding her balance. She parted the curtain of wavy hair and I saw that her eyes were black as two marbles and her face shone with a luminous glow, though whether it came from the booze or somewhere deeper

34

inside was hard to say. The drink was eroding her lush beauty, thickening her features and making her voice jagged and rough.

'And now I really must...'

And she teetered off, eyes unfocused, until she spied a waiter with a tray of margaritas.

'Aaaah,' she said, swiping one. 'Thank you.'

She drank deeply. And in that wet pause, I caught up with her.

'Please help me,' I said. 'I don't know what the actors look like, but I've got to know. Is Catarina here?'

Marisela stopped. Her eyes glinted unpleasantly. And then she did focus on me.

'Why is everyone so obsessed with her?' she said, tossing back her hair. 'Now he can make *me* his muse. I told him not to cast her. I knew she'd destroy everything. And now,' her voice rose triumphantly, 'my warning has come true.'

While I hadn't seen the whole play, it struck me that there was as much melodrama going on offstage as on. If this performance was any indication, Marisela could give Catarina a run for her money in the acting department.

Now a small frown played across Marisela's generous mouth.

'The understudy stepped in. On opening night, what a travesty. This is the end of Catarina's career.' Her voice held barely banked glee.

'So you have no idea where she is?'

'Who are you?' Suspicious now. Bristling with hostility.

'A friend of Silvio Aguilar's,' I said. 'Your husband sent us to Catarina's apartment to look for her. She wasn't there but it looked like someone had broken in. The bedroom window was open and the screen torn and pushed in.'

Marisela's mouth quivered, and her heavy brows drew together.

'Come with me,' she said, dead sober now. 'We must tell Alfonso immediately.'

She grabbed my arm and tugged me through the crowd, which parted before her. Soon we stood next to her husband.

Up close, Alfonso Reventon looked older and had finer features than I had seen onstage. A silver loop hung from one ear. His black hair sparkled with strands of silver. He had small, thin lips and a slender nose. Two horizontal lines ran across his forehead, just above the bridge of his glasses. He turned to us with the practiced smile of an artist greeting his patrons.

'Sweetheart, this is a friend of Silvio's,' Marisela said. 'She was just at Catarina's apartment. Tell him,' she commanded, prodding me in the back.

As the halting words fell from my tongue, Alfonso's smile ebbed. A muscle in his jaw twitched and his body stiffened. I had expected concern. But what I saw looked more like anger. The anger of a control freak who learns his orders have been defied.

'Silvio stayed to talk to the police,' I concluded.

'The police?' Alfonso shook his head. He pulled a cigarette out of his pocket, turned it from end to end, but didn't light it. 'She's probably passed out drunk somewhere. Or shacked up at the Chateau Marmont with some new boyfriend.

36

Unfortunately for my plays, Catarina is a creature of libidinous impulse.'

'Here's to libidinous impulse,' said a voice
behind us. I turned and saw Marisela Reventon,
margarita in hand.

Alfonso tapped the end of the cigarette against
his palm, his gaze fastened somewhere above my
head.

'It's certainly given the understudy a chance to
shine,' he continued, ignoring his wife. 'She
might as well enjoy her moment in the spotlight
until Catarina turns up. What a lucky break for
her,' he finished bitterly.

Marisela's long, wavy hair flew like Medusa's
snakes.

'I told you not to cast her,' she said through
gritted teeth. 'That woman is poison. You deserve
this, Alfonso. It's all your fault.' Then she stalked
off.

I thought I saw Alfonso's eyes narrow, but his
voice was steady. 'My wife,' he said, 'is not well.
She's easily agitated. You must take no notice of
her. She doesn't mean what she says.'

He studied the floor, contemplating some
private sorrow, then slowly raised his eyes to me.

'I should call Silvio,' he said finally, pulling out
his cell phone.

He dialed, then swore as it beeped twice. 'Oh
Christ, battery low, it's not going through.'

He looked around for another phone but I was
already calling Silvio on mine.

'It's me,' I said when he answered. 'She's not at
the theater.'

From the other end came a loud groan.

'Where are you?' I asked.

'At the house. I can't talk long. The police are still here.'

'I didn't realize you had so much to tell them.'

I felt brittle, caught up in a drama of my own. I'd been cast as the jealous girlfriend and was playing it to a *T*.

There was a loud exhalation. 'As soon as I'm finished, I'll fill you in.'

'I'll be all ears.'

'Can I talk to Alfonso a sec?'

I handed over the phone and listened to a highly circumscribed conversation. Then Alfonso walked across the room and talked heatedly and at length.

After hanging up, he looked over and saw I had been watching. His face darkened, but by the time he walked back with the phone, he was smiling.

'Thank you,' he said, and gave a little bow. 'You should relax until Silvio gets here. Have a drink.'

I shook my head. My appetite for alcohol had vanished along with my romantic evening.

'Please,' the playwright said. 'It will leave that much less for my wife.'

He pressed his lips into a smirk, but I wouldn't meet his eyes. Maybe his wife had a drinking problem but it seemed petty and mean-spirited to call attention to it.

'Well then, you'll excuse me...' Alfonso pointed to the line of well-wishers, deferential smiles on their faces, champagne and flowers in their arms.

I gave him an incredulous look. The leading lady was missing on opening night and her apartment showed signs of being broken into – why wasn't Alfonso more alarmed?

'Silvio said you think she's dead or something,' he said, divining my thoughts.

'Does that mean you're actually concerned?' I let the sarcasm dangle between us.

'I'd be more concerned if her Toyota was there. Silvio said it's gone. She went somewhere, that's all.' Petulance filled his voice. 'Just to spite me and ruin my play.'

I crossed my arms and stared at him.

'Women don't usually leave a full purse behind when they take off.'

'Why don't you read your own paper's clips about Catarina,' Alfonso said. 'That will convince you of her flakiness faster than I ever could.'

Just then we heard shrill laughter. The room fell silent.

'I was never his muse,' slurred a female voice.

'If you'll excuse me,' Alfonso said, 'I've got another problem to attend to.'

He took a step toward his wife, stopped, and said, 'For years she's taken acting lessons. She doesn't understand why I don't cast her.'

Then with the air of a condemned man, he took her by the arm and whispered into her ear, caressing her hair. Marisela Reventon's expression softened.

I thought how difficult it must be to be married to a genius. To languish on the periphery of his world and yearn for center stage.

An aide appeared with two chairs. Alfonso settled his wife into one and sat beside her. Then he composed his features and greeted the next well-wisher. His face grew animated, mouth up-turned in a modest smile as the compliments rained down. But I thought that his eyes remained alert and calculating.

The door opened. Two more visitors stepped backstage. They wore badges and uniforms and hadn't come to offer congratulations. But they had the good grace to look apologetic as they cut to the front of the line.

CHAPTER 4

As ripples of confusion spread through the room, I slipped away. The cops would want to question Alfonso and that was one party I couldn't crash. I was anxious to meet up with Silvio but even more curious about the bizarre backstage per-formances of his friends.

And so, despite the late hour, I drove the few blocks to Second and Spring streets, to the Los Angeles Times, the building that never sleeps. I would read the clips and steep myself in Catar-ina's past while I waited for Silvio's call. This had all the hallmarks of a good story, and I wanted to be prepared.

As I drove, a bubble of exhilaration rose inside me. I knew it was wrong, but I couldn't help it. It flooded my capillaries until every bit of me tingled with certainty that came from the viscera, not the brain. Something terrible had happened to Catarina Velosi, and I was being drawn inexorably into the fire.

It was 11:30 when I reached the third-floor editorial offices. I was shocked to see Tom Thompson sitting at the City Desk. He ran the San Gabriel Valley section, where I usually worked, and it was hard to fathom what could have brought him to the mother ship so late.

'Did an airplane go down at LAX?' I asked.

He peered out over his bifocals.

'Why, if it isn't Eve Diamond,' Thompson said, his relaxed tone providing the answer. 'Even considering your slavish devotion to the job, it's a bit late.'

'Had a theater date downtown,' I said. 'But it ran amok.'

'Whassamatter, your date stand you up?'

'He stood himself up. And the play's leading lady is missing.'

Thompson grinned. 'Maybe they ran off together.'

I remembered Silvio's urgent calls for Catarina in that tiny house.

'I'm here to read the clips on her,' I said.

I bit back the impulse to say more. Thompson would want me in the San Gabriel Valley tomorrow, not haring after a missing woman from Echo Park.

'So what brings you to the Velvet Coffin tonight?' I said, using the paper's nickname. Despite being a top-notch place, the *Times* often had an airless, half-dead feel, which is quite a feat for a daily newspaper.

Thompson wearily adjusted his glasses. 'Bunch of paperwork on that new hire. Plus I gotta write

41

condolence letters to everyone else.'

He opened his briefcase, revealing a jagged mountain of cover letters, résumés, and newspaper clips. He had been busy for months, reading and shuffling them like cards and arguing with Hiring and Development. They had told him to hire a minority; he wanted the best person for the job, regardless of color. Meanwhile the barrage kept coming, fat manila files stuffed with hope.

'So who'd you hire?' I asked

'A Met-Pro.' He beamed. 'She was right under our noses.'

Met-Pro was the Minority Employee Trainee Program, which brought talented reporters of color into the newsroom while allowing the paper to observe and hire the best ones. The only trouble was, the deck was stacked with suburban children of privilege, not the truly disadvantaged, but that was something nobody talked about.

'She's been in the Long Beach bureau for two months, broken a few stories. Plus she's working on a nondupe.'

I raised an eyebrow. Nondupes were front-page stories that ran in the paper's coveted left-hand, Column One slot. Even for seasoned reporters, they were hard to land.

'Sounds like she's on the fast track.'

'Let's just say downtown's watching her closely. Anyway, Long Beach already has two minorities on staff, so Jane Sims did a little horse-trading.'

Thompson slapped down a Polaroid and I leaned in to examine it.

The photo showed paunchy Met-Pro director

Barry Patterson standing next to a pretty young woman with mocha skin, high cheekbones, almond eyes, and the bee-stung lips that women in Hollywood pay small fortunes for. Long black hair erupted around her oval face in tight ringlets.

I clicked my tongue.

'She doesn't look that black,' I said, recalling a reporter who had been hired solely because management thought he was black. His clips were heavy with profiles for *Jet*, *Ebony*, and *Essence*. It was only when he walked into the newsroom that the shocked editors realized he was just another white guy.

'She doesn't look that white, either,' Thompson shot back. 'Felice Morgan,' he said, his lips caressing the words. 'Hotshot reporter from the *Fort Worth Star-Telegram*. Wrote a story that got drug convictions overturned for thirty-two black prisoners. Turns out the fat-bellied sheriff trumped up the evidence. Now he's sitting in his own cell block. Oh yeah,' Thompson said, 'she's the real deal. Hiring and Development's hot on her. Sees lots of potential. And as of tomorrow, she belongs to San Gabe.'

I knew he didn't mean it, but it still had an unpleasant ring. I'd heard about the fierce bidding wars that newspapers waged over top minority reporters. It made me think of auction blocks and chattel and the merciless Southern sun.

SOLD! To the Los Angeles Times: *One young, ambitious, intelligent black female reporter. Guaranteed to enhance diversity and improve your institution's credibility with people of color.*

43

I snorted.

'Knowing Patterson, he's probably hot *for* her too,' I said.

Rumors swirled that the man took a personal interest in his prettiest prospects. But with jobs hanging in the balance at one of the nation's largest papers, there were few complaints.

'She starts tomorrow,' Thompson said, 'and I'd appreciate it if you take her out on assignment with you this week, show her how we do things around here.'

Annoyance rippled through me. I should be advancing my own career, not babysitting the paper's latest poster child for affirmative action. I focused on the résumés sticking out of Thompson's briefcase and took several deep breaths.

'It's hard to believe so many reporters want to come here for a lousy bureau job,' I said.

Thompson grinned. 'You forget, ingrate, that this is the *L.A. Times*,' he said. 'When you're slogging through a Buffalo winter and it's so cold the ink in your pen freezes during an interview, the orange groves of the San Gabriel Valley begin to smell mighty fragrant.

'Now about this missing actress gal,' Thompson said, and I knew he hadn't been fooled by my earlier change of topic. 'It's too late for today but write up what you've got for the Overnote,' he said, referring to the nightly memo the late editor left for the morning folks.

'But don't think you're going to cover it,' he said, seeing my eagerness. 'For one, it's out of your geographic beat. And two, there's a personal connection. Am I wrong?'

'You think I can't separate my personal life from my professional?'

'If this thing gets messy, your boyfriend's gonna get hauled in front of the police. So you'd best stay away.'

'Silvio already spoke to them. And I may be next. We were at her house tonight, looking for her.'

Thompson's eyes narrowed and his voice rose. 'Jesus, Eve, why can't you ever stay out of trouble?'

'It was supposed to be a quiet evening at the theater,' I said, remembering that moment by the fountain, which, in retrospect, had been the cultural highlight of my night.

'Well, next time make it a puppet theater.'

Thompson stood up and stretched. 'It's eleven forty-five and this old boy is plum tuckered out.'

He stuffed the papers into his bulging briefcase but one fell out and zigzagged lazily to the floor. I bent to pick it up and read:

Gelatinous pork in a can.
Our taste buds hail
Mama's mystery meat.

'What the heck is this?' I asked, dangling it between thumb and forefinger.

'It's big on the Internet,' he said. 'Spam haiku. People try to one-up each other. I'm still working on the meter.' Thompson reddened.

My grandmother tried to get me to eat Spam once. It was big in Europe after World War II when the Allied food lifts had kept the continent fed. She sautéed it with garlic, but still...

45

'You eat that stuff?'

He laughed. ''Course not. I just like to see how profound I can get in seventeen compressed syllables. Takes the pressure off, after a long day. A true creative challenge.'

He took the paper from my hand and slid it into his briefcase.

'San Gabriel tomorrow morning, Diamond.' He fixed me with a knowing look. 'We don't want to keep Felice waiting.'

CHAPTER 5

After Thompson left, I wrote up my notes about the no-show actress and filed them to the City Desk. Then I punched in Catarina Velosi's name for a LexisNexis search. As the citations began popping up, I wondered what was keeping Silvio.

Deciding to make the most of my time, I clicked on a *Los Angeles Times Magazine* profile of Catarina and soon realized that the drama of her personal life made Alfonso's play look sedate by comparison.

Catarina was a throwaway child from the East Side projects who bounced around in foster care for years before landing in the California Youth Authority for stabbing a foster father who molested her. She got into acting through a drama teacher who had the naivete to think that theater could reform young delinquents. At sixteen she left the system, an emancipated minor, and got her first Equity role in a production by up-and-coming playwright Alfonso Reventon. They became lovers and had to sneak around because she was underage. At first she blossomed under his tutelage. She won awards and critical raves and a college scholarship to study drama. But as the pressure grew, old habits began to re-assert themselves. There were missed rehearsals. Chronic tardiness. She showed up loaded and slurring her words. She imagined insults and provoked fights and Alfonso had to make nice. It was as though she wanted to sabotage her own success. Word got out about her volatility, her wild affairs, and Alfonso's generosity in forgiving them. As her behavior spiraled out of control, it was said she had a death wish.

I glanced at the clock: midnight. Where was Silvio? I frowned and read some more. Catarina was diagnosed as bipolar. She bounced in and out of rehab. She begged people to give her another chance and saw herself as a tragic heroine of epic proportions, a Latin Frances Farmer. Like so many great but troubled artists, Catarina brought pleasure to everyone but herself. She had no insight into her own life and actions. Seeing her was exhilarating, a high-wire performer working without a net. But it was also terrifying to watch a wounded soul bent on immolation.

And through it all, Alfonso kept writing for her. There were dark whispers that he needed the ugly dramas of her life to ignite his work. Their symbiotic relationship unraveled, even as Holly-wood came calling. After getting fired from a TV pilot, Catarina dropped out of sight and there were rumors she had gone to Belize to 'heal.'

Our Lady of the Barrio was to have been Catarina's triumphant return to the Los Angeles stage. The most recent article had talked about the synergy of the actors, of Alfonso brooding in the back row at rehearsals, scribbling new dialogue for his muse. The reporter had found Catarina subdued, and I wondered if she was on medication. Or was there some other, more sinister reason?

I decided to order up Alfonso's clips, then call it a night. While I waited for them to print, I scrolled back through the Catarina stories, stopping at the teacher who had introduced Catarina to theater: Victoria Givens. Here was someone worth interviewing. She worked at Belmont High School, an imploding fortress near downtown where overworked teachers valiantly crammed Civil War battles and quadratic equations into the minds of minority students, a race against time in a place where less than half the population made it to graduation.

I wrote Victoria Givens's name and her school in my notebook. A wave of tiredness hit. My head felt like lead. It was 12:20 a.m. The phone rang.

'It's me.'

'Did she show up?' I asked.

'No.' Something veiled, almost trembly in his voice.

'You don't mean...'

'No. There's nothing.'

I pushed the computer mouse around the desk, watched it light up at my touch. Turning my fingers ruby red.

'I guess that's good?'

'Who knows. It's late. You still want to meet?'

His voice wary. Probing.

I struggled to keep mine neutral. Did I really want to hear this?

'We've got unfinished business,' I said. 'I wouldn't be able to sleep.'

We agreed to meet at my house.

I thought about Silvio as I drove home. He wasn't an easy man to be with. He was proud, stubborn. He held himself to impossibly high standards, then despaired when he failed to meet them. He could be mercurial, moody. Relying on formality and elaborate manners to keep people at bay. I sensed him retreating now, pulling the drawbridges up behind him, letting the alligators loose in the moat.

I knew because I had breached those defenses. I had seen him naked and exposed, in thrall to the passions he took such pains to hide from the world. Our flesh melting and fusing. The cathedral of our bed at night. What he saw as weakness, I saw as strength. That he could give himself so fully completed something in me. I needed him. I needed the free fall of being with him.

It's going to be okay, I thought. No matter what.

CHAPTER 6

The Los Angeles streets are empty and peaceful late at night, dark expanses punctuated by the nova glow of fast-food cubes. Soon I was on Glendale Boulevard and heading home to Silverlake, an eclectic community fifteen minutes northwest of downtown. There was less neon here, just the slanted yellow light of an occasional bar door opening and a patron slipping out for a solitary cigarette.

Silverlake was a mecca for artists and iconoclasts, and I felt proprietary about the place and reveled in its odd charms. The neighborhood wore its age and history proudly, like a tattered vintage dress of impeccable design that had been lovingly restored. Here, ghosts of long-ago movie studios stood watch over Latin *botanicas* and owls and coyotes hunted in the sylvan hills within sight of downtown. Here, flamboyant Haitian drag queens lived next door to Chinese Jehovah's Witnesses and both were welcomed at block parties by the nice Hungarian octogenarian who was rumored to have been a princess before she renounced her birthright in favor of the Marxist struggle.

When I pulled up to my bungalow, Silvio was waiting in my car. From the radio, I heard Agustin Lara crooning a long-ago ballad, and the sound drifted, poignant and melancholy in the dark.

Then Silvio was beside me. He slung his arm low around my waist as we walked into the house, fingers brushing my hipbone, the intimacy sending a queer spark of electricity through my body.

It's going to be okay.

I turned on some lamps and threw myself onto the couch.

'So,' I said.

Silvio walked to the window. Trees made dark shadows against the glass. Far away, a siren started up, faint but insistent. A coyote chimed in. It yipped and howled, voice rising and falling in time with the siren. Another coyote joined the fray. Soon there was a furry-throated chorus at their vespers. Suddenly they fell silent. The air throbbed with emptiness and still he didn't speak.

'Silvio, look at me. Why do you have a key to her place?'

Across the vast expanse of room, he turned. The corners of his mouth sagged. He took a deep breath.

'Because we used to be involved.'

Even though I had suspected as much, it still hit me hard. This was his friend's leading lady, his onetime lover and muse. Small explosions went off in my brain.

'What did you and Alfonso do, share her?' I said coldly to keep my voice from cracking.

'Of course not.' His voice equally cold and flat. 'They had broken up.'

I stared at his sandals, black and made of supple leather. The sandals shuffled. My eyes

51

traveled up the khakis to the crisply ironed shirt, the long ruddy neck. His face half lost in shadow. I felt like an explorer, gingerly setting foot on the dark side of the moon.

'When were you together?' I asked. Such a simple question. And so much riding on it.

His voice thawed. 'Long before we met, if that's what you mean.'

Silvio and I had known each other almost a year but hadn't spent much time together due to lawyers, murders, trials, family troubles, and our respective work. Plus I had been in the hospital. I was fine now, at least physically. We were easing back into dating. But once again, the curtain had thudded down on our plans.

I wondered how well I truly knew this man and whether our physical attraction had blinded me to other things. What if I had kidded myself about the depth of our relationship? If Silvio could sleep with his best friend's woman, where did that leave me?

'Alfonso didn't mind you and Catarina...?' Silvio ran his finger along the glass pane.

'Alfonso doesn't know.'

'Oh, even better. You betrayed your friend with his lover. Pretty shabby.'

'It wasn't like that,' he said softly.

'Then please tell me how it was.'

There was a long silence.

'Well?' I pulled a blanket over my shoulders for comfort. Part of me yearned for him to put his arms around me and reassure me of his love. But another part knew that if he did, I'd push him away.

'Alfonso had broken up with her,' Silvio said at last, his voice catching deep in his throat. 'You have to understand that they had an extremely tempestuous relationship. But it was over. And I'd known her for years. We had too much to drink one night and ... something happened. In hindsight, I can see that she orchestrated the whole thing to get back at Alfonso. She knew how close we were, and how hurt he would be if he found out. So she slept with me.'

'And it was a onetime thing?' I hugged my knees to my chest because I already knew the answer.

'I was young and dumb and she was mesmerizing. Like a cyclone, sweeping up everything in her path. I would have done anything for her. And she liked that. Needed it, even. She's not a good person.'

He shook his head, as if to rid himself of the memory.

'But I didn't see that side of her. All I knew was how beautiful she was, and when I held her in my arms, that body, I didn't want to let go. It was like a sacrament. I didn't realize it was a sacrament she bestowed indiscriminately. She cheated on me. I found out and made a huge scene and she begged me to forgive her and I did. We went on for a while. But eventually she dumped me. There was no challenge to me, she said. No complexity.'

'She was blind,' I said, pinching the skin of my thighs and focusing on the pain. Somehow we had gotten off track.

'What about the key?' I asked again.

53

Silvio made a disparaging gesture.

'She gave it to me when we got together. After we broke up, she'd call me sometimes, late at night, and I'd come over.'

'How long ago was that?'

'Five years. She ran off to Berlin around that time. Then a year later she was back, living with Alfonso again. In that house. It lasted two years before they broke up. And the whole time I was terrified she'd tell him. I hated that she held this power over us. The power she conjured up with her body.'

His voice was thick and slow, drugged with the memory. He closed his eyes and laid his forehead against the glass.

'And you haven't seen her since?' Something inside me flared with jealousy.

'That's right. I finally wised up and realized the person I loved didn't exist.'

His voice oozed resentment and I knew she still had the power to hurt him.

'Swear to me,' I said.

He lifted his head off the window. I thought he might be feigning confusion. 'Swear what?'

'That you haven't seen her since you've known me.'

Something fluttered in his eyes then disappeared like a bat at twilight.

'I swear,' Silvio said. 'I told you. You are asking, and I'm trying to be honest.'

'Then why didn't you throw away the key?'

He looked defeated. 'I'm not really sure. I kept it for a long time out of hope, I guess. Then, after I got over her, throwing it away didn't seem worth the effort. She had no power over me anymore. And the key was a talisman; it reminded me of how lucky I'd been to get free of her. I'm not like Alfonso, who can channel his emotions into the plays. With me it would have bottled up with nowhere to go. She would have destroyed me.'

Silvio walked to the couch and sat down at the far end.

I plucked at the satin hem of the blanket. 'Why didn't you tell me about her before?'

'It was ancient history.'

'Oh, so you would have just sat in the theater with me, watching her and remembering how you once made love to her?'

He winced. 'It might have come up eventually. But it's delicate.'

'Alfonso still doesn't know?'

Silvio nodded.

'Well, it's going to come up soon, knowing the cops.' My brain darted to another topic. 'Speaking of which, did you tell them how you got in?'

'I told them the door was unlocked.'

'What?' I shouted.

He shrugged. 'I guess I panicked.'

Funny, he had seemed quite composed as we said good-bye in front of Catarina's place.

'All I could think of was how it would upset Alfonso,' Silvio said. 'Later maybe, when this is resolved, I'll tell him. He's got too much on his mind right now.'

'But the locked front door suggests that someone broke in through the bedroom window.'

He snorted. 'That screen's always been loose. A

little acrobatic sex would knock it out pretty fast.'

An image rose of Silvio and beautiful, passionate Catarina locked in an embrace on that very bed. I pushed it aside.

'Would a little acrobatic sex leave blood on the sill too?'

Then I thought of something that made me swallow hard. 'What if the police ask me about the front door? Because I don't know if I can lie.'

'Just tell them the truth. I sent you for the screwdriver and when you came back it was open.'

He *was* asking me to lie. Why? He's got motive, a voice inside me nagged. He loved her. They had a nasty breakup. Jealousy can drive men insane. The old 'if I can't have her, no one can.' But then wouldn't he have snapped a long time ago? It didn't make sense. I hated myself for even thinking it, but reporters are natural-born skeptics. In school they teach us that if your mother says she loves you, you'd better find two people to confirm it. What, then, about a lover?

'Won't it be worse if they find out the truth later?' I asked, my suspicions turning to resentment.

'I don't see how they would. Or how that's relevant.'

'Silvio.' My voice rose. 'What if something's *happened* to her?' I was dancing around the *M* word and he had to know it.

'I told you how she is,' he said heatedly. 'By the time we wake up tomorrow, I'm sure she'll have turned up.'

His face was haggard with exhaustion, his eyes crinkled with concern. But for whom? Me? Catarina? Alfonso? Himself and his own credibility? Then he slid over. His arm crept around my shoulder.

'I love you, Eve.'

He leaned in and his lips brushed mine, a soft, warm lingering. My body already believed in him, but my brain wouldn't let me succumb so easily. Years of finely calibrated instinct warned me that something was wrong.

He felt my hesitation and stood up. 'Guess I'll go then. It's late and we both need some sleep.'

'No, stay.'

I stood and wrapped my arms around him, fitting my body against his. I nuzzled his neck, inhaling sandalwood and summer sweat and something new: an acrid fear. He was stiff at first, but slowly his limbs relaxed into mine. It bothered me that he'd asked me to lie but I still wanted the animal comfort of him. I tugged him into the bedroom and we lay down, facing each other but not touching. A wisp of hair curled over his ear, and I had a childlike urge to loop its soft silkiness around my finger. Instead, I ran my fingers along his jaw. His stubble pricked my finger pads and he reached up and grabbed my hand and kissed each fingertip.

Our breathing came soft and still, the tension between us building, an inexorable pull drawing us into each other's gravity. I resisted. I needed to be apart from him until I worked some things out in my head. I could have traced his features blindfolded, every contour of his body. I knew the scent that rose from his skin after making love, the sounds he made, the way his voice cracked as he whispered that he loved me. And yet there was so much about him that I didn't know. Silvio existed apart from me too. He had a history that was not ours. He had secrets. Secrets that were wrapped up somehow with Catarina and Alfonso, and the life he had led before we met.

His other hand lay outstretched on the pillow, smooth and tan against the white cotton. I followed the branching blue tributaries, long, tapering fingers, pink nail beds tipped in white. It was a work of art, disembodied in its sculptural elegance, erotic as Mapplethorpe's calla lily.

And then he reached for me and the calla lily became the hand of my lover. Undressing each other, we made love wordlessly. My spiraling unease and vague fears made things more intense. It can be like that sometimes. But the haunted feeling didn't go away. And in the moments before I drifted off the cliff of consciousness, I wondered where Catarina Velosi was, and whether she was still alive. I wondered if Silvio knew the answers.

CHAPTER 7

Something woke me before dawn. I rolled over and saw Silvio on his side, one thigh slung over the empty space where I had just lain. I felt hollowed out by dread. It took me a moment to remember why.

I got up, made coffee, and crunched granola. My jaw felt rusty. I showered and dried off briskly, feeling my spirit return, settling into the nooks and crannies of my body. I drank a second cup of coffee and my mind quickened. The sun would soon be up.

In the bedroom, a phone rang. Silvio's mobile. I waited for him to pick up, but the unfamiliar chirping continued. What if it was news about Catarina? I walked back to the bedroom.

'Silvio,' I said. He exhaled and pulled the covers up. Afraid the chirping would stop, I answered it.

'Is Silvio there?' Alfonso's voice. Coiled taut.

I shook Sleeping Beauty by the shoulder.

He reared up and I handed him the phone. The clock radio said 5:25 a.m. Silvio listened, then said, 'Was there a body?'

More listening. Minutes passed.

'We'll meet you there.' A pause. 'She's a reporter,' Silvio said. 'She'll be fine.'

He hung up and swung his legs over the bed.

'They found her car three hundred feet down a ravine on Angeles Crest Highway,' he said, already sliding into his pants. 'Empty. They've got a search team combing the area.'

I pictured Catarina prowling her tiny apartment that morning, filled with nervous energy. Then suddenly deciding to drive into the mountains, do a little meditation maybe, tap that inner lightning rod that had always served her so well. Running out the door with only her car keys clasped in her hand. Then, halfway up the mountain, some mechanical trouble, a tire blowout, the steering wheel spinning crazily, Catarina's car plunging off the road. Was she thrown from the car? Had she been injured and gone for help? Was she alive somewhere, nails blackened with earth, pine needles nestling in her blood-caked hair?

But it didn't make sense. Catarina hadn't taken her purse. Her cell phone. And why would she have gone for a joyride up Angeles Crest just hours before her play opened at the city's top theater?

I pulled on my own pants, buttoned a linen shirt, slid into shoes. Dumping the rest of the coffee into a thermos, I grabbed a loaf of bread to soak up the brew in our raw predawn stomachs and we headed out the door.

The 2 Freeway heading into the mountains was so empty we could have parked in the center lane and danced a tango. Within ten minutes, we were climbing Angeles Crest Highway, rising into the San Gabriels, still shrouded by pockets of night. The signs for Mount Wilson appeared.

'He said go a mile past Rocky Flats and we'll see the emergency crew on the side of the road,'

Silvio muttered between mouthfuls of bread. 'God, I hope she's okay.'

I wanted to say, I told you so, I knew there was something wrong in her house yesterday. But we were way past recriminations now.

Angeles Crest was empty and still, the forest not yet dappled with light. Occasionally a car passed in the other direction, plunging into the valley below. Silvio inclined his head.

'They live in Palmdale or Wrightwood and commute into the city. Takes 'em almost three hours.' He shook his head. 'The way some people live.'

'How do you know?'

'A guy who worked in our office bought a cabin in Wrightwood. He did that commute every day for ten years before finally retiring. Loved the mountains. The land he could buy out there. Got up at four every morning to drive in. Said he used the time to meditate.'

I listened with only one ear. I was picturing Catarina on this windy highway. Had she been alone? Had she come of her own free will? Had someone marched her into an isolated clearing, then killed her and ditched the car? In the cool morning air, I shivered.

We passed campgrounds and an occasional ranger outpost, but mainly it was just forest. A funicular train had once carted wilderness-loving Angelenos up to the top of the mountain here, but bad rains and mudslides had destroyed the track some seventy years ago.

After what seemed like a long time, we turned a corner of pine and hit the scene. I counted a paramedic, a sheriff's car, a ranger truck, and a civilian car. We parked and walked over. The foliage was a stunning green, the air crisp, the colors vibrant. It felt like someone had taken Windex to my eyeballs. Alfonso was leaning against a pine tree, listening to a ranger talk into his two-way radio. Marisela was a stone's throw away, sitting on an incline and smoking. I expected that any minute two uniformed paramedics would come hiking up the trail, kicking up dust clouds and carrying a stretcher that bore a dehydrated, exhausted, injured, but very alive Catarina Velosi.

'Thanks for coming, *compa*,' Alfonso said as we walked up. He gave Silvio an elaborate bear hug and ignored me.

Silvio took off his baseball cap and ran a hand through his hair.

'Any sign of her?'

'Not yet, but I'm hopeful. It's the first break we've had.'

'Where's the car?'

'Down the ravine. You can't see it from here.'

Alfonso scratched the back of his neck. He was unshaven and his eyes were bloodshot. He didn't look like a distinguished playwright anymore. He looked like a man who had spent the night being tormented by demon imps.

'Then how did they know it was there?' I asked.

Alfonso's eyes drilled me with an obsidian stare. When he spoke, it was to his friend.

'They got an anonymous call. Motorcyclists use this as a staging ground for races. One of them was on the shoulder over there' – he pointed to the edge of the road – 'and saw something in the

62

bushes below and called it in around sundown. Rescue squad came out last night. There was a call on my machine when I got home. Happy fucking opening night. I waited as long as I could to call you. Hell, it's nice to have some backup.' Alfonso's voice wavered but he got a grip on himself.

I walked over to where he had pointed and looked down. Someone had strung up yellow police tape, which gaily contrasted with the forest green. There were tire tracks and eroded soil, bushes flattened and branches snapped where the car must have gone over.

Down below, two men wearing gloves picked their way through the brush. One squatted on his haunches, scooped something up, and dropped it into his plastic bag. A shard of twisted metal gleamed in the sun. In the foliage, I saw the remains of a rubber bumper and a large, hulking shape that might once have been a car.

I hiked back to Silvio and Marisela. Her hair was matted and her makeup smeared. If anything, she looked even worse than Alfonso.

The playwright saw me checking her out.

'I told her to stay home,' he said under his breath. 'I told her there's nothing she can do, that I need to concentrate on Catarina.'

That's exactly why she came, I thought, wondering how Alfonso failed to see the damage Catarina was doing to his marriage.

The two men I had seen below appeared now, covered in dust and pine needles. They weren't carrying anything big enough to be a human body. Not in one piece, anyway. We crowded around them and Marisela drifted over to hear the news.

'Keys were still in the ignition,' one of them said, stroking an elaborate ginger mustache. 'The airbag deployed. We found some clothes and magazines, but no sign of a body.'

The second ranger bent down to scratch the side of his leg. 'Would have been pretty impossible for anyone to survive, without leaving some blood or tissue or skin behind. And there's no tracks leading from the car.'

Ginger mustache shrugged. 'No human ones, at any rate. Coupla deer and a bobcat came by to check it out.'

'Forensics'll be out soon, and they'll check the car for prints.'

Marisela sighed dramatically, then walked to the incline and lit another cigarette. Alfonso studied her and said, 'I wish there was some way to get her home.'

'I could do it,' Silvio said without enthusiasm.

'No, bro, I'm going to need the moral support if they find her. And maybe more if they don't. I can't help thinking this was all my fault.'

'Why?' I blurted out.

He frowned, and I got the visceral sense that he disliked me. Intensely.

'Why is she here?' he asked Silvio. 'What business is this of hers?'

'She's *my* moral support,' Silvio said. 'And she knows that nothing she sees here goes any farther.'

Alfonso clasped his hands and gave me a pained smile.

'Very well, then, I'll tell you why. We had a fight after dress rehearsal,' he said. 'I'm afraid it might have...' he paused, 'put her in a frame of mind to do something irrational. She always picked a fight before opening night. She fed on the negative energy. I thought it was just the old pattern reasserting itself. But now I'm not so sure.'

'You can't blame yourself,' Silvio said. 'You know how she was. Don't worry, I'll stay.' He turned to me. 'Don't you have to go to work?'

I looked at my watch: 7:45. Thompson would be furious if he knew what I was up to. I was supposed to show that Met-Pro around. I felt balky and aggrieved, wanted to dig in my mental heels. It wasn't fair. I had my own stories to write. Did Josh Brandywine, my downtown rival and colleague, have to baby-sit Met-Pros? I doubted it.

I inhaled deeply, smelling the resinous odor of the pines, that sharp, clean, unfamiliar scent of mountain air. I watched Marisela pick pine needles off her dress, the fastidiousness that city dwellers often display in nature. She intrigued me. I sensed that she knew things. I made a decision.

'I'll take her home,' I told Silvio. 'In your truck. And Alfonso can drop you off at my house when ... this is all resolved. We can switch cars tonight. Here's my car key.'

They looked at each other, considering.

'Could be the best solution,' Alfonso said. 'If she'll go for it.' He went over to ask Marisela.

Maybe she'd say no. Maybe she'd sleep the whole way home and I'd learn nothing. Still, it was worth a try. Let hotshot Felice Morgan cool her jets awhile. A minute later, Marisela and

Alfonso were walking toward us. We said our good-byes and got into Silvio's truck.

Stale alcohol fumes rose from Marisela as she strapped herself into the passenger seat. What was wrong with this woman? At a time when she should be basking in her husband's success, she was killing herself with self-pity and alcohol and jealousy. Why?

CHAPTER 8

'Mind if I smoke?' Marisela asked as we headed downhill. Actually, I did. But a cigarette might relax her and make her more voluble.

'Poor Alfonso,' she said, taking a luxurious drag. She stared out the window and exhaled.

It seemed like a friendly gambit so I took it.

'Because he was close to Catarina or because of the play?'

She looked at me shrewdly.

'I'm talking his heart,' Marisela said. 'He never really got over her, you know.'

'Really?' I slowed for a curve. Suddenly, I wanted to stretch this drive out as long as possible. 'That must be hard on you.'

She sucked furiously on her cigarette and slumped lower in the seat.

'They went back a long time. And they had the street in common. The projects where they grew up and fought their way out of. I could never compete with that.'

I glanced over at her and she sat up straight. 'I grew up in Montebello. Swimming pool, ice-skating lessons, private school, the works. My parents were white-collar. And unlike Alfonso and Catarina, I had two of them.'

Marisela picked a stray wisp of tobacco off her lip. She was just getting wound up. The tense and sleepless night, the alcohol, the long drive, and the surreal circumstances had all conspired to loosen her tongue.

'Is that right?' I said conversationally.

'Yes.' Marisela nodded her head vigorously. 'They were very driven. They wanted to get an education and establish careers before they had children. But when they were finally ready, the kids wouldn't come.' She made a small humming noise. 'So they adopted. I was very spoiled. They gave me everything.'

'They must have loved you so much.'

Her face softened. 'Manny and Dolores,' she said, and a wistful smile played across her mouth. 'They got me at birth, right from the hospital. Manny was a doctor and he knew people. Then Dolores shocked all her professional girlfriends by giving up her job to stay home with me. It was the 1970s. Women's lib and all. She didn't care.' Marisela sighed. 'Yeah, they loved me.'

I sensed an emptiness at the edge of her words. What did any of this have to do with her life now, with Alfonso? I wondered.

'And you loved them?'

'They took me to Sea World and Disneyland, these two middle-aged people schlepping around a toddler all day. Bought me whatever I wanted.

You should have seen my room, full of dolls and toys. I was happy.'

'You don't sound too happy.'

'We had some rough times after I turned thirteen. I got real rebellious and moody. Depressed. They took me to a bunch of shrinks. The doctors asked whether there was a history of mental illness in the family, and of course Manny and Dolores didn't know. That's when they told me.'

'That you were adopted?'

'Exactly. After that, I became even more alienated.'

Marisela picked at her nail polish and said no more. I concentrated on the hairpin turns, blinking at the dappling sunlight. I needed to back up the conversation, get her talking again.

'Most teenagers are moody, aren't they?' I said.

'This was on a whole other level,' Marisela said. 'I couldn't stop thinking about my biological family. How my mother could have given me up. She must have been poor. Young. Desperate. My life would have been so different if she had kept me... I would have grown up in the projects, maybe, turned to drugs or had a baby at fifteen–'

'Doesn't sound so thrilling.'

'Yeah, but then maybe I would have met Alfonso, and he would have loved me first, and I would have become his muse, instead of Catarina.' Her voice rose. 'And we would have fought our way out of the barrio together, instead of him and her. That was my heritage! And it was taken from me.'

Her vehemence suggested there was much

more bubbling under the surface, if only I could calm her and keep her talking.

'But you had a nice childhood and still met Alfonso and he married you, not her.'

Marisela's jaw took on a stubborn cast. 'Yes, he did. But he resents me for not growing up there. It comes out when he talks about the drugs, the gangs, the *abuelas* raising too many grandkids cuz their smacked-out daughters can't. The dads in jail. The tattoos and drive-bys and shaved heads. He's obsessed with it. It's the narrative that drives his plays, where he gets his inspiration. It's certainly not from boring middle-class life in Montebello.

'I can't give him that. But Catarina can. When he writes a scene, he doesn't have to explain it, because she already knows. She lived through it. There's a shared bond. That's why I started...'

Marisela paused and made to throw her lit cigarette out the window – a forest fire waiting to happen. I lunged across and grabbed her arm.

She blinked, then put it out in the ashtray. She seemed far away.

'That's why you started what?' I probed.

But she said nothing. Her hand trembled as she fished for another cigarette. I rounded a turn and saw civilization encroaching on us, the Lego grids of the San Gabriel Valley stretched out below for a flash frozen moment before we were swallowed up again by a forest of pines. But it was a warning sign. The forced intimacy of our ride would not last forever.

I tried to reignite the conversation.

'So what did you start?'

'Nothing,' Marisela said, clutching her unlit cigarette.

'You said you thought a lot about your biological family?'

'Yes,' she said immediately. 'It's only normal.'

'So did you pursue that?'

She slid the cigarette back into its pack, sighed, and rummaged through her purse for gum. She handed me a piece and it tasted faintly of nicotine. We chewed silently for a while. Then she cleared her throat and said, 'When I was a kid, I always felt like I didn't fit in. So when they told me, it was a relief to finally know why. I remember going to the library and reading everything I could on the psychology of adopted children. Manny and Dolores thought I was doing book reports. Anyway, pretty soon I was a quivering mess. I couldn't stop thinking about my birth family. I never told Manny and Dolores, they would have been heartbroken. I could tell, from little things they said. So it was like this big pressure cooker inside of me, building up.'

'Sounds unhealthy,' I said.

'For a long time I kept it under control for their sake. Then two years ago, my parents died in a car crash and all those feelings came roaring back.'

'I'm sorry about your parents,' I said.

'Right after that, Maggie was born. I'd hold her in my arms and feel such a fierce love that I knew I could never give her up, no matter what. And I'd cry and cry that my *mami* had let me go. That's when I knew I had to find her.'

Her eyes held an animation I hadn't seen

70

before; her words came fast and excited. I wondered why she was telling me all this. She seemed to have forgotten that I was a reporter and a close friend of Silvio's.

'Your birth mother?' I said.

'My whole family. Somewhere out there, I had aunts and uncles and brothers and sisters and parents I had never known. They might live five miles away, but we had never met. All of a sudden, I couldn't stand it.'

'Was Alfonso supportive?'

'He thought I had postpartum depression. But I knew it wasn't that. With every day that I looked into my daughter's eyes, it grew more intense.'

We were dropping now with the velocity of a hawk. The pines had thinned. A ratty blanket of yellowish-brown smog hung over the basin. Then, like a gondola car shooting out of an amusement park ride, we were rolling through residential La Canada Flintridge. I downshifted, and the truck's motor revved high on the slope.

I thought about the woman beside me, how she had changed like quicksilver from pathetic drunk to wronged wife to vulnerable little girl. It seemed to me that Marisela was the real actress here, moving fluidly among many different roles.

I thought back to the brittle, inebriated woman of opening night, cracking under the pressure to play the good wife. I found myself liking her more today, admiring her shrewd and dispassionate self-analysis and her hunger to reclaim her history. A history that might heal her and bring her closer to her husband while breaking the bonds that tied him to his muse. Could such ambitions lead to murder?

Marisela looked out the window. Her long hair whipped in the breeze, giving off the scent of honeysuckle. A welcome change from tequila.

'Get on the 210 East here,' she said, and I flipped back into reality, realizing too late that I should have 'accidentally' gotten us lost so as to prolong the conversation.

'Where do you live?' I asked.

'Monterey Park.'

'Isn't that mainly Chinese?'

'We've staked out a presence too. We're up on a hill, overlooking the basin. And we can even see downtown L.A. It's lovely there. No crime.'

'Huh.' I paused. 'So did you find your birth family?'

'I did, yes.' Her voice was a drawer slamming shut.

I pressed on. 'And what happened when you finally met them?'

Her eyes took on a glazed, opaque quality.

'It was utterly humbling. And not what I expected at all.'

'How so?' I forced myself to keep an even pressure flowing from my foot to the gas pedal.

Marisela was silent for so long that I took my eyes off the road to look at her. She stared straight ahead.

'My mother was shocked and overjoyed,' she said in a strangely robotic voice. 'She insisted I come over that evening, when her husband was home. My father.'

'Jesus,' I said, getting the chills just imagining it.

'That night, we sat around the kitchen table and cried and my parents held me. My father was still in his uniform. He's a deputy sheriff. My mother is a counselor for a ... what do you call it, a drug rehab clinic.'

'How overwhelming it must have been,' I said, wondering why she'd had trouble finding the word.

'They have a little house in Pico Rivera, white picket fence and a dog,' Marisela continued. 'Several kids, grown up now with children of their own. My brothers and sisters. I didn't leave until two in the morning. I wanted to cram all those lost years into one night. She was fifteen when she got pregnant with me. A scholarship student at Ramona Convent School in San Gabriel. It would have meant dropping out but the nuns had connections at a local hospital. They convinced my mother's family that it was for the best.'

She stopped and a heavy silence fell over the truck.

'So you lost one family but found another,' I said.

There was another awkward pause.

'Yes,' she said with slow deliberation. 'Now I know where I belong.'

'What does Alfonso think of your family?'

'What he thinks doesn't matter anymore. This is something Alfonso can't steal from me. It's mine. Mine.'

Her voice rose in defiance. And suddenly a child sat in the car with me. A large and morose orphan who clung to her newfound family as

73

fiercely as any security blanket.

'Why would he want to steal them from you?' I asked, bewildered.

Marisela shook herself. She seemed to be coming out of a trance. Something about the tunnel of green sunlight, the shock of early morning, had opened her up to me. But that was over.

'I've got so much to do,' Marisela said. 'And it's the nanny's day off. But first, I'm going to have a warm bath and a nap. We were up all night.'

She stretched her limbs and yawned, then lit another cigarette.

'Even though I can't stand that little bitch, I hope she turns up soon. Dead or alive. Alfonso can't go on like this much longer.'

Mercurial Marisela. So now we were back to the scorned wife. All too soon, we pulled up to her house. It was expensive and new, built in the style of a century-old Spanish hacienda. Two stories high, with overhung balconies and a driveway that held a Jeep, a late-model Saab, and a Toyota Camry. I pulled in behind the Camry.

Marisela gripped my hand in her ringed fingers, thanked me for the ride, and apologized for rambling.

'Not at all,' I said with gusto. Sources who ramble are a reporter's dream.

She strolled up to the gate, her diaphanous robes shimmering in the bright sunlight, and I realized I had better call Thompson. It was nine o'clock and he'd soon be wondering where I was.

I had barely turned on my cell phone when a

plump Latina wearing an oversize T-shirt and leggings walked out the door, a pretty little girl on her hip, a bucket of sand toys dangling from her hand. She strapped the child into a car seat in the Camry and pantomimed that she was leaving. That was odd. Marisela had said it was the nanny's day off.

I backed out and drove halfway down the block before finding a space under a large coral tree. I was on the phone with Thompson, telling him about an imaginary dentist appointment that had delayed me, when a door slammed up the block. Glancing in the rearview, I was just in time to see Marisela Reventon scurry down her walkway. Gone was the earth-mother dress of five minutes ago. She wore tight red jeans, heels, and a clingy blouse and looked like she was late for something. As I watched, she hopped into the Saab and backed out with a loud whine, then thrust the car into gear with a determined jerk and sped down the street.

I remembered her elaborate chatter about a warm bath, then a nap, and I knew I'd been had.

Telling Thompson I'd be in soon, I started Silvio's truck and eased stealthily after her.

CHAPTER 9

I had never tailed anyone before, but it seemed wise to stay a few cars behind Marisela and pray she wouldn't recognize Silvio's truck. Reaching behind the seat, I groped around, found a badly dented Panama hat, and shoved it on my head. Then I lowered the sun visor to hide my face.

Marisela Reventon drove like a woman possessed, oblivious of those around her. I could see her cell phone cradled in the crook of her shoulder, and I momentarily wondered if my great stealth would lead only to the parking lot of the local market.

We were in a seedier part of town now, and the houses were smaller and ticky-tacky, the lawns yellowed, big ugly apartments cropping up. Soon the 60 Freeway approached. I waited to see if she'd get on but instead she turned left onto a frontage road that ran alongside, the cars whizzing past with only a chain-link fence to separate us.

Marisela parked in front of a small bungalow. I shot past, slouching down low. In the intersection, waiting for oncoming traffic so I could turn left, I looked in my rearview and saw Marisela ringing the buzzer. The door opened and she disappeared inside. I made my turn, circled the block, and drove slowly past the bungalow again. Marisela was inside, framed in the picture window. A man stood before her. He was tall, with tattooed and muscled arms that showed through a ribbed white singlet. A shock of black hair fell forward, hiding his face from view, and he threw it back in a broad, sweeping gesture. Marisela reached one arm to pull the curtain shut, and in the brief moment that her face angled toward the window and caught the light, I saw it suffused with anticipation but also great sorrow. Then the drapes fell together and shut her out.

CHAPTER 10

Who could he be? Her lover? Her drug dealer? If it was drugs, she'd be out soon. I parked up the street and jotted down the address of the house. Chanticleer Lane, the street sign read, like something out of a children's fable. And sure enough, over the low roar of the freeway and the screams of children playing on the parched lawns, I heard roosters crowing from backyard pens.

From my spot, I watched the front door. People came and went from other houses but Marisela stayed put. So she had her own secrets. Why did she leave her fancy neighborhood and come to this low-rent part of town to tryst or get high with some guy who looked like a gangbanger? My suspicions peaked – was she paying off a murderer? No, it had to be a lover, I thought, recalling how close they stood, as if about to embrace. A drug buy or payoff doesn't take that long. While Alfonso stood at the edge of Angeles Crest Highway, anxiously awaiting news of his onetime love and muse, Marisela the neglected wife was seeking her own solace.

And that was all I was going to learn right now, unless I wanted to pound the pavement for a new job. Reluctantly I started the car and drove to work.

I was hoping to slip unobtrusively to my desk. But when I walked in, a woman was already sitting there, wearing my headphones and typing away at my computer. I recognized her from the Polaroid. It was Felice Morgan. Her hands joined in supplication as I walked up, and her head rolled to indicate there were no empty desks. Holding up splayed fingers, she mouthed the words *five more minutes* and turned back to her interview.

The office was a hive of reporter activity. Against the back wall, Trevor Fingerhaven was interviewing someone at top volume. Luz Beltran was at the photocopy machine with a stack of documents. Evelyn Chung, the receptionist, was typing a stack of calendar listings into the computer. Tom Thompson was giving Met-Pro director Barry Patterson a tour of the San Gabriel Valley bureau.

'These are the file cabinets,' Thompson said.

'No kidding,' Patterson said with an amused drawl, but I saw his eyes taking in Felice like a long, cool drink on a hot day. Was it true he had a thing for young black women?

I found an empty chair and tried to read the paper but was too annoyed to concentrate. The little hotshot was in my seat, virtuously hard at work in contrast with my own late arrival. On top of that, her gracious request for five more minutes left no room to fume.

I knew I was being petty. Downtown, you sat at whatever desk was empty, and maybe it had been that way at her old job in Fort Worth. She was very young, no more than twenty-three, I guessed, and still had a lot of seasoning ahead of her.

I strained to hear her voice, which was almost a murmur. She would lob a question, then type rapidly, fingers skittering over the keyboard. Then another question, and more typing as she nodded her head and made encouraging sounds into the mouthpiece. But there was no mistaking that despite her velvety voice and regular uh-huhs, Felice Morgan was hammering someone.

'Now let me get this straight,' she said a bit louder, and launched into a recap of the conversation. Then she leaned back in her chair and waited, face alert, fingers poised.

'But I'm confused,' she broke in, her voice smooth and low once more. 'Forgive me, I'm new at this and not familiar with... Uh-huh. Yes, sir. Correct me if I'm wrong, but just a minute ago you said... Oh, is that right? So what you really meant was... He did? I see. Go on.'

A satisfied expression lit up the face of Felice Morgan. She stretched with pleasure and I saw that she was tall and long-limbed, clad in white linen pants and expensive leather loafers. There was a sleekness about her that would have looked at home in a *Town and Country* ad. Her nails were manicured into graceful ovals that glinted with clear polish. The stitched leather of her watchband matched that of her belt. She wore an oversize open shirt of crisp white cotton over a ribbed red tank top whose clinging fabric outlined gentle swells. An Egyptian ankh dangled between her breasts and drew the eye closer. I remembered an Afrocentric theory of history which argued that pharaonic culture had come from black Africa and wondered if she wore the ankh as a political statement.

It wasn't such a leap. Felice's narrow shoulders and long neck evoked Queen Nefertiti. Her chin was small and pointed, her generous mouth set low in her face. Black-rimmed eyes tilted up at the edges, framed by a mass of long, black tendrils spreading in a perfectly fanned cloud. Only her nose called direct attention to her heritage. It had a wide bridge but even here, the nostrils tapered and thinned at the end, with just a hint of a flare.

At some point, I realized she had finished her interview and was watching me stare. Smiling ruefully, she ducked her head and twined her hands between her knees.

'I am *so* sorry,' Felice said, lashes lowered. 'There was nowhere to sit and I had an important interview...'

Then it hit her that she was still in my chair. Gathering a file crammed with documents, she slung a designer bag over her shoulder and jumped up. A ring of keys spilled out. I bent to retrieve them and noted the BMW logo on the chain.

'And now I'm making a terrible first impression,' Felice chided herself. She touched her hair, which gave like cotton candy, then stuck out a thin, shapely mocha hand.

'Felice Morgan.'

Her grip was firm and cool.

'Eve Diamond.'

Suddenly, she let go.

'You're Eve Diamond?' Felice stepped back. 'But...' A small smile played across her face. 'For some reason, I was expecting someone older.'

'You were?'

I wasn't sure whether to feel flattered or insulted.

'Oh, now I'm saying the wrong thing. I mean, you write like a seasoned pro. I've read all your clips and they're dynamite.'

'You've read my clips?'

It made me squirm with embarrassment, as though I had caught her rifling through my lingerie drawer. Part of me realized this was absurd – the *Times* had a daily circulation of 700,000, after all, and everything I wrote went into the public record. Still, it was unsettling to learn that she had scrutinized my stories, not to learn the news, like most readers, but to assess the person reporting the news.

Now it was Felice's turn to look awkward.

'Well, yes, I did.' She jutted her chin. 'When they told me I'd be spending a few days with you, I checked you out. Isn't that what reporters do?'

Yes, I thought. That's exactly what reporters do. But like all practitioners of the dark arts, we feel a bit squeamish when the light we shine on others is suddenly turned upon us.

'What I mean is, I want to watch you work. I've got a million questions. I hope you'll teach me everything you know.'

Her intensity made me step back. It wasn't just her, I was that way with everyone. Pump up the emotional volume and I'm outta there...

'That should take about a day and a half.'

'I'm serious.'

'So am I. It's not like there's a formula.'

Her mouth twitched. 'But whatever it takes, you've got it. I read your stories. I've overheard people talking.'

I knew she was feeding me a line, but I bit anyway.

'You have?'

Felice examined me. 'Not just reporters. Editors too.'

Then why am I still stuck in this godforsaken valley? Why haven't they promoted me downtown?

'Most journalism is just gut instinct,' I said.

She nodded eagerly. Then, to my embarrassment, she got out a notepad and wrote it down. She underlined it twice, then added an exclamation mark, drawing the point as a little circle.

'I'm really looking forward to working with you,' Felice said. 'Don't do anything yet. I'm going to get some coffee and then we can start. Would you like a cup?'

Startled, I stared at her. Reporters didn't fetch coffee for each other; it violated some unspoken principle of newsroom egalitarianism. But the morning's adrenaline was definitely wearing off. I could use a cup.

Felice stood there, smiling. I pictured her in a white maid's cap and apron, carrying in a heavy silver tray and curtseying. Outside, in the languid plantation air, the sun glinted off Corinthian pillars. I blinked. The image was disconcerting, and I vowed that I'd sooner ask Metro queen Jane Sims to fetch me coffee than Felice.

'Already had my quota,' I mumbled ungraciously.

Her head dipped in approval. I got the odd feeling I had just passed some test. Then she walked down the aisle to the lunchroom. She already seemed to know her way.

CHAPTER 11

I settled my ruffled feathers and called Silvio. He answered right away and said there was no news. The search crews were still combing the mountain. He was starting down the hill with Alfonso, who had to get to the theater for a meeting. He hadn't wanted to leave, but the show must go on.

'I had a nice chat with Marisela on the way down,' I said.

'Yeah?' Silvio's voice was noncommittal.

'I didn't know she was adopted.'

'That's the latest. She had to find her birth family. It was going to resolve all her problems.'

'And did it?'

Silvio paused to take a long liquid gulp of something.

'I don't know. She and I don't talk much. She thinks I'm on Alfonso's side.'

I envisioned Silvio's eye roll.

'What?' came Alfonso's muffled voice from somewhere in the car.

'Can we talk about this later?'

I heard the rumble of Alfonso's voice again, and a scrape of stubble against the receiver as Silvio must have turned to his friend.

'*Nada.* Relax, *compa.* We're not talking about you. Eve just says she had a nice talk with your wife.'

Silvio spoke into the mouthpiece again. 'Call me when you're through and we'll get dinner. Maybe they'll know more.'

I hung up and stared at the phone. Who else should I call? Quick, before Felice returned. Her whole earnest demeanor embarrassed me. I was irritated that she was twenty-three and drove a BMW. At her age, I had driven an old Honda Civic that broke down a lot, leaving me to cadge rides to the night classes I attended after my day job. It was clear from her clothes, her diction, her bearing, and her car that Felice was a pampered rich kid. The paper was infested with them. And on top of that she was black, which meant I couldn't even wallow in my resentment, because that would make me a racist. In America, race always trumped class, though we pretended neither one existed. As far as I could make out after thirty years on this earth, class was something we had supposedly shucked off with the yoke of King George III. Race was the sleeping tiger that everyone tiptoed around lest he wake up and demand his due. And over it all hovered the wretched stain of slavery, so that 150 years after the unholy institution was abolished, privileged black kids from Scarsdale still deserved more of a hand up than the most poverty-stricken white hillbilly from Appalachia.

But right now, we were just two reporters feeling our way around each other and I felt uneasy about the halo she had drawn over my head and disturbed at the suspicion that it was calculated flattery. Why would she bother? What could such obsequiousness gain her? Maybe I also winced to see a younger version of myself in her, one that I had since revised. Had I ever been so nakedly enthusiastic? So green? So reverential? Maybe on the inside, but I was convinced I'd hidden it better.

I checked my e-mail and saw that Thompson had us slated to cover an East Side rally demanding that the school district stop dumping problem teachers in poor minority schools. The latest offense: a preschool teacher charged with child molestation for sucking his students' toes.

I read the wire story and saw the defendant faced thirty years to life because prosecutors alleged that he got sexual gratification from the act, toe-sucking being a well-documented fetish. There were multiple counts from eight victims.

'Congratulations,' I said when Felice returned. 'You've got your first assignment. Have a seat and check it out.'

I hopped onto the desk, swinging my legs like a schoolgirl while she read. Would Felice consider it patronizing to have me accompany her on 'Toesucker'? After breaking a big prison story in Texas, she obviously knew her way around C&C – cops and courts.

Felice scrolled through the story and recoiled.

'That is the most disgusting thing I've ever heard,' Felice said.

'Don't people do that in Texas?'

'That creep should get life. The kids will have permanent scars.'

'Not to minimize the crime, but violent rapists often serve less than five years.'

'Multiple victims,' Felice said. 'The counts add up quickly.'

She was a fast study, was Felice. She didn't need me tagging along behind her. I figured it was time to lay that one on the table.

'Hey, um, I'm sorry they want me to hang with you this week. You obviously don't need it.'

'Don't worry, I'm the one who requested it,' she said crisply. 'Let's take my car.'

And for a moment, I wondered who was shadowing whom.

'Do you mind if we grab some lunch first?' I said, as my stomach gave a bearlike rumble. 'There's a great Cuban place on the way; they have wonderful *medianoches*.'

'Say what?'

'It's a Cuban sandwich, with pork and pickles and cheese, and they put the bread between a press and grill it and...'

That's what I wanted. One of those chewy, gooey sandwiches would make me feel right-eously sated.

Felice was wrinkling her nose.

'I don't eat pork.'

'They've got salads and shit too.'

'All right,' she said without enthusiasm, and I realized we were getting off on the wrong hoof. Somehow, I didn't care.

As we gathered our bags, Thompson buzzed me from his office.

'They found the car belonging to that actress,' he said, his voice crackling with excitement.

I know, I wanted to say. I was there.

'No shit,' I said, examining a hangnail. 'Where?'

'San Gabriel Mountains. Off Angeles Crest. The cops have been there since dawn searching for a body. Metro's assigned the story to Josh Brandywine, and he is going to be calling you for some background.'

It figures, I thought, and the toddler inside of me wailed *it's not fair* at the idea of my story being handed to the princeling. Josh was a second-generation newspaper star, the son of a famous *New York Times* correspondent, and on the fast track to his own Pulitzer. With those genes and credentials, he could easily have been a preening egotist, but Josh won people over by sheer brilliance and self-effacement. I enjoyed working with him and felt it was good for my game. But this smelled like outright thievery.

'We can work together,' I said, fighting to keep the pleading out of my voice. 'If they found the car in the San Gabes, it's ours. And I was at her bungalow last night. I know the players.'

'Maybe, but you didn't tell me about the blood on the windowsill and the pillow.'

'What blood on the pillow?'

'A splattering of drops. On the bottom pillow. Someone had obviously tried to cover it up.'

I pictured the pillows piled haphazardly atop one another. I hadn't wanted to disturb a potential crime scene. My instinct had been right, I thought, wishing for once I had been wrong.

'C'mon, Thompson. You know I'll do it justice.'

'Out of bounds, Ace.'

'Why?'

'You're way too close.'

'But Thompson—'

'Listen up. If I find you anywhere near this story, your ass will be grass. You could taint the investigation. So stay away. Hear?'

'Yes,' I said sullenly and slammed down the receiver.

'What was all that about?' Felice asked.

'My media stocks are tanking again.'

As we drove to the café, my disgruntlement grew. I stared out the window, trying to suss out a new way to convince Thompson. But nothing sprang to mind.

'So what's the hot story you're working on?' I asked as the silence in the car grew awkward.

Felice's eyes crinkled.

'A dirty elected official,' she said.

'No way. In our fair city? What'd he do? Suck some toes?'

She blanched. 'I really can't say.'

'Why not?'

'I don't feel comfortable.'

''Cause the investigation is ongoing?'

88

'It's not that.'

A wave of comprehension swept over me.

'Don't worry,' I said. 'I'm not going to steal your story.'

She shot me an alarmed look. 'Oh, I didn't mean...'

Yes, you did.

'Don't worry about it.'

'You don't believe me.'

'It's no big deal.'

'You don't know what it's like for me. I'm new and this place is so intimidating. I don't know who to trust.'

'Well, whatever you do, don't trust me.'

Felice touched her tongue to her lower lip. 'At the *Fort Worth Star-Telegram* there was an older reporter who befriended me. We'd drive around and talk stories. I had a lead on corruption at the greyhound track and he asked me tons of questions about it. Then he presented it to the editor as his investigation. He stole my story.'

I wiggled in sympathetic outrage.

'That's terrible. Didn't you demand a meeting with the editor to explain the truth?'

Felice sniffed and reached for a tissue. With one hand, she dabbed at her eyes.

'This reporter was older and well respected. He told the editor I must have misunderstood. So who do you think the guy believed, his old frat brother from the U of T or *me?*'

The way she huffed out the last word revealed something no less powerful for going unsaid. The good old boys were white; she was young and black. They held the power so their version of the

89

truth prevailed.

'I'm sorry you got burned, but that's not going to happen here.' Suddenly, I wanted her to know that I wouldn't screw her. I was on her side.

A sports motorcycle pulled up in the next lane. The driver wore a purple and white leather suit with racing stripes that matched the colors of his bike. He leaned forward in his seat, twitching impatiently as we idled at the light. Then the purple-helmeted head rotated slowly in our direction and he checked us out through his visor, two girls in a new forest green BMW. I stared back, but the visor and the mirrored shades revealed little more than a sci-fi insect.

Then the light changed and with a full-throttle roar, he was gone. I watched his receding back. Something nagged at me. Motorcycles. Where had I heard something about them recently? Then I remembered. It had been early this morning on Angeles Crest. Alfonso recounting how a motor-cyclist had seen Catarina's car in the ravine.

Suddenly, I felt trapped in the car with Felice and impatient to be done with 'Toesucker.' There was something else I wanted to investigate – a way to help Silvio and Alfonso without incurring Thompson's wrath. Slowly, my plans began to coalesce.

I had seen the daredevil moto demons speeding through the hillside communities en route to Angeles Crest. These were not touring motor-cycles of the self-indulgent yuppie class, nor the hard-core Harley hogs of scraggle-bearded, pot-bellied bikers. This was an androgynous, high-tech tribe unhindered by gravity and speed limits, traveling in brilliant butterfly flocks, lithe figures in skintight suits astride chrome Japanese machines whose peacock hues matched their riders. They wore heavy-duty crash helmets and dismounted with catlike grace to fill their engines at the gas stations along Foothill Boulevard. Then they'd swing a long, leather-clad leg over their steeds, arrange their bodies into a racing Z, and roar off, convinced they were immortal until they found themselves hurtling over the handlebars and into the asphalt at 110 miles per hour.

Perhaps one of them had seen something on that stretch of Angeles Crest Highway where Catarina's car had been found. I would park by one of those gas stations and sooner or later a plumaged moto would roll in, and with any luck, we could talk.

'What's the restaurant address again?' Felice asked. 'I'm starving.'

Snapped out of my daydream, I told her and added that with forty-eight cities and munici-palities in the San Gabriel Valley, it would take her a while to get the lay of the land.

'I already know it,' Felice said. 'I spent last night studying the map.'

'You mean after you finished reading all my clips?'

She snorted, and that little smile played across her face. She reached for the volume knob on the car radio and cranked it, humming along to Aretha Franklin's 'Respect.' I wondered if she was trying to tell me something.

At Havana Nights, I ordered a *medianoche* and a

lemonade. After interrogating the waitress about the *ensalada cubana,* Felice ordered it. But she substituted turkey for ham, asked them to hold the cheese and the egg yolks and bring the dressing on the side. When the food came, she picked delicately at her salad and watched with some alarm as I tore into my molten sandwich. I wondered idly whether she had an eating disorder, especially since she had told me she was starving. I hated when women said that, then barely touched their food.

We discussed 'Toesucker,' and I was impressed to see Felice already looking into expanding this bizarre incident into a national-trend story about sexual fetish laws.

'I think it's a great idea,' I said. 'Pitch it to Thompson when we get back.'

Looking pleased, Felice speared a tomato.

My cell phone beeped, and I saw it was posh Josh. Throwing down some money, I asked Felice to pay the bill and went outside to take the call.

'So,' Josh breathed heavily into the phone. 'Can't even go to the theater without all hell breaking loose. I hear you've got some inside dope for your old pal.'

I looked at the ugly strip mall where I stood and felt the aggrieved toddler stir again.

'I finally get a live one and Thompson yanks it from me because I happen to know some of the players. Tell me, is that fair?'

'Nope, it's journalism. So lay it on me, sistah.'

Would he use that faux black jive on Felice? I wondered. But then, Josh wouldn't know she was black unless he met her, since her Eastern-seaboard accent was utterly race-neutral.

Inside the restaurant, Felice was handing the cashier an American Express Gold card.

'I put everything in the Overnote,' I said, making Josh work for it.

'Just tell me if that playwright ex-boyfriend's gonna deck me when I show up.'

I smiled. Josh had no idea he'd be retracing my steps. I knew that Alfonso would be surly and Marisela would be cryptic. I felt like we were closing ranks, and it reminded me how reporters sometimes see only the whitecaps on the surface of the sea, totally missing the subterranean earthquakes and storms that rage on the ocean floor.

At the cashier's desk, Felice was signing the receipt and I feared she was on her way out. She handed it back and said something. The cashier pointed down a hallway. Felice turned and headed deeper into the restaurant.

'You there?' Josh said.

'I'm here.'

Quickly, I recounted what I had seen last night, which already seemed like eons ago. I didn't mention the peculiar dynamic of Alfonso and Marisela's marriage. I wasn't sure it meant anything. But let him do his own reporting.

We chatted another minute, then Josh said in parting that he owed me one.

'Hold you to it,' I said cheerfully.

I hung up and turned, startled to see Felice standing two feet away.

'Hold who to what?' she asked, head cocked.

'Goddamn it, Felice, you shouldn't sneak up on people like that. Didn't anyone ever tell you it's impolite to eavesdrop?'

She fixed me with a steady gaze.

'I wasn't eavesdropping. I came over because it's time to go. But since we're on the subject, what's this big breaking thing *you're* working on?'

I wondered how much she had overheard. Then all at once the story welled inside of me, wanting to get out. So I told her an edited version.

'Will you take me next time you go out?' she said immediately.

'Metro's handling it from downtown. And you have your hands full with "Toesucker."'

She clicked her tongue impatiently. 'I can do both.'

She thought a moment.

'Wouldn't it be dramatic if it turns out that the ex-lover playwright killed her? With your sources, you could easily find out more.' She batted her lashes at me.

'That's exactly why they're not using me. There's a conflict of interest. Ethical concerns.'

'Hmmm.' She gave me a lopsided grin and waggled a finger. 'But I bet you're investigating anyway. Off the books, of course. Let me help?'

'I am not investigating.'

'I won't tell anyone. I just want to see how you work.'

I looked away, trying out different excuses in my brain.

'Please, Eve.'

'It could be nothing,' I dissuaded her. Why couldn't she take the hint?

'But then at least we'll have tried.'

'I don't think it's a good idea.'

94

'But what if she's still alive? Every moment is precious and two can work faster than one. I'll be your gofer. I'll do anything.'

Somehow, she had intuited my biggest fear. What if there was still time, but the hourglass was running out? I pictured Catarina bound and gagged in a concrete dungeon, her abductor already growing tired of his sadistic games. Didn't I owe it to her, to any woman, to use whatever resources I could? And here was Felice, smart and brimming with energy and eager to help.

'A woman's life is at stake,' Felice said solemnly.

Did she really care? Then again, if we succeeded, what did it matter? Cynicism and urgency warred inside me. I still didn't trust her. But her argument made sense.

'All right,' I said. 'But this is just between you and me. Strictly freelance. And only after we finish "Toesucker."'

'Of course,' Felice said, and her eyes glistened like those of a kindergartner who's scored a huge piece of birthday cake. She was so young and eager, and I remembered myself at twenty-three and hoped that I wouldn't live to regret my decision.

CHAPTER 12

As Felice and I arrived at the decrepit district headquarters of the Del Mar school district, an assemblyman from the East Side grabbed Felice's arm.

'How nice to see you again.' He beamed.

I felt the dogs of uncertainty nip at my heels. How did she know everyone so fast? I had been at the *Times* for several years and I still wouldn't know this man without his name tag.

But Felice seemed as surprised as I did.

'I don't believe we've met,' she said with aplomb. 'But I feel as though we're going to know each other quite well. Felice Morgan, *Los Angeles Times,* and I'm *very* interested in this case.'

Now it was the assemblyman's turn to be surprised.

'But we had a nice talk last week at the reception for Cardinal Mahony,' he said, a perplexed smile on his face. 'And Richard Riordan came up and told that perfectly awful joke about the priest and the mohel.'

Felice looked thoughtful, her features tight and alert. 'That wasn't me.'

'I could have sworn... She looked just like you,' the assemblyman insisted. Something important rode on his being right.

Felice snapped her fingers.

'Oh, I bet it was Antonia Bassett. She covers

religion for the *Times.*'

'There ya go.' The assemblyman beamed, glad the mistake had been resolved. 'At any rate, welcome.' He looked around the sidewalk, which was filling up. 'Ah, there's Matt Johnson. Must have a word.'

Felice was studying her shoes.

'Antonia Bassett?' I said. 'She wears glasses and has short dreads.'

'She's black, Eve.'

'How embarrassing.'

Felice straightened her neck. 'Excuse me?' she said imperiously.

'For him, of course,' I practically sputtered.

'Thank you.' She put slender fingers to her temples and massaged in tight circles. 'I'm used to it,' she said. 'Now let's get to work.'

Inside, we split up and worked the room, recording the outrage of parents who hadn't known that a sex pervert was teaching their children. I began to get a creeping feeling up my back that someone was watching me. I turned and surveyed the clusters of politicians, their minions, and community leaders, but saw nothing out of the ordinary.

Then a hand brushed across my shoulder. A man stood there, his full lips parted somewhere between a smile and a sneer.

'Do I know you?' he asked.

'Possibly. Eve Diamond, *L.A. Times,*' I said, giving him my most blandly professional smile.

We shook hands and the air between us filled with the scent of cheap cologne.

'But it's the woman, not the reporter, who

97

interests me.'

I glanced up to see if I had heard right. His eyes bored deep into mine. He bowed in an elaborate mockery of polite society and the muscles rippled under his pale shirt. He had thick black hair that reared up in a widow's peak, a teardrop tattooed at the corner of his eye. His hand rose to his collared shirt and tugged to loosen the constriction around his neck.

'Baltazar Galvan,' he said in a mock-sardonic voice. 'I'm with the assemblyman.'

Surprised, I took a step back and reassessed him. He certainly wasn't one of the khaki-clad political wonks who draw up policy and meet with constituents. Could he be the assemblyman's bodyguard? His boy toy? I thought, wondering if His Honor might be gay. Or was the assemblyman reaching deep into the grassroots to find a representative 'of the people and for the people,' though Baltazar Galvan didn't look like he was for anyone but himself?

'What do you do for him?' I asked.

His eyes pinned me to the wall like a dead butterfly.

'Whatever he needs.'

Politics attracts a lot of quirky people. But they're usually hardworking and slavishly devoted to their bosses and causes. This guy was barely tame.

'Very nice to meet you, Mr. Galvan. I'd better get back to work,' I said.

'Work hard, play hard,' he said. 'What are you doing later tonight?'

Students holding placards that said *Save Our*

Children and *Dump the Supe* were milling around the dais. Assemblyman Ernie Gutierrez clambered onto the stage, hustling a small child before him.

'My name is Julia,' the child said in a quavering singsong voice. 'I'm four and my teacher did it to me. He sucked my toes. And I didn't like it. It tickled.'

Assemblyman Gutierrez scooped the child into his arms.

'We demand justice for all disenfranchised people of color,' he said, as the pure, high voices below the stage began a ghastly chorus.

'Equal schooling for all, keep predators out of our schools,' they chanted.

I rolled my eyes.

'You find this a cynical manipulation?' Galvan said.

His bluntness surprised me. In politics, it was practically a criminal offense.

'Don't you?'

'Justice must be served,' he said with a sickly smile. 'Perhaps we could discuss the assemblyman's strategy over dinner?'

I wasn't used to being picked up in the middle of a political rally. And especially not by some swaggering political flunky.

'Sorry, I'm seeing someone,' I said.

'So am I.' His smile was vulpine. 'We shouldn't let that get in the way of passion.'

I wanted to laugh at his dimestore-romance dialogue, but something in the way his shoulders bunched up held me back.

'You're lovely when you get angry,' he said. 'Your mouth purses like so, and your eyes get a downward cast that is really quite sexy.' Baltazar touched the parts of his face to illustrate.

'I'm not angry,' I said. 'I'm amused. Now good-bye.'

I walked away without looking back. But as I finished up my interviews, my mind kept returning to Baltazar Galvan. Was he for real? While I wasn't remotely interested, he intrigued me, in an anthropological kind of way. I regretted not giving him a phone number I had memorized years earlier for just such occasions: the offices of Dewey Pest Control.

Now I spied a community activist I knew. I said hello, then inclined my chin discreetly and asked, 'Who is that guy?'

'Oh, he's something with the assemblyman.'

'A field deputy?'

'Naw. One of Gutierrez's "projects." Giving people from the hood a break. But the assembly-man's wise. He only picks projects that can help him.'

'What do you mean?'

The activist pressed a forefinger against one nostril, bent his head forward, and sniffed.

'No!' I said.

He shrugged. 'That's the rumor.'

The activist drifted away and I filed this nugget of intelligence for later. Right now, I itched to get back and see if there was any news about Catarina. I was gratified when Felice came up and said she was ready.

'Done so soon?' I couldn't help needling.

She pretended not to hear but her head rose like a queen's. We walked in silence, reaching the parking lot just as a back door to the building opened. The children's chorus poured out with their parents. They hadn't let us interview the children directly before, but now Felice saw a golden opportunity.

'I'll be right back,' she said, practically skipping off.

Good, I thought. I walked to the Beemer and got out my phone, turning to face the crowd so Felice couldn't sneak up on me. She was having a rough time. Several parents gave her dirty looks as they hustled their children past.

I leaned against the car, called Silvio, and got his voice mail. Frustrated, I punched off. Then I remembered a name I had written down last night. I dialed Information and asked for a home number in Los Angeles for Victoria Givens, the drama teacher who had introduced Catarina to the theater. Glancing over, I saw that Felice had struck up a conversation with an African-American mom whose daughter was playing hopscotch on an imaginary grid. Would that woman have talked to me? I wondered. Or did Felice have an edge because they were both black? Should I even be contemplating this stuff, or was it just going to make my job more difficult? The operator came back with eight listings and I wrote them down.

When I looked up again, Felice was kneeling in front of the child. Then she sat on her haunches, hands on her knees. The child regarded her solemnly, then buried her face in her mother's legs. The mother put her arms around the child. Felice placed her hands on her hips and spoke,

101

her head waggling. The girl peeked out from her mother with a shy smile. Haltingly, she began to speak.

Felice eased the notepad onto her knees and wrote, smiling with encouragement at the child. Several minutes passed. Then she threw her arms in the air and embraced the girl as her mother watched with an alert expression. Felice pushed herself up and shook hands with them both. Then she walked back to the car. Halfway there, she turned and waved. She looked animated and happy.

But as she turned back, the energy drained out of her. Her shoulders drooped and her face seemed to crumple. She threw open the car door, flung herself inside. I got in too.

'These damn allergies,' Felice said, sniffing as she started the car.

'Here.' I handed her a tissue.

'What? Oh, thanks.'

'That was quite a virtuoso performance,' I said, wanting her to know she couldn't put one over on me. 'I'm impressed.'

Felice's eyes narrowed. 'Fucking pervert.'

'Was that little girl involved?'

'Yeah.'

'I'm amazed the mom let her talk to you.'

'I guess she trusted me.'

'It's not just an act with you. You've got the touch.'

'I'm human.' Felice sniffed, this time in triumph. 'But I got the story, didn't I?'

She turned to me, her eyes shiny and wet. 'That mom said one of the parents reported a similar accusation last year and the school never investigated.'

'Really!' I said. 'That makes it a much better story.'

'I know,' Felice said and jammed the gas.

CHAPTER 13

By the time we pulled into the office, she had composed herself. We briefed Thompson and he told the City Desk, which ordered up a longer story. Then I watched Felice bang out eighteen inches in forty minutes.

When she was done, I slid into the chair to back-read. Felice wrote fluidly but made beginner mistakes, spreading the lede out over the first three grafs, which made me wonder how much of her wrongful-conviction-in-Texas story had been her editor's shaping and rewriting. There was no doubt she had killer instincts. But she was still raw.

'You need to attack the story, not back into it,' I said, showing her how to squeeze the main points into the lede.

She nodded and took notes in that damn notebook of hers, then went back to tinkering with the story. I thought about the Alfonso Reventon clips I had printed out the night before. Moving to an empty desk where I could keep Felice in my sights, I started reading.

Like most overnight successes, Alfonso Reventon had actually been around for a while. There were stories dating back ten years, but coverage had heated up recently with the MacArthur 'genius' grant that had anointed him Bard of the Streets, Shakespeare in a singlet and low-slung chinos, playwright laureate of the barrio. His plays mixed time and space like a marble cake and they contained multitudes: old men in yarmulkes stepping out from the shadows in early-twentieth-century Boyle Heights, back when it was a thriving Jewish community and Cesar Chavez Avenue was still called Brooklyn Avenue; multigenerational Latino families that spanned a hundred years; blue-collar midcentury whites; and space-age Japanese-American graffiti artists with handles like Gaijin.

'I don't write about the rich,' Alfonso told *The New York Times*. 'The people I know live in pain. They're angry. They're frustrated. They resent what they see around them, people who got rich on the dot-com boom. These people can't get a seat on the bus. And they don't live in those nice suburbs where the light rail goes.'

'Eve?' Thompson called from the corner office. 'Can you c'mere for a sec?'

I stuffed the clips into my satchel and walked over.

Thompson had 'Toesucker' up on the screen. He also had a new Spam haiku tacked on his bulletin board. *Pink meat mound glistens*, it began, in sixteen-point type.

Jeez, the guy was getting out of control. It was almost obscene.

'Close the door, please.'

104

'How's the poetry going?' I asked.

He frowned. 'I'm stuck on the last line. Got a few ideas. But work before pork.'

I groaned. 'That doesn't even rhyme.'

Thompson turned his attention to the screen. When he finished scrolling through Felice's story, he leaned back in his chair and regarded me.

'This is looking pretty good.'

'I thought so too.'

'You do much work on it?'

'Naw. Just helped her rejigger the lede.'

'Were you with her all afternoon?'

'Like you said.'

'Good. I want you to continue that.'

I crossed my arms over my chest.

'If she's such a hotshot, why does she need my help?'

'She wouldn't normally,' my editor said. 'But this is a sex-crime story full of nasty allegations and Jane wants to make sure all bases are covered.'

'Honestly. She doesn't need a minder.'

'Do I have to spell it out for you?'

I stared at him, hoping I was wrong. 'I guess you do.'

He clasped his hands on the desk like a virtuous schoolboy. 'Then let me put it this way,' he said. 'We're delighted to have found Felice Morgan. The newsroom needs more diversity, and she comes with great credentials. But so did Jayson Blair.'

As no one in any American newsroom could forget, Jayson Blair had been a cocky young black reporter at *The New York Times* who ignited a journalism scandal by plagiarizing and fabricating quotes in dozens of stories. Eventually, *l'affaire Blair* had brought down the top editor of *The New York Times*, Howell Raines himself.

'Has there been any indication that Felice...?'

'Not a whiff. In fact, she's just turned in a nice take-out about black-on-black violence in the inner city. It's very edgy, very street. No one interviewed in the story's pulling any punches. We're considering it for Column One.'

'Good for Felice,' I said, biting back a flicker of envy.

Thompson clucked his tongue. 'And since you're working with her already, Jane had an idea. I want you to know that I was not in favor of this, but Jane suggested, I mean, she'd like...'

My editor stopped and ran his hand through his thinning hair.

'I'm shipping the story to your basket,' he said bluntly. 'Jane wants you to call two sources from the story and read them back their quotes. There is some concern downtown that the community organizer, for instance, sounds too angry. He mentions a "genocidal conspiracy by whites."'

'Some black people do believe that.'

'That's nonsense.'

'But if he said it, what do you want me to do?'

'Jane just wants you to read them back their quotes, Ace,' Thompson said softly.

So Jane Sims was taking out a little job insurance. My canny city editor wanted to make sure she didn't end up in the unemployment line behind Howell Raines. And I was cast as accomplice in their velvet-glove racism.

'Forget it, Thompson. If Jane doesn't trust her, she shouldn't have hired her.'

'Fine.' My editor fixed me with an unfathomable stare. 'I'll let her know.'

I stood up. I was trembling with anger.

'Next you're going to ask someone to check out *my* stories,' I said.

Thompson looked down at his hands. 'One step ahead of you there, Ace.'

I thought the top of my head might blow off.

'What?' I shouted.

'That story about the Asian kids? Jane thought it was too sensational to be true so she made a few calls. I didn't find out until much later, or I would have vouched for you.'

'But—'

'So all I'm saying is don't get your diversity knickers in a knot. It happens.'

'Who did she—?'

'That source of yours, Mark somebody. The counselor.'

Waves of disbelief washed over me. Mark and I had gone out for a while. It had been serious.

Thompson saw the surprise on my face.

'I guess he never told you.'

'There's a lot he didn't tell me, it seems.' I searched my editor's face. 'And he's not the only one.'

Thompson had the grace to flush. 'I didn't know until recently.'

'But that was before Jayson Blair. She had no cause to—'

'Before him, maybe, but not Stephen Glass, Patricia Smith, Mike Barnicle, and Janet Cook. Remember her? She won a Pulitzer for her exposé about an eight-year-old heroin addict. Only problem was, he didn't exist. *The Washington Post* fired her ass.'

'She deserved it,' I said. 'You don't have to make things up. Whatever horrible, perverse scenario you can imagine, it's already out there. You just have to find it.'

As my anger bubbled, my voice grew softer and a small knot of contentment swelled in the pit of my belly. Jane Sims wouldn't be a problem. She might not like me, but now she left me alone. I had something on her that ensured that. Jane had a secret life she didn't want exposed and I agreed to keep the details under wraps in exchange for her keeping my favorite septuagenarian photojournalist safe from forced retirement.

I stepped away from the desk.

'Diamond,' my editor bellowed.

I walked to the door and opened it. Only then did I turn.

'What?'

'I don't blame you.'

CHAPTER 14

I tried to compose my face as I walked back to Felice, then gave up and headed for the bathroom. I needed a few minutes to myself. The exchange with Thompson had made me reconsider what she was up against. I vowed to be nicer and look beyond the youthful insecurities that made her brag and pry.

At the sink, I rubbed my eyes. The door burst open.

'There you are!' said Felice. 'I was afraid you had left.'

Could I get no peace? 'Didn't you see my purse on the desk?'

I flashed to Catarina's purse on the coffee table in her living room. What did it signify?

'I guess I'm not a very observant reporter,' Felice demurred. 'But I was worried you wouldn't get this important message.'

She held a slip of paper. When I saw Marisela's name and the word *urgent* next to it, I had to restrain myself from snatching it out of her hand. A tingle went through me. I felt like Josh, seeing only the whitecaps, while Marisela cavorted on the ocean bottom, swishing her mermaid tail along the cold sand.

'Thanks,' I said, aiming for nonchalance.

'So who is she and why's it so urgent?' Felice peered into the mirror to catch my reflection.

'She knows that missing actress. I'll tell you more when the time is right,' I said, infusing my voice with mystery.

Felice's face glowed with conspiracy.

'Okay. Marisela, Marisela.'

She squinted her eyes, committing the name to memory. I only hoped she wouldn't do the same with the phone number. Quickly, I folded the message and we walked back to the desk.

'Let me call her back, and then we can go.' A hopeful idea stirred. 'You sure you're up for this? It will make it a very long first day and you look tired.'

'I do?' she said, alarmed. 'Well, I'm not. I'm totally up for this.'

Too bad.

'I'll need some privacy,' I said, raising an eyebrow.

'Yes, of course.' She drifted off to the lunchroom.

Quickly, I dialed. A machine picked up and said that Marisela and Alfonso were not at home. I swore, biting it off as I heard the beep. Then I left my message.

At 6 p.m. we got the all-clear from Thompson. Promising to call the copy desk in an hour for questions they might have about 'Toesucker,' we left. I was off the clock and itching to advance the Catarina story. Hopefully, Marisela would call back soon. Meanwhile, we'd stake out the motorcycle riders who frequented Angeles National Forest. If we found any, Felice could help with the interviews.

I wanted to drive, but Felice took one look at

110

Silvio's truck and her nose wrinkled in distaste. So I played copilot again, explaining my motorcycle-tipster theory as she drove. When I finished, Felice wiggled in her seat and told me what a wonderful sleuth I was. My blood pressure rose. Just treat her like you would anyone else, I thought. It would become my mantra.

I took a deep, yogic breath, then let it out slowly.

'If we're going to work together, you have to stop saying shit like that.'

'But it's a great idea.'

'I don't care. Put a lid on it.'

'I'm just trying to be nice,' she pouted.

'That's exactly the problem.'

There was no response. I snuck a peek at her. She looked hurt.

'I appreciate your enthusiasm,' I said. 'But if we're going to be joined at the hip for a while, you've got to just treat me normal. This buddy movie wasn't my idea.'

'I don't mind,' she said. 'Besides,' more quietly, 'I don't blame them.'

I glanced at her again.

'You don't blame who?'

'The editors. For not trusting me.'

I flushed scarlet. Had she somehow overheard the conversation in Thompson's office? Earlier, Felice had claimed it had been her idea to follow me around. Had that been bluster to preempt the truth?

'It's not about trust, it's about experience. Like you said, you're still pretty new.'

She ignored me. 'Can you imagine how it

111

gnaws away at your self-esteem, not knowing if you've been hired because of your color or your talent? And everyone watching and waiting for you to screw up. Maybe you figure, okay, if that's what they want, I might as well blow it big-time.'

Was that some kind of warning? I wanted to warn her in turn, tell her to be careful, but I didn't have the words. To this day, I wonder whether it would have averted disaster if I had.

'You have to realize,' I said instead, 'that Jayson Blair caused tons of resentment at *The New York Times* because he got promoted over more qualified reporters.'

'That's their fault, not his,' Felice said. 'There are plenty of qualified minorities out there but they had to pick him. With one dishonest brush, he's tarred and feathered all of us, set newsroom diversity back a decade.'

Her voice cracked and a sob rose from her throat. 'And it's not fair, I've worked so hard.'

Is she really going to cry, right here in the car? I wondered. I forced myself to look at the road.

'Has anyone said anything to you about...?'

Felice rubbed her sleeve across her eyes, then snorted in disdain.

'They don't have to. It's in the air. And it's happening in every newsroom throughout America,' she said, her voice hardening and growing steadier.

That's right, I thought, move it away from the personal and into the political. Use that rage. We shall overcome. Did people even say that anymore? Or was it a relic from the civil rights era?

'Not here,' I said, unsure why I was defending

112

my evil masters. 'The *L.A. Times* is a merit-ocracy.'

Ah, but did I even believe that myself? There were so many baroque political games in the newsroom, and most had nothing to do with race and everything to do with allying yourself with people whose ascendance would help your own rise. They called it managing up.

'Then why are there so few black reporters?' Felice asked. 'During the 1965 Watts riots, they had to deputize a black ad salesman to have someone to send into the inner city.'

I ticked off the paper's black reporters and editors but quickly ran out of names. 'Well, at least they hired you,' I said, but she only looked at me moodily and did not respond.

Fine, I thought with irritation as we pulled into a gas station at Foothill Boulevard and Angeles Crest Highway. We'll just sit here in silence for two hours. I was itching to call Marisela again but didn't want Felice's big ears flopping all over it.

Instead, I punched the buttons on the car stereo and a ZZ Top song about being under pressure came on. It was a raunchy, kick-out-the-jams song, twin guitars going like machine-gun patter, and I could see the front men of the band, with their wraparound shades and biker beards hanging below their belts. The lyrics were all about cocaine and high heels and guns. It was the aural equivalent of rubbernecking at a car crash, but I couldn't turn it off.

'Ugh!' said Felice, swooping down to change the station. 'How can you stand it?'

113

I flushed.

'I don't really like it,' I admitted. 'But sometimes a corny song can be interesting. It's amazing how those pop hooks insinuate themselves into your brain.'

She snorted. 'Cracker shit best keep it ugly self outta ma brain.'

So now all of a sudden Felice was ghetto? I wondered if she had learned to talk that way from MTV but kept that to myself. She punched the buttons until Nina Simone's molasses voice came on, singing about misfit girls and melancholy love, then leaned back and sighed.

'Save me, Nina,' Felice said. 'Take me away. Oh yeah.'

'I like her too,' I said timidly.

'Then how can you stand that redneck music?' Felice shot back.

Her elocution had returned, each syllable enunciated clearly and grammatically. What was that about? It was like having Marisela in the car again.

'Aw, Felice, they're not singing about race. They're singing about getting high and having sex. That good ole boy shit's probably an act they put on for their fans. I bet they have college degrees and listen to Debussy on the tour bus.'

Felice harrumphed. 'A lot of racists have degrees.'

I tried to see it from her point of view. 'I guess if you're racist, an education just gives you fancier words and more sophisticated arguments.'

'Some of those eugenics doctors even won a Pulitzer. We studied that at Brown.'

114

'That where you went to school?'

'Uh-huh. I got accepted to Howard and North-western but I wanted to be close to my parents.'

'Where do they live?'

'Manhattan. My daddy's a partner in a law firm and my mama's a neonatologist.'

I hadn't asked, but now I pictured her up-bringing and knew my earlier impressions had been right. Prep schools and cashmere sweaters. Cotillion. That black bourgeoisie thing. I considered how young she was, that her frames of reference were still her parents and college. I hoped she wouldn't trot out her SAT scores next.

'They pleased with your choice of profession?'

Felice looked out the window.

'They still hope I'll come to my senses and go to law school. Not much money in journalism, they say. For now,' she sighed, 'they're right.'

'You've got to pay your dues. But you're already at the *Times*. That's a pretty good start.'

She made a face. 'But it's the 'burbs. How long you been here, Eve?'

'Two years.'

'That seems like forever. I'm not going to be here that long.'

A small warning bell went off. She was either too naive to realize she was insulting me, or cold-heartedly announcing she planned to leave me in her dust.

'We'll see,' I said.

I checked my cell phone but neither Silvio nor Marisela had called. Meanwhile, dozens of people filled up their tanks with gas, but not one biker. It was a hot, muggy evening. Maybe they had been here earlier when school let out. Or they were already on the mountain and we'd missed them.

At seven we called in. The copy desk had a few questions. They wanted to put the story under a double byline but I told them to just use Felice's, and she was so thrilled and grateful, you'd have thought I'd given her a million bucks.

As it grew dark, I realized that my gut feeling had been wrong.

'Sorry to have wasted your evening,' I said.

'Oh, you didn't. I like talking to you. But watch out. I made it to the national debate finals three years running at Brown.'

'I should have guessed. Anything else I should know about?'

'Firearms,' she said. 'I'm a dead aim at a hundred feet. Trained with the Finnish biathlon team one winter outside Helsinki.'

I clamped my teeth over my tongue to restrain myself, then told her I had to get back. It had been a long day, starting with the phone call before dawn, and I was beginning to wilt. Felice dropped me off at Silvio's truck. As she pulled away, I called Silvio and told him I was free.

'Good,' he said. 'There's been a development. But I don't want to talk about it over the phone.'

We made plans to meet at a Japanese restaurant.

'Did they find her?' I asked, unable to contain myself.

'No,' Silvio said sharply. 'It's something else.'

116

CHAPTER 15

When I got there, Silvio was already at the bar.

'So how are you?' I asked, leaning in for a wary kiss and smelling tart hops on his breath.

Silvio stared into his beer. He had puffy shadows under his eyes and needed a shave. 'Alfonso's been told not to go on any trips,' he said, launching right in. 'He thinks the cops suspect him.'

Was that what Marisela wanted to tell me?

A kimono-clad waitress with a white-powdered face and a pierced nose arrived to lead us to our table. We sat in silence while she brought edamame, pickled cucumber, water, and iced barley tea.

'Was he still seeing her?' I asked when she left.

'We never talked about that.'

I felt like I was marooned on a dance floor, forced to guess the intricate footwork because I didn't know the steps. And the arms around me were a stranger's.

I changed the subject. 'Why doesn't Alfonso like me?'

'What?' Silvio's eyebrows came together in disbelief. 'Who said that? Of course he likes you.'

'No, he doesn't. It's pretty obvious.'

'He's overwrought, with Catarina disappearing and the play opening. Don't take it personally.'

'It's more than that. He bristles like a porcupine every time he sees me. Is it my personality?

My job? My breath?'

He pressed his lips together. 'You're making too much out of this.'

A seaweed salad and some octopus arrived. Silvio peered into the ceramic dishes and made a selection.

'No I'm not,' I said stubbornly. 'I sense it. Maybe he's...'

Maybe he's afraid I'll ask too many questions and find out the truth.

Chopsticks halfway up to his mouth, Silvio waited for me to finish. But I lacked the guts.

'Maybe every time he sees me he remembers a less-than-glowing review he once got in the *Times*,' I said.

'Eve, don't be ridiculous.'

Silvio tucked the octopus into the side of his mouth, chewed, and swallowed.

'Oh, by the way,' he said, 'the cops are going to find my fingerprints at the house.'

An electric current went through me.

'Of course they will. Because we were there the other day. Right?' Fighting to keep my voice neutral.

'Yes,' Silvio said a touch too quickly. 'They don't want me to go anywhere either. They want to talk to me again tomorrow. Nice and friendly. I'm going to run it past our family lawyer. This is getting too weird.'

Silvio's family had hired a lawyer after his brother was murdered, and while Silvio had never been a suspect, there had been complex family relationships to sort through, trial testimony to prepare for, and many minefields along the way. But I hoped that was all in the past.

'So you think you need a lawyer?'

Silvio took a long swig of his beer before answering.

'Look, I've been around cops enough after what happened with my brother. They're going to try to railroad me into saying something incriminating, either about myself or Alfonso. A lawyer can ride herd on that.'

'But wouldn't bringing a lawyer make it look like you had something to hide?'

For example, that you had a key to the dead woman's apartment and don't want anyone to find out. That you used to be involved with her. That you won't tell me the whole story but expect me to lie for you if the cops inquire.

'Everyone has lawyers these days.'

'You don't have anything to hide, do you, Silvio?' I hated the pleading tone that had crept into my voice.

'Of course not.' He saw my expression. 'Look, *querida*, everything is going to be all right with us.'

But I wasn't so sure.

I excused myself to go to the bathroom.

The sweet smell of the room deodorant invaded my nostrils, making me feel sick. I sat on the anteroom couch and called Marisela again. This time, I got her.

'Are you with Silvio?' she asked.

'Yes.'

'So you know then.'

'Know what?'

'Let him tell you.'

I ran my forefinger along the embossed gold braid of the upholstery.

'Tell me what?'

'He didn't kill her.'

'Who didn't?'

There was a long liquid gurgle on the other end. 'Oh, just forget it. I shouldn't have called. I just panicked when I heard.'

'Heard what?'

'That he's a suspect.'

'Who?'

'Alfonso. But he didn't do it.'

'How do you know she's dead?'

'Oh, she's dead all right.'

I forced my voice to stay calm. 'Why are you so sure?'

There was a pause. I could picture her trying to focus, already fuzzy from the booze. The introspective woman from this morning's car ride had fled. I saw her again framed in the window of the bungalow near the freeway. Should I ask her about that? No, not yet. It might scare her away.

'If she was alive,' Marisela said, 'there's no way on earth she'd miss this limelight.'

'Is Alfonso under arrest?'

'No.'

I might have been annoying her on purpose with my thick questions.

'Well then, what are you saying?'

'They told him to stay close to home. As if he's going to do anything else. With his play premiering at the Mark fucking Taper.'

120

'Silvio told me. Don't worry, I'm sure that everyone who knew her is going to be questioned.'

'Silvio's going to have his own problems. But I'll let him fill you in.'

Her coy cruelty was undermined by a resounding belch.

I pressed my finger deep into the upholstery, watching the indentation grow bigger.

'Why don't *you* tell me, Marisela?'

The phone went dead.

CHAPTER 16

Filled with dread, I pushed off the couch. What kind of forked-tongue wickedness was Marisela up to? I already knew that Silvio and Catarina had been lovers. And of course they'd find his fingerprints. There was an innocent explanation for everything. There had to be. I couldn't let Silvio see how upset I was. I softened my eyes, relaxed my forehead, and forced my mouth into a smile. Then I walked out.

Silvio sat at the table, shucking edamame pods. He didn't ask what had kept me. He seemed millions of miles away.

'So what have you learned at work?' he asked, as I slid back into the booth. Normal and sedate. How could he be so calm? He licked pod salt off his lips and waited.

'Just what's on the wires, and you can read the news feeds as well as me. Besides, I'm too busy baby-sitting a new reporter.'

'But what have you learned in your investigation?'

I wrinkled my brow. 'What investigation?'

Now Silvio looked confused.

'Aren't you doing a story? Talking to the cops? Alfonso isn't just big in the Latino community. He's big, period. And this is his leading lady and the play just opened.'

'Oh, that. Don't worry, the *Times* is on it like white on rice.' I thought about Thompson's disgusting poetry and almost smiled.

'So?'

'But they took me off. On account of you. Said I was too close.'

'Oh.' Silvio hunched forward. 'I was hoping...'

He poked at the edamame shells piled like Mount Fuji in the roughly fired rectangular dish. Finding one still plump with treasure, he shucked it and popped the boiled green soybeans into his mouth.

'I'm a little in the dark here,' Silvio said. 'They've asked me a lot of questions and I'm not sure where it's going. Alfonso and I had to give fingerprint and DNA samples today,' he said casually. He concentrated on his food and refused to look me in the eye.

'What?'

'I suppose they want to test the sheets and all that. They found some kind of residue.'

His voice was neutral. I laid my chopsticks across the glazed green ceramic.

'Like, semen?'

'Maybe. But they also check for blood. Saliva.

122

Pubic hair. Fibers. Whatever.'

'I know they found drops on a pillow that looked like blood.'

The muscles around his mouth tightened. 'I hope they're wrong about that.'

'Do they have any matches yet?'

Silvio swallowed hard. 'Don't you watch those forensics shows? Takes a week or two.'

He unfolded his lemon-scented washcloth and hot steam rose from the table.

'I can't believe they asked you for DNA,' I said, panic surging. Realizing I had been shouting, I leaned in, lowered my voice.

'That means you're a suspect too.'

He wiped his mouth, then threw the cloth down on the table.

'Look, I was happy to oblige. It will clear me off their list that much sooner. It's not me I'm worried about, it's Alfonso. And Alfonso is not a murderer. No matter what anyone says.'

Marisela had just told me the same thing, yet it was getting harder to believe.

'Who says he is?' I asked.

'The police are going to find his fingerprints all over the house too,' Silvio said.

'How recent?'

Silvio sighed.

'What?' I said.

'Oh, it's useless.'

'What's useless?'

'It's all going to come out.'

'What is?'

He looked at me for what seemed like the first time.

'You're driving me crazy with all these questions. I don't want to lie to you.'

'That would be good.'

'But he's my friend. And I'm worried about him.'

'Why?'

I felt eerily like a reporter coaxing information out of a source, not a woman talking to her lover. Reaching for the teapot, I tried to pour some tea. It splashed and sloshed over the cup, a clear wet stain advancing along the tablecloth.

'I hope the cops don't haul you in for questioning, Eve. You're a mess.'

It was the last straw.

'It doesn't make sense,' I said, my emotions erupting. 'You won't tell me what's going on, you're being all secretive and strange, I feel I hardly know you anymore, and despite all that, you expect me to lie for you. Of course I'm a mess.'

Silvio's eyes filled with apologetic sorrow.

'I know, I know.' He hung his head. 'And I feel terrible. But I'm in a real bind. Caught between my girlfriend and my best friend. Don't make me choose.'

Oddly enough, I was growing calmer now that things were finally on the table.

'It's me or him,' I said, half hoping he wouldn't force me to follow through on my threat.

Silvio rubbed his face. 'Okay, the truth of the matter is that Alfonso and Catarina saw each other the morning she disappeared.'

I exhaled slowly. 'Did he tell the cops?'

'Yeah. He says he was there to discuss the play.'

'There's more to it, though, isn't there?' I asked, remembering Marisela's jealousy.

But the heart-wrenching confession I'd been expecting sputtered into silence as Silvio did the food-avoidance thing again, slurping up the fat white udon noodles in his soup. Then he drank the anise-scented broth. This seemed to require all of his attention.

'You need to level with me,' I said, enunciating each syllable.

'He's my best friend, Eve.' Silvio's face took on a pained, pinched look.

'I know that. But I need the truth. Do you know what happened to Catarina?'

He looked miserable and didn't say anything.

'You haven't answered my question,' I said.

'No.'

Before I could parse the semantics of this, he said, 'Eve, there's something I need to tell you.'

My nerves lit up. Was he going to confess something that would change everything?

'What?'

'In the play, a man murders his girlfriend. That was Catarina's role. She dies.'

'So?' I said.

'The police are very interested in Alfonso's script.'

'What does that prove? They shouldn't conflate the playwright with his play.'

Silvio sipped at his barley tea. 'These are guys that majored in criminal justice, not English lit. They're wondering if it shows intent.'

'Oh, for God's sake.'

Quietly: 'He never really broke with her, Eve. I

know. I used to cover for him.'

With his words, the world clicked into sharper focus. I leaned my head against the banquette and considered all the angles. So Marisela wasn't jousting with imaginary demons. She had a very real adversary. And a motive for murder. I thought about the conversation in the bathroom just now. The mangled marriage. The adulterous husband and the jealous wife with a drinking problem and a lover of her own. And Silvio, a supporting player in their vicious drama, trapped in his own lies.

'You think Marisela might have killed her?' I said, eager to embrace any scenario that didn't include him. Finally we were on our way toward a normal conversation again, instead of this awkward pulling of factual teeth.

'No,' Silvio said after a beat. 'She's just a poor lost soul.'

'If Alfonso was still in love with Catarina, why in the world did he marry Marisela?' I asked.

Silvio didn't catch my tone. 'He thought it was over. And he tried to break with her, he really did. But if you met Catarina, you'd understand. She had this hold on people. She's like a witch. She can make water dance.'

I hated her, then, with a vehemence that astonished me.

'Then she should make her abductors bring her back,' I said. 'They can drop her off in front of the theater for a grand entrance.'

He groaned at the cheap shot.

'What really happened when Alfonso went over to Catarina's apartment that morning?' I pressed.

'I don't know. He was always very secretive when it came to her.'

'The police are going to find out,' I predicted. 'And then there will be trouble.'

There was a slight shudder across the table.

I gave him a moment to compose himself, then looked up. A fleck of green clung to his cheek, the soft emerald casing of an edamame. His evasiveness irritated me. His lies and half-truths left me suspicious. Without thinking, I reached across the table to brush the speck off his cheek and he leaned in and submitted patiently. And in the complicity of that gesture, the old tenderness returned. I thought: This is how it will be when we are old and have spent our lives together. This easy intimacy and trust. Because without trust, there is nothing.

I could trust my lover, couldn't I?

CHAPTER 17

In the parking lot, I gave him back the key to his truck and we swapped vehicles. The gulf was reopening between us.

'Silvio?' I bit the inside of my lip. 'Is everything all right? I mean, is there anything else you want to tell me? That I should know?'

He looked pained. 'No, of course not.'

My heart sank. He wasn't leveling with me. I knew it.

Silvio mumbled something about needing a

decent night's sleep in his own bed and I didn't try to persuade him otherwise.

The next morning, I opened the paper over breakfast, eager to see what else Josh had managed to dig up. There was nothing on the front page, but when I turned to Metro, I saw twinned stories about the missing actress above the fold.

CAR OF MISSING ACTRESS FOUND IN RAVINE, the headline on the left screamed, below a photo of what appeared to be a mangled Toyota. The story bore Josh's byline. MOTO RACER SAW STRANGE DOINGS ON ANGELES CREST, said the headline on the right. The accompanying photo showed a motorcycle rider standing in the lengthening gloom of early evening, anonymous inside his helmet. He looked exactly like the guys Felice and I had stalked yesterday along Foothill Boulevard.

That damn Josh, I thought. The park ranger must have told him about the racer who called in the tip, and like any good reporter he'd followed up. But unlike me he'd gotten somewhere. Then I saw the byline: *By Felice Morgan*, Times *Staff Writer.*

My mind went numb. My eyes dropped to the lede and I read, 'A motorcycle racer on Angeles Crest Highway said he drove past two men lifting a large bag out of a car trunk near Rocky Flats, just feet from where the vehicle of missing actress Catarina Velosi plunged down a ravine. The racer, who declined to be identified, said he couldn't see well because he was driving in excess of 100 mph.'

In disbelief I read on.

Recounting his story to a *Times* reporter as night fell amidst the tall pines of the Angeles National Forest, the moto racer said the men wore dark clothes and had black hair and drove a late-model foreign car that was either black or dark blue. The racer said he called authorities anonymously because he didn't want to get caught for violating a court order to stay off the bike for two years after a speeding conviction.

Alfonso and Marisela have a black Saab, I thought, and the words pounded away in my brain, taking up the echo of my heartbeat. *Black Saab. Black Saab.* And two men with black hair? That would fit Alfonso and Silvio. But that was ridiculous. With some effort, I pushed the thoughts back and kept reading.

'We see plenty of weird stuff up in the forest,' the young man said. 'There's a lot of underage drinking and drug use. People come here to have sex and shoot off guns. There's an unwritten rule that unless someone's getting hurt, we respect each other's privacy.'

When asked about this development in the disappearance of Catarina Velosi, one of the city's most popular and acclaimed actresses, Los Angeles Police Detective Saul Solano urged the rider to come forward and said he would ask for prosecutorial immunity in exchange for the rider's cooperation.

'If this guy could give us a better description of

129

the men or the cars, it could break the case wide open,' Solano said.

The detective then demanded that the reporter relinquish her notes and describe the young man to police but was informed that the Shield Law protects journalists from having to reveal such information.

Even without such help, the police may have a difficult time tracking down the anonymous motorcycle racer. Chuck White, a spokesman for the Rincon Rattlers, a group of motorcycle enthusiasts who make weekend runs up Angeles Crest Highway to Mount Wilson, said the road is a popular racing venue. He added: 'We're tired of criminal scum coming up here to dump bodies and cars. It gives a bad reputation to everyone who hangs out here.'

In disgust, I threw the paper down. I couldn't believe that Felice had stolen my story. The story she had begged me to take her on. The story I wasn't supposed to be working on. She must have doubled back to Foothill Boulevard after she dropped me off and waited for some riders to show up.

And not only that, but she had managed to thrust herself squarely into the limelight. By refusing to tell the police about her murky source, Felice was sure to ignite a firestorm of controversy. Journalists had every right to claim that their notes and interviews were privileged, but the courts often tried to force their release.

I pictured the police subpoenaing Felice, her eloquent refusal before a judge to reveal her source, and finally, Felice being marched off to jail, hands cuffed and mouth still zipped tight. And I saw the emergence of Felice Morgan, twenty-three, martyr to the First Amendment, canonized in textbooks, honored by Amnesty International and Human Rights Watch, prayed for in churches and newsrooms throughout America. Upon her eventual release, *The New York Times* would offer her a job and she'd go on to win a Pulitzer.

'No!' I screamed.

In a red haze of anger, I drove to work, trying to calm myself down. Felice was not at my desk this time, she was sitting at a chair, talking on the phone. When she saw me, she slammed it down and ran over.

'I'm so sorry,' she said. 'I can explain.'

I took a deep breath and, as serenely as I could, said, 'Explain what?'

Let her go on the defensive. The cops always say never ask someone something you don't already know the answer to.

'You haven't read today's paper?' Felice said, her voice wavering.

'No, why?'

She bit her lip. 'I did a story last night, on late deadline. Metro asked me to, after what I found out.'

'What did you find out, Felice?' Calm. Measured. Composed. Angry? Who, me?

'About the motorcyclist and what he saw.'

'What motorcyclist?'

'Oh, you'd better just read it for yourself.' She got a paper and thrust it at me. But she couldn't wait for me to finish.

'After I left you yesterday, I felt bummed we hadn't found any racers. It was such a brilliant idea you had, Eve. So I decided to give Angeles Crest one more shot. So I drove in a ways, parked on the shoulder, and pretty soon I heard a motorcycle coming up the mountain. The guy was in a racing outfit, just like you said. I jumped out and waved and he stopped. Maybe he thought I had car trouble. So I ran up and introduced myself. And you were right, Eve. He told me.'

I couldn't look her in the eye.

'What did he tell you?'

'What's in the story.'

'So he wouldn't ID himself, huh?'

'No. He seemed scared.'

'What did he look like?'

'He never took off his helmet, so I couldn't see. And it was pretty dark by then.'

'Did it occur to you to call me at home or run the story by me or anything?'

'Gosh, Eve, I'm sorry. I had to call the Desk first. Because it was breaking news. And then the night City editor made me come in and write it on deadline for the late edition. I did call after I filed but hung up when I got your machine. I was afraid you were asleep. But isn't it great? This may help them find Catarina. What a clip this will be. I told them I was available for a follow-up, if they wanted.'

'That was mighty generous of you.'

'They're going to call us this morning. Of course you'd be in on this too.'

'Yes,' I said slowly. 'Of course.'

132

The phone rang. It was Thompson, calling from his car phone.

'Metro wants you and Felice to collaborate on a daily about these illegal motorcycle racers. Find some more of these yahoos to interview.'

'They want us to collaborate?'

On Thompson's end of the phone, someone was honking.

'Well, originally they just wanted her to do it; she's free and I wanted you to work on the valley-wide crime stats that just came in. But I decided to give it to Trevor and free you up. All right, Ace?'

For a moment, I didn't think I could speak.

Originally they just wanted Felice? Part of a big breaking missing-person story that was beginning to reek of murder. While I, the 'seasoned' staff writer, got stuck with a lowly crime stats story of mind-numbing tediousness.

'Jane Sims is high on her. Keeps saying "she's hungry." They like that downtown. I've heard three people call her that this morning. "She's young and hungry." No wonder the *Times* plucked her out of obscurity in Texas. She's got a nose for it, Eve. Just like you. She was driving around last night, exploring the San Gabriel Valley, when she pulled into a gas station and struck up a conversation with some motorcycle riders. She'd been reading the paper and following the daily budgets, so when she read Josh's sked about how a motorcycle racer called in the car in the ravine, she got a hunch.'

I groaned inwardly. I couldn't tell him it was *my* hunch Felice had usurped. That I had shown her

133

exactly where to go and what to ask. Maybe that was how she planned it.

'So that's your assignment for today, Ace.' I heard honking again. 'And now, if there's nothing else, I better get off this phone and drive.'

I hung up and looked at Felice, whose guileless face quivered with excitement.

'So you told them you just had a hunch, huh? You just happened to be out for a leisurely drive, taking in the sights?'

'I'm sorry, Eve. You swore me to secrecy, remember? I didn't want to get you in trouble. So I made it look like my idea. Did I do the right thing?'

She looked at me with that open face, but I saw only a scorpion, tail upraised and lashing the air. I had a queasy feeling that my sweet little understudy had stepped onto the boards in my place, à la *All About Eve* or *Showgirls*. There's always someone younger or hungrier waiting to push you down the stairs, and I was staring at her.

'Check your machine if you don't believe I called last night. There's a hang-up.'

She was right, I had seen it when I got home. But something told me she would have hung up even if I had answered.

'You realize this could turn into a huge mess,' I said. 'That motorcycle rider is a witness. What if the cops subpoena your notes?'

'I would never hand them over,' Felice said.

'The Shield Law doesn't offer blanket protection. A journalist in Texas recently served a hundred and twenty days for refusing to turn over her notes in a murder case. Didn't you hear

134

about that in Fort Worth? Of course the *Times* lawyers would do their best, but you could be held in contempt of court.' I paused for maximum effect. 'Maybe even go to jail.'

'Really?' she said, shivering. 'Oh, that would be wonderful!'

'What?'

'It would make me a hero. Taking a fall for the First Amendment.'

'So where are the notes?' I said, realizing that my mean-spirited attempt to frighten her had backfired.

Her eyes gleamed. 'In a safe place.'

'Where?'

'I won't say. Not even to the *Times* lawyers.'

'Don't worry. They won't want the burden of knowing.'

But something more ominous nagged at me: What if she didn't want to give up the notes because they didn't exist? What if she had made it all up, just to get a big story splashed across Metro? With the dozens of cyclists who raced along Angeles Crest every day, what were the odds of her finding one who had seen something related to Catarina's abduction? Yet her story was almost impossible to disprove. Without a look at the rider's face or a name, there was no way to identify him and track him down.

'So,' said Felice. 'Where shall we start? I was thinking I'd call that guy Chuck White with the motorcycle club, and see if I can go on a ride-along. What do you see as your part in this story?'

CHAPTER 18

Ignoring her, I stalked to my desk. I knew I had to calm down before I did something I regretted. I looked at the stories again, and this time my eye fastened on the photo credit: *Harry Jack*/L.A. Times.

On impulse, I walked into the darkroom where septuagenarian Harry Jack was living proof that newsrooms had once embraced colorful characters and salty tongues.

'Did you go out with Felice last night?'

Harry looked up from a light table and removed the loupe from his eye.

'Got a call last night to meet her up there, yes, I did.'

'So you were there when this guy' – I jabbed at the photo– 'told her all that stuff?'

'What stuff?'

'Well, about the car he saw parked on the side of the road and the men unloading something from the trunk. For God's sake, Harry, didn't you read the story?'

The old fotog placed his loupe carefully on the light table and turned on his stool.

'As a matter of fact, I haven't. What's the big hurry, anyway?'

'I just want to know if he said anything like that to Felice.'

Harry thought about it.

136

'No,' he said finally.

'Aha. I suspected as much.'

'But then my hearing isn't as good as it used to be,' Harry said.

'You would have heard this, it was pretty explosive.'

'And I did go back to the car for another lens.'

'You mean you weren't there for the whole conversation?'

'That's right. What about it?'

'Oh, nothing.'

'You're in quite a snit there, Eve. You want to live to be as old as me, you'd better go do some yoga.'

A message was taped to my computer when I returned: *Call Victoria Givens,* followed by a phone number. When I got her on the line, she agreed to meet me on her lunch break at a restaurant near Belmont High.

I hung up and blocked out the plays. Let Felice chase the motos; I'd take a spin through Catarina's past, as recounted by her drama teacher and mentor. Calling Thompson on his car phone, I made my pitch.

'And best of all,' I concluded disingenuously, 'this stuff is all in the past, so there's no conflict of interest with the investigation.'

'Felice coming with you?'

'She's arranging a ride-along with that motorcycle club.'

'Well' – Thompson's gears turned– 'I'd rather you two stick together but Metro's hot to advance this puppy so I guess that's okay. Just this once.'

CHAPTER 19

Right at noon, I parked in front of Picholine, a little olive and cheese store on First Street near Virgil. I had been surprised to discover a foodie outpost in the forsaken outskirts of Koreatown, but there it was, tucked inside a Tudor building between a sushi restaurant and an art supply store. It looked as if the owners might live upstairs. Amid the desolation of strip malls and public storage units, the enclave was a hip sanctuary that thumbed its nose at the surrounding ugliness.

Inside, the olive and yellow walls of the café were a model of Gallic understatement. My eye was drawn to the glass displays of oozing cheese and herb-flecked olives. There were also hand-dipped chocolates, elaborately decorated by a patissiere who might suffer from obsessive-compulsive disorder.

I scanned the patrons. A teenager with cat glasses and pink hair sipped from a turquoise bowl of frothy cappuccino. A man with a black widow tattooed across his shaved head poked moodily at a salad. In the corner, a waiter was explaining to an older woman why he couldn't bring ice for her hand-pressed lemonade.

'The owner disapproves of the American obsession with ice cubes, madam,' the waiter said down his long nose. 'It dilutes the taste of his artisanal *citronade*.'

An irritated sigh rippled through the woman.

'For God's sake then, bring me something that's chilled, it's ninety-five degrees outside. You French should really look into this ice business. Then maybe fifteen thousand of you won't die in the next heat wave.'

'Very good, madam,' the waiter said with a small and aggrieved sniff.

He wore a crisp white apron and kept his hands clasped behind his back, no doubt to keep from throttling her.

Figuring that such an eccentric performance could come only from a drama teacher, I walked over. The woman had a tall, wiry athlete's build, a thin face, hawk nose, and graying hair pulled into two long braids. She wore an embroidered skirt and a loosely belted sleeveless top that exposed long, muscular biceps. She looked to be in her fifties.

'Victoria Givens?'

'Yes.' She tugged at a Guatemalan cloth bracelet. She wore black nail polish and bright red lipstick that drew attention to a large mole above her lip. 'You must be the reporter. Sit down. My God, the indignities I subject myself to for a decent sandwich.'

'This place really is quite French,' I said, taking in neatly stacked bottles of olive oil, duck pate, *crème de marron*, and apricot jams.

'Alas, the service is quite French as well.'

She glared at the waiter, who was reaching into a stainless-steel refrigerator, and I got the impression that this was a stylized ritual they played out each time she dined here.

139

'Now let's see how long it takes that nogoodnik to come back here and take your order,' Victoria said.

'Long enough, perhaps, for you to tell me about Catarina Velosi.'

Victoria tapped ebony nails on the table.

'I keep up with her career. Clip the reviews. I'm very proud of her. Use her as an example for my students.'

'Well, if you read the paper, then you know that she's–' I began.

'I only read the Calendar section,' Victoria said imperiously. 'I don't need any more bad news, it's not good for my chakras. But as I told the court at her juvenile hearings, Catarina was the most prodigiously talented student I ever taught. Raw. No filters. It's what kept her alive during high school. Well, the California Youth Authority, I should say. I taught a class there each week. They'd frisk me.'

'Is that right?'

Apparently, she didn't know about her onetime star pupil's disappearance and I didn't want to stop the flow of words and tell her. But a look of caution suddenly fell over Victoria's face, as though she had caught a whiff of danger on the wind. She peered over her spectacles, which were attached by a leash of pink plastic beads that looked suspiciously yanked from a rosary.

'When did you say this article is running?'

I looked blandly at her. 'Tomorrow.'

'But you can't possibly want to hear all this old personal stuff.'

'Of course I do.' Keep her talking.

140

Victoria's hand flew to her mole, fingered it nervously. Seeing me watching her, she grew flustered and yanked her hand down.

I waited.

Victoria shifted in her seat.

'I'm not sure what you want from me that you couldn't just read in the file.'

I popped a tiny green olive into my mouth and worked the pit to one side. Then I spat it into my fist and took a big bite of ragged, crusty bread.

'Juvenile records are sealed by the court.'

'Oh,' Victoria said. Her hand rose toward her face, hovered in the air. She caught herself and brought it back down.

'Well, I suppose I'm not revealing anything earth-shattering that she hasn't already told the press,' Victoria said. 'Catarina and I had a love-hate relationship at the beginning. Every single person she had ever trusted had betrayed her, and she didn't see why I would be any different. It took me a long time to win her over.'

'Who betrayed her?'

Victoria's hand rose, and she sat on it.

'She grew up in the Agua Dulce projects. Never knew her father. Her smacked-out teenaged mother would disappear for days, leaving her with neighbors. One of them molested her. Eventually she was put into foster care. She ran away after stabbing a foster father who tried to rape her. Then it was juvenile hall. She was thirteen. She banged her head against the wall and cut herself, so they locked her in a cage.'

'What do you mean, a cage?'

Victoria's eyes narrowed as the waiter

141

approached. I ordered and he left. Victoria played with her fork.

'Don't you know that's how they discipline the kids there?' she said when he was out of earshot. 'Some of them are in for weeks, twenty-three and a half hours a day.'

'My God.'

Victoria sighed. 'Eventually they diagnosed her as bipolar. Whether she started like that or life made her that way is up for debate. But from then on it was a roundelay of drugs. Chemical straitjackets.'

'How horrible.'

'Drearily predictable, in my experience,' Victoria said. 'But don't despair. This story, at least, has a happy ending.'

'That remains to be seen,' I muttered.

'The day I met her, Catarina had just gotten out of forty-eight hours in the cage for slashing herself with a razor. She was weak and disoriented, and thought she was walking into the TV room when she opened the door. Her name wasn't on my roster. But I took her arm and led her to our circle. That first lesson, she just sat there, slumped over.'

'Not exactly an auspicious beginning.'

'When she didn't return the following week, I hunted down the staff psychiatrist and had him write it into her treatment plan. Theater therapy.'

'And she went along?'

Victoria gave me a pitying look.

'She wanted to be hanging with her *comadres* in the TV room. But she had no choice.'

'So when did that change?'

142

'After I won her trust.' Victoria preened. 'I studied with Sanford Meisner in New York so I know what I'm doing.'

'I bet.'

I wondered if Victoria Givens had anything to teach me or if this lunch was all about stroking her sizable ego.

'I took them to the Forum to see *Zoot Suit*. We went to the beach. They had never seen the ocean before. Fifteen miles away and it could have been fifteen hundred. All Catarina knew of L.A. was the projects and the *tiendas* on Broadway and some storefront Pentecostal church her *abuelita* dragged her to. I stuck a script in her hand and told her to read. She stumbled over some of the big words. But then something from inside took over.'

Victoria Givens tapped at her heart.

'And she was hooked?'

'It wasn't like in the movies. It was chipping away, every day, at that granite exterior. Getting in her face. Tough little b-girl, she was. Eyebrows plucked into nonexistence. That brownish-purple lipstick they all wear. But she had something. She inhabited the role.'

'Don't all actors?'

Victoria Givens wiped her brow.

'She'd never been out of the barrio. But somehow she knew. She could do alcoholic housewives. Mercedes ladies. Spoiled teenagers. Anything you threw at her.'

Victoria paused, struggling to pin down the essence of Catarina's talent.

'She'd do a two-minute scene and take you

through five different arcs of emotion,' the drama teacher said. 'That's very much what life is like, but it's not something we often see in acting. It's not like Meryl Streep or Marlon Brando, building a character brick by brick. Catarina is one of those rare actors who when you watch them, you think, oh, she must be just like that in real life. And then you watch her play ten more parts and realize, wait a minute, she can't be like all those people.'

'I'm sorry I never got to see her onstage.'

Victoria Givens's eyes grew dreamy.

'I remember her first role. When the audience clapped, it was as if God himself was showering her with love. You could see it in her face. She was mesmerized, wouldn't get off the stage. We had to drag her away.'

Victoria's eyes focused, grew more steely. 'Some might say she's lived onstage ever since. Trying on and discarding roles, playing with the emotions of those who love her, even forgetting who put her there...'

Victoria stopped, gave a little chuckle.

I smiled. 'Who put her there in the first place – you mean you?'

She reared her head back, raised her eyebrows.

'I mean God, young lady. Hers is a gift from God. And with that comes obligation. It is her sacred duty to use it for the good, to bring her audiences joy.'

'Oh, I get it. The muse.'

Theater people could be rather tedious, I thought. With that kind of burden, I might run away too, escape to where people didn't know me

144

and expect such grandiose things of me. Maybe that's all it was. A disappearing act. Her swan song into blessed oblivion.

'The talent was there from the beginning, but it needed guidance. Encouragement. She still missed rehearsals. Threw tantrums. Brawled. You can't change a lifetime of conditioning overnight.'

'I read that she was an "emancipated minor."'

'Once she got serious about the stage,' Victoria said, 'the court appointed me temporary guardian.'

Her voice trailed off and I thought I detected something unpleasant at the end of it.

'How wonderful. So she lived with you?'

'For a year. Then she moved in with Alfonso.' Her plastic beads rattled in outrage.

'And you didn't approve?'

'Honey, she was seventeen. It could have been statutory rape.' She buttered a croissant with vigor. 'She's always been strong-willed. There was nothing more I could do except give her wings.'

'But were there hard feelings?'

Victoria sighed. 'Of course there were hard feelings. I had sacrificed so much, and this is how she thanked me? At least I got her on birth control pills before she left.'

'You kept in touch, all these years.'

'I watched her blossom into the flower I had planted. Yes, we kept in touch.'

'Have you talked to Catarina recently?'

'She'd call whenever she broke up with a lover, crying about how I'd been like a mother to her, begging me to visit. I hated those stairs to her bungalow. Tree boughs bending over me in the

145

dark, dripping damp needles down my back. And that unpleasant young fellow next door, scowling through the window, that loud music. And she'd be dancing through those tiny rooms when I arrived, or weeping on the bed, and she'd clutch my hand and thank me for saving her life.'

'How'd you save her life?'

'Haven't you been listening to a word I've said? The theater, my dear.'

'Doesn't sound like she was happy, though,' I probed.

'That's why I was so relieved when she called a few months ago. She sounded ... reborn. "Oh Victoria," she said. "I'm in love. And he's wonderful. He takes me right back to my childhood."

'"Now wait a minute," I told her. "Your childhood was nothing to get excited about."

'"But he loves me. For me. Even if I never step onstage again. I'm the most important thing in his life. Not his goddamn plays."

'And you know who she meant by that.' Victoria fixed me with a steely, disapproving gaze.

'Alfonso?'

'Yes. He had the gift. That was plain to see. But students with talent are fairly common. An artist who makes it big has to be obsessed. Alfonso was obsessed.'

'How well did you know him?'

Her lip curled, and not from the lemonade.

'You didn't care for him?'

'I admired his merciless will to succeed. It burned bright, a core of ruthless ambition, a purity of vision that no one could derail. All great artists have it.'

146

'But as a person?'

'He's selfish. He uses people. You want to understand him and Catarina and that pathetic wife of his, look to the plays. It's the blueprint for their lives. Especially *Our Lady of the Barrio*. It's all buried there. I haven't seen it yet, but Catarina showed me the script last year.'

'Did Alfonso use Catarina?'

'Maybe not at the beginning. She managed to slip inside his heart, just as it was closing off to the world. There was love, but also mutual recognition. They hitched their stars to each other, those two. There were times I felt I was competing with Alfonso, that we were battling for possession of her ... well, her soul.'

'What do you mean?'

'I wanted her to dedicate herself to art. Alfonso demanded total dedication to himself. He manipulated her, wooing her with talk of the plays he'd write for her. How could I compete with that? He wanted her as a muse. But only in the abstract, and onstage. He couldn't deal with the real Catarina. Her fragility, her breakdowns. He wanted his shirts ironed and hot coffee in the morning. And Catarina wasn't like that. You do not domesticate Eleanora Duse. Catarina said this new man understood that.'

'Did this new man have a name?'

'She never said.'

'Where did he live? What did he do?'

We fell silent as the waiter brought Victoria's salad and my *pissaladière*, a Provençal savory made of puff pastry topped with caramelized onions, anchovies, and black olives. Then he

147

plunked down a Pellegrino, and Victoria grabbed it, nails clicking like castanets around the bottle's neck to ensure it was properly chilled.

'She never said. But he's wealthy. Works a few days a week. Family money, maybe. I've been hoping that Alfonso finally sees he has to let her go.'

'They were still seeing each other?'

Victoria Givens looked at me with alarm. 'I didn't say that. But it's her business who she sees.'

'Not anymore.' I was ready to drop the bomb. 'If you read the paper more closely, you'd know that Catarina's disappeared and the police suspect foul play.'

'But...' said Victoria Givens, her eyes large and startled. 'How is... I mean, her play, it just ... oh my God, I didn't know.'

I watched as color stained her pale cheeks. A vein pulsed at her temple.

'I was in Ojai, leading a workshop. I just got back this morning.'

Her alibi came quickly, even though I hadn't asked. 'Then let me bring you up to date,' I said. 'Police found her car two hundred feet down a ravine in the San Gabriels. But no body. They're doing tests on some residue found in her bedroom and have asked Alfonso and several others' – I paused here – 'for DNA samples. The screen was torn and pushed in. She might have been in bed, taking a nap, but there's no sign of a struggle. Everything after that is pure conjecture.'

'My poor, poor Catarina,' Victoria said. 'She

148

doesn't deserve this. No one has fought as hard as her.'

'So the police haven't been by to see you?'

'The police?' Her hand flew to her mouth.

'You've known her longer than just about anyone. I thought they might get your name off the stories, like I did, and see what you knew about her personal life. Especially the mystery lover.'

'Catarina was cagey about him,' Victoria said. 'Which is unusual. Usually she can't hold anything back.' I caught a hint of a smirk.

'What else did she say about him?'

'That's all I remember,' Victoria said. 'I try not to pry. Now I wish I had. Oh God, let her be all right.'

'Tell me, was Alfonso the jealous kind?'

Victoria Givens stabbed at her salad.

'Alfonso isn't what he pretends. It's the quiet ones you have to watch. They can snap.'

We looked at each other.

'You think Alfonso learned about the new guy and got jealous and...'

She looked at her plate for a long time. With one long finger, she wiped some wetness off the corner of her mouth.

'Playwrights don't kill people,' she said finally.

'They don't?'

She laughed. 'Well, they do in their plays, of course. With words. And actors do it onstage. It's really marvelous therapy. That's what I told my students. We–'

'Victoria, you have to go to the police.'

She bent over her salad, hunting for teardrop tomatoes.

149

'I'm from the sixties. We don't go to the police.'

'Fine, then. They'll come to you once my story runs.'

She looked panicked. 'You're going to put this in the paper?'

'Why do you think I came out here to talk to you?'

It still amazed me that people could sit down with a reporter, reveal all sorts of intimate details, then feel betrayed when they saw their quotes in the paper the next day.

'I mean about the new boyfriend,' Victoria said.

'She's missing. And it's a fresh lead.'

Inside, I did a little jig. Take that, Felice Morgan. You're not the only one who can dig up new information. This is going to hit big-time.

Victoria looked primly into the distance. 'I've always been very careful to respect her privacy.'

'Her privacy won't matter if she's dead.'

The drama teacher blanched. 'Don't say that.'

'There's an urgency here you don't seem to be grasping.'

Victoria looked flustered. 'How do I know you're telling the truth? You could be trying to entrap me.'

I eyed her with renewed interest.

'Entrap you into what?'

'Telling you more than I should.'

'What more should you tell me?'

'I think I've had about enough of this conversation, young lady.'

I stood up. 'Well, thanks for your time.'

She shook her head. 'Are you all so rude?'

'All who?'

'Reporters. I've never talked to the press before. It's very unpleasant.'

'It's not all sweetness and light on my end either. But you've been kind to spend your lunchtime with me. Could I call you if I have more questions?'

Victoria's hands went to her braids and toyed with the ribbons.

'I love Catarina and want her found. Alive. So yes, of course. Though I don't know what else I can tell you.'

'Thanks, Ms. Givens. I'm sure I'll think of something.'

CHAPTER 20

Back in the car, I turned the AC on high and drove up Second Avenue to Glendale Boulevard. The heat radiated off the asphalt and pedestrians picked their way along the sides of buildings where the eaves threw off angled shade.

So Catarina had met somebody new. Could he have killed her? Or had they run off together? With a new play opening, I didn't think so. But what if she wanted to spite Alfonso? Or what if Alfonso had found out about the new lover, become insanely jealous, and killed her? Then there was Marisela. Fey Marisela, festering in her own jealousy. Could she have done it? And what about Silvio, the onetime jilted lover, whose behavior last night made it clear he still had feelings for her, and things to hide. Or was it simply a random act of violence? Catarina's house was plenty secluded, up that whitewashed walkway overhung by trees. Anyone could sneak up those stairs, especially at night, without being seen. Then there was the alley outside her bedroom. Providing easy access and getaway. Was it someone she knew, or a burglary gone bad? I had only been to Catarina's house once, and then not long enough to linger. Maybe seeing it again would give me some fresh ideas. Some connection to who she was, how she lived, who might have been angry enough to kill her. Maybe there was something the cops had missed.

I looked at my watch: 1 p.m. If I got back to the newsroom by two, I'd have plenty of time to file. I drove the ten minutes back to Echo Park. Hip realtors had begun touting the area as an 'inner-city suburb' and it seemed to have worked: stretches of Sunset and Echo Park Avenue now bustled with art studios, upscale thrift stores, and coffeehouses. The higher into the hills you went, the more expensive things got. But large swathes of the flats still looked like what they were – a thriving Mexican barrio. Soon I reached Echo Park Lake, where pedal boats skimmed across the surface like iridescent water spiders. At the lake's northern end, lotus plants floated in the shallows, their large flat leaves like a green giant's upturned palm, creamy white petals unfurled to the sun, anatomical and almost obscenely voluptuous.

I pulled over for a moment to gather my thoughts. There was a soft plop in the water, then a frog landed on a lotus pad. Another splash, and an empty beer can hit the lake, metal glinting off the sun. The frog probably had diseases from all the trash people threw in his lake. My primordial marsh dissolved into a horror movie. I pictured a frogman crawling out of this swamp, holding a dazed and dripping Catarina in his slimy black arms. Beauty was always more exquisite when backlit by horror and L.A. was a double helix where the sublime twined with the profane.

Pulling back into traffic, I drove to Catarina's house and hiked halfway up the whitewashed steps, glad for the thick canopy of trees that blocked out the sun. Then I stepped off the stairs and onto the hillside itself, my shoes sliding on a carpet of pine needles. I canvassed the hillside, looking for signs of a tussle. Debris. Empty cigarette packets. Bits of clothing. Anything that might give me a clue.

After twenty minutes, I conceded defeat and hiked back to the stairway and up to the top of the steps, serenaded by Spanglish rap from next door. Catarina's front door was locked and the windows drawn. Enervated by the heat, I sat on Catarina's front porch and pondered my next move. My grand plan had come to nothing.

The rap music got louder, and I started down, moving in rhythm to the staccato sounds until I caught my ridiculous dance moves reflected in the neighbor's window. I could see my ass wiggling in the lower pane. But the window was closed. Unlike two days ago, when I thought I had smelled marijuana through the open window. Silvio said the cops had interviewed all the neighbors and no one had seen or heard anything unusual.

Still, Echo Park was a place where not everyone welcomed the police with open arms. I studied the window. Another song started up. I sniffed the air for chronic but Pot Boy seemed to be on good behavior in case the cops returned. I hiked over and stood under the window. In the beats between songs, I hollered up.

He lifted the sash and stuck his head out. I jiggled my dog tags at him and said we needed to talk. He seemed to mull it over. Then he pulled his head in and turned the music down. I heard thumping as he came down some stairs, then the door opened.

'Yeah?' He pulled at a wispy goatee. 'I already told you guys, I didn't hear or see anything.'

He wore jeans and a T-shirt, and was so thin that his chest and stomach curved inward like a question mark. Coarse black hair grew on the knuckles of his bare toes.

'What guys?' I said, puzzled.

'The Man.'

He looked at where my skirt ended just above the knee. 'So now I gotta talk to "the woman"? Nice uniform, by the way, Officer. They should make that regulation.'

'I'm not a cop,' I said, realizing that from the second floor, he had mistaken my dog tags for some kind of badge. 'I'm a reporter.'

'You one a them chicks reads the news on TV?'

'Newspaper. *L.A. Times.*'

'Oh.' He made a dismissive motion. 'Well, I got no more to say.'

154

'I just want to ask you about Catarina, since you were neighbours. Was she friendly? Did she keep to herself? Was she a night owl? Did she have lots of visitors? I'm Eve Diamond, by the way.'

I smiled and extended my hand.

He studied it for a minute. Finally he took it. His hand was dry and rough and I felt calluses in his palm, small hard bumps that dug into my flesh.

'Steve Herrera.' He dropped my hand, then scratched his shaved head, his nails making a loud rasp.

'Is it okay if I come in?' Once we were sitting down he wouldn't be able to slam the door on me.

'I guess.'

I stepped onto a green shag rug. You could probably get high sniffing the fibers. Color-drenched paintings covered the walls, stuff that a pain-wracked Frida Kahlo might have done on a day when the morphine got the better of her. So Steve was an *artiste*. Good, that gave us something licit to talk about.

Before I could unglue my eyes from the paintings, he whisked something off the coffee table and into a back room. I flashed to high school science lab. Measuring things on a scale. And this was not a guy who counted portions for Weight Watchers.

Pot Boy bustled back into the living room and lit a fat red candle. It gave off an incense of chipotle peppers and cinnamon. Camouflage. He threw himself into a chair and regarded me with suspicion.

I started in and we lobbed the ball back and

forth real easily until he warmed up. He recounted how Catarina had welcomed him to the neighborhood and bummed a cigarette the day he moved in. It was late afternoon, and she had just gotten up.

Did she have a boyfriend?

The question seemed to consternate him, because he frowned, grabbed a match, and began to clean his nails.

I repeated it.

'I don't know. She gets a lot of visitors. I seen men. But I seen women too.'

He gave a lascivious laugh.

'I'm interested in the men.'

Steve said they usually came at night. He didn't know anything about Catarina's romantic entanglements. It wasn't his business, he said with growing irritation.

To distract him, I asked about his art and he told me he painted murals for the county. He'd have more business if he hustled, but somehow he couldn't work up the ambition.

I nodded, as if this were an admirable career goal. I had written enough stories about L.A.'s dwindling arts budget to know that murals couldn't provide a steady living for most artists, much less an unmotivated and only mildly talented one. Steve Herrera either had a trust fund or another source of income.

'I guess the drug business tides you over when things are slow.'

He twitched angrily.

'I don't know what you're talking about,' he said. 'I'm clean and whatever this is, it's over.'

156

He stood up.

I stood up too, because I was starting to feel small and vulnerable. Was he a harmless pothead or a potentially dangerous dealer? I decided to take out a bit of insurance, just in case. 'I don't care how you make your living. And I'm not a cop. I'll prove it.'

I took out my cell phone and called the paper.

'*Times* City Desk,' chirped Luke Vinograd.

Luke was a senior copy messenger who had been at the paper so long that he knew its inner workings better than many editors. We were friends.

'Hi, Luke. This is Eve Diamond. Would you mind repeating that?' I said, holding the phone up so Steve could hear.

'The Lady Eve,' Luke said. 'What can I do you for today?'

'You can humor me for a sec, dollface. Have I called the *Los Angeles Times?*'

'You know you have. And Eve, I've just got to tell you the richest bit of news. Remember that–?'

'Luke, am I a staff writer for the *Los Angeles Times?*'

'Last time I checked, darling. What is this, a joke? Is this call being monitored for quality control and consumer satisfaction?'

'Hardly. I've got someone here who thinks I'm a cop and I need to set him straight. Now write this down and I'll explain later. Ready?'

Good-natured grumbling came from the receiver. I rattled off Steve Herrera's address as my host's red-rimmed eyes narrowed in anger. He made to swipe the phone out of my hands but

157

I had already hung up.

'What the hell was that?' he said. The lacka-daisical demeanor was gone.

'Just a precaution. And now, as you suggested, I'm leaving.'

I made for the door and he followed me, standing uncertainly on the threshold.

'I told you I'm just a reporter,' I said once I was safely outside. 'But I have a personal interest in finding Catarina. The police suspect a friend of mine but they're wrong.'

'Well, I sure didn't do it.'

'But you did sell her dope,' I said, taking a chance.

His eyes searched mine, trying to figure out what I wanted. Then he stepped back inside his apartment and began to shut the door.

'You are one crazy chick,' he said, shaking his head.

I stuck my foot in the doorway.

'You know, I'm getting tired of this,' I said. 'I'm not a cop but I can certainly tell them about the weed I smelled last time I climbed these stairs. And today I saw a scale.'

His mouth opened in denial.

'You weren't as slick as you thought, whisking it away.'

I paused, thinking of his earlier words: *I'm clean.*

'And the cops take drug dealing awfully seri-ously, especially if you already have a strike or two working.'

Slowly, the door opened and I knew that I had gotten very, very lucky.

Steve Herrera stood, glowering at me, but I also caught a whiff of fear, faint but growing at the edge of his anger.

'So I sold her some stuff,' he said with a high whine. 'Big deal.'

'Pot?'

'Jah-love isn't her thing. Pills is.' His words came fast and nervous.

'Prescription pharmaceuticals? Why didn't she just go to the doctor?'

That would explain her volatility, I thought. The great erupting volcano of chaos and instability.

He looked to see if I was for real. 'In those quantities? Are you kidding?'

'What about online?'

Pot Boy rubbed his thumb and forefinger together. 'Dearth of *dinero.*'

'Then how'd she pay you?'

Pot Boy realized he was backed into a corner. A petulant look crossed his face.

'With cash, mostly.'

'But you just said—'

'I deal in bulk. She got it at cost.'

'Even so. She had that kind of money?'

'Depends. Sometimes she was short.'

'So you sold her drugs on credit?'

'Yeah.' He shrugged. 'It's against my policy, but she's my neighbor. Okay, now you've got to go.'

I didn't like doing this. It was ugly and it warped something in my soul. But sometimes it was the only way.

'Fine,' I said. 'I'm sure the cops will find this very interesting.'

159

His shoulders sagged. 'There's nothing more to say. Honest.'

Dishonest people love saying that word. They don't realize what a big tip-off it is.

'How much did she owe you?'

'Not that much.'

'How much?'

'Couple grand.'

I paused. That was plenty to get her killed. Almost unconsciously, I took a step back from Steve Herrera's door.

'That you had fronted?' I finally said.

'I told her she had a week to come up with it. I had people breathing down my neck.' He exhaled hard and long. 'I didn't kill her. It has nothing to do with this.'

'Who says she's dead?'

He stuttered. 'I just assumed... She's been missing so... You have to believe me.'

'The only way I will believe you is if you tell me the truth.'

'I already did. She owed me five grand.'

'So now a couple of grand is five grand. How long ago was this?'

'Last week.'

'Could she have blown town so she wouldn't have to pay you back?'

'Naw, man, she didn't leave town.'

'It doesn't make sense, with her play opening. But how do you know?'

He just stood there, swaying in the door.

'This is going to look really bad if the cops find out,' I pushed.

I tried to look bored, like it didn't matter either

way to me. Dulling my eyes, so he wouldn't see that all my senses were on red alert.

Herrera blinked. Pot Boy was back. He looked like he was itching to get back in his apartment and take the edge off his annoyance with a few bong hits.

'Wait a minute,' I said, snapping my fingers. 'If she owed you five grand, how did you pay your supplier?'

Steve Herrera stared gloomily at the floor. 'I haven't yet,' he said finally. 'They gave me an extension.'

'What civilized people the drug trade attracts these days.'

'It's my cousin in Tijuana. He's got connections with the cartel. But it's coming due.'

'Then you should want to find her as much as anyone.'

'I do,' he said in a mournful voice. 'I was small-time, man. Strictly dope. But she wanted pills. So I started moving pharmaceuticals. A little coke. So she'd have a steady supply. I got in over my head. These people my cousin's with, they're droid killers. Shoot you dead then wash their hands and go eat dinner.'

The skin under his left eye twitched like an insect was in there, trying to work its way to the surface.

'Sounds like you're in big trouble.'

'My cousin will bail me out. But I'll have to move more stuff for him. And I want to ease out of the business, not get deeper in. I need to concentrate on my painting. She left a jacket here a few weeks back, and I'm gonna sell that, even

161

though it's only a drop in the bucket. Wanna buy a black leather jacket?'

'I'd have to see it first.'

'Hold on.'

I thought I heard him talking to someone in the other room but he was back in a minute, a butter-smooth, hand-tooled leather jacket slung over his arm.

I pretended to examine it, admiring the cut and grain of the leather as I dipped fingers into empty pockets. The lining had a vest pocket and I probed that too.

'Sorry, not my style.'

He surveyed me with a grin.

'You'd look hot in black leather. Stilettos. I could paint you.'

Not in this lifetime.

He threw the jacket onto the couch. 'I'm not stupid, you know.'

'I never said–'

'I know what you were doing. Looking for evidence.'

'There wasn't any.' I shrugged.

'I took it out.' He seemed cocky, proud of himself.

'You took what out?'

'She was always so secretive, didn't want me to know anything about her life.'

'What did you find, Steve?'

'I'll show you. Come in.'

He opened the door wide and swaggered into a back room.

Was this a ploy? To lure me back in where he could turn up the Spanglish rap and...

'No thanks, I'm allergic to all that candle incense.' For good measure, I sneezed.

In a minute he was back, something palmed in his hand.

'So what is it?' I leaned forward with casual disinterest.

'Oh no.' He swiped it behind his back like a coy toddler. 'No looksies until we have a deal.'

'Like I was about to say earlier, Steve, you're no fool. Not a half-bad painter, either. Certain Kahlo-esque touches.'

'I prefer Diego Rivera analogies.'

He tugged on his goatee. I could tell he had taken a toke when he put away the jacket. His eyes were shiny. He must feel pretty sure of himself to let down his guard like that. But then, maybe he was just a stoner.

'Two things,' Steve said. 'First, you give me your word that you won't go to the cops.'

'I already told you.'

'Two.' He held up a stubby forefinger, dirt packed under the nail. 'You do a story about me.'

I blinked in stupefaction.

'My paintings,' Steve said. 'How I'm a muralist for the county.'

I shook my head with disbelief that he thought he could leverage his information into a story. He wasn't even good.

'I write news, not features. You'd need to talk to the arts editor.'

'Well, that's no problem. As soon as he sees my work, he'll understand. Papers love stories like mine. Former gangbanger goes straight, discovers his inner Aztlan. I'm the reincarnation of a

163

famous Aztec painter from the royal court of Emperor Montezuma.'

And I'm Marie Antoinette.

'The arts editor is a woman, by the way. The most I can do is send her an e-mail.'

'Okay, but make sure you tell them about my reincarnation. Seven hundred years ago, I painted the great pyramids.'

I rolled my inner eye.

'Right. Now it's your turn. Show and tell.'

He thrust out his hand. Inside was a sweated-up business card, curled at the edges from his humid palm. Gingerly, I picked it up and read: Barry F. Mancuso, president, Skylight Productions. There was a Beverly Hills address.

I looked at Steve.

'Any idea who this guy is?'

'That's your job.'

'It could be someone she met at a cocktail party. On a casting call.'

'Or it could not.' Steve Herrera rocked onto his toes. I fingered the card's frayed edges.

'Did you show this to the police?'

He recoiled, as if I had said something unbelievably vulgar. 'Why should I?'

'Maybe so you don't get slapped with a with-holding evidence charge?'

'I didn't even find it until after they were gone. Worked my nerves big-time, that visit. So if you think I'm going to invite them back, you're dead wrong.'

He rubbed his goatee nervously, then plucked the card out of my hand. 'Sorry, but I have to hold on to this. It's my insurance.'

But I had already memorized its contents.

'Say hi to Montezuma next time you see him,' I said. 'Tell him not to trust that bastard Cortés.'

CHAPTER 21

The shade seemed darker as I hiked down the steps, the wooded slopes on either side thick with the rustle of small animals. Far away, a bee droned. I was glad it wasn't night, when the enchanted forest morphed into something more sinister, bats flapping overhead and shrubs reaching out gnarled hands.

Back on the sidewalk, I felt glass crunch under my feet and saw that the streetlight was busted. I swore inwardly at kids who were so bored they had to shoot out city lights. I went to unlock my car but the key wouldn't go in.

I pushed harder. Could I have the wrong key? No. My finger traced something smooth. Tape. Disbelieving, I rubbed it. Why would someone put tape on my lock? I straightened up.

A figure appeared from behind a parked car. A teenaged boy. He moved across the narrow street toward me. He had a bandanna across his face and held a gun. I considered running but he was too close. Instinctively, I dove onto the hood of the car, sliding along the metal and back down to the sidewalk on the other side, where I whacked my chin hard on the concrete.

'Freeze,' the boy shouted and a bullet exploded

above me.

As he came around, I edged the other way to make a dash for it. But my car was tiny. Unlike a wing-tipped Cadillac, it didn't offer much room to hide.

I heard a huge thump and the rustling of clothing as he jumped onto the roof of my car, and then the gun was staring me down. The sun danced in my eyes, the light bouncing off the metal, blinding me.

'Move and you're dead.'

He had visibility and height. If I tried to run up the stairs, he'd shoot me in the back. If I slid under the car I'd be captive. Could I pull up the bumper and tip the car over? I'd heard of adrenaline making this possible, and my pineal gland was working overtime. But no. He'd pump several pieces of lead into me before I even got my hands around the bumper.

'Got a message for you,' the voice said, cutting in on my thoughts.

In the next fifteen seconds, my brain worked feverishly on several different levels. I probed the voice on top of my car. No accent. Young. Not very educated. A slight serpentine hiss in his *s*, as though a childhood speech impediment had gone untreated. But this wasn't a garden-variety mugging. Those guys didn't stop to deliver messages.

I stood up, took a half step back. I could dive into the shrubbery, maybe make my way into someone's backyard and pound on a door for help. But then my crashing and lumbering through the underbrush would tell my pursuer exactly where I was.

166

'Don't even think about it,' a voice behind me said, and a second teen stepped off the stairs I had just come down.

I swallowed and felt only sour bile burning in the back of my throat. I prayed that someone would come down the stairs or along the block, remembering he needed a quart of milk or had to pick up his kids from school. This was a heavily populated hill. Then I heard footfalls and a soft jingle. The street was curved and I couldn't see who it was yet. I opened my mouth to scream, choking it back as the guy on top of the car leaped with a soft thud, landing beside me. With a fluid motion, he shoved the gun between my ribs, and I wondered what internal organs it was pointing at. The second guy had melted into the shrubbery.

'Don't move,' he said softly, and I smelled beer and tooth decay. He pulled me onto the stairs and shoved me down by a crepe myrtle bush.

I heard the panting of a dog, the scrabbling of toenails. Then sniffing. From where I lay, I could see that the dog and his owner were old and creaky, moving slowly. The dog looked with interest up the stairs and gave a loud *wuff*.

'No squirrels for you today,' the man said, tugging him along. The dog's tags jingled against his collar as he and his owner disappeared around the bend. With a silent glide the second man reappeared at my side.

'All right then,' said my tormentor, shoving the gun butt deeper. 'Stop minding other people's business.'

'What?' My teeth chattered, suddenly outside

167

my control.

'You heard. Or next time we won't miss.'

'W-w-why?' It was out before I realized I had spoken aloud.

'That's the message.'

'Who sent you?'

The gun guy cracked a grin now. He turned to his friend.

'There she goes again.'

'That's exactly what we mean.'

'Miss Nosy.'

'She doesn't get it, does she?'

He turned back to me.

'No more questions. At all.'

I looked away, knowing it was better not to meet his eyes. I didn't answer.

'Got it?' The gun jabbed.

I shook my head up and down, a parody of a nod.

'Or we'll send you to where you can ask Catarina yourself.'

And with that they were gone.

I waited, heart pounding, on my knees, until I heard their feet slapping down the street. Then a motorcycle revved and tore off. The encounter had felt unreal, like an out-of-body experience. Now it hit me in the solar plexus. I was scared and humiliated. I got up, staggered to my car, peeled the adhesive off my lock, got in, and drove to Times Mirror. By the time I got there, the fear had ebbed and the humiliation had channeled into anger.

I parked and took inventory, willing myself to calm down. They hadn't hurt me. They just wanted to scare me off the story. But my nature was stubborn, dogged and contrary. Now I was more determined than ever to get to the bottom of Catarina's disappearance, if only to avenge my hurt pride. I pulled down the sun visor, looked in the mirror. Other than flyaway hair, severely dilated pupils, and a galloping heart, I was okay.

I remembered Herrera talking to someone in the other room. Had he sicced those two hoods on me? And what about the significance of the motorcycle I'd heard as the thugs took off? Could it be tied in with the moto Felice had interviewed? That bizarre story? All of a sudden, things were breaking wide open.

Then there was my best lead yet, Barry Mancuso. Was he the mystery lover Catarina had mentioned to Victoria Givens? Or was Pot Boy merely trying to throw me off the track? I wrote the story in my head as I walked out of the parking lot, deciding I'd lead with the mystery lover but leave out the business card for now. And Mancuso's name. At least until I had talked to him. I felt a twinge of conscience, thinking that I should probably report everything to the police first. But then they'd be all over Herrera and his Barry Mancuso card. And I'd be out a story. Which just wouldn't do.

I was determined to one-up Felice. I knew it was base and venal, but I didn't care. I wanted to save Catarina myself.

CHAPTER 22

My backgrounder on the missing actress turned into a hard news story that began: 'Just months before her disappearance, missing actress Catarina Velosi met a man and embarked on a secret but passionate affair with him, according to Velosi's former drama teacher, who kept in contact with her onetime student.'

After I filed, Metro editor Jane Sims called me over and warned me to expect a call from the police the next day, seeking more information.

'Wouldn't they just go straight to Victoria Givens?' I asked.

'Just keep your notes in a safe place and refer all law-enforcement calls to Corporate Legal.'

I imagined myself being led into the courtroom with Felice, the two of us shackled in chains. They'd put us in the same cell and we'd keep our sanity by reciting poetry and writing our memoirs. Ah, but this was high fantasy. Unlike the mystery moto racer notes, there would be no need to subpoena these. Victoria Givens worked at Belmont High and the police would have no problem finding her.

Waiting for my story to clear, I called Silvio, intending to tell him about the two guys who had threatened me. I wanted comfort, reassurance. But his secretary said he was meeting with his lawyer and would have to call me back. Biting back disappointment, I told her that would be fine.

Just then, Felice strolled out of the Met-Pro office and waved. Jeez, was she stalking me or what? Why was she downtown? But if I feared she'd try to glom on to me, I was dead wrong. Felice pantomimed that she was about to get edited and headed for the City Desk. I waited until she was tête-à-tête with one of the assistant City editors, then ordered up the clips on Barry Mancuso. Sensing someone behind me, I turned and saw Josh Brandywine, briefcase in hand, staring at my computer. Was the producer's name still on the screen? Glancing back in what I hoped was a distracted manner, I was relieved to see that my request had been replaced by the CNS newswire. We smiled at each other, two predators sizing up the possibilities.

He raised a quizzical eyebrow.

'Had a nice chat with Catarina Velosi's high school drama teacher today,' I said.

Josh's face relaxed. A backgrounder. Nothing important. Nothing that would compete with his story. I let him think that. Then I laid it on him.

'She says Catarina had a new mystery lover.'

The eyebrow rose higher. Two lines appeared across his forehead. He looked away. An internal struggle took place. When he looked back, his face was friendly and composed again.

'Good for you, digger,' Josh said. He leaned in, placed his hands on my desk, and said, 'And I've scored an interview with the lead detective on the case later tonight. At the Shortstop.'

A baseball bar down the hill from Dodger

Stadium in Echo Park, the Shortstop was a long-time cop hangout.

Josh nodded. 'They've got me working late shift tonight. So I'm off to grab some dinner.' He pointed a finger at me. 'Don't work too hard.'

'You wish.'

He strode jauntily out the door, and I turned back to the computer. The day had started with a bang when I read Felice's moto story. Since then I had done two interviews and been intimidated by thugs. I hoped the evening would be calmer. It wasn't.

At 6:48 p.m., I was scrolling through the wires when something caught my eye: 'City News Service– The partially clad body of an unidentified female was found on the ocean rocks below a San Pedro cliff around 4:30 this afternoon, authorities say. Police and coroners are investigating and refuse to speculate if she fell to her death from the 60-foot cliffs or was killed elsewhere and the body dumped. The victim is Caucasian and appears to be in her late 20s.'

Dread curled its tendrils around my heart. I picked up the phone and called Silvio's cell phone. As it rang, a blinking message arrived at the top of my computer screen from Sims, Jane. '"Drama" just cleared. You can go.'

Not likely, I thought.

When Silvio came on, I read him the story. I heard a sharp intake of breath, then the muted strum of a guitar from his truck stereo.

'It has to be her,' he said when I finished.

'She's quite a ways from home.'

'I'm going to call Alfonso, and then I think we

172

should get out there,' Silvio said, in a voice not altogether steady. 'I'm downtown, just leaving the lawyer's office.' He didn't even wait for my squawk of alarm. 'Wait for me in front of the Globe Lobby in ten minutes,' Silvio said, referring to the show-case entrance trimmed with marble and gold and dominated by a six-foot-high globe that illustrated how *L.A. Times* coverage spanned the world.

I hung up, feeling dizzy. The world had suddenly tilted and changed. At that moment, a gruff voice on the City Desk called out.

'You still here, Brandywine? Looks like you're going to San Pedro.'

'He just left,' I called out.

'See if you can catch him. Got a hot one here.'

Indeed, I thought, trotting into the hallway and praying it would be empty. It was. An idea was forming. I slowed down, taking it easy to the elevators. Josh was already gone. Too bad, so sad. Diligently, I pressed the buttons, but no elevator came. I waited a reasonable interval, then took the stairs to the service lobby. It was deserted except for the security guard, who looked up with mild interest from the sports pages of *La Opinión*. I walked out to the sidewalk. A block away, a figure clutching a briefcase was striding to the parking garage. I cupped my hands to my mouth, imagining that I had called out for him. Then I turned around, walked back inside. I threw open the stairwell door and raced up the steps, making sure I was panting by the time I arrived at the City Desk.

'Couldn't catch him,' I said.

The night City editor, Boris Johannsen, cracked

his knuckles and swore. 'He's not answering his cell either.' He looked around the room. 'Wonder who I can send. It's getting late.'

I cleared my throat and flung back my hair and he looked at me, as if for the first time. Finally, the light went on.

'Hey, Diamond, what are you doing right now?'

I pretended to think it over for a minute.

'I have a date.'

'Break it.'

I looked out the window like I was wrestling with the idea. 'I don't think I should. We've got tickets ... he'll be furious...'

I stopped. Rueful. The dawning realization that duty came before pleasure. 'But if you need me...'

'I need you, baby. I need you.'

'All right. I'll do it.'

I packed up, but had to walk past Felice, who was huddled over her story, making last-minute changes. She looked up, sniffing the air. I had banked the fires but she was too canny.

'You look pretty electrified,' she said. 'Whassup?'

'A friend just called with an emergency.'

I could tell she didn't believe me. She was already pushing back her chair, heading to the City Desk to find out what was going on.

After sauntering around the corner, I tore down the hallway and through the warren that was the back corridors of the *L.A. Times*, making my ratlike way to the Globe Lobby. This was one assignment I intended to handle alone.

CHAPTER 23

Outside, Silvio was just pulling up in his truck. I jumped in. 'Step on it,' I said, feeling like a dame in a 1940s getaway flick.

He shot me a distracted look. 'Am I that late?'

'No, but I've got to ditch someone who's going to burst out that door any minute now.'

He gunned the V-8 engine and we took off. As he drove, I explained how Felice had hijacked my motorcyclist story.

'Sounds like an honest mistake,' he said.

'That's not the adjective that comes to mind.' *Low-down, cunning, sneaky* was more like it.

'She's just trying to prove herself.'

'There's a fine line between an aggressive reporter and an asshole.'

He put his hand on my knee. Shook it. 'Hey, now. It's not you she's got to impress. It's your boss. And your boss's boss. Imagine what it must be like, everyone watching her, waiting for her to stumble, just because of the color of her skin.'

'As if you've ever dealt with that. You're the *jefe.*'

Silvio made a *tsk*ing sound.

'It happens whenever I step outside my little universe,' he said. 'Take my banker. Blue-chip American firm. My attorney and I meet with him, and no matter what question I ask, he directs the answer to my lawyer, who just happens to be

175

white. Won't even look me in the eye.'

'Fire him,' I said. 'Look, I don't want to fight. We've got more important things to consider, like whose body just washed up on the shore.'

Silvio's jaw twitched. We lapsed into silence and crawled along the aptly named Harbor Freeway, which dumped motorists onto Los Angeles's dueling harbor towns – Long Beach and San Pedro.

'Ever been to this place Point Fermin?' I asked.

Silvio hesitated. 'Yes,' he said. 'Alfonso and I used to hang out there as teenagers. There's a lighthouse and a park at the top of these huge sandstone cliffs overlooking the ocean. It's a one-hundred-and-fifty-foot drop to the rocks below. Lots of signs warning people to keep away from the edge.'

'Hmm. Someone obviously didn't.' I wondered about the pause before he answered. So the body had washed up at Silvio and Alfonso's old stomping ground. My stomach clenched.

The freeway snaked past cheerless suburbs and a factory with a giant smokestack belching out bluish-orange flames. We passed a building from the 1950s, a more optimistic age, that proclaimed *Oil, Chemical, and Atomic Workers Union*. I wondered if the workers' comp division saw older members shuffling in, complaining of strange and inexplicable cancers. The cars thinned and we flew past oil derricks, whimsical black crows bobbing in synchronized pecks, anachronisms in this age of oil platforms and pipelines.

Then the San Pedro harbor rose up, with its monster cranes that stacked ocean-cargo containers as easily as toddlers do blocks. Then belching factories and refineries, a terrorist's wet dream, and finally the lovely, lyrical span of the Vincent Thomas Bridge, which connected San Pedro to its sister community of Long Beach.

Taking the Gaffey exit, we shot past a graceless hodgepodge of fast-food outlets, liquor stores, and boxy apartments. The L.A. City Council must have been on crack when it approved it. The Pacific came into view, a dark, brooding presence lapping the horizon. As the sun set, airborne pollutants turned the sky magnificent shades of teal, pumpkin, and cotton-candy pink. Poisonous blooms for a savage garden in the sky.

I rolled my window down and inhaled the humid tang of the sea. I missed the ocean. I missed its majesty, its limitless expanses. It made me feel insignificant and small in the most wonderful way.

The road dead-ended into a park, a strip of grass at the cliff's edge. I heard the crashing of the waves, the percussive tinkle as the tide sucked back the stones, God's great tumbler, buffing and dragging them to the sea.

'I'll jump out and you can park,' I told Silvio, as an exasperated policeman told us to move along. Instead, I melted into the news-folk, making my way to a spot where erosion had crumbled the sandstone, carving a ravine to the sea.

A motorcycle policeman herded me back before I could see anything. All around us, TV crews spread out like happy picnickers. They joked and tinkered with the angles of their cameras as neighborhood joggers and cyclists stopped, open-mouthed, to gawk. One young woman pointed

177

out media personalities to her baby, who sat up and gripped the bars of his stroller. Several reporters were conducting interviews, but no one had seen or heard anything unusual. I found myself glancing over my shoulder, half expecting to see Felice pop up any minute. It would be just like her.

Crime scenes have their own internal logic and rhythm. When the body was finally brought up, a great hue and cry would erupt as everyone jostled to shoot it being loaded into the ambulance. Then an LAPD honcho would stand behind the barricades and dispense the facts like Halloween candy and reporters would yell themselves hoarse with questions.

I heard a honk and saw Silvio in the distance, beckoning. I hesitated. I didn't want to miss the dénouement but the crews were camped out in a way that suggested hours.

'How much longer?' I asked the mustachioed policeman.

'At least an hour.' His mirrored sunglasses caught and reflected the strobing lights of nearby emergency vehicles.

I ran back to Silvio.

'Get in,' he said. 'I've got a plan.' We drove away from the park and down a hill.

'Where are you taking me?'

'The back way.'

Soon we were in another seaside park. We drove past the unattended parking kiosk, its security bar saluting the sky. Silvio stopped where the grass met the sand and we got out. South of us sprawled San Pedro Harbor with its massive cranes and docks, hulking freighters anchored off the horizon. To the north loomed the cliffs of Point Fermin.

'Where are we?'

'Cabrillo Beach,' Silvio said. 'Welcome to my childhood playground.'

My stomach tightened again. I forced myself to relax. It was only my doubting, second-guessing paranoia at work again. If he was involved in any way, why would he boast how well he knew this place where a woman's body had just been found? It would only invite suspicion.

Oil and tar fumes hung in the air, the essence of heavy industry mixing with the seaweed and salt. In front of us was the Pacific, deep and vast. We hiked past a shuttered community center and a set of rusty swings anchored in the sand. Fifty feet to our right, the cliffs rose, sheer and high.

'We can't climb this.'

He walked to the waterline, bent down. The receding tide had left the beach studded with rocks, shells, and clumps of seaweed.

'It's pretty low,' he said. 'See those rocks at the foot of the cliff, where the waves are crashing? They're covered at high tide. But when it goes out, there are wonderful tide pools. Right now, we can walk on the rocks all the way to Point Fermin.'

'Where the cops and the body are?'

'They won't be expecting anyone to hike around the tide pools. We'll have the element of surprise.'

'I hope they're not so surprised that they shoot us.'

He brushed wet sand off his hands and headed off. 'Just jump in the water and bark like a seal. They're a protected species.'

I followed. The sandstone cliffs had eroded over time, leaving boulders and rocks strewn at the bottom. Rocks and shells scrunched underfoot, and my shoe slipped into puddles of salt water where eons of lapping tides had hollowed out shallow basins. Seagulls swooped low in the dusk, dropping crustacean bombs that shattered against the rocks, revealing succulent mussels and sea urchins within. Then with a flap of wings, they settled down to enjoy their evening meal.

How would we get back if the tide came in? I wondered. We'd have to swim for it or risk getting dashed against the rocks. I blinked and felt cold, salty drops condensing on my eyelashes.

'Alfonso and I spent hours here as kids,' Silvio said, his voice catching with enthusiasm despite our grim mission. 'We'd collect shells and watch dolphins and seals, occasionally a migrating whale if the season...'

A crashing wave drowned out his voice. A shiver of dread. What was it they said about killers returning to the scene of their crime? I tried to keep my eyes on Silvio as I pushed that thought away. The wind whipped my hair into my mouth as I jumped like a sea goat from rock to rock, testing each surface first for slippery algae. Thank goodness I was wearing flats today. The tide pools at my feet teemed with life – hermit crabs, sea anemones, even a probing black tentacle that disappeared as it felt the vibration of my foot.

Silvio was far ahead, picking his way with confidence along the rocks. The coastline curved and he disappeared. I hurried to catch up and saw only another rocky outcropping lashed by the sea. Silvio was a tiny solitary figure in the distance.

'Wait,' I called. He stopped, staring up until I reached him. I followed his gaze. Above us, jagged chunks of collapsed sidewalk lay strewn halfway down the cliffs, sticking out at haphazard angles. It was eerie and beautiful and utterly apocalyptic.

'It's like a civilization died here.'

'Long Beach had a big earthquake in 1931,' Silvio said. 'It sent houses and entire streets tumbling down the cliff. You can still see the stamped signs for the contractors who poured the cement sidewalks back in the 1920s.'

A particularly large wave crashed at our feet, licking our legs with spray.

'I'm glad it's low tide,' I said. Was it my imagination, or was it starting to come in? 'C'mon, let's go.'

We hiked to the next promontory and peered around. A woman's body lay on the rocks.

CHAPTER 24

She was oblivious to the hive of activity surrounding her. Solitary and tragic, she lay on the
rock-strewn stage in her final role, a Cordelia for
the ages. A great artificial sun shone upon her, a
forensics light for investigators to see by. Clouds
scudded across the sky, obscuring the early moon
and cloaking the landscape in intermittent
shadow, as if the light board were being manned
by a grief-crazed King Lear.

A young woman. Petite, not much over five feet
tall. There was no mistaking that she was dead.
Her body was stiff and unnatural, limbs extended
and bloated. This was a grotesque caricature of a
human being. She wore torn boxer shorts and the
remains of a frilly shirt with ruffles at the neck.
Large cuts marred her legs, her skin gashed like
an overripe fruit that had fallen in the garden.
Her skin was a waxy bluish white against the dark
rocks, her oval face framed by long hair fluttering
in the breeze. There was an ugly cut near her
temple, and another on the side of her mouth,
the blood no doubt washed clean by the tides,
nibbled away by tiny fish.

She lay, pliant and docile, as a photographer
took photos and an artist sketched the body.
Several clipboard-carrying men in white shirts
conferred. A woman with thigh-high boots foraged
along the cliff, bending down to poke at the

detritus tossed up by the waves.

'Dear Lord,' Silvio whispered.

'Is it her?'

His head bent and he clasped his hands in prayer.

I put my arms around him, embracing him from behind. He turned, catching me off guard, and we teetered on our rock perch, clutching each other to keep from falling. Quickly, we regained our balance. I felt his heart pounding in his chest. I heard a ragged intake of breath, then a keening, unnatural sound.

'It's her, isn't it?'

He nodded. 'It doesn't even look like her.'

As I stroked his head, I also committed the scene to memory – the details of her red-and-white polka-dotted men's boxers, the tear at the crotch, the cut of the shirt. A wave broke, hitting us with heavy spray. I looked back. The surf was licking the rocks where we had just stood, greedily reclaiming its turf. Then the tide receded and the rocks glistened with water.

Silvio hiked up to the lee of the cliff, where the rocks were still dry. He sat, hunched his knees to his chest, and looked bleakly out over the horizon. I followed his gaze and saw a dorsal fin cut the water not fifty feet from us, then another, three in all, then sleek gray bodies leaping and falling. Porpoises. I wanted to swim out to them, hitch a ride on a smooth rubber fin, and let it take me far away.

'She was so alive. I just saw her. I mean ... who could have...?' He looked up at me, his face abject and disbelieving.

What do you mean, you just saw her?

But the pain on his face stayed me. I swallowed my burning question. Instead, I said with deliberation, 'That's what we're trying to find out, isn't it?'

It came out colder than I had intended. He had loved her once. And now he rocked with anguish, huddled against the coming night, while a bloated mermaid lay broken on the rocks before him.

'We'd better let them know we're here,' I said. 'We can't go back. The tide's too high.'

Night was falling with a vengeance. In the blurry twilight, I saw two men roll Catarina's body onto a stretcher. A wave lapped our feet. Silvio didn't move.

'We're going to get trapped if we stay any longer.'

I pulled him up and we rounded the point and trudged toward the men, me haloo-ing them every ten feet. I knew what could happen if you spooked cops with guns.

We were almost upon them before they saw us.

'Freeze,' yelled a policeman, aiming at us. 'Hands up where I can see them.'

We complied, and I was glad for the dog tags around my neck.

Another cop strode forward. He tore the ID from my neck.

One of the forensics guys threw a towel over the victim's head, but I had already seen what I needed. A third cop was roughing up Silvio, looking for his ID.

'Didn't you see the emergency tape?'

184

'What tape? We hiked from the other side,' I said.

Always play dumb. Ignorant. They might not believe you but they couldn't be sure.

'You a reporter too?' the cop with the gun asked Silvio. We could no longer see each other's face. With a small cry of triumph, the cop pulled a driver's license out of Silvio's wallet.

'Silvio Aguilar. That you?'

A flashlight lit up his face.

'Yes,' said Silvio leadenly.

'Wait here,' he said, striding off.

The forensics guys began struggling up the path with their heavy burden and we parted to let the funeral procession pass. Soon the cop came crunching back down the trail, holding our IDs. He seemed to be the boss.

'Eve Diamond,' he said, stopping in front of me. 'You want to get arrested for interfering with a crime scene?'

His level voice scared me more than if he had been angry.

'No, sir. We weren't interfering. We were far away.'

'I'll be the judge of that,' he said. 'All right, up we go now. March.'

We struggled to climb the hill, slipping in the dry, pebbly sand, the cops right behind us. At the top, we saw the media cameras trained on us, huge industrial things that lit up the darkness and indeed me.

'You going to brief the press now?' I asked the cop, trying for a light, friendly tone. Below, the waves boiled and hissed against the rocks. Then a door slammed, and an ambulance took off, rumbling into the night.

'Yeah,' said the cop. 'In a little bit.' He checked a yellow legal pad and jotted down a few things. 'Now why don't you go wait over there like a good reporter.'

I pulled out my cell phone, ready to call the City Desk and dictate what I had seen. As we made our way to the other side of the emergency tape, the cop grabbed Silvio by the arm and jerked forward.

'Hold it right there, pardner,' he said. 'I meant the little lady. You come with me.'

He shoved Silvio before him. Silvio stumbled. A rumble went up from the waiting crowd.

'Who's that, Chief?' a reporter yelled.

'Give us an ID, wouldja? Hey, fella, turn around.'

I ran to follow.

'Right this way, Mr. Silvio Aguilar,' the cop was saying. 'Well, waddaya know about that. I think there are some folks at headquarters who are mighty eager to talk with you. I understand from my captain that you knew the deceased. Word is you even paid her a visit right before she went missing. And now here you are again, at the dump site. Isn't that an interesting coincidence?'

CHAPTER 25

Putting on a burst of speed, I caught up with them and said, 'He didn't call 911 at the house to report her missing. I did.'

But even as I defended him, all I could think was: What visit? Is that what Silvio meant out on the rocks when he said he had just seen Catarina? After swearing to me that he hadn't.

The cop turned. 'Then why haven't we interviewed you?'

Fear gave me strength. 'I don't know,' I said. 'Why haven't you?' I crossed my arms, glared him down. 'I'm a reporter for the *L.A. Times*. Not exactly hard to find.'

I hooked a thumb at Silvio, who stood there like a caged and demoralized wolf. 'My friend Mr. Aguilar drove me down this evening to cover the story. Our car's over in the Cabrillo Beach lot. Could you give us a lift there? Then we'd be happy to drive to Parker Center and tell you whatever you'd like to know.'

The cop examined me with distaste. 'I don't think so.'

'Are we under arrest? If so, I've got to call the *Times* lawyer and Silvio's got to call his. And if not, then we are going to walk over and get our car.'

I wasn't sure where I got the gall to say this.

'Just a minute,' the cop said. He called another

187

officer over to watch us, then went to talk to a third policeman with a fancy hat. When he came back, he said, 'If foolishness was a crime, you'd both be under arrest. Go get your car. Then you, fella, get your ass to Parker Center. If you're not there by'– he looked at his watch– 'ten, I'm getting a warrant on both of you for obstruction of justice.'

He walked away.

'One more thing,' I called out. 'You said the body was dumped. Was she killed somewhere else, then thrown over the cliff? Or did she die of injuries sustained in the fall?'

The cop looked at me with pure hatred. 'No comment.'

But I knew I had another scoop. Meanwhile, Silvio was coming back to life.

'I don't believe it,' he said between clenched teeth, looking every inch the avenging ex-lover. 'Here I am trying to help, and this is the thanks I get.'

'C'mon.' I grabbed his arm. 'We have to hurry.'

I wanted to ask him about the policeman's words and his own on the rocks, but first, I had a job to do. As we hiked down to the Cabrillo Beach parking lot, I called the City Desk.

Boris Johannsen answered and I gave him a rundown.

'Hold on, let me find someone to take dictation; we've got several dead bodies tonight and it's busy.'

He put me on hold. Then a seductive female voice came on.

'Felice Morgan, I'm ready for you.'

188

'Hey, Felice,' I said weakly. 'It's Eve.'

There was an accusing gasp. 'I thought you had an emergency tonight.'

'I did,' I said grimly. 'And you're about to hear it firsthand.'

'You lied to me.'

'Look,' I said, embarrassed at being caught, 'we can talk about this tomorrow, but right now, we're on deadline, right? Team effort. So you ready for this dictation or not?'

There was an angry *humpf*, and then the professional took over.

'Ready when you are,' she said in a treacly voice. Speaking from memory, I dictated paragraph after paragraph of what we had seen on the rocks of Point Fermin. I described the body, making sure to say that a family friend had informally IDed it as Catarina. How it had been tossed up onto the rocks and jagged chunks of seventy-five-year-old sidewalk. How it had lain there as the sun set and dolphins frolicked offshore, oblivious to the dead mermaid. How the police had hiked down to investigate; then the rickety procession with the stretcher up a rocky incline as the mist came off the ocean and the press pack bayed for details. How a police source said the body had been dumped off the cliffs, but wouldn't confirm whether she had been killed elsewhere.

'That's all I've got,' I said. 'Now could you please patch me through to Boris Johannsen?'

Soon his gravelly voice came on the line. 'Call me back after the press conference. How many more inches you think you'll get?'

'Boris, uh, I can't make the press conference.'

'Why the fuck not? You're right there.'

I hesitated. Silvio was several paces ahead of me, walking with shoulders hunched and head down. Although I could have reached out and touched him, he seemed locked in a force field of grief.

I dragged my feet, and the distance between us grew longer.

I lowered my voice. 'My ride's got to get to Parker Center. He's a friend of the deceased and the cops want to talk to him. He'll be good for a quote, though,' I said, feeling disgusted that I would use Silvio this way.

'Diamond, you're killing me.'

'You can get the conference off the wires,' I said calmly. 'I already got you the exclusive. No one else saw the scene on the rocks. Silvio, uh, the guy who brought me here, he and I hiked around from the south end, from Cabrillo Beach.'

'Next time take your own car, goddamnit.'

'Okay, but I want you to understand, it's thanks to him we got the scoop.'

'All right, all right. Felice can pull the press conference off the wires. Great reporter, that Felice. Never seen an intern so hungry. Refuses to go home. No grumbling from *her* about other plans.'

A loaded silence followed and I had to remind myself that discretion was the better part of valor. I couldn't very well let on that I had tricked him into sending me.

'Mark my words,' Johannsen was saying, 'that little gal is going to go far.'

I thought I might puke.

'Just keep your cell phone on in case the Desk has questions. And call in that quote.'

I hurried to catch up with Silvio.

Was it my imagination, or had he quickened his pace?

I reached out a hand, only to let it drop when I saw his face. Brooding. Closed off. The muscles around his mouth and eyes tensing with some private grief.

'I'm so sorry,' I said. I wanted to comfort him but he seemed frozen, beyond my reach.

Thinking of her.

At the car, I did embrace him, but it felt clumsy and forced. With each moment, he was slipping farther away from me and into some private hell where I couldn't follow. It disturbed me that this woman, who had seemed inconsequential to him while she was alive, could exert such a monstrous hold on him now that she was dead. What did it mean?

We rode in silence, but as the lights of downtown began to shimmer in the distance, I squirmed and hemmed and hawed and finally told him about the quote I needed. Maybe on some level I wanted to hurt him, to shock him into an emotional response. Anything was better than this wall of stone.

He exploded, slamming his hand against the dash. 'Eve, I refuse to take part in this media circus.'

I leaned against the headrest. 'Too late for that, darling, you're dating me.'

'Just make something up then.'

'You know I can't do that.'

191

He shot me a look of annoyance. 'Put it in your own words. You're the writer.'

'That's cheating.'

'So what? You know how I feel.'

The temptation arose, and I saw how easy it would be. Drafting a quote to be approved by the source. Then tweaking a few facts and statements, an improvement, really. What the person had *meant* to say. And finally, a more compelling story altogether, with fictional characters and scenes. Go ahead, the pitchforked devil inside my head urged. Just this once.

'I'm sorry, I just can't,' I said.

'Fine,' Silvio said. 'Then say this: 'The theater world has lost one of its brightest stars and I and everyone who knew her have lost a generous dear friend.'

'That sounds so trite,' I baited him.

'Goddamnit.' He pounded on the wheel. 'I'm down there being dashed against those rocks, drowning with her. My heart's been wrenched out and devoured by sharks. She was so alive, so gorgeous, so sparkly, it was like there was a high-wire voltage running through her. I loved her once, and I'm desolate beyond words that I will never see her again.'

The torment in his voice was almost unbearable.

'Much more heartfelt,' I said, striving for detachment. I wouldn't use it. His words were too raw, unfiltered. The cops would find it too interesting.

He shot me a penetrating look. 'Sometimes I wonder if you're a journalist first and a human

192

being only a distant second.'

I put my fist to my mouth to stifle a sob, but he heard it anyway. In the dark, he groped for my hand but found only my thigh. I felt his warmth through the fabric of my skirt.

'Eve, please don't be jealous. That was long ago. I love you now. So much. I'm sorry this is hurting you. It's hurting me too, though. Please understand.'

'I know,' I said woodenly.

But again I remembered how he hadn't wanted me at Catarina's house when the cops arrived. And how he knew Point Fermin like the back of his hand. And I couldn't forget the cop's sneer as he spoke of Silvio visiting Catarina right before she disappeared. Of my lover's own words on the rocks, in the heat of emotion. *'I just saw her...'*

But as much as I wanted answers, I couldn't ask him now. He had to get himself under control for Parker Center. Which made me complicit in whatever cover-up might be going on.

'It'll be okay with the cops,' I said steadily. 'It's not like you have anything to hide.' My words reverberated with the unspoken question: *Do you?*

'Of course not.'

'Silvio,' I asked, unable to let it go. 'What did you mean back on the rocks, that you just saw her? That cop said it too.'

He looked at me like a man doomed. 'Nothing,' he said flatly. 'Just seeing her at rehearsal, and parties and social occasions.'

'Oh,' I said. *Like hell.*

We drove silently for a while, each of us

absorbed in our own thoughts.

'Why did you drive like a bat out of hell with me to San Pedro tonight, if you don't care about her anymore?' I asked.

He said nothing.

'Can't you see that it looks suspicious?'

Before he could answer, a shadow detached itself from the center divider and darted across six lanes of freeway, diving for the bushes on the other side. I screamed as Silvio jerked the wheel, veering into the next lane and braking hard. I thought we were about to die. The truck fishtailed and spun. I screamed again and put my arm up, closing my eyes. The truck swerved the other way now, as Silvio pulled the wheel, his body slamming into mine. Miraculously, the truck wobbled and straightened, and we were hurtling forward again. Silvio pressed on the gas. I opened my eyes and saw him, hunched forward, hands clenched tight on the wheel, his face white with fury.

'Little homie hazing ritual,' Silvio said.

'What?'

'It's part of getting jumped into the gang. They do it on a dare. To prove what *cojones* they have.'

'*Cojones*, hell. That's a good way to get killed and take a lot of people with you.'

'We may not see each other tonight,' Silvio said after a long minute. 'I imagine I'll be a while.'

'You going to tell them you used to be involved?'

'Do I have a choice?'

'They're going to frame you.'

'But what about motive?'

'The jilted lover. It's only been around for, oh,

194

seven thousand years.'

'If that was the case, I would have killed her long ago. But they need to hear it from me. That's what I was discussing with the lawyer earlier.'

I knew he was right. I also knew the cops would wonder why Silvio hadn't been straight with them from the beginning.

At the *Times* lot, he kissed me good-bye but missed my mouth.

'I don't care what time it is, call me when you're done. I want to know how it went. Promise?'

But I saw in his averted eyes, as he drove off without answering, that he was afraid of making a promise he couldn't keep.

CHAPTER 26

At home, I moved from room to room, too lit up to sleep. I stared out the window at the neon archaeology of downtown. Was some commodities trader on the fifty-third floor standing at a bank of windows at this very moment as he spoke to Tokyo, watching my light twinkle on the dark hillside?

Barry Mancuso, I thought. I had to follow up. No time like the present. I logged on to the *L.A. Times* system, found the Mancuso clips in my electronic basket, and printed them out. Then I picked up the business card and looked at the clock: 10:30 p.m.

I called, expecting to get a recording, and was

startled when a young female voice answered: 'Skylight Productions, Barry Mancuso's line.'

Time to focus. I told her I was doing a survey for the Los Angeles Economic Development Corporation and asked if I could have a few minutes of Mr. Mancuso's time.

'He's gone for the day, can I take a message?'

'Will he be in tomorrow?'

'No, but he'll be calling in.'

I could almost see her sliding my message into her trash can as she spoke.

'Is he in town?'

'Yes. And I'll see he gets the message.'

'And your name is?'

'Angela Mallorca.'

'Are you his partner or something?'

A freezy silence greeted this question. Partners didn't answer other people's telephone lines, much less their own. Partners weren't in the office at this late hour.

'I'm his assistant.'

I hung up and considered that at least I'd just saved myself a trip to the icy reaches of Beverly Hills tomorrow. Mancuso was in town but not in the office. Opening a new computer screen, I typed in 'L.A. County Tax Assessor' and looked up property records for Barry F. Mancuso. There were dozens of Mancusos on the tax rolls but only four with the right middle initial. One owned a 1,400-square-foot property in Agoura Hills but I eliminated him because no self-respecting Hollywood player would live in the Valley and even if he did, his property footage would have another zero on it. The second Barry

F. Mancuso lived in Cerritos and I eliminated him for the same reason. In Hollywood, that was so GU – geographically undesirable – that it made you a nonentity. The third Barry F. Mancuso had an 8,400-square-foot property in Arcadia but that was the wrong neighborhood too. The fourth address came out of Hollywood-mogul central casting: 1357 Sea Cliff Drive in Malibu, with a tax-assessed square footage of eleven thousand. That was my man. With a home address, I could get a phone number from the reverse directory. It might be unlisted, of course, but then I could make like a paparazzo and just show up.

I made a cup of licorice tea and got into bed to read the clips while I waited for word from Silvio. Barry F. Mancuso was forty-six and best known for a comedy franchise that appealed to teen boys with raging hormones. But he had also produced several acclaimed indie films and I noticed his name was often preceded by the word *maverick*. He was twice divorced and had recently married a much younger woman. He had a horse ranch in Virginia and a coffee plantation in Hawaii. There was an arrest at the Burbank airport for cocaine possession but like most of Hollywood, he had gone through rehab. Based on the file photo, he was trim and lean, had an electric shock of spiked hair, and wore a small earring. Since his drug misadventures, he had traded one addiction for another and now lived on a restricted diet of wheatgrass, oat biscuits, and protein shakes, according to his personal trainer.

Mancuso's filmography listed thirty movies,

including an Oscar nominee and a vampire flick that had been attacked for degrading pop culture, if that was even possible anymore. He had an MBA from Stanford and a weakness for starlets. I scanned for something to link him with Catarina. One of Alfonso's clips had mentioned a play being optioned for Hollywood. Was that where Mancuso came in?

I looked at the clock. Alfonso and Marisela had to be up after hearing the news. Would Alfonso be at the morgue, identifying the body? Would they be holding a wake at the theater? On impulse, I picked up the phone and dialed. But there was no one home. I hung up without leaving a message. I wasn't totally insensitive.

I must have fallen asleep with the phone in my hand. Its shrill ringing woke me with a start.

'Hello?' I said, looking at the clock: 1:05 a.m. Silvio had been with the cops almost three hours.

'How are you?' The voice muffled and faraway.

'Silvio?'

'Who else?' Warmer but slightly on edge.

'Well, no one. You just woke me up, I'm groggy.'

'I like you that way.'

'I thought you'd call earlier. I fell asleep.'

'Without me? What a shame. What are you doing right now?'

'I told you, I was asleep. So what did they ask you? Is everything okay?'

'Everything's fine. What are you wearing?'

'A camisole. Why? Do you need me to come get you?'

'Is it silk?'

'Will you be serious? I've been so worried.'

'Want to know what I'm wearing? Nothing.'

'What do you mean?'

'Want to know what I'm doing?'

I struggled to sit up, alarm bolting through me. Suddenly, I was wide awake.

'Who is this?'

'It's Silvio.' The voice mock-intimate.

I slammed down the phone and shivered. I thought the voice had sounded off, but I'd been half asleep and expecting Silvio, which had given some jerk the perfect opening to creep me out. Ugh.

The phone rang again.

I watched it as if it were a tarantula creeping toward my bed.

It rang and rang. Finally I picked up. If the obscene phone caller had been dialing random numbers and it *was* Silvio this time, I needed to answer. My caller ID wasn't showing his number, but what if the cops had confiscated his cell phone and he was calling from jail?

'Hello?'

'Is this Eve Diamond?' the same voice said in a serious and half-mocking professional voice.

'Who is this?'

I scrunched my knees to my chest and pulled up the covers.

'This is Baltazar Galvan. We met yesterday at the press conference, remember?'

The assemblyman's mysterious aide! And part-time pervert.

'Why did you call me and pretend to be, uh, someone else?'

'I'm sorry, I thought you were flirting with me.'

'You know damn well I thought you were someone else.'

'I had a yearning to talk to you.'

'You're insane. It's after midnight. If you have a story to discuss, call me at the office in the morning...' I paused. 'How did you get my home number?'

'The *L.A. Times* operator patched me through.'

'What?'

'I called the switchboard and told them I needed to get ahold of you for a breaking story.'

'You shouldn't have done that.'

I could picture his lips rising in a smile on the other end.

'Don't you think that was resourceful of me?'

'No, I think that was borderline harassment.' Then my journalism instincts got the better of my outrage. 'So, what? Does Gutierrez have some late-breaking time bomb?'

He laughed. 'Hardly.'

'So you lied to the *Times* operator?'

'I just wanted to hear your voice.'

'Well then, listen to these dulcet tones: Don't call me at home ever again.'

He laughed again, louder this time.

'Don't worry, I'm not going to stalk you.'

A leer in his voice. Mocking my vanity to even think of such a thing. 'I don't even have your number.'

'Good. You wanna chat, you wanna leak, call me at the office. Good-bye.'

Heart pounding, I lay there, wishing Silvio would call. I tried his numbers but got only machines. It took me a long time to go back to sleep. Twice I got up and checked all the locks. Everything was tight as a drum.

CHAPTER 27

I woke again, realizing it was 5 a.m. and Silvio had never called. Shivering, I got up and called him. He didn't answer his home phone or his mobile. I called Alfonso and couldn't get him, either. I showered, ate, and drove to Parker Center. They made me sit there until 7:30, when a flack from media relations arrived. Luckily I knew him. Drew Winship. I had once taken him to lunch, specifically to lubricate future requests. And now, voilà. If he realized I was using my press pass to pump him for personal information, he didn't show it.

'They're holding him for questioning,' Winship said, after several hushed calls.

'Is he under...?' I stopped. I couldn't say it.

'Arrest? No. But things are fluid.'

'I need to see him.'

'He your boyfriend or something?'

Winship thought he was just being funny until he saw the blood drain from my face. He leaned back in his chair.

'Well, well,' he said.

'I'm working that dead actress story,' I said truthfully. 'I need to talk to him.'

'Uh-huh,' said Drew Winship.

Not enjoying it, exactly. But flexing his new-found power. I fed him more.

'He's a good guy trapped in a bad situation,' I said, confirmation of our relationship leaking out of my voice.

Drew Winship exhaled. 'Pretty thin ice on that lake.'

'I imagine there's tremendous pressure to come up with a suspect.'

Drew picked up a pen and held it like a baton between his second and third fingers.

'He's in a cell till they figure it out. They can hold him another' – Drew looked at his watch– 'fourteen hours before they have to arrest or release.'

'What about visitors?'

'Not officially.'

'How about unofficially?'

He shuffled papers, avoided my eyes. 'I can try.'

'I'll wait.'

'He'll have to agree. And so will the watch commander.'

'Better get started then.'

The pen hit the blotter. Drew Winship stood up and looked at me from under his brows. Waiting for his tribute.

I made my voice go all husky. 'Thanks, man. I owe you one.'

By 8:15, I found myself sitting across a table from Silvio. He looked gaunt and needed a shave. A caul of humiliation shrouded his eyes.

'The lawyer is hopeful I'll be out soon,' Silvio said without preamble. He ignored the guard who stood just inside the room, watching us.

'This is insane,' I whispered. Now that I saw him in the light of day, detained like a common criminal, my loyalty to him overcame my suspicions and I was ready to fight for his release. Even if he had seen Catarina right before she disappeared, there had to be an explanation, and I would hear it soon enough. He was no killer.

Silvio grimaced and looked away.

'Ever heard of circumstantial evidence?'

'But that's ludicrous. You–'

Silvio held his hand up.

'Let's not talk about it.' He looked around meaningfully.

'We've got to clear your name.'

'Our lawyer is working on it.'

I leaned forward. My heart was beating slowly, powerfully, in my chest.

'I'm going to find the bastard who killed her.'

He grabbed my hand. 'You stay out of it.'

'But–'

His grip tightened. 'Promise me.'

'What are you afraid of?'

He flinched and his grip slackened. I pulled my hand away.

'It could be dangerous,' he said.

'How?'

I felt we were having two conversations here. Dangerous for whom? Me? Or him? Or the killer, if it was someone Silvio knew and loved? I chose Door Number One.

'You think the killer would come after me?' I scoffed, then realized the killer had already sent someone after me. Two someones. And that in the chaos last night, I had forgotten to tell him. Now I couldn't, or it would just convince him he was right.

'Absolutely.'

'I'm a big girl.'

'There are things best left to the police.'

'There are things people don't tell the police.'

'You are being ruled by your emotions, Eve. You'll take chances.'

'Someone is setting you up.'

'Whoever killed Catarina is still out there. You want to be helpful, call the lawyer. Tell him everything you learn. But for God's sake, stay out of it.'

'I've been in it since the day we met.'

I leaned across the table and kissed him before he could pull away. His lips were soft but his stubble scratched my cheek. The guard had disappeared. I walked away. At the door, I stopped and looked back. Silvio was standing up, his hands gripping the edges of the table, a haggard, lost look in his eyes.

'Don't,' he mouthed.

'I love you,' I mouthed back.

In the hall, someone called my name.

'Eve Diamond?'

'Yes?'

It was the guard.

'Watch commander wants to see you.'

I followed him to an office where a uniformed man sat behind a desk.

'Sit down,' he said. I did as he ordered.

'Your boyfriend's a smart guy,' the cop said with a bland smile.

'He didn't do it.'

The smile widened. 'I'm glad you cleared that up for us. Makes our job easy.'

'It's just the truth.'

'Finding the truth is *our* job. Not yours. You meddle in this investigation, we will arrest you. Understand?'

My eyes roved the room, trying not to light on his. It's harder to lie when you're staring straight at someone.

'Yes.'

'Glad to hear it. Always read the *Times*. Read a fine story the other day by someone named Morgan who's going to be hearing from our lawyers. Know the byline?'

'All too well, Officer.'

CHAPTER 28

Back in the car, I thought over the cop's words. His dripping sarcasm at Felice's 'fine story.' Something had nagged at me since I'd read it. But it wasn't until Catarina's body turned up on the rocks of Point Fermin that I began to put my finger on it. About how the moto rider had seen two men lifting a large bag out of a trunk. Now that story seemed full of holes. Had Felice even interviewed a moto rider? And why dump the car in the forest and the body on the coast? Something didn't track. What if the cops and everyone following the case were making assumptions based on a fabricated story? Lives could hang in the balance. I prayed that I was wrong about Felice. But I knew now that she was right about one thing: Jayson Blair had screwed it up for everyone.

I thought carefully about the last twenty-four hours. Yesterday, I had been threatened as I left Steve Herrera's house by someone who wanted me off the case. He had either sicced them on me or he knew who had. He hadn't told me the entire truth. So now, instead of getting on the freeway, I called him. It was 8:40 a.m. and I hoped I was waking him up.

But he answered as if he'd been waiting by the phone. I identified myself, then said, 'Do you know what happened when I left your house?'

'A marauding pit bill attacked you?'

'A human pit bull. Two of them. They held a gun to my ribs and warned me off the story.'

There was a shocked pause.

'Are you serious? That's horrible.'

Even through the phone line, it sounded like an honest response. The first such emotion I had heard from him.

'So that didn't have anything to do with the phone call you made in the back room while I was there?'

'What call?' He spoke slowly, underwater, his reactions a beat too slow, and I thought he might be stoned.

'Don't lie.'

'You don't miss a thing, do you? But no, man. I can't believe someone roughed you up. You okay?'

His need for reassurance seemed genuine.

'Yeah. And it hasn't scared me off. Quite the opposite. I need to talk to you.'

He whined that he was busy so I baited the hook.

'And I was hoping you could bring some photos of your artwork, so I can pass them on to the Calendar editor. I want her to see how talented you are.'

And how talented you're not, I thought.

We agreed to meet at Café Tropical on Sunset in half an hour. After yesterday's little encounter, I was certainly not climbing up those bungalow stairs again.

I went to the counter and ordered a Cuban coffee with foaming milk and a guava-and-cheese pastry from the purple-lidded barista. Gooey and sweet, spiked with the tart cheese and flaky dough, it soon had me licking my fingers. Waiting for Herrera, I felt the rush of caffeine mingling with the sugar jolt and surrendered to the pleasant buzzing in my head.

My private theory was that Castro had ordered Cuban cafés throughout America to spike their coffee with methamphetamine to enslave and addict the population, and in my case, it had worked beautifully. I was utterly and completely hooked on Café Tropical and sought out Cuban roast wherever I went.

Herrera shuffled in ten minutes later and ordered an espresso.

'Make it a double, and put it on my tab,' I told the barista.

Steve Herrera accepted this with the annoying

presumption of his slacker kind.

'Did you read the paper today?' I asked.

'Not yet.'

My expression turned sober. 'They found Catarina's body. On the rocks of Point Fermin in San Pedro. She'd been dead awhile.'

The boho insouciance ebbed.

'Shit,' he said. 'They sure it's her?'

The hope in his eyes was dashed by my expression.

'Family friend IDed her.'

He shook his head. 'Hard to believe. I just saw her—'

'So Steve,' I said, jumping right into the opening he had made. 'I was wondering about that car they found on Angeles Crest.'

He shot me a worried look, then went back to rubbing lemon peel on the rim of his cup.

'I had nothing to do with that.'

'Uh-huh. You know, I promised not to go to the cops. But that was when we still thought we had a missing person on our hands, not a corpse. Things have changed.'

'I didn't kill her.'

'Yeah, so you've mentioned once or twice. Anyway, that's what I got to mulling over. You could be a vicious psychopath, in which case I'm glad we're sitting here, sipping our joe in public. But somehow I don't peg you for a killer. More like a small-time hood. And she owed you money. Cars are worth money. So what I want to know is, what happened to her car, Steve? Did your cousin's friends throw her in it and tell you to look the other way? Cuz I know drug dealers, and I know they don't go away. Even if they're relatives. In fact, they keep coming around, upping the pressure. Or maybe they came after you first. You ran up there to hide and they caught you together and wanted to teach one of you a lesson. Were you in bed? Did Catarina beg them to take her car, and they just had to have her too?'

'That's not what happened!'

'How do you know?'

'Because *I* took her car,' he blurted out.

He stared down at his coffee, his eyes large with panic. A flush grew along his cheeks.

'You what?'

'I took it. As payment. She'd report it stolen and the insurance money would cover her debt to me.'

'So the two of you cooked up this little scheme?'

Steve looked out the window, suddenly interested in a bum pushing a mountainous shopping cart.

'I know some guys who do this for a living,' he said under his breath.

'I'm sure you do. So how did the car end up on Angeles Crest?'

He didn't answer.

'It's me or the cops,' I said softly.

He was getting agitated. His foot tapped against the linoleum. I waited.

'C'mon, Steve. Sing me a song.'

He breathed out, his body collapsing into itself like a punctured balloon.

'I drove it up there with my friend following in his car. We put it in neutral and pushed it over the ravine. It rolled six times before it stopped. We figured it was totaled.'

'Your prints are probably all over that car.'

He sipped his espresso, then put the cup down with a smirk.

'You ain't never heard of gloves, baby?'

'Don't look so self-satisfied. Your plan back-fired.'

'What are you talking about?'

'Auto theft. Insurance fraud. If they even believe it. Jesus, now you're a prime suspect. The neighbor. That guy who was always hanging around.'

I thought about what the motorcyclist had told Felice – two men with dark hair, pulling a large bag out of the trunk of a car. A second car waiting. Late model and foreign.

'What kind of car does your friend drive?'

'Audi. Couple of years old.'

'Your friend have dark hair?'

'Yeah.'

But Pot Boy shaved his head.

'Were you bareheaded that night?'

'What difference does that make?'

'Just answer the question.'

'Wore a black wool cap. Cold in the forest at night.'

It was coming together, except for...

'A witness said two men with dark hair pulled a large bag out of the trunk. All wrapped up. Like a corpse, maybe? That later got dumped over the cliffs in San Pedro?'

I took a long gulp of my coffee and examined him. The callow swaggering artist. If I turned him in, he'd be behind bars soon, and they'd let Silvio go. One warm body in exchange for another. They needed a sacrificial lamb. I needed my lover back. There was something shifty and unsavory about Herrera, and I knew that whatever else he was hiding, the cops would soon worm it out of him. But I had my thieves' honor too.

'That's a lie,' Steve Herrera was saying. 'I wouldn't kill her. I loved her.'

So that's what I had heard in his voice earlier.

'A lot of people kill in the name of love.'

'Not me, man. I'm vegan. I don't even eat eggs.'

Great, a vegan drug dealer in love, now bristling with moral outrage. How dare I accuse him?

'So what did you pull out of the trunk?'

'A duffel bag of her stuff. Gym clothes and books and shit. It's at my house. I can show you.'

'Hmm. Cops'll like that. Killers often keep mementos of their victims.'

Fear made his voice quaver.

'You got it all wrong, lady. I wouldn't hurt her. I wanted to help her. And we hooked up before I ever got her drugs. She's just that way. That's why I was so surprised when she got serious with the latest guy.'

'She used you, Steve. She got you to do something very illegal for her.'

'I would have done anything for her.'

'And she knew it. So this guy? What did he look like?'

'I don't know. He only ever came over at night. I'd hear him walking up the stairs.'

'You think it might have been Mancuso? Did she ever talk about him?'

'No. I told you. She was private.'

Something occurred to him then. He looked back and forth between me and the door, passed his hand across his bare scalp.

'How do I know you're not going to go to the cops?'

'Because I want you to help me find her killer.'

'You believe I didn't do it?' he whined.

'You'd have to be awfully stupid to tell me all this if you did.' I smiled encouragingly at him. 'And I can tell you're not a stupid man.'

'So you won't rat me out?'

He was trembling, and I didn't think it was from the caffeine.

I told him no again, and I left. It seemed easy then to make such promises. But I didn't yet know the whole story.

CHAPTER 29

I drove to the office, feeling torn in half. How could I work with Silvio in jail, under interrogation for murder? A murder he knew something about but hadn't committed. For my own sanity, I had to keep believing that. I had to get him out. But what if in clearing Silvio, I implicated his best friend?

An e-mail from Josh was blinking at the top of my screen when I slunk in late at 10:30. I flinched, the previous night's treachery hitting me full force. I could have caught him in that parking lot. And at that moment, I knew I was no better than Felice. Worse, because I was older and knew better.

Nice deadline work, Lois Lane, Josh wrote. *Hope Metro brings you on to the story full-time, you deserve it. Cheers, Josh.*

I leaned back in my chair, suffused with relief and guilty goodwill toward Joshua Brandywine. Many reporters would have howled at missing such a scoop. But Josh, as cutthroat a reporter as I had ever encountered, had the class to compliment me for a big story I had landed on his watch. It was courtly elegance itself, and not in the least deserved.

'Why didn't you tell me the truth?'

Basking in Josh's high-mindedness, I didn't see Felice storming over and was unprepared for the broadside when it hit.

Hands on hips. Nostrils flared. Face thrust right up to mine, a school-yard edge to her. The polar opposite of Josh in every way. My good mood evaporated.

'This was between me and Silvio,' I said.

'I could have helped.'

'Yeah, you've been a big enough help already, thank you very much.'

'You left me to dangle.'

'You should go home early. Maybe a good night's sleep would put you in a better mood.'

Oh, this was really bad timing, Felice buzzing static in my ear when I needed to concentrate. My computer beeped. An incoming e-mail from Thompson: *See me.*

I smiled at Felice. 'Sorry, the big guy calls.' I

pointed to the screen. Never had I been so glad to escape my desk.

But if I was expecting kudos from Thompson, I was wrong.

'Sit down.'

He rustled a sheaf of papers.

'How did you come to be downtown yesterday?'

I concentrated on the latest batch of Spam haiku pinned to his bulletin board in twenty-two-point type. Some utterly revolting line about basting a Spam meat loaf in Tang.

'I was interviewing that drama teacher near Koreatown. It didn't make any sense to drive all the way back to San Gabe to file.'

He slapped the papers down on his desk.

'Damn it, Diamond. This was no accident. You weaseled your way on to this breaking story after I specifically told you to stick with the backgrounder.'

'That's not true. Johannsen begged me. Brandywine was at dinner and there was no one else to send. Ask him if you don't believe me.'

He looked out the window, then pinched the bridge of his nose. He squinted his eyes shut. When he spoke again, his voice was more gentle.

'If that is truly the case, then I owe you an apology.'

'Well, I *was* dying to do it.'

'Congratulations, then. You've just written yourself back on to the story.'

I steeled my face not to show elation.

Thompson popped his legs onto the desk and clunked the heels of his cowboy boots. 'Over my

214

objection. I told them you're too close. But Metro wants a follow. Initial autopsy results indicate that Catarina Velosi was killed by a single gunshot wound to the head. Josh is doing that one. Metro wants a sidebar. Got any ideas?'

Yeah, I wanted to say. *My boyfriend's about to get charged with murder. I could interview myself about how it feels.*

But there was no way I was going to drop that bomb. Instead, I told him about the leather jacket with Barry Mancuso's business card. Thompson's boots clinked together with increasing enthusiasm.

'Cops know about this?'

'Don't think so.'

'She been in any of his movies?'

'I'm going to check.'

'You talk to him yet?'

'Jeez, Thompson, I just learned about the card yesterday and then I had to write the drama teacher daily and after that all hell broke loose with the body and now I'm here with you. I haven't had a sec.'

He reached for the phone.

'Well, get on it. I'll tell Metro you're chasing a lead out of Hollywood. We'll keep it off the budget so the wires don't report it.'

Back at my desk, I scanned for Felice but the office seemed to have emptied. Even Thompson left, murmuring something about an errand. I picked up the green plastic cactus on my desk and rubbed it for good luck. I went online and cross-checked Catarina Velosi with movies that Barry Mancuso had produced. Nothing. But pairing up Mancuso with Alfonso Reventon gave me a hit. A big studio film called *Borders of the Heart* that had been 'inspired' by a Reventon play. I leaned back in my chair and rocked. Had Catarina visited the set or gone to the premiere, only to meet the man who would kill her? I looked at my watch: 10:50. I called Mancuso's office, left a message. I turned back to the clips. *Borders of the Heart* had been filmed in Vancouver, not East L.A., and the reviews had been tepid. At 11:10, I called Mancuso a second time.

'I had to step out and was afraid I had missed his call,' I said.

'He's very busy, Ms. Diamond.' Through audibly clenched teeth.

'Tell him this isn't about a movie, it's about his personal life.'

I repeated my alphanumerics, hung up, and looked around. Felice was back at her desk and on the phone. Working her moto sources? Or hatching a new story with enough authentic details to make it plausible? Anxiety gnawing at me, I went back to the clips.

The third time I called it was 11:30. Mancuso's assistant claimed she had relayed the messages.

'Does he have voice mail?'

'You're talking to it.'

'I mean at his home office in Malibu. That's where he is today, right?'

An icy pause, then 'I'll see that he gets the message, Ms. Diamond.'

I decided to play the fear card. 'Let me ask you, do you like your job? Do you want to keep it?'

'Excuse me?'

'I need to talk to him about that actress who turned up dead yesterday in San Pedro. Tell him I'm going to the LAPD if I don't hear from him by the end of the day.'

I waited. Mancuso wasn't going to return my calls through normal channels, so I had nothing to lose by being obnoxious. And Hollywood assistants put up with bad behavior because their demeaning jobs are stepping-stones up the industry food chain. While they're fetching their boss's dry cleaning and cleaning up after his dog, they're also making contacts they hope will catapult them into corner offices where they can one day throw tantrums and degrade their own assistants. It's a Byzantine world whose intrigue evokes an eighteenth-century Ottoman court more than a twenty-first-century corporation. You've got your harems, eunuchs, janissaries, jesters, and pages all jockeying for the sultan's favor. And fear keeps everything humming. That's where my churlish little speech came in.

Now suspicion quivered in the assistant's voice.

'Is this June? It sounds like your bullshit, June, and you know there's a restraining order that prohibits you from contacting Barry directly. You have to go through the lawyer.'

Oh-ho, I thought.

'I don't know who June is, but maybe I'll look up this restraining order and write a story about June and Barry. The love that died. Calendar would give it a good ride. Anyway, feel free to Google me. I am very real and if I don't hear from Barry today, he'll need more than a lawyer to get him out of this mess. And you'll be back emailing résumés.'

'That's what you think,' she said smugly. 'Good-bye, Ms. Diamond.'

I hung up the phone and gritted my teeth. Now I had burned my bridges with the assistant. Not that I ever had a chance anyway. Things were not looking good and I needed another cup of caffeine to jump-start my synapses.

Felice and Luz were in the lunchroom, drinking coffee and playing six degrees of separation. I poured my own joe and considered that something sweet might bring me inspiration. The peanut M&M's in the vending machine were calling my name. I heard Luz say, 'How funny. My girlfriend's sister is an oncologist at Mount Sinai too. Does your mom go by Morgan?'

'No,' Felice said after a short pause. 'She uses her maiden name.'

'Which is?'

'Jackson,' Felice said, far off and indistinct.

'My girlfriend's sister is Natasha Ransom. They probably know each other.'

I walked over to the machine, put in my money, and pulled the lever. The candy tumbled down. I picked it up and ambled over to join them.

'I don't think so,' Felice said. A lightning bolt of emotion flashed across her face and was gone. 'She's not there anymore.'

'Natasha's a lifer,' Luz said. 'What years was your mom at the Mount?'

Felice stood up and walked to the soft drinks machine. She studied the display.

'I really don't remember,' she said, flashing a sheepish smile over her shoulder. 'It was during

218

college, and Brown was such an intense experience for me that everything else has blurred.'

Puh-leeze.

Luz leaned back in her chair.

'Well, next time I talk to Natasha I'll ask if she remembers a Dr. Jackson.'

Felice appeared to have decided against a soft drink. She walked back to the table, picked up her purse, and said she had to make a phone call. Her coffee cup was still half full but she seemed done with it. At the door, she stopped and her long fingers gripped the jamb.

'I doubt they ran into each other,' she said. 'My mom worked the night shift. And she taught. She has tenure at one of the teaching hospitals.'

'Small world, Natasha does that too,' Luz said, smiling. 'Which school?'

But Felice was already halfway down the hall.

Luz slurped with gusto at her foul cup of office coffee. 'Kinda makes you want to check the staff names at Mount Sinai going back a few years, doesn't it?' I said.

Luz put her cup down carefully.

'Maybe you should throttle back those killer instincts, just for once. Cut her a little slack.'

I raised a brow, but her eyes had gone all opaque. 'You were the one asking the questions.'

Luz shrugged. 'Just trying to make a little polite conversation.'

'Tell me you believe her mother was a neonatologist at Mount Sinai.'

'I'm willing to go on faith,' Luz said. 'We Latinos are big on faith.' She gave a lazy grin.

'I think she's full of shit. Her and her stories.

I'm surprised she hasn't told us that her daddy's rich and her mama's good-looking.'

Luz sucked her teeth. 'Someone in that family was good-looking.'

'I bet she didn't even go to Brown.'

'She's got that Ivy League veneer, all right,' Luz said. 'But she's just a kid. Imagine how intimidated she must feel. And if embroidering her family's credentials evens the playing field for her, who's it hurting?'

'What if that's not all she embroiders?'

'She just needs to grow into her own skin,' Luz said. 'We all do, present company included. Some of us just have a tougher skin to grow into.'

CHAPTER 30

I had barely sat down at my desk when my mobile rang.

'You the reporter?' The voice was fast and tight, diffidence coiled around a pulsing nerve.

'Yeah. Who's this?'

I heard a sniff. 'Barry Mancuso. You, uh, called?'

My hand caressed the receiver. I cradled it with both hands, afraid I might drop it. I thought of Silvio languishing at Parker Center. I had to feel my way through this with a velvet glove. I didn't want Mancuso to know how little I really had.

'I found something of yours in Catarina Velosi's belongings.'

'Did you, now?'

Not giving anything away. Which told me a lot, actually. He seemed to know exactly who she was.

'I think the police would be very interested,' I said.

'What is this, blackmail? I'm recording this conversation.'

Jerk. 'I'd like to talk in person.'

'Why?'

'She's dead and you knew her.' I paused, went out on a limb. 'Saw her recently, in fact.'

He laughed. 'I see a lot of actresses. It's in the job description.'

Something salacious in his words, like a squirt of whipped cream atop an already sweet pie. He wouldn't be able to feign so well in person.

'What time can we meet?'

'I'm a busy man, Ms. Diamond.'

But he hadn't yet cut me off or referred me to his lawyer. That in itself was unusual and note-worthy.

I looked at my watch. How long would it take to get out there?

'How about one p.m. at your office?'

'Listen, Ms. Diamond. The harassing phone calls are going to stop right now. Or you'll be hearing from my lawyer. Do you understand?'

'Or would you prefer to meet at your home? On Sea Cliff Drive.'

There was a sharp intake of breath. Then, 'I can assure you I have excellent security. Now let's be on record that I've asked you to cease and desist this harassment and you're continuing.'

'Fine, I'll take it to the LAPD.'

From the other end of the phone came a string of expletives. Then he hung up.

I slammed the 'off' button so hard that my headset flipped up and hit me in the nose.

'Ouch,' I yelled, more in frustration than pain.

The rich are different from you and me. They have better security. In the old days, it was castles lined with soldiers who lobbed baskets of venomous snakes and boiling oil at their enemies. Now it was bodyguards trained in martial arts, high-tech electronic eyes, and gated communities patrolled by ex-military men.

But that didn't impress me. Even regular people have security in Malibu. There are too many looky-lous, Goldilocks, and delusionals who break into homes to take a dip in the pool, nap in a high-end bed, or sip scotch on the ocean balcony, convinced they're married to the owner. My fantasies were more mundane. I dreamed of finding a killer.

CHAPTER 31

The phone call had left a sour taste in my mouth. I was restless. Maybe an early lunch would help me collect my thoughts. Felice was on the phone. I let myself out, sighing with relief as I hit the parking lot. Almost there. Then a familiar Miata pulled up and my editor leaned out the window.

'What's up?' Tom Thompson said.

'Lunch,' I said, and kept walking. To my annoyance, the Miata cruised alongside.

'Where's Felice?'

'On an interview. I didn't want to disturb her.'

'She'll want to come.'

No kidding.

'It's lunch, not an assignment.'

Thompson regarded me steadily as the car rolled along, matching me step for step.

'Take her with,' he said. 'You can lob pearls of wisdom at her over burgers.'

He made a snazzy turn into an empty spot, then climbed out. 'I'll let her know you're waiting.'

I fixed my gaze on the San Gabriel Mountains so he wouldn't see the fire raging behind my eyes. Then I kicked the tire of the nearest car and swore under my breath.

'I am not a babysitter,' I screamed once he disappeared inside. Then Felice came running out, purse slung hastily over one shoulder and car keys clasped in her hand.

'Sorry to keep you waiting,' she said. 'I can drive.'

She pointed the key chain at her Beemer and the security locks yelped. We slid into the soft leather seats.

'Where we going?' Felice turned expectantly.

I was about to say something sardonic when my cell phone rang.

'Ms. Diamond, this is Barry Mancuso's assistant. We spoke earlier and–'

It was the same young woman who had cut me off so smugly earlier this morning.

'Barry already returned my call,' I said, retreating into flinty politeness. 'Thanks very much for getting the message to him so promptly. I really do appreciate it.'

'He's an asshole,' she said.

I leaned back against the seat.

Well, well, I thought. What have we here?

'But I wasn't calling to discuss his personality,' she said.

Then what are you calling for? My address so you can serve me with a subpoena?

In the background, I heard cars honking.

'I quit,' she said. 'Walked out. Not ten minutes ago. But here's what I wanted to say. He knew that actress.'

The world shrunk to a one-inch piece of plastic pressed against my ear.

'How well?'

'Well enough to get her a credit card. You should ask him about that.'

'How can I if he won't talk to me?'

'Go to his house.'

'Like he'll let me in.'

'What's going on?' came Felice's voice from the far side of the moon. I put out my hand in a 'stop' gesture and bared my fangs at her.

'I left your name at the guard kiosk,' the assistant was saying. 'Two p.m. That will get you inside the compound. After that, you're on your own.'

'Did they have a relationship?'

'I've got to go.'

'Wait. Can I get your number? I've got so many questions.'

'Look, just know that he's scared. I saw it in his face.'

'Aren't you scared? That he'll find out what you did?'

'I'm done with Hollywood.'

'You must really hate him.'

'He's loathsome,' she said.

'Do you think he killed her?'

There was silence as she considered it.

'I really don't know.'

'Then why did you call him loathsome?'

She choked with remembered indignation.

'He made me take his stool sample to the lab.'

CHAPTER 32

'Will you please tell me what that was all about?' Felice said when I hung up.

I looked around and realized we were parked on a side street. She must have pulled over to wait and I hadn't noticed.

'Big lead just fell into my lap,' I said with my most enigmatic smile. 'And we owe it all to a turd. Now get on the 210 West and drive fast.'

'Excuse me?'

'Please,' I said. 'I'll fill you in on the freeway.'

She shook her head but reached into the glove compartment and pulled out a pair of black mesh driving gloves. With much ritualistic snapping and flexing, she pulled them on.

The words of a song sprang unbidden: *'She makes the Indy 500 look like a Roman chariot race now.'*

Felice gave me an annoyed glance.

'Beach Boys,' I said. 'Never mind. Before your time.'

'I have never been a big consumer of pop culture.'

'But where do you stand on fish tacos?' I asked, the whole California girl, surfer vibe bringing on visions of a beachfront shack that made them as good as anywhere in the Hawaiian Islands. We could hit it on the way back.

Felice's right hand worked the gears.

'You mean do I have a philosophical objection, like am I a vegetarian? You saw me eat turkey the other day.'

'Barely,' I said, remembering how she had pushed her food around the plate.

'What's that supposed to mean?'

If her hands hadn't been so busy shifting and driving, she might have propped them on her waist and had a hissy fit.

'Nothing.'

'There someplace around here that does them good?'

'Santa Monica.'

'That's not around here. It's by the ocean.'

'Mm-hmm.'

'So why we going all the way out there?'

'Actually, it's on the way,' I said, needling her.

'To what?' She snorted. 'China?'

'Malibu. You and me, babe. Don't you want to spend the afternoon in Malibu?'

'Have you lost your mind? You'll get us both fired!'

'It's work, baby. Got us an interview.'

We were on the freeway now, Felice zipping along at eighty miles per hour in the carpool lane. Built for speed, she was. But armored too. Like a Bradley fighting vehicle. There was no way that Felice Morgan was going to let down her guard with me. With her, everything was dead serious and formal. If she had a sense of humor, I'd seen no signs of it. She was so uptight it made me want to scream. I didn't want her along on my interview and I wanted her to know it. At that point, I still assumed I'd be doing most of the talking.

'Well?' Felice said.

Reluctantly, I filled her in, explaining how I'd found Barry Mancuso's business card and what I'd learned from his ex-assistant. To my surprise, it helped to talk it out, made things more concrete in my head. I finished with my favorite question.

'So how do you think we should handle it?'

Felice rubbed a palm against her thigh. 'We have to bluff him.'

'Yes,' I said with impatience. 'I did that earlier. But in exactly seventy-five minutes, it's show-time.'

'For him,' she said. 'Let him make all the moves.'

'Yeah, like kick us out.'

'Eve, to someone like him, you are a complete nonentity.'

I swallowed. Felice had such a direct way of phrasing things.

'What I mean,' she said, 'is that normally he wouldn't even return your calls unless you were

227

writing some Calendar puff piece about his latest film.'

'He only called to tell me he'd sic his lawyers on me if I didn't back–'

'He called, though,' Felice interrupted. 'I think the assistant's right. He's scared. He's got something to hide. We can leverage that. And we have an ace in the hole. That sugar-daddy credit card.'

I noticed the evolving pronoun. In the space of a sentence, *you* had become *we*.

'How are you so sure?'

She gave me a wolfish smile. 'Trust me.'

Soon we were hurtling through the tunnel that announced the western terminus of Interstate 10. As we emerged onto the sunny blue expanse of Pacific Coast Highway, I wondered if Silvio was free yet. I called his mobile but got his voice mail. At Aguilar Entertainment, his father answered and said the lawyer was still working on getting him released. Should I risk calling Alfonso? My hunger to learn the news, any news, about Silvio, led me to dial. He answered on the first ring.

'It's Eve Diamond. I'm sorry to bother you. I'm just wondering... The police have been holding Silvio since last night. Did you know that? They've been questioning him... I'm really worried. Have you heard from him at all? Do you have any idea–'

'Eve.' He drew the word out, then let it drop off a cliff of silence.

'Alfonso, are you there?'

'I'm here,' he said grimly. 'And I don't know any more than you do. But here's the best piece of advice I can offer. Stay out of matters that

228

don't concern you and everyone will remain safe.'

Was he threatening me?

'And if I don't?'

But he had hung up.

Hands trembling, I turned off the phone and put it in my lap. How dare he? It made me suspect him more than ever. Then all at once, a realization hit me and I groaned. I had launched right into *my* questions about Silvio without even offering him condolences on Catarina, whose battered body had been fished out of the surf last night. Alfonso's onetime muse and mistress. How crass, how thoughtless of me. But did that explain his rudeness? Or was there something else at work? My thoughts darted like angry bees in a shaken hive. The police couldn't have enough to arrest Silvio. It was all circumstantial. I had to exonerate him, and interviewing Mancuso was a step in that direction. I had to focus on that, not on Alfonso's veiled threat. Or the paralyzing image of Silvio in some filthy cell, under pressure to confess to a murder he hadn't committed.

We cruised up the coast-hugging highway, crumbling cliffs of sandstone to our right, and pristine white beaches and blue ocean on our left. The air smelled like a briny bouquet of seaweed.

'PCH is so groovy, don't you think?' Felice said, nudging the accelerator past seventy. 'You should drive it like you dance, fast and reckless.'

'All *good* dancers follow the rules,' I said, thinking of my own forays into waltz and cha-cha. Step, glide, step, glide. One-two-three, one-two-three.

'All *great* dancers break them with abandon.'

'Just this once then, let's pretend you're only good.'

'Oh, I almost forgot,' Felice said, pressing a button on the dashboard. With a loud whir, the convertible top accordioned back, exposing blue sky.

'Nice,' I said, luxuriating as the sun flooded in, the breeze keeping things cool.

'Whenever I get a chance, I like to drive around with the top down, pretending I'm Dorothy Dandridge.'

Felice reached into the backseat and pulled out a leopard-print chiffon scarf that immediately unfurled in the wind and flapped like a rowdy kite. She lifted one knee and pressed it against the steering wheel, freeing her hands to tie the scarf around her neck.

Aghast, I lunged and grabbed the wheel. 'What are you doing? That's a good way to kill us both.'

'Then we'll go in a blaze of glory.' She tucked the scarf in artful layers, took the wheel again, and tossed her head back, tight curls flowing out behind her like streamlined confetti.

'With the wind whipping my face and the sun sparkling off the ocean, I feel just like a movie star. This is a place where anything is possible.' Felice took a deep breath of salt air and exhaled happily. 'I love the Eastern seaboard, but it's so stuffy. Centuries of rules and propriety weighing everyone down. It's stifling. But L.A. is like a big stage where every role is up for grabs.'

I examined her with surprise, wondering what

role she had chosen for herself. Even hard-boiled Felice sensed the intoxicating power of this place, where you could effortlessly shrug off your old skin and slip into a newer, more glamorous one. We were all chameleons, struggling out of the Precambrian ooze, and I didn't think that 'ingenue girl reporter' would be in Felice's repertoire much longer. Her sights were set much higher.

But she was certainly right about Los Angeles. There was something about this city that turned everyone into actors, pining for the role they couldn't have. Raised in privilege, Marisela yearned desperately to transform into *chola* girl. Alfonso used his barrio roots as a badge of authenticity for his plays, gaining fame and fortune on the backs of the people whose lives he exploited. Escaping childhood horrors through the stage, Catarina revisited the barrio each night, tearing her heart open for adoring fans while keeping her real life hidden. Victoria Givens used the make-believe of theater to seduce wayward teens from their grim realities while she basked in the reflected glory of her most talented pupil. Everyone moved fluidly between the real world and the stage until the two grew so blurry that no one knew the truth anymore. One day, I thought, the curtain is going to fall like a guillotine, severing the players from their adoring public.

'This coast reminds me of the Côte d'Azur,' Felice said, breaking into my reverie. 'That's in France,' she said after a beat.

Jesus Christ, the woman thought I was a

complete idiot.

'My mother lived in Nice,' I said wearily.

'Oh, *moi j'adore* Nice,' Felice purred. 'In college, I did a semester abroad in Paris and traveled as much as I could. But then, France has always had such an evolved view of race relations. Just think of the haven it provided to James Baldwin, Langston Hughes, Josephine Baker...'

'I hear they have a little skinhead problem now.'

She grew thoughtful. 'In the outlying suburbs, yes. I was warned about that. Luckily most of the clubs were in central Paris.'

'Between that and your studies, you must have kept pretty busy.'

'And my *Post* internship.'

'*The Washington Post?*' I felt a flash of irritation. Was there anything this girl hadn't done?

'Yeah. But mainly it was grunt work for the Paris bureau chief.'

'Some things never change.'

'I did get a few bylines. I profiled Jean-Claude "Baby Doc" Duvalier.'

'The exiled Haitian strongman?'

She turned to me, eyes glittering. 'I read in the French papers that he lived in a ruined villa above Antibes and had lunch every day at the same café. For twenty years, he had refused to talk to the press. So I waited until the bureau chief went on vacation, then e-mailed the foreign editor. I said Baby Doc moved around a lot so it was a one-of-a-kind opportunity.'

'Did he move around a lot?'

'How do I know? That's not the point. I didn't hear back, so a few days later I told him I was

232

going to Antibes on vacation. Reminded him that I spoke fluent French. The next day I got the green light.' She sighed happily. 'I showed up at his favorite café, making sure to wear a short skirt and a belly top. I'd seen photos of his ex-wife, Michelle, she's from a wealthy Creole family and there was a certain resemblance. Five minutes after I sat down, Baby Doc sent over a bottle of sparkling wine. That was telling; in the old days it would have been a magnum of Cristal. Eventually he invited me back to the villa. Easiest interview I ever did.'

'Were you scared to be alone with him?'

Felice laughed. 'I hired the biggest, most muscular French photographer I could find and told him what we were in for,' she said. 'So I wasn't exactly alone. But, oh my God, Eve, you wouldn't believe his place. The International Monetary Fund estimates he and his Tonton Macoutes stole five hundred million dollars from Haiti's treasury. Just looted it. And now he cooks his dinner on a hot plate in a kitchen where the plaster's peeling off the walls.'

'Did he tell you where the money went?'

'Claims his wife got a pile in the divorce and bodyguards and courtiers robbed him blind. He dreams of going back, you know. He's very bitter about being run out on a rail.'

'A solid-gold rail.'

'Yeah, but I almost pitied him. The pathos of the deluded dictator, hunched over his hot plate, dreaming of bloodstone days.'

'So why do you think he talked to you?'

She shot me a sly look. 'He thought I was a

233

little French slut who was going to make his day. I think he's more lonely than horny these days. After the second bottle, he didn't seem to care that the tape recorder was running.'

'You must have had quite an exclusive on your hands.'

'I wrote it in the Antibes Hotel. The story had to get slotted before Farley got back from vacation and killed it.'

'Why would he have killed it?'

She gave me a pitying look. 'You've obviously never worked in a foreign bureau before. Because it wasn't *his* scoop, of course.'

'So you made your deadline?'

'It ran front page center, on Sunday,' she said smugly. 'Farley was on a plane coming back from the Seychelles when he read it. About busted a gut.'

Felice gave me a Cheshire grin.

'He wanted to fire me, but the foreign desk wouldn't let him. It was just the break I needed.'

CHAPTER 33

We turned inland on Loma Prieta Canyon and found ourselves in a different world. In the high brush, cicadas sang their summer song of indolence. A breeze ruffled the tops of the trees. The hills and dales stretched out, gold and green and yellow.

The road climbed and soon we saw glimpses of

234

the Pacific again, vast and placid, the air a perfect seventy-five degrees from the cooling sea breezes while the inland valleys baked at more than a hundred. The vegetation grew lush, hinting at hidden sprinklers. One final turn and we emerged onto Sea Cliff Drive and a promontory that offered breathtaking views of the Pacific. We pulled up to the guardhouse and I leaned across Felice and gave my name.

The guard was a black man in his twenties with pinnacle cheekbones, buzzed hair, and designer glasses. He was reading *Daily Variety*. He checked a clipboard and ran his finger along a name. He frowned. Something was wrong. He twined his fingers into a steeple.

'He isn't back yet.' To my surprise, his voice was low and melodious with a strong French accent.

My hand gripped the door. 'We can wait inside.' I hated how my voice rose a hopeful octave and wavered.

'He left me no instructions.'

'This is ridiculous,' I said, feigning umbrage. 'What are we supposed to do, pick wildflowers until he arrives?'

'That would be fine, mademoiselles. Just do not venture too close to the edge of the cliff. There was a lot of erosion in the last rains and we are not responsible for accidents.'

Felice smiled at the guard. *'Pouvons-nous attendre à l'intérieur?'* she asked sweetly.

The guard started. Earlier, he had addressed all his comments to me. Now he gave her a long look, drinking her in, but also trying to decipher her ethnicity and her place in this pecking order.

235

Had he mistaken her for my driver?

'You also have a meeting with Mr. Mancuso?' he said, and a lot seemed to ride on the answer.

'*Mais oui*,' Felice said sweetly.

The guard pretended to make a call. He talked quietly into the phone. When he hung up, he was smiling.

'Go right ahead, mademoiselles,' the guard said in gallant French.

Felice thanked him in the timbre of a coquette, her voice chirpy and pitched toward him alone. Then the electronic gate swung open and we drove onto a cobblestone road lined with tall cypress trees leading to a Mediterranean mansion painted in the palest peach. We pulled up before a carved marble fountain with a stone statue of Poseidon holding up his trident, clamshells opening in obeisance, cherubs frolicking.

Felice killed the engine and turned to me.

'Good thing you brought me along.'

'Where do you think he's from?'

'Côte d'Ivoire,' she said. 'Only because I've been there.' She examined a tendril of hair.

'Maybe I should have spoken French to him.'

'Wouldn't have mattered,' she said simply.

'Because I'm not...'

'That's right.'

She threw open the car door. 'Let's gawk for a while, before Mancuso comes back. Have you ever seen such a spread?'

There was glee and something else in her voice. Excitement. Envy. A vow that some day she, too, would own such a property.

We watched the sea below. White sails skimmed

across the ocean, passing sturdier vessels, anchovy boats out of San Pedro whose crews still chugged out each day to earn their living.

Then we heard the roar of a powerful engine and a red Ferrari zipped up the cobblestones. Mancuso didn't notice us, standing behind a clump of palms, but I got a good look at him – a tanned man with a shock of black hair and an open-collared shirt. He wore rimless sunglasses. With a loud purr, the Ferrari disappeared into the garage, and I considered what a sad irony it was that you almost never saw young men driving these cars. Only once they were past their prime, starting to sag and sprout hair from strange orifices, did they have the bucks. To me they were little boys galloping on peg ponies. Relying on horsepower and Viagra to restore the virility of youth.

The garage closed with a whisper of well-oiled springs, and soon the front door – a huge arched wooden slab studded with cast iron – swung open.

'You ready?' Felice said hoarsely. She looked lit up from the inside, like she was marching off to battle.

I shrugged. Fey and oblique was my preferred starting position. Mildly sympathetic with a touch of ADD. Lull them as you scrutinize from behind the mask. I drew a bead on him now. *Überproducer, prince of Malibu tides, are you the one? Is there a killer inside?*

Felice was snapping her fingers in my face.

'Yo, Eve. Get your war on.'

Annoyed, I pushed her hand away. I had felt

myself getting close to something. Now it was gone.

'Curb your enthusiasm,' I said.

'Show some. Here comes the advance guard.'

A middle-aged Latina housekeeper in a crisp white uniform was walking toward the trash cans, holding a plastic bag. She dumped it and headed back.

'Excuse me,' Felice called.

The woman turned. The initial alarm in her eyes faded to a dim steady pulse as she took us in, two neatly dressed young women. This was Malibu. We could be jewel thieves, call girls, or development executives.

'May I help you?'

'We have a two o'clock appointment with Mr. Mancuso.'

'This way, please,' the maid said.

We followed her inside, and I wanted to ask her what it was like to be a housekeeper in Malibu and how much they paid her and what secrets she knew. Did she go down to the beach on her lunch hour or just gaze through the window and brood over her children, being raised by relatives in a Managua hovel while she spent her days in luxury?

Instead, I followed her into a sunken living room, where the housekeeper twisted the end of her tea towel and stood uncertainly. The entire western wall was plate-glass windows that over-looked the ocean. PCH curved north like a girl's hair ribbon, all the way to Ventura. To the south rose the jutting promontory of Palos Verdes Peninsula. Between them lay the Santa Monica

Bay. At night, lights lit up the waterline and formed a garland called the 'Queen's Necklace' because houses with those views went for a royal ransom.

Then Barry Mancuso stepped into the living room. Up close, he was less airbrushed than his file photo suggested and short, no more than five foot seven. He had jet black hair, a neatly barbered beard, and a tanned face dominated by large blue eyes, startling in their clarity and framed with thick black lashes. His body was trim and compact, brimming with masculine energy. He had changed into jeans and a snug-fitting black T-shirt, and the thin material drew attention to his sculpted upper body. There was a tautness around his eyes and mouth where delicate instruments had tampered with nature.

'Who are these people, Mercedes?' Barry Mancuso said. 'And what are they doing in my house?'

CHAPTER 34

'Your two o'clock appointment, sir,' Mercedes said.

She curtsied and left the room.

Mancuso circled us, wary as a shark, before gliding over to a claw-footed desk that would have looked at home in a Hapsburg palace. A photo of an attractive blonde with two small children stared out at us. My gaze flickered to his ring finger and found a thick band of gold. He picked up a phone, ready to dial.

'Friends of Bethany's?' he said with hearty insincerity.

'No, Mr. Mancuso.' Felice flashed him a demure smile.

'I didn't think so.' He frowned. 'I don't have a two p.m. And I've never seen either of you before. But give me your names, so I can tell the police when they arrest you for trespassing.'

'I don't think you want to do that, Mr. Mancuso,' I said.

At the sound of my voice, he reacted. I could see him trying to place it.

'Eve Diamond, *L.A. Times*,' I said, saving him the trouble. 'And I was led to believe you were expecting us. You'll find my name on the authorized guest list for two p.m. We've been invited here.'

'Not by me, and I'm the only one who counts.'

He started punching numbers on his phone.

'We're here to ask you about Catarina Velosi's credit card,' I said. 'You know, the one in her name whose bills get forwarded to your office.'

Mancuso got very still. So still that his fingers stopped dialing. Then with great delicacy, he put down the phone.

'I don't know what you're talking about,' he said.

'She left some of the receipts at a friend's house,' I bluffed. 'Must have fallen out of her purse.'

His eyes went to a briefcase by the desk, and I wondered if it held a gun.

'Don't worry,' I said. 'They're in a safe place. With very explicit instructions on what should be done if anything happens to us.'

I stepped up to the desk now, swiped the photo of the blonde, examined it. Felice had settled, uninvited, into one of the embroidered chairs.

'This your wife?' I raised my eyebrows. 'Your kids?'

He saw where I was going, pretended he hadn't.

'Yes. I'm a lucky man,' he said with false heartiness. 'She and my two youngest are in Kona. She's overseeing the remodeling of our home there, it's one of the original nineteenth-century coffee plantations. They're due back early next week.'

I set the photo down. I knew that no matter how many gorgeous women he married or estates he bought, he'd still hunger for more women and more land. Some lusts can never be assuaged.

'It would just break her heart to find out, wouldn't it?' I said. 'I hope it doesn't come to that.'

Mancuso swallowed, his Adam's apple bobbing. His eyes tracked from me to Felice, finally settling on me.

He cleared his throat. 'So what can I do for you, Ms. Diamond?' At once, Felice leaned forward in her chair and twined her hands together in that bashful way that no longer fooled me in the least.

'No, Mr. Mancuso, it's what we can do for you. We'd like to help you with this, uh, situation.'

Mancuso was too polished, too sophisticated,

to show his annoyance. He smiled coldly and addressed me.

'You didn't mention you were bringing an assistant.'

Felice's smile grew broader and she showed her teeth.

'It's a pity we got cut off earlier,' I said, 'because then I could have explained. This is Felice Morgan and she's an *L.A. Times* reporter too. We don't have assistants in journalism.'

She's an albatross around my neck, if you want to know the truth, Mr. Mancuso, and I'm supposed to keep an eye on her all week and make sure she isn't fabricating stories.

Mancuso gave us an incredulous look.

'So what is this? A gang bang?'

He gave a salacious laugh. Felice crossed her legs at the knees, showing some skin.

· 'Only if you don't play straight with us,' she said sweetly. Her voice had been high society, her elocution razor sharp and brimming with privilege. Now it changed. 'Catarina's got four cousins in Eighteenth Street, that's a gang, yo, and they're simply deranged with grief about what happened to their *prima*. Homies just itching for a payback. Y'all had a scene like that in one a yore movies. They tied up the perp and messed with him real bad for a coupla days before drilling him. But I wouldn't sweat it. Buncha them is on parole. On account of a drive-by. They ain't gon' do nothin' stupid.'

Felice leaned back and crossed her arms. Mancuso licked his lips. He turned to me. 'I agreed to meet with you on the understanding

242

that it would forestall any problems.'

I loved how he suddenly decided he had invited us. Probably did the same thing when he stole the idea for a script.

I shrugged. 'I said I wouldn't go to the cops. Family is different.'

'Can I speak to you alone?'

I can't say I wasn't tempted to shut Felice out. But it just didn't seem like the right thing to do, and I'd been unethical enough for one day.

'We're a team,' I said.

Mancuso sat down. The sun was slanting in through the glass, sending a ray of light into the room. Dust motes danced along its path, oblivious to his torment.

'First of all,' he spluttered, 'you tell Catarina Velosi's homie cousins that I didn't kill her. This is just insane.'

'Funny how nobody killed anyone. Huh?' I said. 'You're just lucky I'm in front of the cops on this one. Aren't you worried about fingerprints, DNA?'

He pressed his lips together. 'I didn't do anything.'

'When did the affair start?' Felice asked.

Mancuso's glance went to an oil painting on the far wall. It was a lush re-creation of a Fragonard, who had done those Rococo paintings of Marie Antoinette, and it took me a moment to recognize the creamy-bosomed woman with the long, golden locks, sitting in a garden bower, her lips parted in laughter, cherubs tumbling at her feet. Mancuso's much younger trophy wife. He had so much to lose.

'She was just a young lady I was trying to help.'

'That's not what her neighbors said.'

'What do they know?'

'You were screwing her,' Felice said. 'That makes you a suspect.'

Mancuso looked like an animal in a trap, weighing whether to gnaw off its leg.

'Just tell us when it started,' I said softly.

It was hitting me suddenly, the possibilities of Felice and me playing good cop, bad cop. Or in our case, good hack, bad hack.

Mancuso stood up. 'I think you'd better go.'

Felice stood up too. Swaggered a bit. 'Nice crib you got here.' Her eyes swept over the period furniture, the antique vases, the elaborate Oriental carpets. 'Awful to see it get messed up. But have it your way. You'll be hearin' from the boys. C'mon, Eve.'

I stood.

A battle was raging behind Mancuso's eyes. He cast a nervous glance at the artwork. His type of power came from money and a hermetically sealed environment, not brute strength. But his involvement with Catarina had broken the air lock, placing him outside the protective dome. I could almost hear his calculations. He could hire bodyguards and put in a better security system. He could install bulletproof glass. But one day, where he least expected it, the fictional cousins would come for him.

'I'm sorry we couldn't reach some accommodation, Mr. Mancuso,' I said.

Felice was staring out the window at the Pacific. From somewhere far away came the whir

244

and suck of a vacuum cleaner.

'Why should I tell you anything?' Mancuso said finally, and I knew we had won, though it would take time and patience to reel him in.

We waited and the air throbbed with silence.

'My lawyer told me under no circumstances was I to even talk to you. Much less meet with you.'

'I suppose he doesn't know the whole story,' I said faux-sympathetically.

Mancuso shook his head. 'He doesn't understand.'

'Of course not.' Felice turned. 'That's not their job, to understand. It's ours.'

'I didn't do anything to her.'

'We know you didn't,' I said.

'I didn't even see her that week.'

'I believe you,' I said soothingly.

'I, however, am not so sure,' said bad cop Felice. She walked across the room and sat down again, folding her hands primly in her lap.

'She wasn't just another lay.'

'Oh no?' said Felice. 'Then what was it, Mr. Mancuso? Wedding bells?'

The sarcasm echoed around the room and I feared that this time, she had gone too far. But a funny change was taking place in Barry Mancuso. The meaner Felice got, the meeker the producer grew. She was some kind of alpha dog, making him submit. But just in case, I intended to keep playing good cop.

'I wanted to help her, to save her,' Mancuso said.

I turned to Felice. 'She had that effect on a lot

of men,' I said.

'In my job,' Mancuso said, 'everybody wants something from me. A movie part. Jewelry. Another house.' Brief glance at the oil portrait again. 'Everyone except Catarina. She was pure.'

'Pure trouble, maybe.' Felice examined her nails.

'For her it was all about the art. She hated what I did for a living. She called me the corrupter, the debaser of culture. It killed me that I couldn't have her.'

'I thought you were involved,' Felice said.

'Oh, I could have sex with her. But I couldn't possess her. None of this' – he gestured around the room– 'made a damn difference to her.'

Something thrilled inside me as the mystery lover finally stepped out of the shadows into the light of a Malibu afternoon.

Felice leaned forward. 'And now she's dead, Mancuso. Do you really want the cops tramping around your fine house, knocking on the neighbors' doors? How will you explain it to your lovely wife?'

'When did you start seeing her?' I said.

Mancuso didn't say anything.

'Our next stop is Parker Center,' Felice said.

Mancuso put his hands to his face and rubbed hard. 'I've known her for five years,' he said finally, his words barely audible. 'From when I bought Alfonso's play. Last year, when the movie came out, I invited her to a screening.'

He got up and walked over to the window. The sun glinted off the Pacific.

'She hated the movie. Mocked it. Threw a glass

of champagne in my face at the after-party. But that night she went home with me. It lasted three months.'

'But you saw her more recently,' Felice said.

Mancuso hesitated.

'We know you did,' I bluffed.

'I called her one night. Flipping through my address book after a couple of drinks. She was haughty. Told me I could come by if I wanted. Imagine, to that shack, bringing my Ferrari. But I have a Lexus, too. The next morning the window was smashed in and the stereo was gone, but it was worth it.'

'When was that?'

'May twenty-eighth.'

'A week before she disappeared,' I said.

'But you saw her after that,' Felice said.

'Two nights later. We fought. I stormed out. But I didn't kill her. I'm not capable of ... that's why I make movies. Get my aggressions out on-screen.'

'Did she ever tell you she was scared?'

'She was afraid of Alfonso.'

I looked at Felice.

'He hit her or something?' she asked.

'No. She was afraid to get sucked back into his orbit.'

'Who else was she afraid of?'

'Nobody.' He looked bewildered. 'She seemed happy. She had a new boyfriend.'

Hold on, I thought. Another mystery lover?

'And his name was?'

'She never said.'

'Where did she meet him?'

'She never said.'

'Ever get introduced? See a picture?'

'No.'

'What else can you remember?'

'Nothing. Honest. She was secretive. Compartmentalized her life.'

'We all do that, Mr. Mancuso,' Felice said. 'Or we'd go crazy.'

'Okay, let's talk about the credit card,' I said. It had been the wedge that got us through the door and now it seemed almost beside the point.

'She promised she wouldn't go crazy with it.'

'And did she?'

'No. She'd charge plays and meals. Sometimes clothes, but nothing compared to my wife. I mean, you should see–'

'Why didn't you go to the police when you read that she was missing?' I asked, knowing full well.

He looked pained. 'All the usual reasons.'

'They're going to find out sooner or later. They'll connect it back to you through the card.'

'I've canceled it.'

'We need to see all the statements,' Felice said. Smart girl.

Mancuso looked like he might put up a fight.

'We've already got the one,' I pointed out.

He picked up the phone and made a call, requested the bills be faxed to his home, and told the person on the other end where to find them. He hung up and rubbed his eyes.

'It'll be a few minutes. My assistant quit today. That's the thanks I get, after all I've done for her.'

She was especially thankful for the opportunity to drive your stool sample around town.

The maligned assistant had done me a huge favor, even if it was out of spite. The least I could do was keep her secret.

The fax machine began to whir in the next room. Mancuso excused himself, and returned with a series of photocopied bills.

'Any activity since she disappeared?' I asked.

He wrinkled his nose. 'It's too early to tell. This one is from last month.'

'Let's call them.'

He got on the phone and jotted some things down. When he hung up, he had a strange look on his face.

'Yes,' he said. 'There's a record store on Whittier Boulevard. An auto body shop. A place called La Serenata di Garibaldi.'

I swallowed hard. La Serenata was an upscale Mexican seafood restaurant, all curved arches and mosaic floors, tiled fountains tinkling on the sunny garden patio. I knew because Silvio had taken me there several times. The sauces were refined, the fish exquisitely fresh, the margaritas infused with watermelon and mango. It was one of his favorite places for a romantic evening, Silvio would say as we raised our glasses and toasted each other.

As I pictured him there with her, jealous hackles rose and formed a ridge along my heart. But a lot of people ate there. It was a big East Side hangout for artists, politicians, and businessmen with taste as well as money.

Just then a young woman walked through the French doors and into the living room, wearing a string bikini and toweling her long blond hair. The smell of coconut oil filled the air and glistened off her wet form. She had the voluptuous curves of a teen starlet who has not yet lost her baby fat.

She walked up to Mancuso and he put his arm around her waist and whispered in her ear. Then he spun her around and sent her out of the room with a pat on the butt. Well, isn't that just something, I thought. Gorgeous wife, two little kids. But that's not enough. So he starts an affair with the wild actress Catarina. He loved her. She was no casual lay to him. Yeah, right, he must have paused for a moment longer than usual before returning to the ever-plentiful well for this little Pop-Tart.

At the door, the girl turned. Her fleshy pink mouth opened, revealing a row of straight, white teeth. She yawned and stretched luxuriously.

'I'm going to take a nap,' she announced to no one in particular. Mancuso's face filled with pride and ownership and something I couldn't quite fathom.

He sighed. 'Beautiful, isn't she?'

'Yes. You auditioning her for your next film after we leave?' I said.

He looked shocked.

'Ms. Diamond,' he said stiffly, 'that's my daughter, Bethany.'

CHAPTER 35

'Where did you learn to lie like that?' I asked Felice when we were back on PCH. It was late afternoon and the light was glorious.

Felice tossed back her scarf. 'I minored in drama at Brown. The student paper said I was the best Blanche Dubois in memory.'

It served me right for asking, I thought, squirreling away this new knowledge. Felice lied effortlessly. Magnificently. I had to keep that in mind. And more important, I should never, ever trust her again.

'You think he did it?' I said.

Felice tapped her fingers on the steering wheel. 'Hard to cut through all that fear. Is it guilt or because this thing could ruin him if it gets out?'

We drove for several miles, me brooding about the memory of Silvio in La Serenata, his arm raised to make a toast, except it wasn't me sitting across from him, but Catarina.

At Santa Monica, we waved good-bye to the sea and headed back into the smog. I called Silvio's office again and his dad said there was nothing new.

'We should visit some of the places on the credit card receipts,' Felice said when I hung up. 'I'll order a photo of Catarina from the library to take around, see if they remember her.'

There was no way to pull Felice off the story.

251

She had tasted blood in Malibu, and like any good reporter, she craved more. It was after six when we drove into the deserted parking lot.

We ordered in pizza and got busy with phone books and maps, plotting the evening's itinerary with the itemized charges on Mancuso's credit card. I called the LAPD and was told they were not releasing any information about Silvio Aguilar. I left messages with Alfonso and the Aguilar Entertainment lawyer. Maybe they were downtown, picking him up.

Outside, the sky turned orange and purple. The office buzzer rang, startling me. A thin man was at the door, holding a square box. Felice beat me to the entrance, opening her wallet as she went.

'Let me,' she said, propping the door open for the delivery guy.

'Large veggie pizza. Felice Morgan, yes?' the man said in a thick Middle Eastern accent.

I checked him out. He had a bottlebrush mustache and thinning hair under a tweed cap, and may have been handsome once, before a threadbare existence wore deep grooves along his face. His pants hung too loose and ended above his ankles, and I could see fabric pilling on his polyester-blend sweater. Beads of moisture clung to his temples. He took out a grayish rag and dabbed at his forehead, balancing our pizza in his other hand.

'That's right,' Felice said, waving a twenty-dollar bill. 'How much?'

While she paid, I checked out his car. It was an old beater that had seen a few crashes. One of the headlights was smashed and the passenger door was bent and fastened shut with twine. A small American flag sprouted from the driver's window.

'I bring change.' The man stepped toward the car.

He saw me studying the flag and adjusted the angle to make it more jaunty.

'The wind, it how you say...' He made a tearing motion with his hands. 'Next week I buy new one. Payday.'

He smiled, exposing gold teeth, then put a hand over his heart. I noticed a sticker on the dented rear bumper and stepped sideways to read its red, white, and blue logo: *United We Stand.*

'Here,' he said, rolling his *r.* 'You take menus. For next time.'

He thrust something into my hands and I read down the list: pizza, hamburgers, falafel, chow mein, dolmades, fried chicken, and hummus. The United Nations of take-out.

The deliveryman was counting out change to Felice. He seemed transfixed by her hair. Tentatively, he reached out one hand, touched it. Felice pulled back.

'Hey,' she said.

'Where from?' he asked. 'You.'

When she didn't respond, he tucked his chin into his neck like a turtle and repeated the question.

The pizza box was warm in my hands. 'She's from here. America,' I said.

'You look my wife,' the little man said huskily. He shook his head. 'Four years no see.'

Felice's face softened. 'Where are you from?'

'I, Tunisia,' the man said. 'But many childs.' He

put his hand out to demonstrate varying heights. 'Six sons. I come here work.'

'Yes,' Felice said.

The man doffed his tweed cap at us. 'Good night, Felice Morgan,' he said. Then he bowed and got in his car. I heard the springs squeak.

'Wait.' Felice ran after him, a five-dollar bill flapping in her hand. 'Take this. Thank you.'

I brought the pizza inside and was placing big gooey slices onto paper plates when she walked in.

'Some people will do anything for a tip,' I said, to cover up the squishy feeling that had suddenly risen in my chest.

'You should be ashamed of yourself, Eve Diamond.'

We divvied up the evening's tasks over dinner. I wanted to find Alfonso and ask him about Barry Mancuso. Felice would visit businesses and see if anyone remembered Catarina and a mystery man.

She asked for my cell phone number. 'I want to be able to reach you around the clock.'

'That's what I'm afraid of.' I grimaced, but recited it. She programmed the number into her autodial with a little smile, then gave me her cell number in turn.

'This means you call me as soon as you learn something,' I said, reaching for a second slice of pizza. 'Before you run to the City Desk. No excuses. And for God's sake, be careful.'

'I promise,' Felice said, her eyelashes fluttering like twin butterflies alighting on a flower.

CHAPTER 36

I drove to the Mark Taper Forum as the sun took its final bow, the curtain coming down in sherbet swirls on the horizon. Using my press pass, I talked my way backstage and asked for Alfonso. He was around somewhere, I was told. Not knowing my way through the labyrinth, I walked down corridors and opened doors. On my third try, I found him in an empty room, talking urgently on the phone. He looked haggard, like a character from one of his own plays who has jousted with fate and lost. He saw me, said a hurried good-bye, and clicked off.

'You again,' he said, with none of the ferocity he had shown earlier on the phone.

'I'm sorry about Catarina,' I said. 'I should have mentioned that when I called you before.'

'Yes.' He stared at his shoes and blinked twice, but his eyes were dry.

'Any news about Silvio?' I asked.

Alfonso rubbed his eyes. 'He's innocent.'

I wondered how he was so sure. 'Since when is that a passport out?'

'Like I told you earlier, we will leave it to the police. They are the experts.'

Did he know about the new lover? Catarina's affair with Barry Mancuso? Her dalliance with Pot Boy? Why her car had been found on Angeles Crest?

'Listen, Alfonso, I've spent the day looking into Catarina's life and asking questions, and it seems that–'

'No!' he said sharply.

'What?'

Alfonso regarded me with dark, steely eyes. He couldn't stand me, didn't trust me, hated my meddling. Was it me, or because he had something to hide?

Alfonso seemed to be eavesdropping on my thoughts.

'Sorry I snapped at you on the phone. Catarina's dead, my best friend is in jail, and my wife is headed for a nervous breakdown.'

He glared at me like it was all my fault. 'And meanwhile I'm the toast of the fucking town with this play. Tonight was sold out, with will-call lines around the block. The Taper phone's been ringing off the hook.'

He walked across the room, slipped behind a makeshift bar, and pulled out a bottle and two glasses. He poured two fingers of golden liquid into each glass and brought them to the table. The air filled with the aroma of honey and anise.

'Here.' He handed me one, raised a second glass to his lips. The liquid sloshed as his hand shook.

'You've got to listen to me,' I said. 'Catarina was having an affair.'

'No!' Alfonso said with such vehemence that I thought he might strike me. 'And I don't appreciate what you wrote in the paper. Never believe anything that witch tells you. It's a pack of lies.'

'What witch?'

'That drama teacher. Victoria Givens. Always interfering, thinking she knew best. She had an unnatural hold on Catarina. I told her so, but Catarina would never listen to me.'

'But I heard it from a second person today, that–'

'Lies,' Alfonso said. 'How dare you slander the dead with your filthy rumors? You don't know the first thing about Catarina.'

Alfonso walked out, slamming the door behind him. It was clear that this wasn't his first drink of the evening. By the time I recovered enough to follow, the hallway was empty.

I ran in the direction he had turned, opened a door and found myself watching the play from the wings. Onstage, an older woman had joined the young actress who played Angelica. Her hair hung in graying stands, but she prowled the shabby living room with a ferocious energy that mesmerized me.

'I know I wasn't around much when you was growing up,' the older woman said to Angelica. 'But look how much I love you, *m'hija*. Just had it done. Cost me a whole week's pay.'

She turned her back to the audience and with one swift movement, pulled up her T-shirt.

She lifted her head and struck a pathetic pose, all stringy muscle and curved spine. Tall gothic letters scrolled across her back, forming the name Angelica.

'How 'bout that, huh? Your old *mami* loved you so much she got your name tattooed across her shoulders. No mother ever loved her daughter more.'

She pulled her shirt down, faced the audience again, and smiled, revealing blackened teeth. Then she strutted to the coffee table and took a long, thirsty swig of beer.

I heard a footfall and knew someone was right behind me.

CHAPTER 37

'Terribly poignant, wouldn't you say?' Marisela murmured, blowing out smoke. She crossed one arm over her chest, cradling her elbow, and lifted the cigarette to her mouth.

'Creepy is more like it,' I said.

'Who are you to pass judgment?' She took an angry toke.

'Well, I haven't seen the whole play yet, I just...'

I could smell her perfume, sweet and acrid as it mingled with the oils of her skin. Her eyes were bloodshot.

'Come with me,' Marisela said. Her fingers closed over my wrist and tightened.

'Where?'

'I want to show you something.' She pulled me toward her, and I stiffened. She swayed, her damp fingers like coiled springs around my flesh. *Take your hands off me*, I wanted to yell, but the words died in my throat, held back, unaccountably, by my desire not to disturb the play. Instead I pulled the other way, trying to wrench myself out of her sweaty grasp.

'There's something you need to see,' Marisela said sharply. 'It's not far. We'll take my car. I was going there anyway.'

She turned and tugged me along like a toy on a string. Her voice was calm and matter-of-fact, but her eyes blazed with anger.

'I don't think you're in any condition to drive.'

'I'm sober, if that's what you mean,' she said, punctuating each word with another tug. 'Unlike my dear husband.'

She stopped. Her eyes grew narrow and cunning. 'Wassamatter, you scared of me?' She gave a high-pitched laugh.

'Of course not.'

'Then c'mon. I dare you.' She let go. Suddenly thrown off balance, I stumbled and fell. She crossed her arms and looked down at me.

'Get up. I won't hurt you.'

'Of course not,' I said.

'You're a reporter, aren't you? I promise you'll find it interesting. Hmmm?'

I scrambled to my feet. She fished in her purse, pulled out a stick of gum, and popped it nonchalantly into her mouth. What did she want to show me? I recalled the nagging certainty, driving back with her from Angeles Crest, that Marisela knew a lot more than she was telling.

'All right,' I said. 'Let me leave Silvio a message.'

It would be my insurance, so that someone would know I was with her. For all the good it did. I was about to see fantasy and reality collide in a way I hadn't imagined possible.

259

CHAPTER 38

Marisela drove, cigarette dangling from her mouth as she sped east over the Fourth Street Bridge, which spanned the L.A. River. The vast and silent railroad yards sprawled below us, a rusting testament to the city's industrial heritage. There was a melancholy honesty to this landscape, a reminder that Los Angeles had once made things like cars and beer and tires. In these eastern wastelands, the city's blue-collar past still stood, even though the hulking Pabst brewery had been converted to artist lofts, the redbrick jail to a gallery. The region had become a studio back lot for the more glamorous city to the west, a place stuffed with props and relics where one could sift through the past like an archaeologist.

Now we were in East Los Angeles, traveling down broad boulevards, then past neat stucco homes and into the sprawling projects of Agua Dulce. I wondered how Felice was faring and when I'd hear from her. If I'd hear from her.

Marisela parked next to a cluster of modular buildings painted leaf-rot green. She popped the trunk and walked to the back of the car, stared inside. By the time I joined her, she had slammed it shut.

'This way,' she said, hiking to a concrete path that wound through yellowed grass toward the apartments. The architectural style, if you even bothered to dignify it with a name, was sixties institutional, with cheap stucco, aluminum windows, and plywood doors. Marisela walked fast. From open windows came the sound of rap music, *corridos*, and crying babies. The smell of stewing meat and frying onions. The blue glow of TV illuminating the necklace of a family around a table, heads bent over dinner plates to say grace.

We came to a community center. A maintenance man in beige overalls perched on a ladder, painting over graffiti. Teenaged boys preened on the remains of a playground while saucy-eyed girls in hot pants and platform shoes giggled into their hands. Several more chased toddlers around the weed-choked sandlot where empty chains dangled from the armature of swing sets. An older boy spun lethargically on a merry-go-round whose rusting plates curled upward, an invitation to tetanus. A child's red sneaker lay next to something pale and rubbery that looked like a deflated balloon, but wasn't.

I wondered how bad things could be in a place where grass still grew. Where people cleaned up graffiti and said grace and ate dinner as a family.

Marisela stopped at a door that said 23B. She rapped and the sound came back hollow, like striking an empty gourd.

Ranchera music seeped through the barred window. An ancient air conditioner played percussion, rattling in perfect time. Marisela turned the knob and stepped inside and I followed, wondering if I was being set up.

261

Inside smelled like stale grease and nicotine. I saw movement in the deep corner of the room and tensed. It was only a fan, blowing dirty air. Flies buzzed around an open liter of soda.

The TV blared, a musical variety show in Spanish. In its flickering glow, I made out a woman on an upholstered couch, two fat cats curled like bookends around her. Her face was seamed, her long hair thin and graying, her eyes deeply recessed. But she wasn't that old, you could see it in her long, wiry limbs, the cutoff jeans and man's shirt she wore. An open can of beer nestled between her legs.

'Hello,' Marisela said. She stood in the living room, arms hanging at her sides. The woman stared zombielike at the TV. Her head sagged, and she seemed about to nod off. Marisela walked to a coffee table piled high with empty plates and ashtrays. She grabbed the remote and turned the TV off.

The woman's head jerked upright. 'Hey,' she said, 'I was watching that.' Her eyes focused on Marisela. 'Oh, it's you. How are you, baby? What did you bring me?'

She smacked her lips, then noticed me.

'An' who's this?' She shot me a wall-eyed look, trying to cock her head at an insouciant angle, but it wobbled too much and finally she gave up and eased it back onto the couch.

'Friend of mine,' Marisela said. 'I wanted her to meet you.'

'How nice,' said the woman, the last word eroding into a hiss. She put down her beer with exaggerated care. 'I'm down to two a day.'

Marisela snorted. Slowly, the woman pushed herself into a standing position and stepped toward me, one hand pressed against her back.

'Pleased to meet you,' the woman said. She had the skinny frame and potbelly of a longtime alcoholic. 'Any friend of Marisela's is a friend of mine.'

The woman wagged a crooked finger at Marisela and I could smell the sour hops coming off her, see the scrim of dirt under a ragged fingernail.

'Why don't you help yourself to a beer.'

'No thanks,' I said, feeling a horrible sense of déjà vu coming on.

'Suit yourself. She won't drink with me either. But I still love her. You wanna see how much I love her? Check this out.'

The woman turned her back to me, leaned forward, and hiked up her shirt.

'Got her name tattooed across my back. Look how much I love my darling child.'

I stared at the barrio scrawl, the flanges of bone jutting out in reproach of a lifetime's bad nutrition. The woman before me blurred and I saw only an actress on a darkened theater stage, shouting out the same words.

'She shows it to everyone,' Marisela said. 'She's so proud.'

I shook my head. 'He had no right,' I said. 'It's monstrous.'

And for a moment I was paralyzed by the travesty of it all. I didn't know what I found more repellent, that this was Marisela's real mother, or that Alfonso had ripped the words out of her life and put them into his play. I remembered Victoria Givens saying it was all laid bare in the plays. The truth of their sad, twisted lives. Finally, I began to understand.

The corners of Marisela's mouth tightened as she watched her mother.

''Cause I do love you, baby,' Marisela's mother said. 'You know that, don'cha?'

She shuffled closer to her daughter, her eyes pools of confusion. She had expected approval, maybe an admiring whistle. Not this silence that seeped into the apartment like gloom on a winter's day.

'You loved me enough to give me away,' Marisela said. Her voice was soothing, the way you talk to a child.

'And look how wonderful you turned out. My precious darling girl. You're not mad at your old mom?'

The woman's voice was wheedling, her mouth open in a half smile, revealing snaggled teeth. She stepped closer.

'No ... Mother,' Marisela said, embracing the older woman. 'Shh, it's okay. You did the right thing.'

Marisela's mother lifted her head and her eyes were wet. 'Damn straight I did. I wanted to keep you, *m'hija*, but they talked me out of it. Said you'd have a better life...'

'Yes, that's right.'

The woman broke free and walked back to the table. She scooped up her beer and took a swig. 'Now whadya bring me, dollface? The money goes fast now that I'm eating for two.'

With a start, I looked at her belly again, where it pressed against the seams of her shirt. Lord in heaven, I thought. She's pregnant.

Marisela opened her purse and pulled out some bills. Without counting, she shoved them into the woman's calloused hand.

'Aw, my darling daughter takes care of her mama. I'ma go out right now and buy some groceries.'

Marisela's mouth set into a thin line.

'I've got stuff in the car. You'll help me unload it, won't you, Eve?'

'Of course,' I said, thankful that at this moment, nothing more was required.

In silence, we trekked back to the car and opened the trunk and then I saw what Marisela had been pondering. We returned with vegetables and fruit, sacks of rice and beans, bread, and cold cuts packed in ice, and loaded most of it into the fridge, which held only a crusted jar of relish and some hot dogs. And a case of cheap beer.

Marisela put the sandwich fixings on the table and watched her mother roll up a slice of turkey and chew absently. 'We have to go now,' she said.

On the drive back, I tried to think of something to say that wouldn't sound stupid. My thoughts kept returning to Marisela's quest for her biological family and where it had led.

What if you found your blood family after longing for them for so many years and instead of the wholeness you so desperately craved, the emotional salvation that you hoped it would bring, you found only rot and horror? A twisted fun-house image of what your life might have been like. And what if that horror then reached out and dragged you in? A Pandora's box of misery. What would you do then?

'It must have taken a lot for you to bring me there,' I finally said, staring straight ahead.

Marisela lit a cigarette. She took a long puff.

'I wanted you to see. So you'd understand.'

'She's drinking and smoking.' I shuddered. 'What about the baby?'

'I got her into a parenting program. Social worker comes by each week and so do I. She's really improved.'

Her voice grew tentative and almost trailed off. 'I'd like to adopt the baby if she'd let me.'

'Won't it have problems? Like developmental delays or' – I swallowed – 'fetal alcohol syndrome?'

Marisela gripped the steering wheel until her knuckles shone white. But her face looked serene. 'In that case, a loving family and early intervention are even more important.' Marisela shook her head. 'She's like a cat, you know. Whose kittens get taken away. She just gets pregnant again and hopes she can keep the next one. She's desperate for something she can love and care for.'

'She can't care for herself.'

'Of course. The times she tried, it was a disaster. But if she understood that, there wouldn't be a problem.'

'And the father?'

'She has no idea.'

'So you have brothers and sisters?'

266

'Three half-brothers. Two died in their teens from gang shootings. The one that's left, I'm trying to help.'

Marisela's lips curved down in a sad smile. 'Alfonso calls me crazy, but for my family, I'm quite sane.'

'I can see that.'

'My biological father died in prison,' she said, unwrapping a new pack of cigarettes. The cellophane crackled. 'He stabbed a guy in a bar. His father died by the knife too. And my mother's been in and out of the Big House.' She lit up, inhaled. 'It's a family tradition. Guess I'm next.'

Something in her voice put me on guard. 'Why would you be next?'

She shrugged. 'It's bred in the bone.'

'That's ridiculous. You were raised in a nurturing family that loved you.'

Marisela hunched her shoulders. 'But what if it's handed down genetically? Like an evil heirloom, down through the generations? Scientists say the brains of killers are different from normal people's.'

'Whoa,' I said. 'Maybe so, but they don't know if killers are born that way or if abuse and violence changes their brains. A scientist once told me that violence can change the biochemistry of a child's brain. But mother love can mitigate the damage. Isn't that amazing? That love can chemically alter a child's genes?'

'So mothers who hold and love their infants can't raise murderers?'

'I don't know. But it's fascinating.'

'Nature, nurture, what does it matter, if the end

267

result is a murderer?' Marisela said.

'But we have choice. Free will.'

She shot me a sideways glance. 'Less than you'd think.'

'What about all the people with shitty childhoods who don't become murderers? Who get raped and beaten and still grow into decent human beings?'

'They deserve medals.'

'I'm trying to be serious,' I said.

'So am I. Scientists should study my brain.'

I gave her a canny look. 'What would it show?'

She looked glum. 'A mess.'

'But a murderer?' Keeping it light. Insouciant. But waiting avidly for the answer.

'Maybe on my bad days.'

'Are you trying to tell me something?'

She laughed and stubbed out her cigarette, already reaching for another. 'I didn't kill Catarina, if that's what you mean. I grew up in a loving, nurturing family, remember?'

'Touché.'

We drove in silence, sandwiched between tractor-trailers that groaned and rattled with their full loads, heading for the warehouses that ringed downtown.

'I can't believe he stole your story,' I said.

Marisela shrugged. 'That's what he's like. A vampire, sucking everybody dry. I told you that first day, when you drove me home.'

'It isn't right.'

'He calls it transubstantiation. Turning the ugly reality of life into art. And he's the high priest. Honestly, I see his plays up there on the stage, and sometimes I don't know which is real. He says there's more truth in them than in our lives. Maybe that's the reality and our life here is the illusion. Who knows? At times I think he married me just to have someone crazier around. Alfonso isn't well. He just hides it better than me.'

'What do you mean?'

'Well, his temper, for one.'

My antenna quivered. I had caught a glimpse of those volcanic depths earlier. But I had attributed it to his sorrow over Catarina.

'He seems like the calm one to me,' I goaded her.

She chewed at her lower lip.

'He broke my arm once.'

She held it out, pliant and smooth, heavy with silver bangles, a testament only to its own loveliness. The swine, I thought, hiding behind the mask of the sensitive artiste.

'He thought I was flirting with one of the actors.'

I recalled Victoria Givens saying that Alfonso was not what he seemed. At the time, I had put it down to professional jealousy.

'Did you call the police?' Even though I already knew she hadn't. The cops would be mighty interested to learn his history of domestic violence. Was this what Silvio was hiding?

'He begged me not to. Fell to his knees. Sobbed and said it would never happen again.'

'And has it?'

She exhaled loudly. 'I'd be lying if I said yes.'

'So he just ... stopped?' Finding it hard to believe.

'Oh, he's pushed me around once or twice.'

'As in down the stairs? Against the wall? What?'

'Shoved, I should have said.' Her voice filled with concern. 'But I deserved it. I said terrible things.'

I snorted. 'Textbook response. Nobody deserves it.'

'He's so tightly wound. Deep inside, he's still that little boy in the hood, terrified he'll never get out. It's not his fault.'

'Marisela, stop making excuses. He's abusive.'

'He says I knew how he was when we married. But I told him if he ever hit me again, I'd take Maggie and leave. That scared him. It's important for him to keep up appearances.'

'And just like that, it stopped?'

She slumped down in the seat. 'Now he just breaks things.'

'What was your relationship with Catarina?' I asked.

She gave me a sharp look. 'What, am I under suspicion now?'

'Of course not.' *Well, maybe not.*

'It was ... frosty.'

'When did you see her last?'

'Two weeks ago. At the theater. I've already told all this to the police.' She gave an elaborate yawn. 'They had started up again, you know. He saw her all the time.'

I played dumb. 'The lead actress in his plays, of course he did.'

'Don't be thick, Eve. The lead actress in his bed.'

'How did you know?'

'He had rehearsal one night and said he'd be home late. So I drove past her house. His car was there.'

She looked at me triumphantly. 'Maybe I'd make a good reporter. Or a cop. I have hunches too.'

Or a good murderer, I thought. Hell hath no fury, after all.

'Sure he wasn't there to discuss the finer points of her role?'

'At midnight?' She gave a hyena laugh.

'It must have been tough for you.'

'It would have been, even a few months ago, but not since...'

'Not since what?'

'Since I got on with my own life. Besides, it wouldn't have lasted. Right before she died, I heard she was leaving him. For good this time. Maybe he couldn't accept that. He's a control freak. And she was the one thing he couldn't control.'

'Does he control you?'

'Ah, that's different. Me, he doesn't love.'

'What exactly do you know, Marisela?'

She ticked off a list on her fingers. 'So you take the pressure from the drama world. His mistress dropping him. His wife about to' – she paused– 'put her life in order.'

'That is not what you were going to say.'

Her eyes were coy. 'Of course it was.'

'You're leaving him too?'

She twisted a strand of hair.

'That's our business and no one else's.'

'I know you have a lover.'

271

'Don't be ridiculous. Did Alfonso tell you that? As if he has any right, that adulterer.'

'I saw him. That house overlooking the freeway. I followed you the other day, after I dropped you off at home.'

She licked her bottom lip again and I saw that it was red and swollen.

'You've got it all wrong.'

'Do I?'

'That part.'

'But you *are* leaving Alfonso. Does he know?'

She paused. Considered. I got the feeling she was dying to tell someone. 'I'm waiting for the right moment to break the news.'

We were quiet, then. My thoughts raced. What did it all mean? I wish I could have seen the whole picture. I never would have let her go so easily.

Then we were pulling into the parking lot of the Mark Taper Forum. Marisela dropped me at my car and zoomed off. I searched for my keys. A car went by, tires squealing on the smooth concrete. Automatically, I stepped back, almost tripping. Then with a screech of brakes, the car stopped and reversed, coming straight toward me.

CHAPTER 39

I scrambled up onto my car and crouched there like some disheveled hood ornament, heart racing. The car skidded to a stop. The tinted window came down. I found myself staring at Alfonso.

'What in the hell is going on?' a familiar voice called, and Silvio leaned over his friend, his haggard face lighting up as he saw me.

Between the gallops of my heart, I gasped, so relieved that the cops had let him go.

'Thank God,' I said. 'So you're clear? I was so worried.'

Alfonso stared straight ahead, his fingers flexing on the black leather mesh of the steering wheel.

'C'mon, Silvio, let's get going,' he said.

'Not so fast,' Silvio replied, and I heard a door slam. Then he was beside me, helping me down.

He held me for a long minute.

'Of course they let me go,' he whispered. 'Alfonso just picked me up.'

'Why didn't you call?' My hands plucked at his shirt.

'I was about to. I just got off with my father.'

His arms tightened, enveloping me.

'What's wrong with you? Did you actually think we'd run you over?'

I clutched him, felt the steel of his body against mine. I thought my trembling legs might give way.

'No, of course not.' I focused on the linen weave of his shirt. 'Just jumpy, I guess. You were never a real suspect, were you?'

He shook his head. 'It sure felt that way, though. They asked the same question ten different ways. Then someone else grilled me. It was impossible to sleep. They wanted it that way. Wear you down. Disorient you. And all the while, the lawyer's screaming bloody hell about lawsuits and false imprisonment. Hey, hey, *querida*, you're shaking.'

I rubbed my cheek against his shirt.

'Too much coffee, I guess. It's been a long twenty-four hours for me, too. And I was waiting for you to call...'

'I was about to.' He grinned. 'But homeboy over there needed some calming down.'

'Silvio,' I said, shooting a meaningful glance at Alfonso, 'I've learned some things.'

'Good. You can brief us both.'

It was more of a command than an invitation. And so for the second time, I found myself hurtling into the night with people who seemed to know more about this murder than they let on. What made it so spooky was that these weren't strangers but people I knew and, in Silvio's case, loved. They were bound up in Catarina's murder, by ties of sex and jealousy, in ways that I had yet to unravel. Somewhere, buried deep among these relationships, lay the key. Because the more I learned, the more I believed Catarina had been murdered by someone who knew her intimately.

CHAPTER 40

We drove to a graceless hotel on Figueroa and Eighth Avenue that I had passed a thousand times without really noticing. Like so many downtown, it might once have been grand, but not in anyone's living memory.

'Why are we here?' I asked, as Alfonso pulled into a narrow alley behind the hotel. My hackles went up. My mouth felt dry, my fingers twitchy as they groped for the metal door handle, more out of reflex, I told myself, than fear.

Silvio turned and gave me an enigmatic smile that I found unsettling.

'You'll see.'

He held the car door open, took my arm, and shepherded me around oily puddles and a Dumpster lashed shut with thick chains. The smell of decaying trash hit my nostrils and I thought I might be sick. Then we were walking past a clump of cactus, along a bougainvillea-covered wall, and up to an iron door where a handlettered ceramic sign announced *Hotel Figueroa*.

'C'mon,' Alfonso said.

He pulled open the door and we stepped inside, my senses on red alert. I don't know what I expected to find, but it wasn't a riotous jungle of greenery, a tiled pool, and wrought iron tables lit by candles and latticework lanterns. I heard the slow drip of water, glimpsed azure depths lit by underwater lights. At the pool's far end I saw brocaded pillows and carpets, a bower out of the *Arabian Nights,* fit for Scheherazade. I half expected to see Paul Bowles sitting cross-legged on a carpet, puffing a narghile.

We walked along a path lined with tall urns, cactus, and fronded plants, into a dimly lit bar. A couple perched on rattan stools, drinking something overflowing with mint leaves. I gripped the dark, oiled wood of the bar and willed myself to relax. The plaster walls were splashed with yellow and ocher and blue paint, and inlaid with tiles. The room was lit by ornamental iron chandeliers and glass lamps placed atop wooden chests. Everything was antique, beautiful, lovingly restored. In the midst of the parched outskirts of downtown, I had stumbled onto an oasis.

A thought pulsed through my overloaded brain: I ought to call Felice and see how she was doing. It had been a few hours. But then Silvio handed me a drink.

'Eve's been digging around,' he told Alfonso. He turned to me. 'Why don't you tell us what you've found.'

Alfonso sipped his drink, then placed the glass carefully on the coaster, fixing his eyes somewhere above me. 'I would like to speak first, if I may.'

He looked at Silvio, who nodded.

'When I was fourteen,' Alfonso began, 'I was standing on the corner with a friend when a car came by, spraying bullets. My friend was killed. I got a permanent part seared into my scalp and a shattered kneecap.'

I looked at Silvio, then at Alfonso. What was this all about? Silvio made an almost imperceptible hand motion that said, Let him finish.

'When I got home from the hospital, my *abuelo* pushed me hard into a chair and told me I had cheated death. He spoke in his usual quiet way, but his words were clenched with fury. "You shouldn't be alive, *m'hijo*," he said, "but God in his wisdom has given you a second chance. You have to earn this new life. Starting today."'

Alfonso gulped loudly at his drink.

'It's like yesterday, you know? My grandfather's tears, my friend lying on the sidewalk, blood leaking out of his head. My shame at having survived.

'It should have been me on that sidewalk, see. I had joined the Vatos Locos; they had jumped me in the week before. My friend who died? He was an A student. Wrote poetry and shit. Even won some award. We wouldn't have been friends much longer. I can't remember why we were even together that day. But we were, and along came Eighteenth Street, and they recognized me. And my friend took the bullet meant for me. So I owed him. Because he wasn't alive anymore and I was. And that day, I promised myself I'd make it up to him. To all of them. That's when I started telling their stories.'

Alfonso looked at us, but I knew he was far away, still on that sidewalk. In many ways, he always would be.

'Do you know the intensity that grips a kid at that age when he decides to do something? The purity of it, the ruthlessness?'

Alfonso lifted his glass and squinted, seeking enlightenment in its murky depths.

'Do you understand what I've spent my life becoming? And how I allowed nothing, but absolutely nothing, to derail me? And now to be hit with this. At the moment of my greatest triumph, I face an apocalypse.'

'What do you mean?' I said. Was this the real Alfonso talking, or an elaborate character?

'I am the envy of every playwright who ever was,' Alfonso said, and his voice rang hollow and mirthless. 'I have a runaway hit on my hands, and audiences have the spectacle of a lifetime. People who have never entered a theater before – at least one that doesn't serve popcorn – who don't know a one-act from an entr'acte, are flocking. They come for the stench of scandal. For the frisson of knowing the actress they were meant to see is dead, her killer still at large. Perhaps they hope to see Catarina herself, drifting onstage like Hamlet's father, wailing and bleeding and hungering for revenge. They salivate like dogs. Maybe I'll break down as I take my bow. Or sink to the floor in grief and bash my head against the boards. Or better yet,' Alfonso said, eyes glinting, 'confess my crime as the full house draws a collective breath of horror, then fall on my sword. The lust of blood is upon them. I can sense it, smell it. And why not end it? She's gone, and I will never write again.'

He put his head in his hands, and his hair fell like a curtain, obscuring his face. His fingers raked through it, pulling it back, stretching the skin taut against his skull.

'Carrion birds,' he said. 'They will devour me and peck my heart out. And I will be laid bare upon the rocks for eternity.'

'For God's sake, Alfonso, cut the dramatic soliloquy and get a grip,' Silvio said, shaking his friend's shoulders. 'You're headed for a nervous breakdown.'

Alfonso looked up.

'Is my dear wife the only one entitled to such lapses?'

'You'd better not let the cops hear you babbling like that,' Silvio said. 'They'll think you killed her.'

Alfonso addressed the ceiling.

'In many ways, I did. Years ago. Killed her spontaneity, her youth, her enthusiasm. By demanding that she consecrate herself to me and my art. She was my most glorious creation.'

'Stop talking about her like some puppet on a stage,' I said, irritated by his superiority. Then more coldly, because of what I had learned today, 'You didn't create her or control her. She was a flesh-and-blood woman. She made her own decisions. And sometimes they didn't include you.'

'This is not helpful,' Silvio said, as his friend shot me a baleful look.

'Do you know who came backstage last night?' Alfonso asked Silvio. He snorted. 'That producer. Weaseling and glad-handing around. Offered to buy the rights to *Our Lady of the Barrio* for six figures. Pulled out a contract and wanted me to sign right there in the dressing rooms.'

I grew very still and examined my nails.

'Not the—' said Silvio.

'Yeah, homes, *Pinche* Mancuso. That slime. I had Cesar's boys throw him out on his ass. The gall.'

Now I concentrated on the interesting floral patterns of the tile floor.

'Who's Mancuso?' I said.

Alfonso looked at me like I was an insect that needed exterminating.

'Some Hollywood guy. I met him backstage when *Borders of the Heart* came out. He thought the time was right for a big-budget movie about Latinos, to be carried by Latino actors. He introduced me to all his West Side pals. They became some of my biggest supporters. And sources of raw material.'

I pictured Alfonso in Bel Air mansions, drumming up support for his projects as uniformed Latina maids spooned lamb vindaloo onto hand-fired Japanese plates.

'Tell her about the bed,' Silvio said.

'Oh yeah,' Alfonso said. 'This Brentwood couple was really upset to learn that their housekeeper's fifteen-year-old daughter slept on the floor because the family couldn't afford a bed. So they bought one and drove it over. Some homeboys helped them carry it in.'

'And that night while her parents were at work,' Silvio said, 'the daughter broke in the bed with one of the delivery boys. Six weeks later, she's knocked up. They're Catholic so abortion's out. The Brentwood do-gooders are left wringing their hands at good intentions gone awry. It was a great scene. He put it in *Riding Shotgun with Jesus.*'

280

'I'm surprised they still want to fund your plays,' I said.

'Are you kidding?' Alfonso said. 'It's cheap penance.'

'But you and Mancuso fell out?'

'There was a long honeymoon period,' Alfonso said, loosening up a little. 'We did a deal and he insisted I write the screenplay at his place in Malibu. But I got up there and couldn't write a thing. Ended up drinking beers with the gardeners. Finally I sat down with some crystal for a long weekend and powered through a draft. He loved it. Couldn't say enough good things. My back was sore, he was slapping it so much.'

Alfonso stared moodily out into the night.

'So did it get made?' I asked.

'He showed it to his money men and they wanted some changes. So I made them. Then he wanted more changes. I made those. Then more. Each time it was like he was chipping off part of my heart. But the money kept flowing. It's seductive. You get to depend on it. Then Mancuso tells me he's hired a veteran screenwriter, a pair of them, to do a quick polish.'

'Nothing major,' Silvio said dryly.

'The pair turns into six,' Alfonso continued. 'Then a dozen. All taking their whack. But still I didn't worry. Because Mancuso was my buddy, *mi compadre,* and he got it. He was loyal to the *art* of it. He was committed to the Latino movie. This would be my "coming out." Like a debutante ball. It would open the floodgates to the Latino market. Finally we'd see people who looked like us on the screen.'

'Uh-huh,' Silvio said.

'Then, while I was in New York, getting ready for the off-Broadway run of *Riding Shotgun with Jesus*, I heard that the lead role went to that famous Latina Michelle Pfeiffer. Michelle fucking Pfeiffer. Oh, and they hoped I didn't mind, but they had changed the setting from East L.A. to Santa Monica. I couldn't believe it. After almost two years, my *mano-a-mano* pal, my blood brother, my fine Hollywood friend, had fucked me up the ass.'

'I couldn't believe he didn't see it coming,' Silvio said.

'I thought I had a bad run with that TV pilot' – he shook his head– 'but it was nothing compared to the movies. TV pays well but you sell your soul. The movies? You sell future generations.'

'Catarina warned him,' Silvio said, as Alfonso nodded. 'She would never be suckered in like that by Hollywood. She hated artifice of any kind.'

Little do you boys know, I thought.

'The only good thing,' Silvio said, 'is that the movie tanked, big-time.'

'And Hollywood just uses that as proof that the world is not ready for a Latino film,' Alfonso added. 'Why are you so interested in this guy?'

'Yeah, Eve, tell us what you found out today. Alfonso's been doing all the talking.'

But suddenly, I was cautious. I didn't trust Alfonso. I wanted to tell Silvio later. Alone.

'I talked to Catarina's neighbors and her drama teacher.' I shrugged. 'They gave me some background.'

Alfonso grew agitated. 'That witch Victoria? She's psycho. Don't believe anything she says. It's a pack of lies.'

'Oh?'

'She tried to get Catarina under her thumb. Thought she knew best. She's always hated me and she's grown increasingly upset about her waning power over Catarina.'

Gee, Victoria only had nice things to say about you, too.

'She always struck me as a harmless eccentric who was just a little too enamored of her star pupil,' Silvio said peaceably.

'That's because you didn't know her like I did,' Alfonso said, growing more agitated. 'I told Catarina to cut it off with her, that pathetic excuse for a friendship. But she refused. She felt sorry for her old teacher. But this is exactly what I'm talking about. Eve shouldn't go meddling. Let's leave it to the police.'

'They don't tell us anything,' Silvio said. 'Don't you want to find who killed her?'

Alfonso brought his glass down so hard it almost shattered. 'I want to find him and strangle him with my bare hands.'

'This isn't one of your plays, you crazy *vato*,' Silvio said. 'It's real life. And the cops have lots of murders to solve. Eve can *help* you. But you're going to have to lay it on the line.'

'Lay what on the line?' I asked, intrigued.

'You are the crazy one,' Alfonso said. 'The cops are crawling all over this case.'

'Then why haven't they solved it yet?' Silvio asked.

'Because no one will talk straight with them.' Alfonso shrugged.

'Exactly my point. But you can be straight with Eve.'

Alfonso surveyed me coldly. 'Are you kidding? She's a reporter. She'll run to the paper first chance she gets.'

'No, I won't,' I found myself saying. 'They don't want me near it. The only way I'll write it is with your okay.'

I was going to add that he had my word, but I bit my tongue. Could I really promise that?

Alfonso took a long drink, put down his glass. 'No,' he said.

'You're making a mistake,' Silvio said. He stood, stretched his legs, said he'd be right back.

Alfonso and I watched him go, uneasy without the buffer of his presence.

I turned back to my drink and took a careful sip. I smoothed out my napkin and tried to think of something to say. Alfonso's silence grew moodier by the second. Then he tapped me on the hand, three short, hard jabs. Startled, I looked up. His face was not beautiful at all right now, or tragic. It was simply menacing. Marisela's words about his temper came floating back.

'I'm warning you,' he said. He slid off his stool and stood so close that I could smell his citrusy cologne mingling with the heat of his body. 'No slinking around, asking people questions, digging up dirt. *Comprende?*'

CHAPTER 41

Alfonso swayed, then grabbed at the table to steady himself. Instead his fingers landed on my wrist. His grip tightened, squeezing until it hurt. And in those seconds, a lot of ideas went through my head. I knew he was a playwright who wrestled with issues of life and death, lauded by critics and lavished with awards for giving us insight into the Latin Street. An artist who wrote dramatic soliloquies for the stage and might sometimes confuse them with what was appropriate in real life. On top of that, he was a longtime friend of Silvio's. None of it made me feel much better about what might happen next.

'Get your hands off me,' I said.

I tugged my arm but he held on tight. Craning my neck, I looked in vain for Silvio.

'Did you hear me?' Alfonso said thickly, shaking my wrist.

I focused on the rhythm. The next time he pulled my wrist toward him, I followed through, socking him under the jaw with our combined hands. Then I hooked one leg around his and jerked him toward me, pulling his weight out from under him. I doubt it would have worked if he had been expecting it. Or if he had been sober. But the evening had finally caught up with him. He lay sprawled on the floor beneath the table.

'Barrio this, Mr. Esteemed Playwright. Next

time you touch me, I'll call the police. Unlike your wife and your dead mistress, I'm not cutting you any slack. And if you don't like it, go home and write a play.'

I took off through the dimly lit hotel, searching for Silvio. Turning a corner, I almost collided with him. A lazy Moroccan oud played somewhere nearby.

'What's going on?'

My heel caught in the valley between the saltillo tiles and I tripped. He reached out, trying to steady me as I slammed into him.

'Alfonso just–' I began, but he whispered, 'Don't worry, he'll wait,' and put his lips over mine, and they were soft and warm and yielding and I stopped, my breath coming too quick for words anyway. The adrenaline rush of fear and anger pumping through me surged, transforming into something else.

'I was so worried about you,' I said into his ear, inhaling the scent of him, musky sage along a sunbaked road where car tires kick up dust. I licked his skin and felt him shudder. He pulled me toward him, and I felt him rise against me.

He glanced over his shoulder and we saw a brocade curtain hanging over an arched doorway. He tugged me backward, through the doorway, the curtain whispering against our faces, and we found ourselves in an anteroom. Flickering candles gave off shadows that danced against the walls.

'In here,' he said, maneuvering me toward a wooden door that said *Ladies*.

'Silvio, what...?'

'Shhh.'

He closed the door behind us and locked it. I saw a carved wooden chair and a long tile counter with an azure sink. Behind it hung a huge mirror framed in filigreed iron. Hidden hands plucked at the strings of the oud, making a reverberation that started in my lower belly and radiated outward until I felt dizzy. Silvio put his hands under my bottom, gathered me up, and placed me on the counter.

'What if someone needs to get in?'

He leaned me against the mirror.

'They'll wait,' he murmured, unbuttoning my blouse and pulling up my bra. He nuzzled my breasts and hiked up my skirt. The shadows from the iron lanterns danced against the corners of the room. A fever was upon me. I reached for his zipper but it was already undone.

He tilted me back and pulled aside the crotch of my panties, thrusting into me. I shivered and wrapped my legs around him, and he cradled my buttocks and pulled me back and forth in a delicious rhythm, the warmth and wet and excitement growing until I thought I would scream. I tore open his shirt, biting back my cries with his flesh. His breath came faster and then he shuddered and was still.

For a long moment we leaned against each other, catching our breath. Then he turned and zipped up his pants and I slid off the counter, tugged down my skirt, and patted back my hair. The warm yellow light enveloped us, the mirror reflecting a disheveled young woman flushed with surprise and secret pleasure. I saw Silvio come up behind me, gather my hair in his hands, and nuzzle my nape with dreamy concentration.

'We better get out of here,' he said, his breath hot on my neck. I reached behind me, encircling his waist. 'All of a sudden you're worried about keeping your friend waiting?'

'Yes.' Silvio grabbed my hand and opened the door.

A young woman stood on the other side. She gave us a disapproving look as we slipped past her and back into the lobby.

I rubbed my wrist and considered how to tell Silvio what Alfonso had done. But when we got back to the bar, the playwright was gone, a twenty-dollar bill tucked beneath his empty drink.

Silvio looked around.

'We were only gone' – he looked at his watch– 'a few minutes.'

'I think your friend had too much to drink,' I said finally.

'Poor Alfonso, these emotions have over-whelmed him,' Silvio said. 'He's under incredible pressure.'

I lifted my wineglass, then reconsidered and went for the water. After a big, thirst-quenching gulp, I said, 'Silvio, just how well do you know Alfonso Reventon?'

CHAPTER 42

Silvio's leg danced with agitation.

'He didn't do it, Eve. I would swear it on my life.'

'Maybe so, but he just grabbed my arm while you were in the bathroom and threatened me if I investigated this any further. That's why I went chasing after you back there.'

Alarm flared in his eyes. He gave me a searching look.

'I must apologize for his behavior,' Silvio said finally. 'He's distraught. He feels guilty his play is doing so well in the light of this horrible—'

I leaned forward. 'You don't understand, Silvio. He roughed me up. Your supposed good friend,' I enunciated carefully. 'And you still haven't answered my question.'

Silvio sighed. 'We went to high school together. We were like brothers.'

'But since high school. How close have you been?'

'We're best friends,' he insisted, but it was starting to sound thin.

'I appreciate your loyalty. But I thought he was on the East Coast for a while.'

'When we see each other, time melts away.'

'But in those intervals, people can change.'

Silvio shook his head. 'I've known him for more than twenty years, and I've never heard that story about the shooting until today.'

'That's what I'm saying.'

'He's a very private person. We both are. There are things that wouldn't come up.'

I fixed him with a stern look. 'Like how he broke Marisela's arm, maybe?'

'What?'

'She told me today.'

'That was a mistake,' he said under his breath.

'What? Him breaking her arm or her telling me?'

'I mean it was an accident,' Silvio said. He looked steadily at me, willing both of us to believe.

I gave it right back. 'She says he flies into rages.'

'I've never seen that side of him.' Silvio rocked on his stool.

'You've never crossed him.'

'I'm his friend. Why should I? I'm there to support him.'

It told me a lot about their relationship. Of Silvio's pride in his friend, his need to believe in Alfonso and everything his success stood for. I began to understand how Silvio might turn a blind eye to things about Alfonso that he didn't want to see.

'If he could get angry enough to strike his wife, could he get jealous enough to kill his mistress if she left him for someone new?'

'What?' Silvio's stool came down with a crash.

'Three people have told me that now. That she had a new lover.'

I recounted my talk with Victoria, the interviews with Barry Mancuso and Steve Herrera, the visit to Marisela's birth mother. As I spoke, Silvio's mouth took on a rigid cast. He propped his chin on his hand.

'There's something I haven't told you. But it's all going to come out soon.'

I pushed my drink aside and looked squarely at him. 'This story is like an onion,' I said. 'Every time we talk about it, you peel off another layer and I want to cry.'

'Do you want to hear it or not?'

'Of course.' I crossed my arms and buttoned my lip.

'You know how the cops took DNA samples? From me and Alfonso?'

'Yes.'

'Well, they're going to find matches in the apartment.'

'Of course they are. You already told me. Fingerprints. Mine too, probably. We were there, remember?'

'Not that.'

'What?'

Silvio sighed, as if he were announcing a death warrant. 'Eve, the police are going to make a significant DNA match.'

I almost couldn't breathe.

'Is it ... your blood on the windowsill? The pillows?'

'No.'

'What then?'

'Semen.'

There was a loud roaring in my ears, like a tidal wave crashing down, sweeping away everything I knew and held dear.

'They found your semen at the apartment? But how can that–'

'They're going to find Alfonso's semen on the bed.'

'What?'

'He had been there that morning. With her.' Silvio gave a sad, twisted smile. 'So you see how it doesn't look good for him.'

'He killed her, didn't he? And you've been covering for him. That's why you've been so goddamn secretive and weird.' I clenched my fists and fought back tears.

'Will you stop jumping to conclusions?'

'The cops are going to jump to the exact same conclusion.'

'Hear me out, Eve.'

I wondered what could possibly come next.

'So they had sex that morning. Then they fought. Alfonso stormed out without his wedding band.'

'Why did he take it off?'

'She wouldn't sleep with him when he was wearing it.'

'So he took it off, then forgot it. What an idiot.'

Silvio pressed his lips together in disapproval, but I wasn't sure if it was at me or his friend's carelessness. Then he continued.

'He thought it would set her off if he went back. But he was afraid she'd flush it down the toilet if he didn't. And then Marisela would wonder. He asked me to go by and pick it up.'

Silvio looked sideways at me and I glanced away, unable to meet his eyes.

'Go on,' I said.

'Catarina was crying when I got there. We sat and drank tea and then I took the ring and left. The mugs were still on the table when the police got there and started tagging everything. One of them is sure to have my saliva on it. But that's not all. I sneezed into a tissue that morning. I remember balling it up and throwing it into her trash can.'

'Your cat allergies,' I said, remembering his violent reaction when Catarina's beast darted out of the bungalow.

'They're going to find that. And then it's not going to go so good for me either.'

I tried to think like a cop. They had done her in together, these two old friends, or maybe Alfonso had killed her in a fit of rage, then called Silvio to help dispose of the body. I remembered the moto rider that Felice had interviewed up on Angeles Crest, the story about the two men with dark hair who had hauled a large bag out of a trunk. And I knew that no matter what angle I considered it from, things looked bad.

'You can see why I've called in the lawyer can't you, Eve?'

My lover sat, shoulders hunched, making patterns with the change that the waitress had left on the table. I couldn't believe that just ten minutes ago, we had been making frenzied love in the bathroom. I was furious at him for all the lies. But to my great surprise, another strange and protective fury was also welling up inside me.

'We have to find the real killer,' I said. 'Before the DNA evidence comes back. That's the only way.'

'Should be a snap,' Silvio said, pushing around a quarter.

'But first I need to know' – I put my hand to his face– 'is this finally the whole story? All there is?'

Silvio's eyes bored into mine.

'That's all of it.'

I held his gaze but he didn't look away. Finally, I broke it off. I was so weary.

I looked at my watch. It was 12:30.

'So what are you going to do?' Silvio asked.

'Right now? Go home and get some sleep.'

I paused, then threw down the gauntlet. 'You joining me?'

I meant it as a challenge. *Are we in on this together or not?* But Silvio said he needed a shower and change of clothes after his night in jail, and I didn't insist. Later, I would regret my decision. Things might have turned out differently.

CHAPTER 43

There was a message from Marisela on my machine when I got home.

'Hi, Eve, hope I'm not disturbing you. I wasn't quite straight with you tonight.'

Big pause. Then a *glug-glug* sound.

'There's something else I should tell you. In person, I mean. It's too complicated over the phone. I'm going to sleep now, but call me in the morning.'

I played it back five times, parsing each word.

What new secret would Marisela unveil now? I checked my watch: 1 a.m. I was itching to call and wheedle it out of her. But waking her up might piss her off so much she'd never tell me.

I showered off the day's sweat, brushed my teeth, and climbed into bed. I felt jumpy, unmoored. A thousand tiny fish of anxiety nibbled at my flesh.

The phone rang.

'Hi, Eve,' a familiar female voice said.

Oh no. Amid the evening's tumult, I had forgotten all about her. But then she spoke again. 'It's Jayson.'

'What is that supposed to mean? Knock that shit off, Felice. You should have called me ages ago. Where are you? Is everything okay with–?'

'Jayson Blair,' she interrupted. 'I'm sorry about earlier. I lost track of the time.'

What the hell? Her smooth-as-butter voice didn't fit with this weird role-playing thing she was doing. Why would Felice ever associate herself with Jayson Blair? I thought back to our conversations about the disgraced *New York Times* reporter. What had she said about him? That he had set minorities in newsrooms back a decade. That he had tarred and feathered all of them. That *The New York Times* was equally at fault for being so blind. Was this no-nonsense Felice's idea of a joke? I was not in the mood.

'Felice, what's with the Jayson bit? It's late. I'm tired.'

She ignored me. 'I got some good stuff, Eve.'

'So you're not going to answer me? If you're calling yourself Jayson because you're afraid I won't believe you, you can rest easy. I'm all ears. What did you find? Did anyone recognize Catarina's picture?'

She was creeping me out. Disappearing for half the night, then calling to whisper strange things in my ear. I got the feeling she might be trying to set me up. But for what?

'At La Serenata,' Felice said. 'But that's not all.'

The restaurant in East Los Angeles that had shown up on Catarina's last credit card bill. Where Silvio and I had gone.

'Are you okay? You sound really weird.'

There was a strange dislocation between her voice and her words. Knowing Felice, she should have been crowing with glee. Instead, her tone was measured, flat. Maybe she didn't want to be overheard. I strained to catch background noises but heard nothing.

'I'm just fine. But you'll never guess who pulled into the parking lot as I was leaving.'

'Who?'

'Your boyfriend.'

I pulled the phone away from my ear for a moment in disbelief. First calling herself Jayson, now saying she had just seen Silvio? This was some kind of mind game. How could I believe anything this smooth liar said?

'That's impossible, Felice. I was with him until an hour ago.'

'This was earlier. Right after we left the office.'

A dull thudding started up in the pit of my belly. I thought Silvio had been at Parker Center until ten with Alfonso. Had they lied to me? Or was Felice lying now? I stood up, and the blood rushed to my head. Then I was across the room, looking out the window at the colorful circuit board that was the downtown L.A. skyline with no idea how I had gotten there.

'How do you even know what Silvio looks like?'

'I had the library e-mail me his photo along with Alfonso's and Barry Mancuso's. Just as a precaution. You taught me that, Eve. Be skeptical of everyone. Came in handy tonight.'

'You don't need to be skeptical of Silvio.'

'It's funny,' Felice said, her words coming out elongated, like she was speaking through a smile. 'Turns out you did a story on his family's business a while back, that's why they had the pic on file. I'm confused, though, because I thought you weren't supposed to sleep with sources. Maybe you can explain the ethics of that. 'Cause I know you're big on ethics. You lectured me about that, remember?'

'That was a coincidence,' I said stiffly.

Was this some kind of big payback Felice had cooked up? A way to sabotage me? My mind churned with possible scenarios.

'Oh.' A throaty laugh. 'Well then, that's okay. I've had a few of those myself.'

Ripples of irritation heightened my anxiety. It was late and I was emotionally drained, and there was something here that I was not catching at all.

'Will you please get to the point?'

'Sure. I followed him. You'll never guess where he went.'

'Where?'

'A motel off Interstate 10. And Marisela's car was in the lot.'

Her voice was casual, like we were playing some kind of game.

'How do you know what kind of car she drives?'

'I had DMV run her plates. Alfonso's too.'

'It's after midnight, Felice. DMV is closed.'

'I did it yesterday.'

'You what?'

She gave an exasperated sigh. 'Why do you persist in thinking you're the only one working this case?'

'You're not stealing this story from me, I'm warning you.'

'*Au contraire,* Eve. I'm sharing it with you. That's why I called. Anyway, Silvio left for a while. But now he's back. Come see for yourself.'

She gave me the address, her voice gliding over the words like a skater on newly groomed ice. I felt my blood pressure rise.

A new fear rose, a pairing I hadn't foreseen and found hard to imagine. Silvio and Marisela? Had Felice found them in bed together? Or could she mean something worse? I pictured their bodies sprawled lifeless on the ground. But no, I had just seen him, made love to him. How could he be with her?

'Why should I?'

'You'll see.' Smug and self-contained.

'Why can't you tell me over the phone? Why do I need to go out there?'

'It's a professional courtesy. You should know what's coming down the pike before I write the story.'

A red ball of anger burst inside me. 'Whatever's happened out there, it's going under a double

298

byline. And only after I vet it. People's lives, their reputations, are at stake.'

From the other end of the phone came a low chuckle. 'Oh, I see. Unlike stories where you don't know the perps so it doesn't matter whose life you ruin?'

She was lobbing grenade after grenade, and they were detonating where I lived. I searched for the right biting words but they didn't come.

'I'm waiting for you,' she said. Then the line went dead.

I hurled the phone against the wall. It hit like a projectile, chipping the plaster and clattering in pieces onto the hardwood floor. I ran to it, crouching as I tried to put it back together. Now what had I done?

Felice's baiting infuriated me. At that moment, I hated her. Who did she think she was? And why should I go out there, when she was so clearly lying? I remembered her boasting about how she had tricked the *Washington Post* bureau chief to get the Baby Doc story into print. I had seen her in action at Barry Mancuso's this afternoon. And what about her background – the many things that didn't track? None of her bullshit made sense.

Côte d'Ivoire. Only because I've been there.

Trained with the Finnish biathlon team one winter outside Helsinki.

She was only twenty-three. She could not possibly have packed that much into one short life. Could she? Maybe Felice and her jet-set moneyed friends crisscrossed the globe as easily as I traversed the Valley.

But no, it had rung false then and it rang false now. She was lying. But why? The only thing I could be sure of was that whatever went down tonight, Felice would rig it to come out in her favor. She'd cast herself as the star. It was probably a big con, just like her scoop about the moto rider, unidentified to this day. My initial doubt about that story had reared up again after Catarina's body had turned up miles away at Point Fermin, but I hadn't wanted to think her truly capable of fabricating a story. I didn't want to be a racist. She turned my instincts against me. Jayson Blair indeed. That bitch.

Propelled by anger, I threw on some clothes and stalked back into the night.

The motel where Felice waited – El Dorado – had been built about fifty years ago to look like a ranch with rooms arrayed as a horseshoe. A twenty-foot cowboy towered over the buildings, tossing a neon lasso. Tourists from Iowa and Ohio had stayed here once on their way to Disneyland. Now the tenants were sad-faced Mexican families and poor white trash, and for them El Dorado was a destination, not a one-night stopover.

There were a few cars near the motel office, but Silvio's truck and Marisela's Audi were not among them. There was more parking in back. I swung through the lot and saw Felice's BMW at the far end. She had backed it up to the chain-link fence that separated the motel from the freeway. As the cars whizzed past on I-10, their headlights cascaded over the Beemer like the aurora borealis, illuminating a dark figure within.

I parked next to Felice and got out. The motel squatted in the shadows fifty feet away, the lasso flickering above us. The giant cowboy looming above felt almost menacing. I wondered why Felice didn't come out.

Just then, the window whizzed down and her head popped out. 'Here I am, it's me, Jayson.' She gave a sharky smile. 'C'mon inside and let me brief you before we go up and knock.'

I was rounding my car now, approaching the canyon between our two vehicles. She must have seen the puzzled expression on my face because she said it again, with more urgency in her voice. But all I could think of was Jayson Blair. A reporter who made things up. Who couldn't be trusted. And then I knew. I felt my throat constrict.

'I forgot something in the car,' I said, gripping my keys tightly. 'I'll be right back.'

Down came the Beemer's back window, and I found myself staring into the metal nostril of a gun.

'You heard what the little lady said,' a voice said from the depths of the car. 'Get in.'

They are going to kill me if I get in that car, I thought, so I might as well die trying to escape.

'Felice,' I screamed, shoving my hand upward. My open palm connected with the metal barrel as the gun discharged above my head.

Zigging and zagging like a hare, I ran to my car as gunfire exploded in the motel lot. I threw the door open and fumbled the key into the ignition. I heard something strike the car, a dull thud as metal absorbed metal. The side window shattered, and a bullet sailed over my head on its way out. Throwing the car into gear, I floored it but forgot that in my hasty parking job a few minutes earlier, I had neglected to straighten my wheels. The car shot forward with a sickening twist, slamming into the left front end of the Beemer with a crunch of metal.

The bullets stopped. Unfortunately, so did my motor. Start, oh please start, I prayed, and it did. I jerked the car into reverse, spun the wheel around, and threw it into drive again, burning rubber out of the lot and into the darkened streets, hunching low in case the bullets started up again.

CHAPTER 44

Although I am not a religious person, I made the sign of the cross, shuddering at the thought of Felice still trapped in her car with a killer. Please forgive me for abandoning you, Felice. One of us has got to get help.

It was hard to believe I had just been shot at. I called 911 as I drove, running the possibilities through my brain. Felice had been driving around East L.A. tonight, asking pointed questions. Had she unwittingly stumbled onto Catarina's murderer? Had he panicked and taken her hostage, then used her as bait once he learned we were working on the story together? Or did he know because it was someone I had already interviewed?

302

The 911 operator patched me through to the police and I gave them the motel's address and Felice's name and the make and model of her car. By this time, I was on the freeway headed for home, but the policewoman and I realized at the same time that home might not be so sweet. She asked for my address and promised to have someone waiting by the time I got there.

Forty minutes later, I was relieved to see a flashing red light in front of my house as I pulled up. Shakily, I recounted my story to Officer Tom Lesher, who told me the police had already put out an APB for Felice's car with the LAPD, county sheriff, and California Highway Patrol. Law enforcement in surrounding counties had also been alerted.

I went to my satchel and pulled out copies of the credit card records, which we had made at the office. I told Lesher about our visit to Barry Mancuso in Malibu, feeling no guilt at naming him. Once bullets got involved, all bets were off. By the time I finished, Lesher had a car headed up to Malibu and another waking up the owner of La Serenata di Garibaldi. It was 3:04 a.m.

'Can you call in and see if they've found the car yet?' I asked, not letting myself think about what else they might find. But there was no news.

Lesher asked to see my car, so we walked outside and he shone his flashlight around, then squatted by the trunk, where there was a hole. He asked me to pop it, then looked inside, the light casting strange shadows. He motioned me closer. A bullet glittered under the bright beam.

Lesher got a plastic ziplock baggie and dropped

it inside.

I replayed the events in my head, Felice's frozen grin, the gun's muzzle raised in my direction. The thought began to prickle through me again that something was weird here. Felice wouldn't go so far as to set up a fake shooting, would she? That would mean the end of her journalism career, and maybe a trip to jail. I shook my head. It was crazy to even think this way. Felice was in danger. The cops had to find her before she showed up dead.

Clearing his throat, Lesher suggested I'd be safer staying with a friend until they caught Felice's kidnapper. And here I'd let Silvio go without so much as a *please*.

'Hurry up and pack a bag. I sure as hell don't want to get called back here tomorrow because they've found a body,' he said, lapsing into the black humor that cops and reporters use to make their work bearable.

His beeper went off. He made a quick call while I hovered, unable to move.

'I'm sorry,' he said when he got off.

My heart did a flip. 'Is there a break? Did they find her?'

'No, but someone ran over a transient in Hollywood. I've got to go.'

I bit back the urge to beg him to wait. The house already felt hollow and empty, watched by hidden eyes.

'Finish packing and go,' Lesher said, more serious now. 'I don't want you hanging around.'

I promised him I would, then turned the deadbolt after him and hooked the chain. When

I dialed Silvio, I got his machine. Unease coursed through me. Probably he had turned off his phone to sleep after being up all night with the cops. Probably. But what if Felice really had seen him earlier tonight? She was out there somewhere. A second missing woman. Kidnapped, maybe being tortured and held captive. Catarina. Felice. As in one of those logic puzzles that measure IQ, I saw the next person in the set. Me. There had to be some clue staring me in the face, one the killer figured I already knew. And that made me a liability.

I packed my toothbrush and a change of clothes. I would drive over to Silvio's house and surprise him. He had to be home. I didn't have a key.

I carried my stuff to the living room and peered out through a slit in the curtain. The front yard looked as it always did at night, lit up by the yellow beam of the halogen streetlight. There were no suspicious cars parked in front of the house. No friendly lights burning in my neighbors' homes, either. I envisioned walking the twenty paces to my car, my footsteps echoing in the still night, alerting whoever might be waiting in the bushes. I'd insert the key, turn the lock, and feel a hand on my shoulder. A whispered command. I twitched away this paranoid nightmare. No, I'd insert the key, turn the lock. Start the engine. Then pull out, free and clear. I swallowed and my throat felt dry. I nodded to my reflection in the hall mirror, gripped my bags, and walked out. My shoulders prickled as I turned to lock the door, exposing my back to the silent street. I stepped away from the porch light. The night was at its deepest, the mouth of a cave that went back forever. Blackness washed over me as I walked, the night swallowing me. Twenty steps to my car. Fourteen, thirteen, twelve, eleven. I was almost there. I was entering a pool of light, the street-lamp buzzing loudly above me. Far away a cat yowled. I stuck my key into the car door and turned it.

At the same time that I heard the welcome click, another, louder sound rattled like a steel drum. I was so wrapped up in my sinister scenario, it took me a minute to realize it was only my cell phone going off in my purse.

Now what? Did I stop to answer it, or jump into the car, lock myself in, drive off, and pick it up once I was safely on the road? What if it was someone calling to distract me? But what if it was Felice running for her life and calling to tell me where she was?

In the end, I opted for something in between. Each ring counting off precious seconds, I wrenched the car door open, slid in, slammed it shut, and locked it with my elbow while reaching for the phone.

The number on the display was not one I recognized. I hit 'talk' but heard only background noise. I strained to hear more. Sitting in my dark car, alone on my dark street, in the middle of the dark night, I listened. I didn't dare turn the engine on for fear of missing something. The rhythmic droning was unsettling. Was this some kind of a trap?

A man spoke in my ear and I jerked upright in

my seat. But his voice was far away and it rose and fell, the receiver catching only stray words.

'You thought ... smart ... lay some big trap ... I'd fall...?'

The words horrified me, playing right into my deepest fears. What trap? I wanted to say, but the words didn't come. I peered through the windshield, saw only the night pressing down. My hand trembled so much I could barely hold the receiver to my ear. I was about to speak when the voice grew jeering, its tones cruel. 'Well, now ... who's trapped?'

CHAPTER 45

I twisted in the car seat but didn't see anyone looming up behind me. My free hand crept to the key in the ignition. I wanted to turn it, to get out of there, but I didn't dare breathe. Over the ambient machine sounds came a moan, then muffled panting. My first instinct was to yell *hello, hello* but something stopped me: the sudden realization that the malevolent voice was not aimed at me. My momentary relief was spiked with a new fear. What had the city's crossed microwaves spliced me into? The taunting voice sounded slightly familiar, but I couldn't place it. With effort, I controlled my breathing, willing myself into silence.

I groped for the car door, imagined pulling the handle. Could I do it silently? A series of grunts started up, muffled and indistinct, and I jumped, knuckles hitting the door with what seemed like a loud bang. Now what?

Then I had a brilliant idea. I pressed a button on the mobile to display the incoming call again. Instantaneously, it appeared in fluorescent digital green. I stared at the numbers, willing them into a sequence I might recognize, a code that translated into someone I knew. But I came up blank. I bent my ear to the phone again. The white humming noise was back. I had to get inside my house and call the police.

Stealthily, I opened the car door and slid out, holding the phone like a crown jewel. I walked back to the front door and silently let myself in, turning the lock behind me.

Still clutching the phone, I crept to my address book, hoping a match would reveal itself.

As I turned to the *As*, I thought about my evening, about Marisela, Silvio, Felice, and Alfonso. The phone was silent now, except for the low rubber roar. The voice didn't belong to any of them, anyway. Steve Herrera? Barry Mancuso? No. Their voices lacked the high malice of this one.

Wisps of memory floated toward me.

'Get in the car.'

The Beemer, in the deserted parking lot. The man with the gun in the backseat. Felice's abductor.

I found my purse, reached inside, ransacking it for the scrap of paper with Felice's cell number. After examining a dozen receipts, I found nothing. But wait. Back in my car. On my notepad? I knew I had scrawled it somewhere. Anxious not to make any noise and alert whoever was on the line that he had an electronic eavesdropper, I put the phone down on my bed, tiptoed back out to my car, leaving the front door open this time. Far away, an owl hooted. Then an answering hoot, raptorian dialogue echoing through the trees.

Not bad. And how many mice did you catch tonight?

I slid into the car and flipped the pages of my notepad, back to the end of Mancuso's interview. Yes. There it was. Felice's number. It matched. The call was coming from Felice's cell phone. Lord in heaven. And I might be missing some crucial clue on the phone while I sat in my car. My colleague Felice, held hostage by some maniac, had somehow managed to dial my number in a silent plea for help. Clever Felice. I cringed to think I had ever doubted her.

Back inside, the phone was still engaged, the grunting more muffled. I heard the low, canned sound of people talking, then a barely audible 'We'll be right back.' Then a louder voice, someone talking fast. It was ... a commercial. I was listening to a car radio. The steady whir began to make sense. It was the ambient sound of driving. Felice was traveling in a car. Trussed up and gagged? I pictured the driver, turning in his seat to taunt her. Somehow, she had called me. I remembered her coy request for my number, her long brown fingers punching it into autodial.

What if the person who had killed Catarina was now driving to an isolated and remote area to kill Felice? The thought sent me scurrying to call the police on my land line. It lay in disarray, where I

309

had thrown it against the wall.

I jammed the pieces of plastic together and dialed. The call didn't go through. I cursed and hung up. Tried again. No dial tone. I jiggled the pieces and heard something click into place. Please God. I tried once again and held my breath. This time, it rang. Within minutes, I was patched through to Officer Lesher. Alarmed by my voice, he asked if I was all right. I said yes and struggled to explain the incoming call.

'You can track her through the cell phone, can't you? By what switching station the signal's bouncing off? Like a global positioning device?'

'We'll do our best,' Lesher said, and asked for the number of Felice's cell phone. I read it off and he put me on hold, then came back on and said he would be at my house in fifteen minutes.

I paced until I heard him pull up, then ran out and put my finger to my lips. We walked back in, and I noticed his hand resting casually on his holster, just in case I wasn't as harmless as I seemed.

In the bedroom, I showed him the phone number displayed on the screen. We stared down at the small silver instrument. From it came a faint and steady whir. I beckoned him out to the kitchen.

'I heard a man threaten her,' I told Lesher. 'He said, "Now look who's trapped." I'm sure it's the same guy who kidnapped her and shot at me from her car.'

Lesher wrote everything down, then we stood there for a while but heard nothing more. He excused himself to call his dispatcher. I worried he was writing me off as a nutcase. He was half-way out the door when a low moan came from the phone.

CHAPTER 46

We froze, then started a grotesque tiptoe ballet back to the phone.

A man laughed cruelly. 'You ... had ... coming...'

I grabbed Lesher's arm and jabbed at the phone. See, see, I wanted to say. I'm not insane. Something horrible is going to happen if you don't find her.

We heard another moan and a crackling, like a heavy weight had just rolled over the phone. There were multiple beeps, then the line disconnected.

Gingerly, Lesher picked up the phone.

'I'll have to take this. In case she manages to call back, we can monitor it.'

'But you've already put a trace on it, right?'

His face was grim. 'They can track it up to the point the line goes dead. From there, it's anyone's guess.'

Lesher looked at me. 'Any idea what he meant by that comment?'

'Felice was going to stop at all the businesses and restaurants listed on the credit card bill,' I said. 'You've got to go to each of those places. Maybe they'll know something.'

'She started at the top of the list?'

'I don't know,' I said. Why hadn't I paid closer

311

attention? I had been so focused on my own mission.

'Wait,' I said, remembering the maps. 'She'd probably do it geographically. Whatever was closest to the office. But she also mentioned La Serenata. You're checking that, right? And California Highway Patrol can check the freeways. Do you think she's in that car? That he's driving her around?'

'I wouldn't want to hazard a guess,' the cop said. 'But we've got an APB out. If they drive around long enough, we'll find her.'

We said good-bye on the porch, a strange intimacy drawing us close for an awkward moment as night turned imperceptibly into dawn. With the light, danger seemed to retreat.

Lesher said he'd send a car to surveil the property, just in case. I drew the blinds and curled up on the sofa with a blanket. My thoughts drifted. A bird trilled, one clear note. The sky outside grew lighter. I heard more birdcalls, tentative at first, then swelling in a triumphant symphony as dawn broke.

I woke in hot, panicked guilt. Had they found Felice? Praying she was still alive, I reached for the phone. Officer Lesher was unavailable but they patched me through to a detective who launched into our conversation with a pop quiz to make sure I wasn't some random reporter on a fishing expedition. Then he grudgingly told me a few things off the record. Cell phone transmissions had tracked the car west along Interstate 10 from Rosemead to San Gabriel, through East L.A., and into downtown. There, at California's biggest freeway interchange, a concrete prayer wheel shooting off in every direction, Felice had broken off contact.

If I wasn't so worried, I might appreciate the irony. Felice, who lived for the limelight, had finally gotten her wish – a huge breaking story. It would be splashed across the front page. Only this time we'd be reporting on one of our own. Foolish, foolhardy Felice. She'd never be anonymous again. She'd be immortalized as the reporter abducted while chasing the scoop. She'd write her memoirs. Eventually, Philip Glass would turn it into an avant-garde opera. If she lived to tell the tale, that is. I realized with a jolt that it could easily have been me in that car. Only chance had sent me to the theater last night instead of following a trail of restaurant and auto shop receipts. I knew that I had to find her.

I made coffee and nuked some black beans, the aroma of sizzling cumin and garlic reviving me. I added a wedge of feta cheese and bread and sat down to eat. I wanted to call Silvio but was afraid to wake him. I felt terrible for doubting him, for resenting his long-ago relationship with Catarina. None of that mattered anymore.

Then I saw the red light blinking on my phone machine. Marisela's message. I had forgotten all about it. I played it back while I ate, heard her nervous, fluttering voice. She wanted to tell me something important.

From outside came the low hum of voices. I froze. When I finally screwed up the courage to peek out the window, I saw it was only gardeners, getting an early start next door. They chugged tamarind soda and passed around something wrapped in a banana leaf. It was 6:50. If I drove out to Marisela's, I'd get there around 7:30, a perfectly decent time to knock on someone's door. I knew I should call first but my gut said just show up, before she rethinks that impulse to confess. But what if Alfonso answered? After last night, he'd slam the door in my face. On the other hand, he was probably sleeping off a hangover.

From outside came sharp metallic sounds, the loamy scrunch of earth being displaced by shovels. Looking out, I saw they were digging a trench, a pyramid of dirt growing alongside. It looked like a backyard grave, I thought, dismissing the omen. Instead, I gathered my things and drove east. On the radio, a DJ was announcing that his station played only upbeat music. But what if you wanted music to slit your wrists by?

As I drove, I replayed the scene with Marisela and her mother in that fetid apartment. A place where dreams go to die. Where the fantasy of the happy family disintegrates into a nightmare. I felt sad yet strangely honored that she had taken me there. Finally, I was piercing her caustic exterior. But I wondered whether the vulnerability I had seen in her eyes was just another manipulation.

I pulled onto Alfonso and Marisela's street, parking behind a white van with a ladder lashed to the top. The kind you see all over suburbia on weekdays, hauling tools and workmen around. I walked up to the house, unlatched the grillwork gate. Inside was a tiled courtyard framed with

314

bougainvillea and exotic palms. The front door was massive, hewn of oak and studded with iron hinges. It could have graced a medieval church. I clanged the knocker and felt the sound reverberate in my rib cage.

Deep in the backyard, a dog barked, something small and aggrieved. I banged louder.

'Marisela,' I shouted. 'It's me, Eve Diamond.'

In the recesses of the house, floorboards creaked. Someone upstairs? The steps retreated. I heard muffled voices.

'Who is it?' Marisela called.

'It's Eve Diamond. You said you wanted to talk. In person.'

'Just a minute.' Commanding. Peremptory.

Someone padded away. I heard a muffled conversation. Back and forth it went, a whispery debate. Then some kind of resolution.

Marisela's disembodied voice came back, closer this time, and I knew she was right on the other side of the door.

'You'll have to come back later.'

'I can't. I'm on my way to the office. A colleague of mine was abducted last night while investigating Catarina's murder. Please, we have to talk now.'

Again the muffled footfalls. Another murmur of voices. Probably that goddamn Alfonso, telling her not to talk to me.

'Whatever you've got, I need to hear it now,' I told the door, surprised at the reasoned tone in my voice. 'Or my colleague may die.'

'No,' Marisela said sharply. I didn't think she was talking to me.

Then the door creaked open and she stood there, hair askew and snaking off like Medusa's locks, smeared mascara making her look like a raccoon. Face powder clumped around each nostril flange. Through the musk of her perfume, I smelled sour sheets and sweat.

'Now what?'

She clung to the door and I stepped past, brushing against her peignoir, which clung to my skin for a moment in a crackle of electricity before releasing the hairs on my arm.

Then she closed the door and blew by me with a swish of silk. I followed her deeper into the house, noting the carved wooden tables, the grand piano, the painted porcelain chandeliers.

Marisela clutched at her robe, hand curling into a fist over her heart.

'You called me last night,' I said.

The rings on her hand clinked in assent.

'It was a mistake. I was drunk.'

Somewhere in the house, a door shut with a decisive click. Above us, I heard steps.

Marisela stepped into the sunken living room, where brocaded curtains held back the morning light. A giant Persian rug dominated the space, bloodred and shot through with fiery sunset hues. The color of flames, of the Inquisition and the Catherine Wheel, of Aztec conquests and bodies flung from the tops of pyramids.

'Come.'

She led me past wrought-iron candleholders where lit tapers flickered and dripped waxy tears. Sorrowful Madonnas reproached me from gilt-edged icons. A triptych hung from the wall, the bloody-thorned heart of Jesus. Standing urns overflowed with desiccated rose petals, filling the air with sweet musk. Marisela paused before a church pew carved with cavorting demons and angels, and I imagined she might kneel, clasp her hands together, and confess to killing her rival.

Instead, she clutched her throat and looked sad and strangely resigned.

I realized that whatever impulse had prompted her to call me last night had flown. I had to get her talking again.

I lifted my chin to the ceiling.

'Alfonso up yet?'

Marisela patted her voluptuous locks.

'No. Uh, yes. I guess so.'

Nice and easy, I thought. Don't spook her.

'They finally let Silvio go,' I said. 'Alfonso told you, right?'

'Yes. Of course.'

The sun's golden fingers stole through a crack in the curtains, illuminating the bloodred carpet. Thick adobe walls kept the house cool, a cave that never lost its chill, even in summer.

'He didn't come home last night,' Marisela blurted out.

I fixed her with a steady gaze.

'He does that sometimes,' she said hurriedly. 'He's got a cot in his office. At the Taper. He writes best at night, that's when he's most inspired. He says I' – she paused, looked away – 'distract him.' Marisela plucked at the collar of her robe. 'He's been doing it more and more lately.'

So who was upstairs? I wondered. Then I remembered their daughter. The nanny.

317

'So you haven't told him that you're ... leaving?'
'No.'

She beckoned me to the couch, spreading her layers of silk, and we sat down, the swirling rosettes of velvet upholstery pressing into the backs of my thighs. She clasped her hands in her lap and waited.

'I need to hear what you know.'

The hands squeezed together.

'I told you, I'd been drinking.'

'Alcohol certainly makes people chatty.'

'It was a mistake. There's nothing to tell.'

'What's changed, Marisela?'

'Nothing. Everything.'

I waited, but she was silent.

'My colleague Felice Morgan may have been abducted by Catarina's killer. He used her as bait to lure me out to a motel in El Monte last night. She's going to die if we don't find her. Do you want that on your conscience?'

'You don't understand,' she cried.

I had to goad her into revealing what she knew.

'You helped kill Catarina, didn't you?'

'No!'

'Maybe you did it yourself. Neat trick. Kill your husband's mistress, then set him up to take the fall. He goes away for a really long time and you're free to enjoy his money with a new lover.'

Marisela's eyes blazed with scorn.

'Isn't that a bit extreme, when all I have to do is divorce him?'

'But the wronged party gets a bigger settlement. Nobody likes a cheating murderer. So you're keeping a boy toy stashed away until this

318

is all over.'

'That's ridiculous.'

She reached for the pack of cigarettes on the coffee table, lit one, brought it to her mouth. Sucked with the intensity of a baby at her bottle.

'Then enlighten me. Who kidnapped my colleague and shot at me last night?'

'I don't know.'

'I'm writing a story for tomorrow's paper. I want to get it right.'

'That would ruin everything.'

'We'll let the cops decide.'

'You write that story, you better watch your back.'

'You threatening me?'

'No comment.'

I stood up.

'Give me a ring if you change your mind. I'll be in the office.'

'No, you won't.'

It was a man's voice. Familiar. Conversational as he stepped into the room, holding a gun. Baltazar Galvan.

I stared at him, paralyzed, a mouse before a cobra. Trying in vain to puzzle it out.

A keening wail came from Marisela. She jumped up.

'No,' she said. 'You promised.'

Baltazar's jaw twitched. A shadow passed across his face.

'Things have changed,' he said.

'What are you doing here?' I said.

'You don't know yet, do you?' Trying to sound suave and amused but betrayed by bloodshot eyes.

'Stop it, Baltazar, I beg you,' Marisela said. 'Why didn't you stay upstairs?'

Baltazar leaned lazily against a pillar.

'I couldn't help myself.'

The smile widened into a smirk. I remembered his lecherous late-night phone call. His oily, seductive voice, insinuating itself into my nightmares. The same voice that had ordered me into Felice's car last night.

'Where's Felice?'

'Somewhere she won't cause any more trouble,' he said, in a voice that chilled my heart.

Marisela gave him a startled look but said nothing. Baltazar stepped up to a mirror, preening like a rooster. All the while, staring at me in the reflected glass, his gun at the ready. Just try it, his posture seemed to say.

'It was you in the car, wasn't it?' I said.

'What?' Marisela said, recoiling. 'You know her?'

'What have you done with her?' I said.

Baltazar turned. His lips pressed together in annoyance.

'Not your business.'

'Alive? Is she alive?'

'How do you know her?' Marisela repeated. I sensed a flare of possessive jealousy.

'We met at a press conference,' Baltazar said. 'You know the work I'm doing for the assemblyman.' He turned to me. 'And yes. For now, she is alive.'

I felt my body go limp with relief, but only for a moment.

Something about his ragged insouciance scared

me more than if he had held the gun to my temple. The only way out of the living room was past him.

Baltazar ran his free hand through his hair like some kind of jailhouse dandy and I recognized that gesture from ... from the picture window on the day I had followed Marisela to the bungalow near the freeway.

'Marisela,' I said in disbelief. 'So this is your lover? The man who tried to kill me last night and took a reporter hostage?'

As I spoke, I sized up the gun. Should I make a run for the front door?

'Soon to be two hostages,' Baltazar said conversationally.

'No,' Marisela said. 'This has gone far enough.'

She took a step toward me, her hands smoothing the layers at her chest.

'You were right,' she said. 'I killed Catarina.'

Every reporter dreams of this. The satanic choir, voices raised in exultance, as the sinner confesses. But the words tumbling out of her mouth were all wrong.

'Shut up, Marisela,' Baltazar snapped.

She began to weep.

'I was eaten away by jealousy. Time and again, she destroyed my life.'

'So you took hers?'

'Imagine what it was like for me. The humiliation. Everyone knowing about her and Alfonso. But I lived with it. Until she started up with...'

Grief erupted across Marisela's face and she said no more. I glanced at Baltazar. He stood still, listening with the intensity of a child eavesdropping on his parents.

I held my breath.

'She took the one thing that was all mine, just because she could,' Marisela said. 'She toyed with his emotions. To her it was just a game.'

'Catarina stole Baltazar from you? Is that why you killed her?'

She gave me a terrified look.

'Because that won't solve the problem, Marisela. He'll just betray you again, with someone else. It's him you should be angry at, not Catarina.'

'No. You don't understand.'

Her anguished denial flooded over me. I could feel the shame and anger that emanated from her. The thirst for revenge. But not the act itself. No, Marisela was protecting someone.

'I understand that your lover is a lying piece of criminal shit,' I said.

From the corner of my eye, I saw Baltazar's arm twitch.

'He's not my lover.'

'Don't lie, Marisela. It's written all over your face. But there's still a chance for you. Save yourself. Make him put down the gun. Turn yourselves in.'

'He's not my lover–'

'Don't be ridiculous; your eyes are shiny with love. I saw it that first time.'

She bent forward. Great heaving sobs came from her. Baltazar moved toward her and placed one arm around this woman he'd betrayed. He seemed stunned, transfixed by her confession.

Slowly Marisela raised her head. Her face was

blotchy with tears and her eyes had gone all glassy and faraway.

'He's not my lover–'

'Don't,' said Baltazar.

'He's not my lover.'

'Of course he is.'

'He's my ... brother.'

There was a long silence.

I stared at her, skeptical that this was yet another lie to throw me off balance. Then I scanned his face. Could it be? There was an undeniable resemblance in the mouth, full and sensuous, but what was voluptuous on Marisela presented as cruelty in Baltazar. Each had a high forehead, a widow's peak. But whatever genetics had knit together, environment had undone. Baltazar's eyes were sly and darting, his body a collection of quivers and tics, his manner at once preening and servile, with none of Marisela's haughty queenliness and grace.

Still, their combined stillness convinced me, as no words could. They stood before me, offering only themselves as proof. The silence was eloquent, and terrifying.

'How...?' I said after a long moment.

'After I met my real mother,' Marisela said, 'I was desperate to find the rest of my family, so I hired a private investigator. He found out that two of my brothers had been killed. Baltazar was the third. My baby brother.'

'And Pandora's box gaped open,' I said.

'It wasn't like that at all,' Marisela said, and she smiled at him through her tears with a ferocity that made me look away.

'Marisela, don't,' Baltazar said.

She ignored him. Hands clasped together, she spoke like a schoolgirl reciting a wretched poem.

'From birth, he never had a chance. I read the files. Our mom didn't know how to be a mother. She was just a child herself. She traded the government-issued formula for drugs and fed him bottles of sugar water. She'd disappear for days, partying, and he'd crawl into people's houses through the pet doors, looking for food. Or she'd bring home boyfriends who abused him. One of them burned him with a curling iron. Remember what we talked about, Eve? Last night in the car?'

I winced.

'That was his life. And it would have been mine, if our mother hadn't given me up for adoption. I escaped my fate. So I had to help him. Don't you see? I, who had everything. And he, my blood brother, who had nothing.'

I looked at Baltazar. The gun drooped. He seemed embarrassed, cowed, hushed. And suddenly I didn't see the brute. I saw a humiliated, snot-dribbled child, with welts and old scars. Crying for his mommy, for milk. And inside, I wept at the ruin of a life so twisted and stunted that he had grown up learning to lash out before he was hit, to numb himself to the pain, to see the world as predators or prey. Like a beaten dog gone slightly insane.

'He was living in a van when I found him. Alfonso and I helped him get his own place.'

'The bungalow by the freeway,' I said slowly.

'Yes,' Marisela said, and the words came out in a tumbled rush. 'We had so many years to make up for. All that deprivation. I told him to dream big. We were there to make it come true. Alfonso wasn't crazy about it but he went along. We introduced him to our friends, took him to plays and nice restaurants. He had just gotten out of prison, seven years for robbery and assault.'

'I told you it was self-defense.' He made an angry motion with the gun. 'Both times.'

She soothed his brow. 'Of course. You know we believed you.'

Then to me: 'He just needed a break. A chance to get on his feet, to be treated as a human being with respect and dignity. Something he had never had before. A family who could help him and broaden his horizons with art, with culture, with ... love.'

Baltazar was gazing at his sister with pity, and something else. Shame, perhaps. But I didn't lose sight of the gun. Or of the fact that Felice was alive. I had to keep them talking, somehow get free and sound an alarm.

'And then what happened?'

'He wanted to go back to school and get his GED, so we paid for that. When he took classes at the community college, we were so proud. We gave him two thousand dollars a month, and he swore he'd pay it back. Then he got an internship with the assemblyman. We were overjoyed. Finally he was getting his life on track.'

'That's enough, Marisela,' Baltazar said.

'He wasn't working for the assemblyman, except as a fixer and drug dealer,' I said. 'As for going to school, you should have demanded to see the grades. The tuition receipts.'

Marisela regarded her brother calmly. 'We trusted you. We didn't need to see proof. You just needed time, because of everything you've been through.' She shook her head ruefully. 'And that's what we just didn't have enough of. I didn't dream that it would be so hard. I thought love would make it right.'

A bitterness crept into her voice. 'Instead, how did you reward us? You slept with my husband's mistress.'

'Stop it, Marisela,' Baltazar said.

'No, I won't.' She turned to me. 'They met at one of our parties. And that was it. All my hopes and dreams for our future went up in smoke.'

I knew I had to ride the tension coiling up beneath them, the recriminations and accusations. Because at last I saw it laid out clearly. What had only been a glimmer before.

'You didn't kill Catarina. He did.'

'No,' Marisela said steadily. 'It was me. I was disgusted. My own brother, sleeping with that slut. I gave him money for school, for clothes. And he used it to show her a good time. I could have wept. Instead, I killed her.'

'It doesn't hold water, Marisela. He's your brother, not your lover. Blind, passionate jealousy just doesn't apply.'

'You're wrong,' she screamed.

'He's a predator, Marisela. A murderer. And you're a fool. Save yourself. I know you're innocent.'

'If you put a wolf in with a bunny, it's not the wolf's fault that it kills the bunny. That's all it knows. It's the same with Baltazar. He never had a chance. And I did. Now it's my turn to pay.'

'The cops will never believe you killed Catarina. They'll go for Mr. Two Strikes over here.' I inclined my head to Baltazar, who listened with strange fascination to our exchange. 'Her lover with a rap sheet and a history of violence.'

Finally, Baltazar roused himself. 'Listen to the pretty reporter, Marisela,' he said. 'There's no need for this.'

'They'll put you away for good. Just when I've found you. I can't let that happen.'

'Nothing is going to happen. I'm innocent. I may be a lot of things, but I'm not a killer. Why won't you believe me? My own sister.'

He began to weep.

Marisela stroked his arm. 'Hush, darling, you can't help what God made you. I'm here, I'll protect you.'

'The police know that a man abducted Felice last night,' I said.

'Who?' Baltazar looked blank.

'My colleague, Felice Morgan.'

'She told me her name was Jayson.'

Clever Felice, I thought, feeling a stab of guilt. Hoping the name would be enough to warn me. Too bad I wasn't half as clever in my turn.

'Oh, right. Jayson.' I hit my head with my palm. 'That's her nickname. Can't you let her go? She doesn't know anything.'

'She was at the restaurant, asking questions. It was all going to come out.'

'Baltazar, I beg you, on all that is holy, don't do this to me,' Marisela said.

'Will you please shut up,' he said laconically.

'What was going to come out?' I asked.

'They don't care if I did it or not, they'd nail me anyway. And I ain't going down again.'

He had given me an opening. Since a woman with a gun pointed at her has few options, I locked eyes with him and bled sincerity.

'I don't want to accuse you of anything you didn't do, Baltazar,' I said in as steady a voice as I could manage.

His eyes pinballed away. 'You'd be the only one, then.'

'Why would the cops think you killed her?'

'Because I was there, man. That morning.'

Marisela moaned and slid to the floor.

'What do you mean, you were there?'

His voice wavered but took on a hardened cast as he recalled the scene. 'I found her. Dead. Laying across the bed. Bullet hole right here.' He pointed to the back of his head. 'I rolled her over. Her eyes were open, staring at me. I knew she wasn't the type to off herself. So then it's murder. And I loved her but there was nothing I could do. I can't go back to the Big House. I booked, man. Didn't even call 911. What's the point, she's gone already.'

I got very still. This didn't jibe with what I knew. I reminded myself that Baltazar was a criminal and a sociopath, adept at telling people what they wanted to hear.

'So she was killed at home?'

'That's what I'm saying.'

'Then how'd she get to Point Fermin? That's where they found the body.'

He grew agitated. 'How do I know?'

'The murderer must have come back after you left to dispose of the body. Who would do that? And why?'

'I have no idea,' Baltazar said. 'We were going to leave that night. Run off, after her big return to the stage. She promised me. She wanted to stick it to Alfonso. I just dropped by to tell her break a leg.'

'Did you have a fight?'

He took two steps closer and his eyes filled with rage.

'She was dead, I told you.'

'But you had a volatile relationship?'

'Doesn't everyone?'

'What did you fight about?'

'I didn't like the way Alfonso bossed her around. That's why we were going away. She was tired of L.A. All the games. Everyone wanting a piece of her. We would go someplace new, where nobody knew us.' His voice spiraled down into a hoarse mutter. 'I'd work and she'd stay home. Have some babies. She was going to give up the stage.'

Marisela choked off a laugh. 'Not likely. She lived to be the center of attention.'

'What did you know about her?' he screamed. 'What did anyone know?' The words stuttered out of him. 'I loved her. She was the only one, ever.' He looked at the bundle on the floor. 'Other than you, Marisela. But you're my sister.'

Marisela struggled back to her feet. 'I have not found my brother after all this time, only to lose him like this, for a crime he didn't commit.'

'If he didn't murder anyone, then why did he kidnap a reporter?' I asked.

Baltazar gave me a wild look, then ran his hand through his hair in that nervous gesture again. 'Because I freaked when the Jayson chick came into La Serenata, asking questions. Okay? That's why. I was in there having a drink, and she barrels over, starts showing pictures to the manager,' he said. 'Nosing around.'

'So instead of just taking off, you kidnap her?'

'I wasn't planning on it. But she gave me this look, like she *knew*, man. It was a stone-cold look.'

'She gives everyone that look.'

'I guess I panicked.' He shrugged. 'No impulse control. That's what they say.'

'So then what happened?'

'I told her I had some photos of Catarina in my car that she might find interesting. And she went for it. I have a way with the ladies.'

It took all my willpower not to roll my eyes. I imagined Felice, wanting a break in the story so badly that her usual street smarts failed her.

'Then I went to my van and got them. And my gun.'

'And then what happened?'

'I showed her the photos. Her face turned kind of sicklike, when she recognized who was in most of them, his arm around Catarina. Yup, it was me.' He snickered at the memory. 'I had the gun on her by then. I made her get in the car and drive us to a motel off I-10 where I knew the manager wouldn't give us any trouble. I had to find out what she knew.'

'And Fe– um, Jayson told you?' Somehow I was disappointed. I had thought her made of sterner stuff.

'She had a gun in her ribs, prying it out of her, word by word. When she told me about you, I wanted to drive to your house but she didn't know where you lived. So we called instead.'

I remembered Felice's cockiness. She had meant to goad me, to warn me, in the only way she could.

'And I fell for it. I drove out.'

'Yeah. But you bolted. Had to shoot at you. So you'd be scared enough to drop the story.'

'So then what did you do?' I didn't want to tell him about Felice's phone call.

'I tied her up and drove back to the restaurant to get my van. I knew the cops would be looking for her car. So I put her in the van. I drove around for a while. Then I came here.' He inclined his head. 'She's outside. In the back. And then what do my ears hear this morning but that other nosy reporter, pissing round my sister's door. I just had to come down and say hello.'

He grinned at his own brilliance.

'Look,' I said. 'I can tell you're very smart. But you're just digging yourself a deeper hole. Now they're going to add kidnapping, assault, and attempted murder to Catarina's murder rap.'

'It doesn't matter anymore. I'm getting out of here. And you and that chick in the van...' Baltazar's voice trailed off and I worried that he was contemplating killing us.

'The cops are going to find you.'

He smirked. 'I'm headed for Mexico. There's no extradition treaty with the U.S.'

'That's not going to stop some bounty-hunter cowboy from tracking your ass down to wherever you've holed up. Turn yourself in. Tell them the truth.'

'They'll never believe him,' Marisela said with sad resignation.

Play it up, I thought. I wanted to make her crack. It was my only chance at escape.

'Yeah, I guess you're right. And with good reason. Your brother is an animal, Marisela. Whatever happened to him back there in that apartment did its damage. You found him thirty years too late.'

Beneath the bravado, something was beginning to crumble. Baltazar's free arm twitched almost imperceptibly. There was a red cast to his eyes. I prayed he wouldn't shoot me.

Marisela began to cry. 'I've ruined everything,' she said. 'It's all my fault.'

Her sobs grew louder. She seemed to be losing control.

'Here's a good story for you,' Marisela said. 'A hell of a play. Once there was a man who clawed his way out of the dangerous, poverty-stricken place where he had grown up. He remade himself, won honors and fame, was accepted into the highest levels of society. And he did it without turning his back on his roots. But at the height of his glory, his past caught up with him, attacked him where he was weakest. It dragged our hero back down into the mire, never to be seen again. They could call it *The Ballad of Alfonso Reventon*.'

'Marisela,' I said. 'You are not to blame for any of this.'

'But I killed her. I already told you.'

'No, you didn't.'

'You don't believe it?' She looked around, wild-eyed. The light of madness and desperation was in her eyes. 'Then maybe I'll have to kill you, too. Will that make it more plausible?'

She grabbed at Baltazar's gun, tried to wrestle it away. He was stronger but she had the element of surprise and the ferocity of a cornered animal.

'Marisela, no,' Baltazar screamed.

It was now or never. Operating on sheer adrenal instinct, I sprinted past them for the front door. Then something came crashing through the picture window and exploded. Clouds of thick, toxic smoke filled the air. I threw myself to the ground, my head slamming against something hard.

'This is the police. The house is surrounded. Come out with your hands up and you will not be harmed.'

Then I knew no more.

CHAPTER 47

I felt the sun on my face and stirred.

'You're awake,' Felice said.

I lifted my head. It felt tender, emptied out. Felice lay in a bed across from me, purple welts blooming along her face and neck.

'What happened to you?'

'Oh,' she said cheerfully. 'I'm fine. They're doing some X-rays, but I don't think anything's broken. How do *you* feel? They said you have a concussion.'

I squinted. 'I'm okay. Though that light is

awfully bright.'

'How many fingers am I holding up?' Felice extended her entire hand.

'Um, five?'

A stricken look crossed her face. 'No, Eve, just one.'

I looked again and saw she was right. 'Oh God,' I said, holding my head.

She laughed, her voice a tinkling bell. 'I'm just messing with you.'

I lay back down and stared at the ceiling. 'Glad to see some things never change,' I said tartly.

'Doc says we'll be out of here in a few hours,' came the peace offering from the far side of the room.

'How long have we been here?' I struggled to see the hospital clock: 12:20 p.m. But what day?

'Since yesterday,' Felice said. 'You hit your head pretty hard, I guess.'

I struggled into an upright position. The room didn't swim.

'But now that you're up, I just have to ask: Couldn't you have run out to that van and untied me before all hell broke loose? I blew my fifteen minutes of fame.'

The last thing I remembered was hitting the ground.

'He pulled you outside. We think he was going to use you as a human shield. But the SWAT sharpshooters got him first.'

'Glad I don't remember.' I paused. 'Is he dead?'

'Oh yeah. Thank God. It was him all along. He killed Catarina. They were having an affair and she wanted to cut it off. Marisela finally admitted it under questioning. She and Alfonso are in seclusion now.'

'Oh.'

'Eve, I have to tell you something.'

'Yes?' Wary now.

'I'm sorry.'

'For what?'

'For leading you into that trap. He made me call you. He had a gun on me the whole time.'

'Oh,' I said stupidly, focusing on a bouquet of flowers.

'They're from Silvio. He was here all morning. We had a nice chat about you. He'll be back soon to see how you're doing.'

It was amazing how Felice managed to insinuate herself into every aspect of my life. I didn't want her getting all cozy with my boyfriend, the two of them fretting over my recovery.

'I tried to warn you,' Felice continued. 'I figured you'd catch on if I called myself Jayson. You know, code for someone who made things up. That and all the awful things I said, you'd realize something was wrong.' She saw my blank look. 'You caught on, didn't you?'

I didn't say anything.

'Or maybe you didn't?' Softly now. 'Maybe my clever plan backfired.'

All I could think of was how furious I had been at her. 'You hate me, don't you? You've never trusted me since that moto story. You think I made that up too, don't you?'

'You're awfully ambitious, Felice.'

'But to lie like that? How could I face my conscience?'

335

I shrugged.

'How could you think so badly of me?'

'Guess I'm just an evil racist.'

'Yeah.' She nodded briskly. 'Maybe you are.'

'But you know what, Felice? If you were white, I'd still find you obnoxious.'

'You're the one who's obnoxious. The way you condescend to me. And treat me with suspicion. What do I have to do to make people in this godawful profession trust me? I might as well get out now.'

She let out a banshee howl that brought the nurse running. 'I want a sedative,' she declared.

The nurse bustled out to get it. Felice grabbed a newspaper on the table. Then she let out a gasp. I turned.

'What?'

'Oh my God, I'm in the paper. There I am, being carried out on a stretcher into an ambulance.'

'You crossed that sacred line, baby. You became the news. We both did.'

'I don't even remember waving to the cameras like that.'

'You must have been in shock.'

'I should e-mail the *Columbia Journalism Review*, propose a first-person account.'

'Get out!'

'I'm serious.'

I sighed. There was no taming Felice Morgan.

'How did the cops know where to find us?'

She cracked a thin smile. 'I called them.'

'I thought you were tied up and gagged.'

'It took me hours. I wiggled like a worm to get

the right angle. Do you know how hard it is to work a cell phone with your chin? I messed up so many times. Then I had to find the 'clear' button and start all over. I had such a knot in my neck. Anyway, finally I was able to dial 911. I couldn't get the gag off but I knew they'd trace it. It took them long enough.' She rolled her lovely chocolate eyes. 'As soon as they untied me, I told them he was in there.'

'How did you know whose house it was?'

'I remembered Marisela's address.' She smiled with satisfaction. 'The cops said that helped them immensely.'

The nurse came back to wheel Felice off for one last X-ray. Lulled by the tedium, I dozed until a woman who looked to be in her fifties poked her head into the room.

'Is this Felice Morgan's room?' Her voice was shy, the accent flat and upper Midwest.

She wore white pants and a shiny polyester shirt that tied at the front in a bow. Orthopedic shoes with support hose. Her forehead had two deep horizontal lines and she wore blue eye shadow and red lipstick that glistened against her black skin.

Curious to get a better look at Felice's visitor, I pushed myself into a sitting position.

'Yeah, but she's having an X-ray.'

'Mind if I wait?'

'Please.'

I shifted uneasily, trapped into making awkward small talk.

'I had no idea until I saw her picture on the

news,' the woman said. 'I caught the first plane, had the taxi bring me straight from the airport.'

The urgency in her voice set off my radar. 'I'm sorry, I didn't catch your name.'

She smoothed her palm on her pants, then extended it. 'Pardon my rudeness. I'm Mrs. Ruth Morgan. Felice's mother.'

A shock wave went through me. This decidedly unglamorous creature, with her humble demeanor and down-market attire, was Felice's mother?

'Pleased to meet you,' I said. 'Felice should be back soon. She'll be so happy to see you.'

Mrs. Morgan gave a long sigh. 'It's almost five years since I've seen her. We're estranged. But I think about her every day, wonder how she's doing. My baby girl.'

'Is that right?'

'Oh, I know I wasn't always the best mother. I had my ... troubles.' Her voice took on a confessional tone. 'Took to the bottle after their father left, four kids and no money. Providence is a cold, hard place to be on your own. But I've been sober four years, God bless.'

For a moment, I wondered if someone was playing a practical joke. Whether Felice would come rolling in, jeering that I had fallen for it yet again. But there was a ring of truth to this woman's words that I had never felt with her daughter.

'We all make mistakes,' I told her. 'What counts is that you're here... What do you do in Providence?'

'I'm a janitor,' she said, unaware that the question was rigged.

Had I heard her right?

'You mean, like, cleaning?'

She gave me a bemused look. 'That's right. Oh, they gave us a fancier title a few years ago. But I believe in plain speech.'

'That's admirable,' I was able to spit out. I tucked my chin into my neck. 'So where do you work?'

'At the college.'

'Brown?'

'That's right. I worked the night shift when Felice was growing up. I hated to saddle her with the little ones, but she was so good with them. Told them stories. Lord, the things she came up with. I'm not surprised she's become a famous *L.A. Times* reporter. Even as a child, she had a way with words. And people.'

We were getting close to something that had once seemed very important.

'And Felice went to Brown?' I asked, holding my breath.

Mrs. Morgan thought about it for a minute.

'She took a few extension classes the summer after high school. That was about the long and the short of it.'

I had to nail it down. 'Do you think she kept going after you lost touch?'

Mrs. Morgan's eyes twinkled. 'Honey, janitors know everything that goes on at that school. Including which professors are carrying on with their students. You wouldn't believe what we find in the broom closets. But no, they wouldn't have taken her. Her grades weren't good enough. And I know for a fact that she was living in Texas. She sent postcards. About how she was working for the paper.'

The air around my head hummed, and I wondered whether my concussion was flaring up.

Instead of being elated at finally catching Felice red-handed, I felt only dismay.

We heard the muttering and creaking of the chair as Felice was wheeled back into the room.

When Felice saw her mother, all the color drained from her face.

'What are you doing here?' she finally asked, in a voice so hard and cold that I winced.

'Your mother and I were having a chat,' I said, filled with such sadness for both of them that I wanted to cry.

I dared a glimpse at Mrs. Morgan. She was gazing at her daughter with mingled fear and hope.

'Your mother was telling me how worried she was when she saw you on the news. She took the next flight out.'

Felice looked at her mother, then out the window. She blinked rapidly, and her mouth tightened.

'You should have called first, Ma,' she said. 'I gave you the number.'

'I did,' Mrs. Morgan said apologetically. 'Over and over again. But I only got your machine. For all I knew you could be dead. I had to see you.'

She walked up to Felice, then stepped back, as if she had taken too many liberties. She put out one hand, let it hover near her daughter's face. Caressed the air.

'How are you, sweetpea? I've missed you so much.'

'Aw, Ma,' Felice said.

Then with a brisk tug, the orderly pulled the curtain between us closed.

'How 'bout we give them some privacy, honey,' she said.

Then she brought the chair around to me and helped me into it.

'Your turn now. X-ray.'

As she wheeled me out, a low murmur came from the other end of the room. I thought I could hear quiet sobs.

When we returned, the curtain was still drawn.

The orderly settled me into bed, then left.

I listened for voices but heard nothing. 'Hey, Felice,' I finally asked, 'is your mother still here?'

There was a long silence.

'Felice?'

'She left,' came the reply.

'She loves you.'

'Yeah, right. You weren't there when I was growing up.'

Big sigh. Then her voice tentative, slowly growing in assurance.

'I wish she'd dress a little better, it's embarrassing. I'm constantly giving her gift certificates to Barney's and Saks. She volunteers at an inner-city clinic and doesn't want to stand out from the patients.'

It seemed fitting, somehow, that we were talking across a curtain that concealed us from each other. Felice's whole life, I knew now, had been an Oscar-worthy act.

'Felice,' I said gently. 'Your mom told me what

she does for a living.'

There was silence on the other side. 'She was putting you on. She does that with white folk sometimes. You so racist you fell for it?'

Could it be true? I thought about Mrs. Morgan. Her weary but steady gaze. Her quiet dignity and simple answers.

'C'mon, Felice. The whole thing is over.'

From the other side of the curtain came angry huffing. 'I just saved your life, you ungrateful bitch. This the thanks I get?'

'You didn't grow up in New York.'

'Course I did.'

'And you didn't go to Brown. Your mother told me. You didn't have the grades. You just took some extension courses one summer.'

'Yo' pushin' yo' luck there, girl.' The ghetto only growing stronger the more frantic she got.

'Is that right, Felice? Should we call up the Brown Alumni Association? The registrar? Get your transcripts?'

I held my breath at my meanness, but I couldn't help it. I was so angry at all the tricks she had played on me.

To my surprise, she burst into tears.

'What right does she have, barging in on my life?'

I knew she didn't mean me.

'She wants to make her peace with you,' I said. 'Tell me something, Felice. Don't you realize that growing up poor and black gives you way more street cred than being from a rich family? You've had so many more obstacles to overcome.'

She moaned and I heard the bed creak as she

342

tossed. Her voice took on a plaintive tone.

'Ever since I was little, I'd pretend I was a rich girl who had been snatched away at birth and given to a poor family to raise. A girl out of a fairy tale. My mother, neighbors, the kids at school, they said I put on airs. But it's what got me through. I knew I didn't belong there. I left as soon as I could. Started a new life where no one knew me. Where I could make it all come true. And I did. You have to promise not to tell, Eve. I'll be ruined.'

'I don't know if I can do that,' I said. 'You almost got me killed back there. And for what? To impress some editor?'

'But I'm good at this,' she said. 'It's all I ever wanted to do, be a big-city journalist. And I made it. Please don't take that away from me.'

'You could have made it on your own merits, Felice. You didn't have to lie. People are out there, trawling the schools for bright disadvantaged kids like you.'

'Uh-huh. I must have been too busy taking care of my brothers and sisters the day they came to campus. 'Cause I never saw them. But I made it on my own anyway. Moved to Detroit with my boyfriend after high school and got a job at a paper. Lied about my age, my credentials. Worked my way up. Dumped the guy. Within two years I was in Fort Worth. On my way.'

'But you weren't who you said you were.'

I heard a thump as her legs hit the floor. She yanked the curtain open, stood there, eyes blazing with anger.

'The *Times* wouldn't have hired me if they knew

343

the truth. They wanted a hotshot Ivy League overachiever,' she said. 'I just gave them what they wanted.'

'You got hired because you did good work. That series in Texas.'

She rolled her eyes. 'But I'll never know, that's the shame of it. You can't tell. Please, Eve.'

I wondered what right I had to out her. Whether it would be out of prissy self-righteousness or because I really felt a gross miscarriage of justice had occurred. Hadn't she proved herself?

Just then, Silvio appeared in the doorway.

CHAPTER 48

He stopped in his tracks when he saw that I was sitting up in bed. Then, with a choked exclamation, he was at my side.

'*Querida,* you're awake. Thank God. If only I had stayed with you last night, this never would have happened.'

I leaned into him, felt his arms envelop me, inhaled his familiar scent. It was finally over. The killer had been flushed out of the shadows. Now he was dead. My fears and suspicions about Silvio had come to naught. We were safe, our love intact. I took a deep breath. It felt as if, after a long time wandering, I was finally back home.

'I know,' I said, remembering how I had charged out the door in a jealous rage, thinking I was about to confront Silvio and Marisela at a motel. I swallowed. What kind of a fool had I been to doubt him?

'When I think of that sleazebag, holding you at gunpoint, I feel I ... I'm glad he's dead, Eve. I would have killed him myself, for what he did.'

If he had a sword, Silvio would have brandished it. But he couldn't protect me against the world or from my own venality and professional skepticism. No one could. I had misjudged him. I had misjudged them all. At least I had lived to see the error of my ways.

'Don't say that.' I shivered. 'There's been too much death already.'

He caressed my hair. 'How do you feel? Is your vision blurry?'

Maybe just my inner compass is blurry, I thought.

I swayed against him.

'Whoa, *querida*, you're dizzy. Oh my God, Felice, call the nurse, she's fainting.'

I laughed with joy, the pure adrenaline rush of being loved.

'I'm okay,' I protested.

Not fully believing me, he grabbed my shoulders and scanned my face. Felice pulled the curtain across and I was grateful for the privacy. I didn't want her to see the besotted look in my eyes.

'Honestly.' I held up a hospital form. 'The doctor's released me.'

Silvio read it carefully. 'Then let's go,' he said. 'I had one of my guys drive your car back to your house. Felice's car is still at La Serenata; we can drop her off. By the way, she says she saved your

345

life back there at Alfonso's house.'

'She did,' I said. 'And I owe her for it.'

The curtain drew back.

'Could you repeat that?' Felice said, the old smile creeping back across her lips. She was dressed in her own clothes and ready to go.

'And I'm considering' – I turned to Silvio, articulating every word – 'what would be the most appropriate way to pay her back.'

'Are you sure you're okay to drive?' Silvio asked Felice as he pulled up to La Serenata twenty minutes later.

Felice smiled, put her hand to her cheek. 'It looks a lot worse than it feels. I just want to get home, shower, and then swing by the office, see if they need me for anything.'

She slid out of the car, then leaned her elbows on my window. 'How about you, Eve? Gonna take it easy today?'

My competitive instincts stirred. Catarina's funeral was tomorrow. I knew there'd be plenty of new stories to write now that Baltazar was dead.

'Naw. I'll see you there later this afternoon.'

'You ladies are crazy,' Silvio said, shaking his head. 'If I'd been through what either of you have, I'd take the whole week off.'

Felice and I exchanged conspiratorial looks. If you've got the news jones, you know. If you don't, it's hard to explain.

After we pulled away, Silvio kept glancing at me, reassuring himself that I was really there. Then he grabbed my hand in a way that told me he'd been dying to the whole way from the hospital.

At home, he took me in his arms. 'You have to let me make it up to you,' he said huskily. 'All the evasions and half-truths. I'm so sorry.' His lips brushed my skin and I felt dizzy in a way that had nothing to do with concussion. I thought I might not make it to work after all.

His phone rang. He ignored it for a while but it kept ringing. Finally he tore away, cursed, and answered. I heard a male voice on the other end, though I couldn't make out the words.

'Yeah. Yeah. Okay,' Silvio said, after listening for about twenty seconds. His voice was tense. 'See you soon.'

He clicked off and ran his hand through his hair. Avoiding my eyes, he said, 'It looks like this is going to have to wait. There's an emergency at work. I'll deal with this, you deal with your news-paper, and we'll see each other tonight, okay?'

Now what? I thought. It couldn't have anything to do with Catarina, could it? Baltazar was dead. The whole thing was over. But even as I won-dered, part of me was secretly relieved. I was antsy to get to the newsroom, see what I had missed.

'You sure you're well enough to drive?' he asked doubtfully.

'You read the hospital release. It isn't even a real concussion. I'm fine.'

With a final wave, Silvio zoomed off. Forty-five minutes later, freshly showered, I was on the freeway to work.

Felice was already there when I got in, sitting in Thompson's office, both of them huddled over a computer printout.

'That playwright friend of yours?' Thompson said when I walked in. 'The lab found his DNA inside the dead actress.'

Shit. Silvio had warned me about this. But just because Alfonso had slept with her last didn't mean he killed her.

'They've put out an APB on him,' Thompson said. 'Cops are beginning to wonder if they killed the wrong man.'

Was that the emergency that had sent Silvio speeding away? I got a queasy feeling in my gut, wondering whether he was helping Alfonso evade the police. That would make him an accessory.

'Sic me on it,' I said.

'That's what I said,' Felice said in a resigned voice, and walked out.

Thompson looked at her receding back, then turned to me.

'You reporters have barely gotten out of the hospital, and look at you, cruising for another bruising.'

'So we're masochists. Sue us.'

'What I need you to do, Ace, is swing by that drama teacher's house. She's promised us some old photos of Catarina. See if you can get a fresh quote while you're there.'

'That's glorified copy messenger work,' I said, resentment smoldering.

'Docs said you need to take it easy for a while. Now are you part of this team or not?'

I went back to my desk and called Victoria but

the number was busy. I waited ten minutes then tried again. If she was online or something, I'd have to show up unannounced, feeling like an even bigger jerk than I already did. I came back to the office for this? I sensed someone behind me, looked up, and saw Felice hovering.

'You doing anything on "Semen"?' she asked.

I hesitated. 'Not really.' I shrugged.

'Bummer,' she said. 'Brandywine's already at the cop shop. Thompson wants me to watch the wires. Can you believe that?'

'He's trying to keep us out of trouble.'

'Good luck,' she said, giving me that piercing look, the one that had spooked Baltazar into kidnapping her. 'What are you up to?'

'Gotta pick up some photos for tomorrow's paper,' I said, walking away.

'Whose photos? Where?' Felice called.

But her answer was the office door slamming shut. I didn't owe her anything anymore. I didn't have to cart her around with me or put up with her endless scheming. I was free at last. But as I got onto the freeway, I forgot she wasn't there and found myself talking to the empty passenger seat. At least Felice had been entertaining.

Victoria Givens lived in a gingerbread bungalow in Larchmont, a tidy district of well-kept single-family homes in the center of town. Daisies and black-eyed Susans lined the walkway and bees buzzed lazily in the noonday heat. From inside came the faint strains of music.

I knocked and the screen door rattled against the wooden frame. I heard footsteps. Then a figure appeared on the other side.

'Yes?'

I stuck my face up to the screen, introduced myself, and reminded her we had met before. Then I asked about the photos.

Victoria Givens stroked the ends of her braids. 'Don't you people call first?'

'The line was busy. We need them for tomorrow's paper. They've made a DNA match.'

'Oh?' she said.

'Semen.'

'Hmph.'

'It's not what everyone thought.'

'Isn't it?'

She didn't invite me in and I stood there, straining to see into the dark rooms where music played, haunting and familiar.

'Don't you want to know whose DNA they found?'

'What does it matter?' Victoria Givens said bitterly. 'She's dead. It won't bring her back.'

I jotted down the quote but yearned for something fresher. More gut-wrenching. A Euripidean lament from the drama teacher who had discovered Catarina all those years ago and now grieved that her star protégé was no more.

'Ms. Givens, while you get the photos, could I please use your bathroom?'

It would give me an excuse to get inside and chat her up. Victoria Givens turned and surveyed the living room. 'Of course,' she said after a long moment. 'Come in.'

She made no attempt to open the door so I grabbed the handle and let myself in. The screen creaked unpleasantly. Inside, I blinked as my eyes plunged into the penumbra.

'This way,' she said peremptorily.

I followed her through the living room and saw framed photos on the fireplace mantel and crowding every table. Then we were in the hallway. Victoria stopped and turned, and I smacked right into her bony chest.

'Umphf, sorry,' I said.

'Okay, whose DNA was it?' she asked.

'Alfonso's. They want to arrest him if they can find him.'

A gloating look came over her face. She propped up her chin with one hand.

'I'm not surprised,' she said. 'I told you he had a temper. He always interfered between me and Catarina. From the very beginning. He was obsessed with her. But she was leaving him. She must have told him that morning. And his jealousy couldn't take it. Without her, he was nothing.'

I thought of Alfonso. His blind rage. What if at this very moment he was skulking around Victoria's house, aiming to kill one last person before he fled? The woman who had long thwarted him in the battle for Catarina's affection. No, that was silly. He was probably hundreds of miles away already. Or already in police custody.

'Come along, then,' Victoria said, and led me farther into the house, the faint music serenading us as we walked. 'Bathroom's over there.' She pointed. 'I'll be waiting on the back porch.'

I closed the door and stood in Victoria's bathroom, taking in the black and yellow California tiles. Deco cabinets. Little sachets of lavender and lemon verbena.

I watched two minutes tick by on my watch. I flushed the toilet and ran some water. Then I walked through the hallway and emerged into the light of a sunporch where Victoria sat in a rocking chair, a box of photos on her lap.

The room was devoted to her life in the theater. There were promotional stills from the stage, Polaroids taken in dressing rooms, signed head shots, cast photos of Victoria with young actors. On the wall hung framed posters for bygone productions of *Macbeth* and *Singin' in the Rain*, *Zoot Suit* and *Speed the Plow*, *Arcadia* and *Noises Off*. Bouquets of dried flowers tied with satin ribbons. The memento mori of a life consecrated to the Muse.

'So,' said Victoria, giving me a look that peered into the corners of my soul. 'How do you like my wall of fame?'

'Your devotion is ... admirable,' I said.

'Sit here beside me, Ms. Diamond,' she said, and rifled through her box. 'You know, all this would be nothing if not for Catarina. It's her I'm most proud of.'

She thrust something into my hands.

'Here she is in high school. A class photo. And here's her first play. In juvie. She was a comely maid in a 1920s bedroom farce. How we laughed. But even then, I knew she had the gift. It was I who molded her, who formed her. Alfonso takes credit, but in his heart, he knows it was my doing.'

She handed me a sheaf of old photos. 'Take whatever you want for the newspaper,' she said. 'I'll be right back.'

I flipped through the photos, pulling out a handful. Victoria returned with a garment bag.

'Her first costume.'

With great care, Victoria unzipped the bag. Inside layers of paper was a rough-hemmed skirt and bodice, the smell of trapped dust and mothballs and something stale and sweet rising into the open air. Victoria held the garment to her face and inhaled.

'It still bears the scent of her.'

This was getting weirder by the minute.

Victoria ran her fingers reverentially along the outfit.

'Catarina never cared about these things, but I had it washed and pressed and put in acid-free paper. To preserve it.'

She placed the outfit back inside, then zipped the bag gently.

'I'll just go and hang it up.'

I heard footfalls moving through the house. I thought of the photos in the living room, how Victoria had hurried me past. I got up, slipped through the open door, and worked my way back to the front room.

The music grew louder as I walked, maddeningly familiar. I had an overpowering sense of déjà vu.

I puzzled over the song, standing with my hand on the bathroom doorknob in case Victoria came back. The men's voices twined in romantic lament.

'What are you doing?' she said, stepping into the hallway.

Then I had it.

'That music,' I said.

'I was just going to turn it off,' Victoria said. 'It's giving me a headache.'

I pictured the front door. My car. Zooming away.

She opened a bedroom door and the sound floated out, timeless and silvery, the voices crooning in controlled passion.

'*You are a carnivorous flower...*'

'I know that song,' I said, my body quivering with memory. Of standing in Catarina's house, with Silvio prowling its tiny rooms, as a record played on a scratchy turntable.

'It's beautiful, is it not?' came Victoria's voice, slow and faraway.

'Yes. Yes, it is.'

'It was Catarina's favorite song. It was I who introduced her to Trio Las Palmas.'

'*In a savage garden...*' The intertwined voices rose and fell as they sang, sugary sweet to belie the poisonous words.

'It's haunting,' I said.

'I introduced her to a lot of things.'

'*Beautiful but deadly,*' the male voices warbled.

'I'm sure you did.'

'It was I who made her what she was. She came to me unformed, a child. I unlocked the artist within her. But she never appreciated all I did for her. How I sacrificed. She wanted to throw away her great gift.'

'*As you devour my heart.*'

Then I knew that I had to be very, very careful.

With elaborate casualness, I strolled past her and into the living room, but she was right behind me, her breath hot on the back of my neck.

The room was dark, heavy curtains obscuring the blazing light of afternoon.

'How would she have thrown away her gift?' I asked, infusing my voice with curiosity. I wanted to keep her reminiscing. Anything to keep her from thinking too hard about the present.

'Alfonso, I could tolerate. At least we saw things the same way. He wanted what was best for her as an artist.'

'Did he?'

'And that film producer. Catarina and I thought he would help her career. That was okay too.'

After the bright light of the sunporch, my eyes were slowly adjusting to the shadows of the living room. Enough to make out the framed photos that covered every available space of the walls. There was an eerie pattern to them and it took me a moment before I realized why: every single photo was of Catarina Velosi. The room was a veritable shrine to Victoria's most famous pupil.

'But Baltazar?' I said softly.

Victoria Givens gave a scornful laugh.

'That scum. He was going to take her away. Some nonsense about starting over, a new life without the stage. How could she not realize? The stage was her life. It was the life I created for her.'

'And you couldn't let that happen,' I said, willing her to continue.

Her eyes narrowed. She plunged her right hand into her overalls and fingered something deep inside. Slowly, her face relaxed.

'That's right. You see how it is, don't you?'

I did. The missing piece of the puzzle dropped into place. It had eluded me for so long.

'It wasn't Baltazar at all, was it? Or Alfonso?'

'Of course not.' Her voice was hard now. 'I created her. I had to destroy her before she could destroy herself.'

'Destroy herself, how?'

'Baltazar wanted to bring her back down to what she was before I discovered her. A pregnant barefoot *chola*. I couldn't allow that. I did it for the theater. I did it for love.'

'Love?'

'I loved her. She was like a daughter to me. And I was the mother she never had. In some ways, Alfonso was like her father. But lately he had become too possessive. He knew there must be someone else, and it drove him crazy. Of course, there were always other men, but Alfonso was smarter than me in some ways, he sensed that this one was different. He had been there that morning, before I got to her. I think they slept together. She never could resist him. I wanted to plan a little accident for him, but Catarina told me not to bother. It didn't matter anymore. That's when she told me she was leaving. We had a terrible row.'

'Did she realize how upset you were?'

Victoria lifted her chin and fingered her mole. She was long past caring what I thought.

'No,' the drama teacher said. 'Catarina just laughed and put her arms around me and said, "Oh, Victoria, I do believe you're jealous, you old silly. And you mustn't be. Don't treat me like a goddess on a pedestal."

'But to me she was. A glorious goddess. She needed someone to worship her. To take care of her. For years I had done that. But now she wanted to cast me away. So I had to destroy my creation. My most beautiful, wonderful creation.'

Her voice faltered and broke. She stood, hand rubbing obsessively at her chin, lost in twisted memory.

'But why?' I said. 'It was opening night, her glorious return to the stage. It would have made her a star.'

'Don't you understand yet?' she said spitefully. 'It was all arranged between her and Baltazar. Their flight. The ultimate fuck-you to all of us who had worked so hard for so long.'

'But it was her life,' I said, 'and you took it from her.'

'It was poetic, don't you think? Now instead of betraying her audience, her death is a tragedy for the ages. Struck down on the eve of what should have been her greatest triumph.'

'So you killed her?'

'It was an accident,' Victoria said dismissively. 'She wanted to get away, clear her head, and she called and asked me to take her to Point Fermin.'

'Where the body was found,' I said.

'She loved it there. Alfonso had introduced her to it years ago. Standing on that cliff, on the edge of a continent overlooking the sea. It was majestic.'

'And you drove?'

'I brought the car around to the alley. She didn't want anyone to see us, she owed money to that boy next door. So she climbed out the bedroom window.'

'What happened on that cliff?'

'We walked. It was deserted and empty, the wind was up. She told me her mind was made up about leaving. I couldn't persuade her. We argued. She said hateful things. It made me frantic. I grabbed her arm. Until that moment, I didn't know what I would do. I was mad with grief and loss. Her back was to me. And I pushed her. She lost her balance and staggered over the edge.

'"No, Victoria," she screamed as she fell, but the wind blew her words away.'

The drama teacher dipped her head, then spread her arms like a tragic player on center stage.

'And I fell to my knees and wept. I couldn't believe what I had done. My child was gone, and I wanted to throw myself after her. I crouched there like an animal, for a long time, before I could bear to leave her forever.'

I knew from the anguish in her voice, the dilation of her pupils, that we had finally hit bedrock. But something in this elaborate melodrama infuriated me.

'She died from a gunshot to the head, Victoria. This was premeditated. You shot her in her own bedroom. You planned it.'

'That's a lie.'

'And after you killed her, you took out the window screen and hiked back down to your car. You drove around the block and into the alley. Then you climbed back into her apartment, hauled her body out the window and into your car. She was tiny, and you're tall and wiry. Muscular. You've got the strength. Then after it got dark you drove to San Pedro and threw her body over the cliff.'

'It's not true.'

'Yes, it is. There was a kind of witness. Baltazar went to Catarina's house that morning to wish her good luck. He just missed seeing you drive away. He let himself in as he usually did, saw Catarina lying there dead, and didn't stick around to see any more. If he had, he might have killed you with his bare hands.'

'The word of a dead felon? Who'll believe that?' Her eyes narrowed.

'The forensic guys can fix time of death, angle of the bullet. Plus the blood on the pillow. The windowsill. It'll prove you killed her in her own bed and dragged her out.'

'No one would have known,' Victoria said. 'But you had to keep asking questions. You knew when you heard the music. I saw it in your eyes.'

'You're insane,' I said, edging for the door.

'Don't you see there was no other way for her?' Victoria Givens advanced toward me.

'No, I guess you don't.'

In the dim light, she pulled her hand out of her pocket and extended her arm, and I saw something small palmed inside it. Something that would put a hole in a body, leave maybe a spray of blood, but not come out the other side.

I had to keep her talking. Compliment her.

'It was you who sent those thugs after me, wasn't it? After we met at that café? Pretty clever.'

She stopped and looked almost proud.

'They were students of mine. I said it was a

practical joke, and you were in on it. The guns had blanks.'

'You should turn yourself in, Victoria. Explain what happened. You might get clemency. You've lived your life through her for too many years, and it's warped your mind.'

Victoria's lips pursed and her face closed down like a beach-front before a hurricane.

'I've worked inside the justice system too long to believe that,' she said. 'Now sit down on that couch until I decide what to do with you.'

I felt the gun prod into my back and we both moved forward.

I wondered if I should make a run for it. Then I heard a crash and a muffled groan. The gun went off. I dove, rolling as I hit the carpet, and saw Victoria Givens crumple, an alabaster lamp bouncing off her head as it shattered to the floor.

CHAPTER 49

Behind her stood Felice Morgan, hyperventilating with pure terror.

'Oh God, she's dead.'

I scrambled up and we both rushed to the prone body. Victoria lay unmoving, gun still gripped tight. I squatted to touch the back of her head and my hand came away bloody. But when I pressed my fingers against the inside of her wrist, I felt a steady pulse.

'She's alive,' I said.

I got on the phone to call an ambulance.

'Get the gun away from her in case she comes to,' I told Felice, 'but be careful not to smudge any prints.'

Felice crouched over the body, hands pressed against her cheeks.

'I can't.'

'Why not?'

'I'm ... I'm afraid of guns.'

Finnish biathlon team indeed.

Squatting by the body once more, I gingerly slid the gun from Victoria's fingers along the barrel, using the tail of my shirt so as not to smear the prints. I carried it to the kitchen table. Then I helped Felice up and led her to the couch. I patted her hand.

'How did you know I was here?'

Through her tears, it came out. Felice had watched me call Victoria after I left Thompson's office. When I wouldn't give her any details, she got suspicious. She waited for me to leave, then hit 'redial' on my phone to see the last number I had called. She used the reverse phone directory to get the address. Knowing that the big profile of Catarina was running the next day, she decided to drive out and see what I was up to. When she got to the house, she stood at the open door and heard us talking. Something in my tone alarmed her and she soon heard enough to understand why. She let herself in and hid behind a door. When Victoria ordered me onto the couch, Felice waited until we walked past, then jumped out and hit Victoria on the back of the head with the only weapon that presented itself – the heavy alabaster lamp.

As she finished her story, Felice doubled over, retching and moaning. A tremor ran through her. 'Oh my God, oh my God. What have I done?'

'A pretty good day's work,' I said. 'You knocked out Catarina's murderer and saved my life. Thanks, pal, I really owe you now.'

Felice looked up. Wet tracks ran down her cheeks. 'Really?' she said.

'Yup.'

She grabbed my hand. 'Then don't tell anyone.'

Her family. I paused, sensing an advantage. 'I'm still considering it.'

Her mouth set in a stern line.

'You just said you owe me one.'

I thought about it a long minute.

'Okay,' I said. 'But on one condition.'

'Anything,' she said.

'You saved my life, and I'm grateful. But if you ever follow me again, or eavesdrop on any of my conversations, or stick your nose into my business, or try to cop any of my stories, on purpose or otherwise, the deal is off. Are we straight?'

From far away, we heard the approach of sirens. Felice's face underwent a change. Slowly the terror left her eyes. Anticipation suffused her features. She seemed to have forgotten all about me and the body sprawled five feet away.

'Well?' I said.

Her eyes glittered as she turned.

'It's a deal,' she said.

Then Felice Morgan pushed herself off the couch, dusted alabaster powder from her pants, lofted her head, and stepped out to greet her audience. The curtain was about to rise, and this time, she was ready.

As for me, I stayed behind. I wanted to make sure Victoria didn't stir before the cops arrived. Besides, they were playing our song:

You are a carnivorous flower
In a savage garden.
Beautiful but deadly
As you devour my heart.

ACKNOWLEDGEMENTS

I would like to thank Ellen Slezak, Kerry Madden-Lunsford, Lienna Silver, Diana Wagman, Leslie Schwartz, Donna Rifkind, Heather Dundas, and Diane Arieff for their comments on an early chapter of this work. Thanks also for the theater lore, Heather; any mistakes are mine.

Thanks to my agent, Anne Borchardt, and my longtime editor, Susanne Kirk. I'm going to miss you, Susanne. But I'm extremely blessed to gain Sarah Knight, whose perceptive comments, questions, and suggestions made the manuscript stronger.

Thanks to Susan Moldow, Louise Burke, and Maggie Crawford for support and encouragement. You guys rock.

My hat is off to Suzanne Balaban, Erica Gelbard, Melissa Gramstad, P.J. Nunn, and the gang at BreakThrough Promotions and Kim Dower, who helped pull it off. Blake Little, you're a genius with the lens.

I couldn't have done it without the team of Bryan Christian, John McGhee, John Fulbrook, Paulo Pepe, and Henry Sene Yee.

Thanks to Mary Lou Wright for putting me up in Lawrence, Kansas, and to *comadre* Julia Spencer-Fleming for being my minder on the

Murdering Mommies of Mystery Tour. Ross Hugo-Vidal, you get a hand too.

Lastly, thanks to Adrian, Alexander, and David Garza. You make my life complete.

The publishers hope that this book has given you enjoyable reading. Large Print Books are especially designed to be as easy to see and hold as possible. If you wish a complete list of our books please ask at your local library or write directly to:

Magna Large Print Books
Magna House, Long Preston,
Skipton, North Yorkshire.
BD23 4ND

This Large Print Book for the partially sighted, who cannot read normal print, is published under the auspices of

THE ULVERSCROFT FOUNDATION

THE ULVERSCROFT FOUNDATION

... we hope that you have enjoyed this Large Print Book. Please think for a moment about those people who have worse eyesight problems than you ... and are unable to even read or enjoy Large Print, without great difficulty.

You can help them by sending a donation, large or small to:

**The Ulverscroft Foundation,
1, The Green, Bradgate Road,
Anstey, Leicestershire, LE7 7FU,
England.**
or request a copy of our brochure for more details.

The Foundation will use all your help to assist those people who are handicapped by various sight problems and need special attention.

Thank you very much for your help.